D1316842

Twentieth-Century Short Story Explication

Supplement II to Second Edition, 1970-1972

Compiled by
WARREN S. WALKER
Horn Professor of English,
Texas Tech University

THE SHOE STRING PRESS, INC.
1973

Library of Congress Cataloging in Publication Data

Walker, Warren S
   Twentieth-century short story explication; interpretations,
1900-1966.

— ——Supplement I-II. 1967-1972.
   1. Short story—Bibliography. I. Title.
Z5917.S5W33 Suppl   016.8093'1   67-24192
ISBN 0-208-01341-5

©1973 by The Shoe String Press, Inc.
Hamden, Connecticut 06514

Printed in the United States of America

PREFACE

Supplement II of the second edition carries forward the coverage of *Twentieth-Century Short Story Explication* through the three years from January 1, 1970, to December 31, 1972. Included with the recent explications are a few older ones which were overlooked or were previously unavailable for examination. For reprintings of interpretive studies listed in earlier volumes of this bibliography, the original sources plus all intervening reprintings have been given in order to provide complete documentation.

The term *short story* here has the same meaning it carries in the Wilson Company's *Short Story Index:*" . . . a brief narrative of not more than 150 average-sized pages." By *explication* I suggest simply interpretation or explanation of the meaning of a story, including observations on theme, symbol, or structure. This excludes from the bibliography what are primarily studies of sources, biographical data, and background materials. Occasionally there are explicatory passages cited in works otherwise devoted to one of these external considerations. Page numbers refer strictly to explicatory passages, not to the longer studies in which they may appear.

Although the entries refer primarily to materials written in English, the reader will also find citations for important studies in other languages, most frequently for articles in such readily available foreign-language journals as *Monatshefte, Modern Language Notes, Hispania, French Review,* and *Slavic and East European Journal.* The Index of Short Story Writers in this Supplement includes 65 authors for whose works explications are listed for the first time in this bibliography.

The increased flow of literary criticism at a time of inflated costs for book production has compelled us to choose between two alternative courses of action: increase substantially the price of each volume of *Twentieth-Century Short Story Explication,* or devise a more efficient utilization of printing space. We have (not without reluctance) taken the latter option and adopted a simple coding system. All books are cited by author or editor and a short title; the full title and the publication data are provided in the Check List of Books at the end of the volume. For an article in a journal the full publication information is provided the first time the study is cited. In subsequent entries only the critic's or scholar's name and a short title are used as long as these entries appear under the name of the same short story writer; if an article explicates stories by two or more writers, a complete initial entry is made for each writer.

Compilation of this volume was made easier by the work of numerous colleagues in literary research, especially the bibliographers of *PMLA* and *Modern Fiction Studies* and the contributors to *Abstracts of English Studies*. To more than 100 American publishers I wish to express appreciation for their willingness to lend me copies of their new books; to the reference librarians at Texas Tech University Library, my gratitude for their patient pursuit of elusive journals. As always, my greatest debt is to my wife, Barbara K. Walker.

Warren S. Walker
Horn Professor of English
Texas Tech University

JAMES AGEE

"A Mother's Tale"
Larsen, Erling. *James Agee,* 12-15.
Ohlin, Peter H. *Agee,* 175-182.

"The Waiter"
Mizener, Arthur. *A Handbook* . . . *"Modern Short Stories* . . . *Revised Edition,"* 88-90; rpt. *A Handbook* . . . *"Modern Short Stories* . . . *Third Edition,"* 103-105.

"A Walk Before Mass"
Larsen, Erling. *James Agee,* 10-12.

SCHMUEL YOSEF AGNON

"Agunot"
Hochman, Baruch. *The Fiction* . . . , 32-35.

"The Betrothal Oath" [same as "Betrothed"]
Band, Arnold J. *Nostalgia* . . . , 367-382.
Hochman, Baruch. "Agnon's Quest," *Commentary,* 42 (December, 1966), 45-46; rpt. in his *The Fiction* . . . , 3-5.

"And the Crooked Shall Be Made Straight"
Hochman, Baruch. *The Fiction* . . . , 35-38.

"Edo and Enam"
Hochman, Baruch. "Agnon's Quest," 46-47; rpt. in his *The Fiction* . . . 5-8.

"The Fathers and Sons"
Hochman, Baruch. *The Fiction* . . . , 48.

"The Legend of the Scribe"
Hochman, Baruch. *The Fiction* . . . , 38-42.

"Thus Far"
Hochman, Baruch. *The Fiction* . . . , 172-177.

"The Whole Loaf"
Hochman, Baruch. *The Fiction* . . . , 165-168.

1

"With Our Youth and with Our Aged"
Hochman, Baruch. *The Fiction* . . . , 83-93.

ILSE AICHINGER

"The Bound Man"
Hays, Peter L. *The Limping Hero* . . . , 212-213.
Minot, Stephen, and Robley Wilson. *Teacher's Manual* . . . , 8-9.

"Eliza, Eliza"
Lübbren, Rainer. "Die Sprache der Bilder: Zu Ilse Aichingers 'Eliza, Eliza,' " *Neue Rundschau,* 67 (1965), 626-636.

MARK ALDANOV

"For Thee the Best"
Lee, C. Nicholas. "The Philosophical Tales of M. A. Aldanov," *Slavic & East European J,* 15 (1971), 286-290.

"Punch Vodka"
Lee, C. Nicholas. " . . . Tales . . .," 281-286.

"The Tenth Symphony"
Lee, C. Nicholas. " . . . Tales . . .," 270-281.

SHOLOM ALEICHEM

809,933 "Dreyfus in Kasrilevke"
W 816 ∂/ Wisse, Ruth R. *The Schlemiel* . . . , 44-46.

NELSON ALGREN

"A Bottle of Milk for Mother"
Silkowski, Daniel R. "Alienation and Isolation in Nelson Algren's 'A Bottle of Milk for Mother,' " *Engl J,* 60 (1971), 724-727.

GLENN ALLAN

"Boysi's Yaller Cha'iot"
Starke, Catherine J. *Black Portraiture* . . . , 71-72.

SHERWOOD ANDERSON

"Almost"
Ciancio, Ralph. " 'The Sweetness of the Twisted Apple': Unity of Vision in *Winesburg, Ohio*," *PMLA*, 87 (1972), 1004-1005.

"Death"
Ciancio, Ralph. " 'The Sweetness . . . ,' " 1005.

"Departure"
Gochberg, Donald. "Stagnation and Growth: The Emergence of George Willard," *Expression*, 4 (Winter, 1960), 35.

"The Egg"
Mizener, Arthur, Ed. *Modern Short Stories* . . . , rev. ed., 427-430; rpt. 3rd ed., 469-470.
————. *A Handbook* . . . "*Modern Short Stories* . . . *Revised Edition*," 114-116; rpt. *A Handbook* . . . "*Modern Short Stories* . . . *Third Edition*," 130-132.

"Godliness"
Bort, Barry D. "*Winesburg, Ohio:* The Escape from Isolation," *Midwest Q*, 11 (1970), 446-448.

"Hands"
Bort, Barry D. "*Winesburg, Ohio* . . . ," 444-445.
Ciancio, Ralph. " 'The Sweetness . . . ,' " 997-998.
Gochberg, Donald. "Stagnation . . . ," 32.

"I Want to Know Why"
Lesser, Simon O. "The Image of the Father," *Partisan R*, 22 (1955), 380-390; rpt. in his *Fiction* . . . , 224-234; Phillips, William, Ed. *Art* . . . , 237-246; Meridian ed., 237-246; Malin, Irving, Ed. *Psychoanalysis* . . . , 98-107.

"Loneliness"
Ciancio, Ralph. " 'The Sweetness . . . ,' " 998-999.

"Paper Pills"
Bort, Barry D. "*Winesburg, Ohio* . . . ," 445-446.
Ciancio, Ralph. " 'The Sweetness . . . ,' " 1002-1004.

"Queer"
Gochberg, Donald. "Stagnation . . . ," 30-31.

"Responsibility"
  Ciancio, Ralph. " 'The Sweetness . . . ,' " 999-1000.

"Sophistication"
  Gochberg, Donald. "Stagnation . . . ," 34-35.

"The Thinker"
  Ciancio, Ralph. " 'The Sweetness . . . ,' " 1000.

"The Untold Lie"
  Rideout, Walter B. " 'The Tale of Perfect Balance': Sherwood Anderson's
    'The Untold Lie,' " *Newberry Library Bull*, 6 (1971), 243-250.

JUAN JOSE ARREOLA

"The Switchman"
  Leal, Luis. "The New Mexican Short Story," *Stud Short Fiction*, 8 (1971),
    14.

MIGUEL ANGEL ASTURIAS

"The Crystal Mask"
  Callan, Richard J. "Miguel Angel Asturias: Spokesman of His People,"
    Stud Short Fiction, 8 (1971), 98-99.

"Juanantes, the Man Who Was Chained"
  Callan, Richard J. " . . . Spokesman . . . ," 95-96.

"The Legend of the Singing Tablets"
  Callan, Richard J. " . . . Spokesman . . . ," 99-101.

"The Looking Glass of Lida Sal"
  Callan, Richard J. " . . . Spokesman . . . ," 101-102.

"Quincaju"
  Callan, Richard J. " . . . Spokesman . . . ," 97-98.

"Torotumbo"
  Callan, Richard J. "The Dynamics of Myth in 'Torotumbo' by Miguel
    Angel Asturias," *Romance Notes*, 12 (1971), 307-311.

ISAAC BABEL

"The Story of a Horse"
Carden, Patricia. . . . *Isaac Babel*, 121-122.

"The Story of My Dovecot"
Carden, Patricia. . . . *Isaac Babel*, 154-171.

JAMES BALDWIN

"Previous Condition"
Bluefarb, Sam. "James Baldwin's 'Previous Condition' : A Problem of
Identification," *Negro Am Lit Forum*, 3 (1969), 26-29.

"Sonny's Blue"
Ognibene, Elaine R. "Black Literature Revisited: 'Sonny's Blue,' " *Engl J*,
60 (1971), 36-37.
Reilly, John M. " 'Sonny's Blue' : James Baldwin's Image of Black
Community, " *Negro Am Lit Forum*, 3 (1969), 56-60.

HONORÉ DE BALZAC

"The Vicar of Tours"
Mozet, Nicole. "Le personnage de Troubert et la genèse du *Curé de
Tours*," *L'Année Balzacienne* (1970), 149-154.

JOHN BARTH

"Ambrose His Mark"
Hauck, Richard B. *A Cheerful Nihilism* . . . , 207-208.

"Menelaiad"
Hauck, Richard B. *A Cheerful Nihilism* . . . , 203-204.

"Night-Sea Journey"
Hauck, Richard B. *A Cheerful Nihilism* . . . , 204-207.

DONALD BARTHELME

"The Balloon"
Minot, Stephen, and Robley Wilson. *Teacher's Manual* . . . , 15-16.

AUGUSTO R. BASTOS

"Borrador de un Informe"
  Rodrĩguez-Alcalấ, Hugh. "Official Truth and 'True' Truth: Augusto Roa
  Bastos' 'Borrador de un Informe,' " *Stud Short Fiction*, 8 (1971), 141-
  154.

SAMUEL BECKETT

"Assumption"
  Webb, Eugene. *Samuel Beckett* . . . , 31-32.

"Dante and the Lobster"
  Robinson, Michael. *The Long Sonata* . . . , 65-67.
  Webb, Eugene. *Samuel Beckett* . . . , 39-41.

"Ding Dong"
  Robinson, Michael. *The Long Sonata* . . . , 73.
  Webb, Eugene. *Samuel Beckett* . . . , 36.

"Draff"
  Robinson, Michael. *The Long Sonata* . . . , 75.

"Enough"
  Mood, John J. " 'Silence Within': A Study of the *Residua* of Samuel
  Beckett," *Stud Short Fiction*, 7 (1970), 386-390.
  Webb, Eugene. *Samuel Beckett* . . . , 170-171.

"Fingal"
  Robinson, Michael. *The Long Sonata* . . . , 72-73.

"Imagination Dead Imagine"
  Lamont, Rosette. "Beckett's Metaphysics of Choiceless Awareness," in
  Friedman, Melvin J., Ed. *Samuel Beckett Now*, 200-201.
  Mood, John J. " 'Silence Within' . . . ," 390-393.

"Love and Lethe"
  Robinson, Michael. *The Long Sonata* . . . , 73-74.

"Ping"
  Mood, John J. " 'Silence Within' . . . , 393-401.
  Webb, Eugene. *Samuel Beckett* . . . , 171.

"Walking On"
Robinson, Michael. *The Long Sonata* . . . , 74.

"A Wet Night"
Robinson, Michael. *The Long Sonata* . . . , 73.
Webb, Eugene. *Samuel Beckett* . . . , 36-37.

"What a Misfortune"
Robinson, Michael. *The Long Sonata* . . . , 74.

"Yellow"
Webb, Eugene. *Samuel Beckett* . . . , 38-39.

SAUL BELLOW

"Seize the Day"
Dutton, Robert R. *Saul Bellow,* 83-97.
Gross, Theodore L. *The Heroic Ideal* . . . , 253-256.
Guttmann, Allen. *The Jewish Writer* . . . , 198-201.
Scheer-Schäzler, Brigitte. *Saul Bellow,* 62-71.

"The Trip to Galena"
Scheer-Schäzler, Brigitte. *Saul Bellow,* 32-33.

STEPHEN VINCENT BENÉT

"Freedom's a Hard-Bought Thing"
Starke, Catherine J. *Black Portraiture* . . . , 180-181.

AMBROSE BIERCE

"The Affair at Coulter's Notch"
Grenander, Mary E. *Ambrose Bierce,* 115-119.

"Chickamauga"
Grenander, Mary E. "Bierce's Turn of the Screw: Tales of Ironical
Terror," *Western Hum R,* 11 (1957), 261-262; rpt. in her *Ambrose
Bierce,* 95-96.

"The Death of Halpin Frayser"
Grenander, Mary E. *Ambrose Bierce,* 106-114.

"The Famous Gibson Bequest"
Grenander, Mary E. *Ambrose Bierce,* 89-92.

"Haïta the Shepherd"
Grenander, Mary E. *Ambrose Bierce,* 80-84.

"A Horseman in the Sky"
Grenander, Mary E. *Ambrose Bierce,* 123-130.

"Jupiter Doke, Brigadier-General"
Grenander, Mary E. *Ambrose Bierce,* 131-138.

"The Man and the Snake"
Grenander, Mary E. "Bierce's Turn of the Screw . . . ," 263-264; rpt. in her
Ambrose Bierce, 97.

"An Occurrence at Owl Creek Bridge"
Bahr, Howard W. "Ambrose Bierce and Realism," *Southern Q,* 1)1963),
309-331.
Grenander, Mary E. "Bierce's Turn of the Screw . . . ," 261-262; rpt. in her
Ambrose Bierce, 94-95.

"One Officer, One Man"
Grenander, Mary E. "Bierce's Turn of the Screw . . . ," 263-264; rpt. in her
Ambrose Bierce, 96-97.

"One of the Missing"
Grenander, Mary E. "Bierce's Turn of the Screw . . . ," 264; rpt. in her
Ambrose Bierce, 94.

"Parker Adderson, Philosopher"
Grenander, Mary E. *Ambrose Bierce,* 84-88.

"A Son of the Gods"
Grenander, Mary E. *Ambrose Bierce,* 119-123.

"A Tough Tussle"
Grenander, Mary E. *Ambrose Bierce,* 102-106.

"A Watcher by the Dead"
Grenander, Mary E. *Ambrose Bierce,* 138-141.

HEINRICH BÖLL

"The Balek Scales"
Fetzer, John. "The Scale of Injustice: Comments on Heinrich Böll's 'Die
Waage Baleks,' " *Germ Q,* 45 (1972), 472-479.

"The Bread of Spring"
Hanson, W. P. "Heinrich Böll: 'Das Brot der frühen Jahre,' " *Mod Lang*
(London), 48 (1967), 148-151.

MARIA LUISA BOMBAL

"The Tree"
Debicki, Andrew P. "Structure, Imagery, and Experience in Maria Luisa
Bombal's 'The Tree,' " *Stud Short Fiction,* 8 (1971), 123-129.

SHERWOOD BONNER

"The Gentlemen of Sarsar"
Skaggs, Merrill M. *The Folk . . . ,* 135-136.

"Lame Jerry"
Skaggs, Merrill M. *The Folk . . ,* 59-60.

JORGE LUIS BORGES

"The Aleph"
Alazraki, James. "Kabbalistic Traits in Borges' Narration," *Stud Short
Fiction,* 8 (1971), 90-92.
Carlos, Alberto J. "La Ironía en un Cuento de Borges," *Revista de
Estudios Hispánicos,* 2 (1972), 211-224.
Stabb, Martin S. *Jorge Luis Borges,* 108-111.

"The Approach to Almotásim"
Alazraki, James. "Kabbalistic Traits . . . ," 83-84.
Stabb, Martin S. *Jorge Luis Borges,* 106-208.

"The Babylonian Lottery"
Lang, Berel. "On Borges: The Compleat Solipsist," *Columbia Forum,* 1
N.S. (Summer, 1972), 7-9.
Stabb, Martin S. *Jorge Luis Borges,* 115-117.

EDWARD BULWER-LYTTON   13

"Tlön, Uqbar, Orbis Tertius"
    Stabb, Martin S. *Jorge Luis Borges,* 100-106.

"The Zahir"
    Alazraki, James. "Kabbalistic Traits . . . ," 86.
    Stabb, Martin S. *Jorge Luis Borges,* 111-112.

ELIZABETH BOWEN

"The Demon Lover"
    Guerin, Wilfred L., *et al. Instructor's Manual . . . "Mandala" . . . ,* 27.

RAY BRADBURY

"The One Who Waits"
    Minot, Stephen, and Robley Wilson. *Teacher's Manual . . . ,* 20-21.

GEORG BRITTING

"Der Schneckenweg"
    Jäger, Dietrich. "Der 'verheimlichte Raum' in Faulkners 'A Rose for
    Emily' und Brittings 'Der Schneckenweg,' " *Literatur in Wissenschaft
    & Unterricht,* 1 (1968), 108-119.

MICHAEL BROWNSTEIN

"The Plot to Save the World"
    Minot, Stephen, and Robley Wilson. *Teacher's Manual . . . ,* 25-26.

EDWARD BULWER-LYTTON

"The Haunted and the Haunters; or, the House and the Brain"
    Kelly, Richard. "The Haunted House of Bulwer-Lytton," *Stud Short
    Fiction,* 8 (1971), 581-587.

ANTHONY BURGESS

"The Muse: A Sort of SF Story"
Cullinan, John. "Anthony Burgess' 'The Muse: A Sort of SF Story,' "
Stud Short Fiction, 9 (1972), 213-220.

GEORGE W. CABLE

"Jean-ah Poquelin"
Egan, Joseph J. " 'Jean-ah Poquelin': George Washington Cable as Social
Critic and Mythic Artist," *Markham R,* 2 (May, 1970), 6-7.
Stone, Edward. *A Certain Morbidity . . . ,* 85-97.

ALBERT CAMUS

"The Fall"
Engelberg, Edward. *The Unknown Distance . . . ,* 230-241.
Lakich, John J. "Tragedy and Satanism in Camus' 'La Chute,' " *(Albert
Camus II) Symposium,* 24 (1970), 262-276.
O'Brien, Conor C. *Albert Camus . . . ,* 61-106.
Onimus, Jean. *Albert Camus . . . ,* 91-97.
Petrey, Sandy. "The Function of Christian Imagery in 'La Chute,' " *Texas
Stud Lit & Lang,* 11 (1970), 1445-1454.
Sperber, Michael A. "Camus' 'The Fall': The Icarus Complex," *Am
Imago,* 26 (1969), 269-280.
Tucker, Warren. " 'La chute': Voie du salut terrestre," *French R,* 43
(1970), 737-744.

"The Guest"
Fortier, Paul. "Le Décor Symbolique de 'L'Hôte' d'Albert Camus,"
French R, 46 (1973), 535-542.

"The Renegade"
Douglas, Kenneth, and John Hollander. "Masterpieces of Symbolism and
the Modern School," in Mack, Maynard, *et al.,* Eds. *World
Masterpieces,* II, 3rd ed., 1387; Continental ed. rev., 1021-1022.
Johnson, Patricia J. "An Impossible Search for Identity: Theme and
Image in Camus' 'Le Renégat,' " *Research Stud,* 37 (1969), 171-182.
Rysten, Felix S. A. *False Prophets . . . ,* 59-60.

"The Stranger"
  Abbou, André. "Les paradoxes du discours dans 'L'étranger': De la parole
    directe à l'écriture inverse," *La Revue des Lettres Modernes,* 212-216
    (1969), 35-78.
  Albrecht, Joyce. " 'The Stranger' and Camus' Transcendental
    Existentialism," *Hartford Stud Lit,* 4, 1 (1972), 59-80.
  Champigny, Robert J. *Sur un héros païen, passim;* Am. ed., *A Pagan
    Hero . . . , passim.*
  Curtis, Jerry L. "Camus' Outsider: Or, The Games People Play," *Stud
    Short Fiction,* 9 (1972), 379-386.
  Dibble, Brian. "Camus' 'The Stranger, Part II,' " *Explicator,* 29 (1970),
    Item 29.
  Friedman, Maurice. *Problematic Rebel . . . ,* 2nd ed., 420-425.
  Hamalian, Leo, and Edmond L. Volpe, Eds. *Ten . . . Short Novels,* 642-
    644; rpt. 2nd ed. (retitled *Eleven . . . Short Novels),* 630-632.
  Johnson, Roger. "A Note on Camus' 'The Stranger,' " *Southern Q,* 10
    (1971), 41-42.
  Knoff, William F. "A Psychiatrist Reads Camus' 'The Stranger,' "
    Psychiatric Opinion, 6 (February, 1969), 19-21, 24.
  Leites, Nathan. "Trends in Affectlessness," *Am Imago,* 4 (1947), 89-112;
    rpt. Phillips, William, Ed. *Art . . . ,* 247-267; Meridian ed., 247-267.
  O'Brien, Conor C. *Albert Camus . . . ,* 11-34.
  Onimus, Jean. *Albert Camus . . . ,* 110-115.
  Rysten, Felix S. A. *False Prophets . . . ,* 24-26.
  Slochower, Harry. "Camus' 'The Stranger': The Silent Society and the
    Ecstasy of Rage," *Am Imago,* 26 (1969), 291-294.
  Stamm, Julian L. "Camus' 'Stranger': His Act of Violence," *Am Imago,* 26
    (1969), 281-290.
  Suther, Judith D. "Red Color Imagery in 'The Stranger,' " *Descant,* 15
    (Fall, 1970), 41-46.
  Sutherland, Stewart R. "Imagination in Literature and Philosophy, a
    Viewpoint on Camus' 'L'étranger,' " *Brit J Aesthetics,* 10 (1970), 261-
    274.
  Wagner, C. Roland. "The Silence of 'The Stranger,' " *Mod Fiction Stud,*
    16 (1970), 27-40.

TRUMAN CAPOTE

"Among the Paths of Eden"
  Nance, William L. *. . . Truman Capote,* 83-87.

"Children on Their Birthdays"
  Nance, William L. *. . . Truman Capote,* 65-72.

"A Christmas Memory"
Nance, William L. . . . *Truman Capote,* 78-83.

"A Diamond Guitar"
Nance, William L. . . . *Truman Capote,* 73-75.

"The Headless Hawk"
Nance, William L. . . . *Truman Capote,* 23-29.

"House of Flowers"
Nance, William L. . . . *Truman Capote,* 75-78.

"Jug of Silver"
Nance, William L. . . . *Truman Capote,* 72.

"Master Misery"
Nance, William L. . . . *Truman Capote,* 32-38.

"Miriam"
Nance, William L. . . . *Truman Capote,* 20-22.

"Shut a Final Door"
Freese, Peter. "Das Motiv des Doppelgänger in Truman Capotes 'Shut a Final Door' und Edgar Allan Poes 'William Wilson,' " *Literatur in Wissenschaft & Unterricht,* 1 (1968), 41-49.
Nance, William L. . . . *Truman Capote,* 29-32.

"A Tree of Night"
Nance, William L. . . . *Truman Capote,* 17-19.

WILLIAM CARLETON

"The Three Tasks"
Ibarra, Eileen S. "Folktales in Carleton's 'The Three Tasks,' " *Tennessee Folklore Soc Bull,* 36 (1970), 66-71.

ALEJO CARPENTIER

"El Acoso"
Giacoman, Helmy F. "The Use of Music in Literature: 'El Acoso' by Alejo Carpentier and Symphony No. 3 (*Eroica*) by Beethoven," *Stud Short Fiction,* 8 (1971), 103-111.

WILLA CATHER

"The Bohemian Girl"
Woodress, James. *Willa Cather* . . . , 148-149.

"Double Birthday"
Woodress, James. *Willa Cather* . . . , 140-141.

"Old Mrs. Harris"
Woodress, James. *Willa Cather* . . . , 21-24.

W. A. CAWTHORNE

"The Kangaroo Islanders"
Healy, J. J. "The Treatment of the Aborigine in Early Australian Fiction, 1840-1870," *Australian Lit Stud,* 5 (1972), 244-245.

JOHN CHEEVER

"The Swimmer"
Auser, Cortland P. "John Cheever's Myth of Man and Time: 'The Swimmer,' " *Coll Engl Assoc Critic,* 29 (March, 1967), 18-19.

ANTON CHEKHOV

"About Love"
Kramer, Karl D. *The Chameleon* . . . , 170-171.

"An Anonymous Story"
Kramer, Karl D. *The Chameleon* . . . , 43-46.

"An Artist's Story"
Speirs, Logan. *Tolstoy and Chekhov,* 160-161.

"At Home"
Kramer, Karl D. *The Chameleon* . . . , 77-78.

"An Attack of Nerves"
Conrad, Joseph L. "Unresolved Tension in Čexov's Stories, 1886-88," *Slavic & East European J,* 16 (1972), 62-63.

"Gooseberries"
  Kramer, Karl D. *The Chameleon* . . . , 168-171.

"The Grasshopper"
  Kramer, Karl D. *The Chameleon* . . . , 126-127.

"Happiness"
  Kramer, Karl D. *The Chameleon* . . . , 85-86.

"The House with a Mezzanine"
  Kramer, Karl D. *The Chameleon* . . . , 165-166.

"In the Ravine"
  Speirs, Logan. *Tolstoy and Chekhov,* 166-168.

"The Kiss"
  Kramer, Karl D. *The Chameleon* . . . , 82-85.

"Late-Blooming Flowers"
  Kramer, Karl D. *The Chameleon* . . . , 37-40.

"Lights"
  Speirs, Logan. *Tolstoy and Chekhov,* 156-159.

"Live Merchandise"
  Kramer, Karl D. *The Chameleon* . . . , 31-32.

"The Man in a Case"
  Kramer, Karl D. *The Chameleon* . . . , 168-169.

"Misery"
  Conrad, Joseph L. "Unresolved Tension . . . ," 56-57.
  Kramer, Karl D. *The Chameleon* . . . , 65-67.

"My Anniversary"
  Kramer, Karl D. *The Chameleon* . . . , 28-29.

"My Life"
  Kramer, Karl D. *The Chameleon* . . . , 148-150.

"Name Day"
  Kramer, Karl D. *The Chameleon* . . . , 94-96, 100-102.

"Two in One"
Kramer, Karl D. *The Chameleon* . . . , 54-55.

"An Unpleasantness"
Kramer, Karl D. *The Chameleon* . . . , 99-100.

"Vanka"
Conrad, Joseph L. "Unresolved Tension . . . ," 57.
Rosen, Nathan. "The Unconscious in Cexov's 'Vanka,' " *Slavic & East European J,* 15 (1971), 441-454.

"Verotchka"
Conrad, Joseph L. "Čexov's 'Veročka': A Polemical Parody," *Slavic & East European J,* 14 (1970), 465-474.
Kramer, Karl D. *The Chameleon* . . . , 67-70.

"Vint"
Kramer, Karl D. *The Chameleon* . . . , 58-59.

"Ward No. 6"
Kramer, Karl D. *The Chameleon* . . . , 129-133.

"The Wife"
Kramer, Karl D. *The Chameleon* . . . , 124-126.

"The Witch"
Conrad, Joseph L. "Unresolved Tension . . . ," 57-58.

"A Woman's Kingdom"
Kramer, Karl D. *The Chameleon* . . . , 162-163.

CHARLES CHESNUTT

"The Conjure's Revenge"
Baldwin, Richard E. "The Art of *The Conjure Woman,*" *Am Lit,* 43 (1971), 392-394.

"The Goophered Grapevine"
Baldwin, Richard E. "The Art . . . ," 387-391.
Lid, Richard W. *Instructor's Manual* . . . , 22-23.
Starke, Catherine J. *Black Portraiture* . . . , 56-59.

"Her Virginia Mammy"
  Starke, Catherine J. *Black Portraiture* . . . , 95-96.

"Hot-Foot Hannibal"
  Baldwin, Richard E. "The Art . . . ," 394-395.

"Mars Jeems's Nightmare"
  Baldwin, Richard E. "The Art . . . ," 395-398.

"Po' Sandy"
  Baldwin, Richard E. "The Art . . . ," 391-392.

"The Web of Circumstance"
  Skaggs, Merrill M. *The Folk* . . . , 97-98.

KATE CHOPIN

"Desirée's Baby"
  Arner, Robert D. "Pride and Prejudice: Kate Chopin's 'Desirée's Baby,' "
    Mississippi Q, 25 (1972), 131-140.

"In and Out of Old Natchitoches"
  Skaggs, Merrill M. *The Folk* . . . , 183-184.

"In Sabine"
  Skaggs, Merrill M. *The Folk* . . . , 41-42.

"A No-Account Creole"
  Skaggs, Merrill M. *The Folk* . . . , 182-183.

"Vagabonds"
  Arner, Robert D. "Characterization and Colloquial Style in Kate
    Chopin's 'Vagabonds, ' " *Markham R,* 2 (1971), 110-112.

KAY CICELLIS

"The Way to Colonus"
  Lee, L. L. "*Oedipus at Colonus:* The Modern 'Vulgarizations' of Forster
    and Cicellis," *Stud Short Fiction,* 8 (1971), 561-567.

WALTER VAN TILBURG CLARK

"The Anonymous"
  Westbrook, Max. *Walter . . . Clark,* 134-135.

"The Buck in the Hills"
  Westbrook, Max. *Walter . . . Clark,* 135-136.

"The Portable Phonograph"
  Cohen, Edward H. "Clark's 'The Portable Phonograph,' " *Explicator,* 28
  (1970), Item 69.

"The Rapids"
  Westbrook, Max. *Walter . . . Clark,* 133-134.

"Why Don't You Look Where You're Going?"
  Westbrook, Max. *Walter . . . Clark,* 134.

JOHN COLLIER

"Thus I Refute Beelzy"
  Minot, Stephen, and Robley Wilson. *Teacher's Manual . . . ,* 13-14.

JOSEPH CONRAD

"Amy Foster"
  Andreach, Robert J. *The Slain . . . God,* 29-43.

"An Anarchist"
  Schwarz, Daniel R. "The Lepidopterist's Revenge: Theme and Structure
  in Conrad's 'An Anarchist,' " *Stud Short Fiction,* 8 (1971), 330-334.

"Il Conde"
  Carter, Ernest. "Classical Allusion as the Clue to Meaning in Conrad's 'Il
  Conde,' " *Conradiana,* 3 (May, 1971), 55-62.
  Dolan, P. J. " 'Il Conde': Conrad's Little Miss Muffett," *Conradiana,* 1
  (1969), 107-111.
  Dowden, Wilfred S. *Joseph Conrad . . . ,* 109-112.

"The End of the Tether"
  Pinsker, Sanford. " 'The End of the Tether': Joseph Conrad's Death of a
  Sailsman," *Conradiana,* 3 (May, 1971), 74-76.

"Falk"
> Johnson, Bruce. *Conrad's Modes* . . . , 52-53.
> Schwarz, Daniel R. "The Significance of the Narrator in Conrad's 'Falk,' " *Tennessee Stud Lit,* 16 (1971), 103-110.

"Gaspar Ruiz"
> Martin, W. P. "Gaspar Ruiz: A Conrad Hero," *Conradiana,* 3 (September, 1971), 47-48.

"Heart of Darkness"
> Addison, Bill K. "Marlow, Aschenbach, and We," *Conradiana,* 2 (Winter, 1970), 79-81.
> Andreach, Robert J. *The Slain . . . God,* 44-53.
> Brashers, H. C. "Conrad, Marlow, and Gautama Buddha: On Structure and Theme in 'Heart of Darkness,' " *Conradiana,* 1 (1969), 63-71.
> Chiampi, Rubens. " 'Heart of Darkness,' " *Humanidades* (Brazil), 5 (1969), 52-68.
> Cook, William J. "More Light on 'Heart of Darkness,' " *Conradiana,* 3 (September, 1971), 4-14.
> Dowden, Wilfred S. *Joseph Conrad . . . ,* 71-85.
> Faulkner, Peter. "Vision and Normality: Conrad's 'Heart of Darkness,' " *Ibadan Stud Engl,* 1 (1969), 36-47.
> Garrett, Peter K. *Scene and Symbol . . . ,* 164-172.
> Gertzman, Jay A. "Commitment and Sacrifice in 'Heart of Darkness': Marlow's Response to Kurtz," *Stud Short Fiction,* 9 (1972), 187-196.
> Hamalian, Leo, and Edmond L. Volpe, Eds. *Ten . . . Short Novels,* 194-195; rpt. 2nd ed. (retitled *Eleven . . . Short Novels*), 149-150.
> Johnson, Bruce. "Names, Naming, and the 'Inscrutable' in Conrad's 'Heart of Darkness,' " *Texas Stud Lit & Lang,* 12 (1971), 675-688; rpt., with slight changes, in his *Conrad's Modes . . . ,* 70-88.
> ————." 'Heart of Darkness' and the Problem of Emptiness," *Stud Short Fiction,* 9 (1972), 387-400.
> Kisner, Sister Mary R. "The Lure of the Abyss for the Hollow Man: Conrad's Notion of Evil," *Conradiana,* 2 (1970), 85-99.
> Lincoln, Kenneth R. "Comic Light in 'Heart of Darkness,' " *Mod Fiction Stud,* 18 (1972), 183-197.
> Low, Anthony. " 'Heart of Darkness': The Search for an Occupation," *Engl Lit in Transition,* 12 (1969), 1-9.
> ————. "Drake and Franklin in 'Heart of Darkness,' " *Conradiana,* 2 (1970), 128-131.
> Meyers, Jeffrey. "Savagery and Civilization in *The Tempest, Robinson Crusoe,* and 'Heart of Darkness,' " *Conradiana,* 2 (1970), 171-179.
> Mizener, Arthur. *A Handbook . . . "Modern Short Stories . . . Revised Edition,"* 1-8; rpt. *A Handbook . . . "Modern Short Stories . . . Third*

Edition," 1-8.

Montag, George E. "Marlow Tells the Truth: The Nature of Evil in 'Heart of Darkness,' " *Conradiana,* 3 (May, 1971), 93-97.

Pavlov, Grigor. "Two Studies of Bourgeois Individualism by Joseph Conrad," *Zeitschrift für Anglistik und Amerikanistik,* 17 (1969), 229-238.

Rael, Elsa. "Joseph Conrad, Master Absurdist," *Conradiana,* 2 (1970), 163-170.

Roussel, Royal. *The Metaphysics* . . . , 72-79.

Ryf, Robert S. *Joseph Conrad,* 16-21.

Saveson, John E. "Conrad's View of Primitive People in *Lord Jim* and 'Heart of Darkness,' " *Mod Fiction Stud,* 16 (1970), 163-183.

Stein, William B. " 'The Heart of Darkness': Bodhisattva," *Orient/West,* 9, v (1964), 37-49.

Yoder, Albert C. "Oral Artistry in Conrad's 'Heart of Darkness,' " *Conradiana,* 2 (Winter, 1970), 65-78.

Zak, William F. "Conrad, F.R. Leavis, Whitehead: 'Heart of Darkness' and Organic Holism," *Conradiana,* 4 (January, 1972), 5-24.

"The Idiots"

Dowden, Wilfred S. *Joseph Conrad* . . . , 107-109.

Schwarz, Daniel R. "Moral Bankruptcy in Plouman Parish: A Study of Conrad's 'The Idiots,' " *Conradiana,* 1 (1969), 113-117.

"Karain"

Dowden, Wilfred S. *Joseph Conrad* . . . , 31-33.

Johnson, Bruce. *Conrad's Modes* . . . , 28-29.

"An Outpost of Progress"

Dowden, Wilfred S. *Joseph Conrad* . . . , 33-35.

Johnson, Bruce. *Conrad's Modes* . . . , 35-39.

"The Planter of Malata"

Johnson, Bruce. *Conrad's Modes* . . . , 179-204.

"The Return"

Dowden, Wilfred S. *Joseph Conrad* . . . , 35-37.

Roussel, Royal. *The Metaphysics* . . . , 33-37.

"The Secret Sharer"

Andreach, Robert J. *The Slain* . . . *God,* 39-44.

Bidwell, Paul. "Leggatt and the Promised Land: New Reading of 'The Secret Sharer,' " *Conradiana,* 3 (May, 1971), 26-34.

Brown, P.L. " 'The Secret Sharer' and the Existential Hero," *Conradiana,* 3 (September, 1971), 22-30.

Carson, Herbert L. "The Second Self in 'The Secret Sharer,' " *Cresset*, 34, i (1970), 11-13.

Dowden, Wilfred S. *Joseph Conrad* . . . , 141-145.

Foye, Paul F., Bruce Harkness, and Nathan L. Marvin. "The Sailing Maneuver in 'The Secret Sharer,' " *J Mod Lit*, 2 (1971), 119-123.

Hamilton, S.C. " 'Cast-Anchor Devils' and Conrad: A Study of Persona and Point of View in 'The Secret Sharer,' " *Conradiana*, 2 (Spring, 1970), 111-121.

Rael, Elsa. "Joseph Conrad . . . ," 163-170.

"The Shadow Line"

Dowden, Wilfred S. *Joseph Conrad* . . . , 145-148.

Zuckerman, Jerome. "The Architecture of 'The Shadow Line,' " *Conradiana*, 3 (May, 1971), 87-92.

"A Smile of Fortune"

Dowden, Wilfred S. *Joseph Conrad* . . . , 135-138.

"Typhoon"

Kisner, Sister Mary R. "The Lure of the Abyss . . . ," 85-99.

"Youth"

Crawford, John. "Another Look at 'Youth,' " *Research Stud*, 37 (1969), 154-156.

Dowden, Wilfred S. *Joseph Conrad* . . . , 85-87.

JULIO CORTÁZAR

"Las armas secretas"

Gyurko, Lanin A. "Man As Victim in Two Stories by Cortázar," *Kentucky Romance Q*, 19 (1972), 317-335.

"La Autopista del Sur"

Echevarria, Roberto G. " 'La Autopista del Sur' and the Secret Weapons of Julio Cortázar's Short Narratives," *Stud Short Fiction*, 8 (1971), 130-140.

"Instruccione para John Howell"

Gyurko, Lanin A. "Man As Victim . . . ," 317-335.

HUBERT CRACKANTHORPE

"A Fellside Tragedy"
Peden, William. " 'A Fellside Tragedy': An Uncollected Crackanthorpe
Story," *Stud Short Fiction,* 9 (1972), 401-402.

STEPHEN CRANE

"Billy Atkins Went to Omaha"
LaFrance, Marston. *A Reading . . .* , 71-72.

"The Blue Hotel"
Beards, Richard D. "Stereotyping in Modern American Fiction: Some
Solitary Swedish Madmen," *Moderna Sprak,* 63 (1969), 329-337.
Cady, Edwin H. *Stephen Crane,* 155-157; rpt. Katz, Joseph, Ed. *Stephen
Crane . . .* , 100-102.
Cox, James T. "Stephen Crane as Symbolic Naturalist: An Analysis of
'The Blue Hotel, ' " *Mod Fiction Stud,* 3 (1957), 147-158; rpt. Katz,
Joseph, Ed. *Stephen Crane . . .* , 48-60; Gullason, Thomas A., Ed. . . .
Evaluations, 452-464.
Dillingham, William B. " 'The Blue Hotel' and the Gentle Reader," *Stud
Short Fiction,* 1 (1964), 224-226; rpt. Katz, Joseph, Ed. *Stephen Crane.*
. . . , 119-121.
Gibson, Donald B. " 'The Blue Hotel' and the Ideal of Human Courage,"
Texas Stud Lit & Lang, 6 (1964), 388-397; rpt. in his *The Fiction . . .* ,
106-118; Katz, Joseph, Ed. *Stephen Crane . . .* , 109-118.
Gleckner, Robert F. "Stephen Crane and the Wonder of Man's Conceit,"
Mod Fiction Stud, 5 (1959), 271-281; rpt. in part Katz, Joseph, Ed.
Stephen Crane . . . , 79-88.
Greenfield, Stanley B. "The Unmistakable Stephen Crane," *PMLA,* 73
(1958), 565-568; rpt. Katz, Joseph, Ed. *Stephen Crane . . .* , 61-65.
Gullason, Thomas A. "Stephen Crane's Short Stories: The True Road," in
Gullason, Thomas A., Ed. . . . *Evaluations,* 480-481.
Holton, Milne. *Cylinders . . .* , 233-241.
Itabashi, Yoshie. " 'To Be a Man'—A Study of Fear and Courage in
Stephen Crane's Stories," *Tsudi R* (Tokyo), 10 (November, 1965), 38-
44.
Johnson, George W. "Stephen Crane's Metaphor of Decorum," *PMLA,*
78 (1963), 254-255; rpt. Bassan, Maurice, Ed. *Stephen Crane: . . .* , 75-
77; Katz, Joseph, Ed. *Stephen Crane . . .* , 104-106.
Klotz, Marvin. "Stephen Crane: Tragedian or Comedian: 'The Blue
Hotel,' " *Univ Kansas City R,* 27 (1961), 170-174; rpt. Katz, Joseph, Ed.
Stephen Crane . . . , 89-93; Gullason, Thomas A., Ed. . . . *Evaluations,*
465-469.

LaFrance, Marston. *A Reading . . .* , 221-232.

Maclean, Hugh. "The Two Worlds of 'The Blue Hotel,' " *Mod Fiction Stud,* 5 (1959), 260-270; rpt. in part Katz, Joseph, Ed. *Stephen Crane . . .* , 71-78.

Narveson, Robert. " 'Conceit' in 'The Blue Hotel,' " *Prairie Schooner,* 43 (1969), 187-191.

Osborn, Neal J. "Crane's 'The Monster' and 'The Blue Hotel,' " *Explicator,* 23 (1964), Item 10; rpt. Katz, Joseph, Ed. *Stephen Crane . . .* , 107-108.

Roth, Russell. "A Tree in Winter: The Short Fiction of Stephen Crane," *New Mexico Q,* 23 (1953), 194-195; rpt. Katz, Joseph, Ed. *Stephen Crane . . .* , 39-40.

Satterwhite, Joseph N. "Stephen Crane's 'The Blue Hotel': The Failure of Understanding," *Mod Fiction Stud,* 2 (1956), 238-241; rpt. Katz, Joseph, Ed. *Stephen Crane . . .* , 43-47; Gullason, Thomas A., Ed. . . . *Evaluations,* 447-451.

Solomon, Eric. *Stephen Crane: . . .* , 257-274; rpt. in part Katz, Joseph, Ed. *Stephen Crane . . .* , 125-135.

Stallman, Robert W. *Stephen Crane . . .* , 482-483; rpt. in his *The Houses . . .* , 108; Katz, Joseph, Ed. *Stephen Crane . . .* , 37-38.

Stein, William B. "Stephen Crane's *Homo Absurdus*," *Bucknell R,* 8 (May, 1959), 173-174; rpt. Katz, Joseph, Ed. *Stephen Crane . . .* , 66-67; Gullason, Thomas A., Ed. . . . *Evaluations,* 232-234.

Stone, Edward. *A Certain Morbidity . . .* , 53-69.

Sutton, Walter. "Pity and Fear in 'The Blue Hotel,' " *Am Q,* 4 (1952), 73-76; rpt. Katz, Joseph, Ed. *Stephen Crane . . .* , 34-36.

Walcutt, Charles. . . . *Divided Stream,* 72-74; rpt. Katz, Joseph, Ed. *Stephen Crane . . .* , 41-42.

Ward, J. A. " 'The Blue Hotel' and 'The Killers,' " *Coll Engl Assoc Critic,* 21 (1959), 1, 7-8; rpt. Katz, Joseph, Ed. *Stephen Crane . . .* , 68-70.

Weinig, Sister Mary A. "Heroic Convention in 'The Blue Hotel,' " *Stephen Crane Newsletter,* 2 (Spring, 1968), 6-7; rpt. Katz, Joseph, Ed. *Stephen Crane . . .* , 136-137.

West, Ray B. "Stephen Crane: Author in Transition," *Am Lit,* 34 (1962), 223-227; rpt. Browne, Ray B., and Martin Light, Eds. *Critical Approaches . . .* , II, 173-177; rpt. in part Katz, Joseph, Ed. *Stephen Crane . . .* , 94-96.

Westbrook, Max. "Stephen Crane's Social Ethic," *Am Q,* 14 (1962), 593-595; rpt. Katz, Joseph, Ed. *Stephen Crane . . .* , 97-99.

"The Bride Comes to Yellow Sky"
  Barnes, Robert. "Stephen Crane's 'The Bride Comes to Yellow Sky,' "
    Explicator, 16 (1958), Item 39; rpt. Gullason, Thomas A., and Leonard
    Casper, Eds. . . . *Short Fiction,* 2nd ed., 603-604.
  Bernard, Kenneth. " 'The Bride Comes to Yellow Sky': History As Elegy,"
    Engl Record, 17 (April, 1967), 17-20; rpt. Gullason, Thomas A., Ed. . . .
    Evaluations, 435-439.
  Cook, Robert G. "Stephen Crane's 'The Bride Comes to Yellow Sky,' "
    Stud Short Fiction, 2 (1965), 368-369; rpt. Gullason, Thomas A., and
    Leonard Casper, Eds. . . . *Short Fiction,* 2nd ed., 607-609.
  Folsom, James K. . . . *Western Novel,* 91-94.
  Holton, Milne. *Cylinders . . .,* 226-233.
  LaFrance, Marston. *A Reading . . . ,* 210-214.
  Stein, William B. "Stephen Crane's *Homo Absurdus,*" *Bucknell R,* 8
    (1959), 184-186; rpt. Gullason, Thomas A., Ed. . . . *Evaluations,* 236-
    238.
  Tibbetts, A.M. "Stephen Crane's 'The Bride Comes to Yellow Sky,' " *Engl
    J,* 54 (1965), 314-316; rpt. Gullason, Thomas A., and Leonard Casper,
    Eds. . . . *Short Fiction,* 2nd ed., 604-607; Gullason, Thomas A., Ed. . . . ,
    Evaluations, 430-434.
  Vorpahl, Ben M. "Murder by the Minute: Old and New in 'The Bride
    Comes to Yellow Sky,' " *Nineteenth Century Fiction,* 26 (1971), 196-
    218.

"The Clan of No-Name"
  Holton, Milne. *Cylinders . . . ,* 262-266.

"Death and the Child"
  Holton, Milne. *Cylinders . . . ,* 183-192.
  Itabashi, Yoshie. " 'To Be a Man' . . . ," 44-47.
  LaFrance, Marston. *A Reading . . . ,* 214-221.

"An Episode of War"
  LaFrance, Marston. *A Reading . . . ,* 238-240.

"An Experiment in Luxury"
  LaFrance, Marston. *A Reading . . . ,* 78-79.

"An Experiment in Misery"
  Holton, Milne. *Cylinders . . . ,* 67-69.
  LaFrance, Marston. *A Reading . . . ,* 43-48.

"Four Men in a Cave"
  LaFrance, Marston. *A Reading . . . ,* 27-29.

"George's Mother"

Brennan, Joseph X. "The Imagery and Art of 'George's Mother,' " *Coll Lang Assoc J*, 4 (1960), 106-115; rpt. Wertheim, Stanley, Ed. . . . *"Maggie"* . . . , 125-134; Gullason, Thomas A., Ed. . . . *Evaluations*, 372-381.

Geismar, Maxwell. *Rebels* . . . , 92-94; rpt. Current-García, Eugene, and Walton R. Patrick, Eds. *Realism* . . . , 440-442; Wertheim, Stanley, Ed. . . . *"Maggie"* . . . , 121-124.

Holton, Milne. *Cylinders* . . . , 55-63.

Itabashi, Yoshie. " 'To Be a Man' . . . ," 23-29.

Jackson, Agnes M. "Stephen Crane's Imagery of Conflict in 'George's Mother,' " *Arizona Q*, 25 (1969), 313-318.

LaFrance, Marston. *A Reading* . . . , 84-93.

Solomon, Eric. *Stephen Crane* . . . , 49-67; rpt. Gullason, Thomas A., Ed. . . . *Evaluations*, 382-394; rpt. in part Wertheim, Stanley, Ed. . . . *"Maggie"* . . . , 135-149.

Stallman, Robert W., Ed. *Stephen Crane* . . . , 19-20; rpt. Wertheim, Stanley, Ed. . . . *"Maggie"* . . . , 118-120.

"A Ghoul's Accountant"

LaFrance, Marston. *A Reading* . . . , 28-30.

"A Grey Sleeve"

LaFrance, Marston. *A Reading* . . . , 180-181.

"An Indian Campaign"

LaFrance, Marston. *A Reading* . . . , 179-180.

"Killing His Bear"

LaFrance, Marston. *A Reading* . . . , 31-33.

"Maggie: A Girl of the Streets"

Ahnebrink, Lars. *The Beginnings* . . . , 249-264, 378-381; first passage rpt. in part Bassan, Maurice, Ed. *Stephen Crane's "Maggie"* . . . , 123-125; Wertheim, Stanley, Ed. . . . *"Maggie"* . . . , 31-33.

Berryman, John. *Stephen Crane*, 51-65; Meridian ed., 51-65; rpt. in part Bassan, Maurice, Ed. *Stephen Crane's "Maggie"* . . . , 125-128; Wertheim, Stanley, Ed. . . . *"Maggie"* . . . , 27-30.

Bradbury, Malcolm. "Romance and Reality in 'Maggie,' " *J Am Stud*, 3 (1969), 111-121.

Brennan, Joseph X. "Ironic and Symbolic Structure in Crane's 'Maggie,' " *Nineteenth Century Fiction*, 16 (1962), 303-315; rpt. Gullason, Thomas A., Ed. . . . *Evaluations*, 323-334; rpt. in part Wertheim, Stanley, Ed. . . . *"Maggie"* . . . , 54-64.

Cady, Edwin H. *Stephen Crane,* 104-111; rpt. in part Bassan, Maurice, Ed. *Stephen Crane's "Maggie"* . . . , 149-151; Wertheim, Stanley, Ed. . . . *"Maggie"* . . . , 50-53.

————. "Stephen Crane: 'Maggie: A Girl of the Streets,' " in Cohen, Hennig, Ed. *Landmarks* . . . , 172-181.

Fitelson, David. "Stephen Crane's 'Maggie' and Darwinism," *Am Q,* 16 (1964), 182-194; rpt. Bassan, Maurice, Ed. *Stephen Crane's "Maggie"* . . . , 157-166; Wertheim, Stanley, Ed. . . . *"Maggie"* . . . , 68-79.

Ford, Philip H. "Illusion and Reality in Crane's 'Maggie,' " *Arizona Q,* 25 (1969), 293-303.

Holton, Milne. "The Sparrow's Fall and the Sparrow's Eye: Crane's 'Maggie,' " *Studia Neophilologica,* 41 (1969), 115-129.

————. *Cylinders* . . . , 35-54.

Itabashi, Yoshie. " 'To Be a Man' . . . ," 9-15.

Katz, Joseph. "The 'Maggie' Nobody Knows," *Mod Fiction Stud,* 12 (1966), 200-212; rpt. Wertheim, Stanley, Ed. . . . *"Maggie"* . . . , 93-107.

LaFrance, Marston. *A Reading* . . . , 50-66.

Martin, Jay. *Harvests* . . . , 57-59; rpt. Wertheim, Stanley, Ed. . . . *"Maggie"* . . . , 89-92.

Overmyer, Janet. "The Structure of Crane's 'Maggie,' " *Univ Kansas City R,* 29 (1962), 71-72; rpt. Bassan, Maurice, Ed. *Stephen Crane's "Maggie"* . . . , 153-154; Wertheim, Stanley, Ed. . . . *"Maggie"* . . . , 65-67; Gullason, Thomas A., Ed. . . . *Evaluations,* 320-322.

Pizer, Donald. "Stephen Crane's 'Maggie' and American Naturalism," *Criticism,* 7 (1965), 168-175; rpt. in his *Realism* . . . , 121-131; Bassan, Maurice, Ed. *Stephen Crane* . . . , 110-117; Wertheim, Stanley, Ed. . . . *"Maggie"* . . . , 80-88; Gullason, Thomas A., Ed. . . . *Evaluations,* 335-343.

Stein, William B. "New Testament Inversions in Crane's 'Maggie,' " *Mod Lang Notes,* 73 (1958), 268-272; rpt. Bassan, Maurice, Ed. *Stephen Crane's "Maggie"* . . . , 134-137; Wertheim, Stanley, Ed. . . . *"Maggie"* . . . 45-49; Gullason, Thomas A., Ed. . . . *Evaluations,* 315-319.

"Making an Orator"

Monteiro, George. "With Proper Words (or Without Them) the Soldier Dies: Stephen Crane's 'Making an Orator,' " *Cithara,* 9 (May, 1970), 64-72.

"A Man and Some Others"

Deamer, Robert G. "Stephen Crane and the Western Myth," *Western Am Lit,* 7 (1972), 118-120.

"Manacles"

Holton, Milne. *Cylinders* . . . , 202-203.

"The Men in the Storm"
LaFrance, Marston. *A Reading* . . . , 83-84.
Monteiro, George. "Society and Nature in Stephen Crane's 'The Men in
the Storm,' " *Prairie Schooner*, 45 (1971), 13-17.

"The Mesmeric Mountain"
LaFrance, Marston. *A Reading* . . . , 33-34.

"The Monster
Gullason, Thomas A. "Stephen Crane's Short Stories . . . ," in his . . .
Evaluations, 481-482.
Hafley, James. " 'The Monster' and the Art of Stephen Crane," *Accent*, 19
(1959), 159-165; rpt. Gullason, Thomas A., Ed. . . . *Evaluations*, 440-
446.
Holton, Milne. *Cylinders* . . . , 204-213.
Itabashi, Yoshie. " 'To Be a Man' . . . ," 33-38.
LaFrance, Marston. *A Reading* . . . , 205-210.
Monteiro, George. "Stephen Crane and the Antinomies of Christian
Charity," *Centennial R*, 16 (1972), 102-104.
Osborn, Neal J. "Crane's 'The Monster' and 'The Blue Hotel, ' "
Explicator, 23 (1964), Item 10; rpt. Katz, Joseph, Ed. *Stephen Crane*
. . . , 107-108.

"Moonlight on the Snow"
Holton, Milne. *Cylinders* . . . , 241-242.

"A Mystery of Heroism"
LaFrance, Marston. *A Reading* . . . , 192-195.

"An Ominous Baby"
LaFrance, Marston. *A Reading* . . . , 74-75.

"The Open Boat"
Adams, Richard P. "Naturalistic Fiction: 'The Open Boat,' " *Tulane Stud
Engl*, 4 (1954), 137-145; rpt. Gullason, Thomas A., Ed. . . . *Evaluations*,
421-429.
Gerstenberger, Donna. " 'The Open Boat': Additional Perspective," *Mod
Fiction Stud*, 17 (1972), 557-561.
Gullason, Thomas A. "The New Criticism and Older Ones: Another Ride
in 'The Open Boat, ' " *Coll Engl Assoc Critic*, 31 (June, 1969), 8.
Holton, Milne. *Cylinders* . . . , 150-168.
Itabashi, Yoshie. " 'To Be a Man' . . . , " 29-33.

Kissane, Leedice. "Interpretation Through Language: A Study of the Metaphors in Stephen Crane's 'The Open Boat, ' " *Rendezvous*, 1 (Spring, 1966), 18-22; rpt. Gullason, Thomas A., Ed. . . . *Evaluations*, 410-416.

813.4   LaFrance, Marston. *A Reading* . . . , 195-205.

C89/ru Metzger, Charles R. "Realistic Devices in Stephen Crane's 'The Open Boat, ' " *Midwest Q*, 4 (1962), 47-54; rpt. in part Gullason, Thomas A., Ed. . . . *Evaluations*, 417-420.

Monteiro, George. "The Logic Beneath 'The Open Boat, ' " *Georgia R*, 26 (1972), 326-335.

Munson, Girham. *Style and Form* . . . , 159-170; rpt. in part Gullason, Thomas A., Ed. . . . *Evaluations*, 239-242.

Napier, James J. "Land Imagery in 'The Open Boat, ' " *Coll Engl Assoc Critic*, 29 (April, 1967), 15.

White, W. M. "The Crane-Hemingway Code: A Reevaluation," *Ball State Univ Forum*, 10 (Spring, 1969), 15-20.

813.4   "The Pace of Youth"
LaFrance, Marston. *A Reading* . . . , 76-78.

C891ru Schellhorn, G. C. "Stephen Crane's 'The Pace of Youth, ' " *Arizona Q*, 25 (1969), 334-342.

"The Price of the Harness"
Holton, Milne. *Cylinders* . . . , 258-261.

"Shame"
Holton, Milne. *Cylinders* . . . , 219-221.

"The Squire's Madness"
Holton, Milne. *Cylinders* . . . , 203-204.

813.4 "A Tent in Agony"
C891ru LaFrance, Marston. *A Reading* . . . , 30-31.

"Twelve O'Clock"
Holton, Milne. *Cylinders* . . . , 242-243.

"The Upturned Face"
Dillingham, William. "Crane's One-Act Farce: 'The Upturned Face, ' " *Research Stud* (Wash. State Univ.), 35 (1967), 324-330.

813.4   Holton, Milne. *Cylinders* . . . , 269-272.
C891ru LaFrance, Marston. *A Reading* . . . , 240-242.

"War Memories"
    LaFrance, Marston. *A Reading* . . . , 232-238.

"Why Did the Young Clerk Swear? Or, The Unsatisfactory French"
    Solomon, Eric. *Stephen Crane* . . . , 7-8; rpt. Gullason, Thomas A., Ed. . . .
    Evaluations, 245-246.

ISAK DINESEN [BARONESS KAREN BLIVEN]

"Ehrengard"
    Saul, George B. *Withdrawn in Gold,* 47-48.

FYODOR DOSTOEVSKY

"The Double"
    Lord, Robert. *Dostoevsky* . . . , 218-220.

"The Dream of a Ridiculous Man"
    Lord, Robert. *Dostoevsky* . . . , 188-189, 233-234.

"The Eternal Husband"
    Lord, Robert. *Dostoevsky* . . . , 222-226.
    Pratt, Branwen. "The Role of the Unconscious in 'The Eternal
    Husband,' " *Lit & Psych,* 21 (1971), 29-39; rpt. *Lit & Psych,* 22 (1972),
    13-25.

"The Gambler"
    Lord, Robert. *Dostoevsky* . . . , 71-73.

"A Gentle Creature"
    Lord, Robert. *Dostoevsky* . . . , 231-233.

"Notes from Underground"
    Engelberg, Edward. *The Unknown Distance* . . . , 230-241.
    Friedman, Maurice. *Problematic Rebel* . . . , 99-109, 257-260; 2nd ed., 152-
    161, 216-219.
    Lord, Robert. *Dostoevsky* . . . , 35-47.
    Merrill, Reed. "The Mistaken Endeavor: Dostoevsky's 'Notes from
    Underground,' " *Mod Fiction Stud,* 18 (1973), 505-516.
    Peace, Richard. *Dostoyevsky* . . . , 5-18.
    Wellek, Renē. "Masterpieces of Realism and Naturalism," in Mack,
    Maynard, *et al.,* Eds. *World Masterpieces,* II, 1712-1715; 3rd ed., 726-
    729; Continental ed., 1429-1434; Continental ed. rev., 504-508.

ANNETTE VON DROSTE-HÜLSHOFF

"Die Judenbuche"
Bernd, Clifford A. "Clarity and Obscurity in Annette von Droste-Hülshoff's 'Judenbuche,' " in Mews, Siegfried, Ed. *Studies*..., 64-77.

ANDRÉ DUBUS

"The Doctor"
Minot, Stephen, and Robley Wilson. *Teacher's Manual*..., 4-5.

PAUL L. DUNBAR

"The Scapegoat"
Starke, Catherine J. *Black Portraiture*..., 181-183.

ESTEBAN ECHEVERRÍA

"El Matadero"
Foster, David W. "Paschal Symbology in Echeverría's 'El Matadero,' " *Stud Short Fiction*, 7 (1970), 257-263.
Mirinfgo, Mariano. "Realidad y ficcion de 'El matadero,' " *Humanitas* (Tucumán), No. 18 (1965), 283-318.
Queiroz, Mari de Jose. " 'El matadero,' pieza en tres actos," *Revista iberoamaricana*, 33 (1967), 105-113.

HARRY STILLWELL EDWARDS

"Elder Brown's Backslide"
Skaggs, Merrill M. *The Folk*..., 89-90.

"His Defense"
Skaggs, Merrill M. *The Folk*..., 92-94.

GEORGE ELIOT [MARY ANN EVANS]

"Janet's Repentance"
Sprague, Rosemary. *George Eliot*..., 143-147.

"Mr. Gilfil's Love Story"
Sprague, Rosemary. *George Eliot* . . . , 137-142.

"The Sad Fortunes of the Reverend Amos Barton"
Sprague, Rosemary. *George Eliot* . . . , 131-137.

RALPH W. ELLISON

"Battle Royal"
Douglas, Kenneth. "Masterpieces of the Modern World," in Mack, Maynard, *et al.*, Eds. *World Masterpieces*, II, 3rd ed., 1389-1390.
Mizener, Arthur. *A Handbook* . . . *"Modern Short Stories* . . . *Third Edition,"* 15-18.

"Flying Home"
Trimmer, Joseph F. "Ralph Ellison's 'Flying Home,' " *Stud Short Fiction*, 9 (1972), 175-182.

"King of the Bingo Game"
Minot, Stephen, and Robley Wilson. *Teacher's Manual* . . . , 7-8.

WILLIAM FAULKNER

"Barn Burning"
Hays, Peter L. *The Limping Hero* . . . , 163-164.
Wilson, Gayle E. " 'Being Pulled Two Ways': The Nature of Sarty's Choice in 'Barn Burning,' " *Mississippi Q*, 24 (1971), 279-288.

"The Bear"
Adamowski, T.H. "Isaac McCaslin and the Wilderness of the Imagination," *Centennial R*, 17 (1973), 92-112.
Adams, Richard P. "Focus on William Faulkner's 'The Bear': Moses and the Wilderness," in Madden, David, Ed. *American Dreams* . . . , 129-135.
Brumm, Ursula. "Wilderness and Civilization: A Note on William Faulkner," *Partisan R*, 22 (1955), 349-350; rpt. Utley, Francis L., *et al.*, Eds. *Bear* . . . , 2nd ed., 251-252.
Dussinger, Gloria R. "Faulkner's Isaac McCaslin as Romantic Hero Manqué," *So Atlantic Q*, 68 (1969), 377-385.
Gelfant, Blanche H. "Faulkner and Keats: The Ideality of Art in 'The Bear,' " *Southern Lit J*, 2, i (1969), 43-65.
Hoffman, Daniel. "William Faulkner: 'The Bear,' " in Cohen, Hennig, Ed. *Landmarks* . . ., 341-352.

Howe, Irving. *William Faulkner* ..., 186-189; rpt., rev., in 2nd ed., 253-259; rpt. in original form in Utley, Francis L., *et al.*, Eds. *Bear* ..., 348-352; rpt. in rev. form in Utley, Francis L., *et al.*, Eds. *Bear* ..., 2nd ed., 124-126.

Howell, Elmo. "Faulkner's Elegy: An Approach to 'The Bear,' " *Arlington Q,* 2 (1970), 122-132.

Kinney, Arthur F. "Faulkner and the Possibilities for Heroism," *Southern R,* 6, N.S. (1970), 1110-1125; rpt. Utley, Francis L., *et al.*, Eds. *Bear* ..., 2nd ed., 235-251.

Lewis, R.W.B. "The Hero in the New World: William Faulkner's 'The Bear,' " *Kenyon R,* 13 (1951), 641-660; rpt. Feidelson, Charles, and Paul Brodtkorb, Eds. *Interpretations* ..., 332-348; Utley, Francis L., *et al.*, Eds. *Bear* ..., 306-327; 2nd ed., 188-201; rpt., rev., Lewis, R.W.B. *The Picaresque Saint,* 193-209; Keystone pb. ed., 193-209; Warren, Robert P., Ed. *Faulkner* ..., 208-218.

Lydenberg, John. "Nature Myth in William Faulkner's 'The Bear,' " *Am Lit,* 24 (1952), 62-72; rpt. Utley, Francis L., *et al.*, Eds. *Bear* ..., 280-289; 2nd ed., 160-167; Vickery, John B., Ed. *Myth* ..., 257-264.

Madeya, Ulrike. "Interpretationen zu William Faulkners 'The Bear': Das Bild des Helden und die Konstellation des Charaktere," *Literatur in Wissenschaft und Unterricht,* 3 (1970), 45-60.

Millgate, Michael. *William Faulkner,* 73-74; Am. ed., 73-74.

Nagel, James. "Huck Finn and 'The Bear': The Wilderness and Moral Freedom," *Engl Stud in Africa,* 12 (March, 1969), 59-63.

Nestrick, William V. "The Function of Form in 'The Bear,' Section IV," *Twentieth Century Lit,* 12 (1966), 131-137; rpt. Utley, Francis L., *et al.*, Eds. *Bear* ...,2nd ed., 298-305.

Page, Sally R. *Faulkner's Women* ..., 186-187.

Prasad, V.R.N. "The Pilgrim and the Picaro: A Study of Faulkner's 'The Bear' and *The Reivers,*" in Mukherjee, Sujit, and D.V.K. Raghavacharyulu, Eds. *Indian Essays* ..., 210-214.

Simpson, Lewis P. "Isaac McCaslin and Temple Drake: The Fall of New World Man,"*Louisiana State Univ Stud,* 15 (1965), 88-106; rpt. in part Stanford, Donald E., Ed. *Nine Essays* ..., 92-97; Utley, Francis L., *et al.*, Eds. *Bear* ..., 2nd ed., 202-209.

Starke, Catherine J. *Black Portraiture* ..., 192-193.

Stephens, Rosemary. "Ike's Gun and Too Many Novembers," *Mississippi Q,* 23 (1970), 279-287.

Stewart, David H. "The Purpose of Faulkner's Ike," *Criticism,* 3 (1961), 333-342; rpt. Utley, Francis L., *et al.*, Eds. *Bear* ..., 327-336; 2nd ed., 212-220.

Utley, Francis L. "Pride and Humility: The Cultural Roots of Ike McCaslin," in Utley, Francis L., *et al.*, Eds. *Bear* ..., 233-260; 2nd ed., 167-187.

Vickery, Olga W. *The Novels* . . . , 130-134; rpt. Utley, Francis L., *et al.*, Eds. *Bear* . . . , 323-327; 2nd ed., 209-212.

"A Courtship"

Cantwell, Frank. "Faulkner's 'A Courtship,' " *Mississippi Q,* 24 (1971), 289-295.

"Delta Autumn"

Adamowski, T.H. "Isaac McCaslin . . . ," 92-112.

Douglas, Kenneth. "Masterpieces of the Modern World," in Mack, Maynard, *et al.*, Eds. *World Masterpieces,* II, 3rd ed., 1381-1382.

Harter, Carol C. "The Winter of Isaac McCaslin: Revisions and Irony in Faulkner's 'Delta Autumn,' " *J Mod Lit,* 1 (1970), 209-225.

Kinney, Arthur F. "Faulkner . . . Heroism," 1110-1125.

Mizener, Arthur, Ed. *Modern Short Stories* . . . , 465-468; rpt. rev. ed., 545-550; 3rd ed., 625-628.

"Dry September"

Page, Sally R. *Faulkner's Women* . . . , 99-103.

Vickery, John B. "Ritual and Theme in Faulkner's 'Dry September,' " *Arizona Q,* 18 (1962), 5-14; rpt. Vickery, John B., and J'nan M. Sellery, Eds. *The Scapegoat.* . . , 200-208.

"Elly"

Page, Sally R. *Faulkner's Women* . . . , 95-96.

"The Fire and the Hearth"

Mizener, Arthur. *A Handbook* . . . *"Modern Short Stories* . . . *Revised Edition,"* 135-140; rpt. *A Handbook* . . . *"Modern Short Stories* . . . *Third Edition,"* 155-160.

Starke, Catherine J. *Black Portraiture* . . . , 193-194.

"Hair"

Page, Sally R. *Faulkner's Women* . . . , 176-177.

"Miss Zilphia Gant"

Pitavy, François L. "A Forgotten Faulkner Story: 'Miss Zilphia Gant,' " *Stud Short Fiction,* 9 (1972), 131-142.

"Mr. Arcarius"

Gresset, Michel. "Weekend, Lost and Revisited," *Mississippi Q,* 21 (1968), 173-178.

"Mistral"
Clark, Charles C. " 'Mistral': A Study in Human Tempering," *Mississippi Q,* 21 (1968), 195-204.

"Old Man"
Hamalian, Leo, and Edmond L. Volpe, Eds. *Ten . . . Short Novels,* 559-560; rpt. 2nd ed. (retitled *Eleven . . . Short Novels),* 537-538.

"The Old People"
Adamowski, T. H. "Isaac McCaslin . . . ," 92-112.
Kinney, Arthur F. "Faulkner . . . Heroism," 1110-1125.

"Raid"
Mizener, Arthur. *A Handbook . . . "Modern Short Stories . . . Revised Edition,"* 143-149; rpt. *A Handbook . . . "Modern Short Stories . . . Third Edition,"* 163-169.

"Red Leaves"
Howell, Elmo. "William Faulkner's Chickasaw Legacy: A Note on 'Red Leaves,' " *Arizona Q,* 26 (1970), 293-303.

"A Rose for Emily"
Brooks, Cleanth, and Robert P. Warren. *Understanding Fiction,* 409-414; 2nd ed., 350-354; rpt. Locke, Louis, William Gibson, and George Arms, Eds. *An Introduction . . . ,* 187-191; 2nd ed., 451-455; 3rd ed., 443-446; Inge, M. Thomas, Ed. *William Faulkner . . . ,* 25-29.
Campbell, Harry M., and Ruel E. Foster. *William Faulkner . . . ,* 99-100; rpt. Inge, M. Thomas, Ed. *William Faulkner . . . ,* 43.
Clements, Arthur L., and Sister Mary Bride. "Faulkner's 'A Rose for Emily,' " *Explicator,* 20 (1963), Item 78; rpt. Inge, M. Thomas, Ed. *William Faulkner . . . ,* 64-65. 1962
Going, William T. "Chronology in Teaching 'A Rose for Emily,' " *Exercise Exchange,* 5 (February, 1958), 8-11; rpt. Inge, M. Thomas, Ed. *William Faulkner . . . ,* 50-53.
————. "Faulkner's 'A Rose for Emily,' " *Explicator,* 16 (1958), Item 27; rpt. Inge, M. Thomas, Ed. *William Faulkner . . . ,* 54-55.
Hagopian, John V., W. Gordon Cunliffe, and Martin Dolch. "A Rose for Emily," in Hagopian, John V., and Martin Dolch, Eds. *Insight I . . . ,* 42-50; rpt. Inge, M. Thomas, Ed. *William Faulkner . . . ,* 76-83.
Happel, Nikolaus. "William Faulkners 'A Rose for Emily,' " *Die Neueren Sprachen,* 9 (1962), 396-404; rpt. in part Inge, M. Thomas, Ed. *William Faulkner . . . ,* 68-72.
Holland, Norman. "Fantasy and Defense in Faulkner's 'A Rose for Emily,' " *Hartford Stud Lit,* 4, i (1972), 1-36.

Howe, Irving. *William Faulkner* . . . , 2nd ed., 262-265; rpt. in part Inge, M. Thomas, Ed. *William Faulkner* . . . , 58.

Howell, Elmo. "Faulkner's 'A Rose for Emily,' " *Explicator,* 19 (1961), Item 26; rpt. Inge, M. Thomas, Ed. *William Faulkner* . . . , 59-60.

Johnson, C. W. "Faulkner's 'A Rose for Emily,' " *Explicator,* 6 (1948),Oct. Item 45; rpt. Inge, M. Thomas, Ed. *William Faulkner* . . . , 35. / Vol.7

Kempton, Kenneth P. *The Short Story,* 104-106; rpt. Inge, M. Thomas, Ed. *William Faulkner* . . . , 30-31.

Magalaner, Marvin, and Edmond L. Volpe. *Teachers' Manual* . . . , 16-17; rpt. in part Inge, M. Thomas, Ed. *William Faulkner* . . . , 63.

Nebeker, Helen E. "Chronology Revised," *Stud Short Fiction,* 8 (1971), 471-473.

————. "Emily's Rose of Love: Thematic Implications of Point of View in Faulkner's 'A Rose for Emily,' " *Bull Rocky Mountain Mod Lang Assoc,* 24 (March, 1970), 3-13.

Page, Sally R. *Faulkner's Women* . . . , 99-103.

Ross, Danforth. . . . *Short Story,* 36-37; rpt. Inge, M. Thomas, Ed. *William Faulkner* . . . , 61-62.

Snell, George. "The Fury of William Faulkner," *Western R,* 11 (1946), 35-37; rpt. in his *The Shapers* . . . , 96-99; Inge, M. Thomas, Ed. *William Faulkner* . . . , 32-34.

Stafford, T. J. "Tobe's Significance in 'A Rose for Emily,' " *Mod Fiction Stud,* 14 (1969), 451-453; rpt. Inge, M. Thomas, Ed. *William Faulkner*. . . , 87-89.

Stewart, James T. "Miss Havisham and Miss Grierson," *Furman Stud,* 4 (1958), 21-23; rpt. Inge, M. Thomas, Ed. *William Faulkner* . . . , 56-57.

Stone, Edward. *A Certain Morbidity* . . . , 85-100.

Sullivan, Ruth. "The Narrator in 'A Rose for Emily, ' " *J Narrative Technique,* 1 (1971), 159-178.

Watkins, Floyd C. "The Structure of 'A Rose for Emily,' " *Mod Lang Notes,* 69 (1954), 508-510; rpt. Inge, M. Thomas, Ed. *William Faulkner* . . . , 46-47.

West, Ray B. "Faulkner's 'A Rose for Emily,' " *Explicator,* 7 (1948), Item 8; rpt. Inge, M. Thomas, Ed. *William Faulkner* . . . , 36-37.

————. "Atmosphere and Theme in Faulkner's 'A Rose For Emily, ' " *Perspective,* 2 (1949), 239-245; rpt. in his *The Art* . . . , 197-203; Hoffman, Frederick J., and Olga W. Vickery, Eds. *William Faulkner*. . . , 259-267; Inge, M. Thomas, Ed. *William Faulkner* . . . , 38-42.

"Spotted Horses"

Houghton, Donald E. "Whores and Horses in Faulkner's 'Spotted Horses,' " *Midwest Q,* 11 (1970), 361-369.

Page, Sally R. *Faulkner's Women* . . . , 158-160.

Rea, J. "Faulkner's 'Spotted Horses,' " *Hartford Stud Lit,* 2 (1970), 157-164.

"The Tall Men"
Howell, Elmo. "William Faulkner and the New Deal," *Midwest Q,* 5
(1964), 323-332.

"That Evening Sun"
Hermann, John. "Faulkner's Heart's Darling in 'That Evening Sun,' "
Stud Short Fiction, 7 (1970), 320-323.

"Victory"
Smith, Raleigh W. "Faulkner's 'Victory': The Plain People of
Clydebank," *Mississippi Q,* 23 (1970), 241-249.

F. SCOTT FITZGERALD

"Absolution"
Cross, K. G. W. *F. Scott Fitzgerald,* 73-74; Am. ed., 73-74.

"Babylon Revisited"
Mizener, Arthur. *A Handbook . . . "Modern Short Stories . . . Revised
Edition,"* 10-14; rpt. *A Handbook . . . "Modern Short Stories . . . Third
Edition,"* 10-13.

"First Blood"
Drake, Constance. "Josephine . . . ," in Bruccoli, Matthew J., Ed.
Fitzgerald/Hemingway Annual, 1969, 9-10.

"Winter Dreams"
Cross, K. G. W. *F. Scott Fitzgerald,* 72-73; Am. ed., 72-73.

"A Woman with a Past"
Drake, Constance. "Josephine . . . ," in Bruccoli, Matthew J., Ed.
Fitzgerald/Hemingway Annual, 1969, 10-11.

GUSTAVE FLAUBERT

"Bouvard and Pécuchet"
Cross, Richard K. *Flaubert . . . ,* 163-173.

"Herodias"
Jasinski, René. "Le Sens des *Trois Contes,"* in Cormier, Raymond J., and
Urban T. Holmes, Eds. *Essays . . . ,* 117-128.

"St. Julien"
  Bancroft, W. Jane. "Flaubert's *Légende de Saint Julien:* The Duality of
    the Artist-Saint," *L'Esprit Créateur,* 10, i (1970), 75-84.
  Cross, Richard K. *Flaubert . . . ,* 31-32.
  Jasinski, René. "Le Sens des *Trois Contes,"* in Cormier, Raymond J., and
    Urban T. Holmes, Eds. *Essays . . . ,* 117-128.

"A Simple Heart"
  Cross, Richard K. *Flaubert . . . ,* 17-25.
  Denommé, Robert T. "Félicité's View of Reality and the Nature of
    Flaubert's Irony in "Un Coeur Simple,' " *Stud Short Fiction,* 7 (1970),
    573-581.
  Jasinski, René. "Le Sens des *Trois Contes,"* in Cormier, Raymond J., and
    Urban T. Holmes, Eds. *Essays . . . ,* 117-128.

E. M. FORSTER

"The Eternal Moment"
  McDowell, Frederick P. W. *E. M. Forster,* 60-61.

"Other Kingdom"
  McDowell, Frederick P. W. *E. M. Forster,* 59-60.

"The Point of It"
  McDowell, Frederick P. W. *E. M. Forster,* 62-64.

"The Road from Colonus"
  Lee, L. L. *"Oedipus at Colonus:* The Modern 'Vulgarizations' of Forster
    and Cicellis," *Stud Short Fiction,* 8 (1971), 561-567.
  McDowell, Frederick P. W. *E. M. Forster,* 60-61.

"The Story of a Panic"
  McDowell, Frederick P. W. *E. M. Forster,* 59-60.

"The Story of the Siren"
  McDowell, Frederick P. W. *E. M. Forster,* 61-62.

JOHN FOX

"Grayson's Baby"
  Skaggs, Merrill M. *The Folk . . . ,* 202-204.

"A Purple Rhododendron"
    Skaggs, Merrill M. *The Folk* . . . , 144-145.

MARY E.WILKINS FREEMAN

"The Three Old Sisters and the Old Beau"
    Toth, Susan A. "Mary Wilkins Freeman's Parable of Wasted Life," *Am
    Lit*, 42 (1971), 564-567.

ALICE FRENCH

"Trusty, No. 49"
    Skaggs, Merrill M. *The Folk* . . . , 95-96.

ROBERT FROST

"The Cockerel Buying Habit"
    Geyer, C. W. "A Poulterer's Pleasure: Robert Frost as Prose Humorist,"
    Stud Short Fiction, 8 (1971), 595.

"A Just Judge"
    Geyer, C. W. "A Poulterer's Pleasure . . . ," 592-594.

"Old Welch Goes to Show"
    Geyer, C. W. "A Poulterer's Pleasure . . . ," 596-599.

"The Original and Only"
    Geyer, C. W. "A Poulterer's Pleasure . . . ," 594.

"The Same Thing Over and Over"   .
    Geyer, C. W. "A Poulterer's Pleasure . . . ," 595-596.

"Trap Nests"
    Geyer, C. W. "A Poulterer's Pleasure . . . ," 590-592.

CARLOS FUENTES

"Chac Mool"
    Leal, Luis. "The New Mexican Short Story," *Stud Short Fiction*, 8 (1971),
    17-18.

ERNEST J. GAINES

"The Sky Is Gray"
  Mizener, Arthur. *A Handbook . . . "Modern Short Stories . . . Third Edition,"* 181-184.

HAMLIN GARLAND

"Rising Wolf—Ghost Dancer"
  Folsom, James K. . . . *Western Novel,* 151-153.

"The Silent Eaters"
  Folsom, James K. . . . *Western Novel,* 149-151.

"The Story of Howling Wolf"
  Folsom, James K. . . . *Western Novel,* 154-155.

WILLIAM GASS

"The Pederson Kid"
  Kane, Patricia. "The Sun Burned on the Snow," *Critique,* 14, ii (1972), 89-96.

ANDRÉ GIDE

"Geneviève"
  Cordle, Thomas, *André Gide,* 146-150.
  Ireland, G. W. *André Gide . . . ,* 377-392.
  Painter, George D. *André Gide . . . ,* 153-155; rpt. with changes in his . . . *Critical Biography,* 105-107.

"El Hadj"
  Cordle, Thomas. *André Gide,* 46-50.
  Ireland, G. W. *André Gide . . . ,* 171-177.

"The Immoralist"
  Brennan, Joseph G. "Three Novels of Dépaysement," *Comp Lit,* 22 (1970), 223-236.
  Cordle, Thomas. *André Gide,* 84-92.
  Ireland, G. W. *André Gide . . . ,* 178-198.
  Painter, George D. *André Gide . . . ,* 64-70; rpt. with changes in his . . . *Critical Biography,* 40-44.

"Isabelle"
Painter, George D. *André Gide* . . . , 92-95; rpt. with changes in his . . .
Critical Biography, 59-62.

"Marshlands"
Cordle, Thomas. *André Gide*, 50-55.
Ireland, G. W. *André Gide* . . . , 103-119.
Painter, George D. *André Gide* . . . , 41-44; rpt. with changes in his . . .
Critical Biography, 23-25.

"The Pastoral Symphony"
Cordle, Thomas. *André Gide*, 100-107.
Hamalian, Leo, and Edmond L. Volpe, Eds. *Ten* . . . *Short Novels*, 423-
427; rpt. 2nd ed. (retitled *Eleven* . . . *Short Novels)*, 403-405.
Ireland, G. W. *André Gide* . . . , 283-308.
Painter, George D. *André Gide* . . . , 120-125; rpt. with changes in his . . .
Critical Biography, 80-84.

"The Return of the Prodigal Son"
Cordle, Thomas. *André Gide*, 81-84.
Ireland, G. W. *André Gide* . . . , 222-236.
Painter, George D. *André Gide* . . . , 83-85; rpt. with changes in his . . .
Critical Biography, 53-55.

"Robert"
Cordle, Thomas. *André Gide*, 144-146.
Ireland, G. W. *André Gide* . . . , 377-392.
Painter, George D. *André Gide* . . . , 151-153; rpt. with changes in his . . .
Critical Biography, 104-105.

"School for Wives"
Cordle, Thomas. *André Gide*, 138-144.
Ireland. G. W. *André Gide* . . . , 377-392.
Painter, George D. *André Gide* . . . , 149-151; rpt. with changes in his . . .
Critical Biography, 103-104.

"Strait Is the Gate"
Cordle, Thomas. *André Gide*, 92-100.
Ireland, G. W. *André Gide* . . . , 199-221.
Knecht, Loring D. "A New Reading of Gide's 'La Porte étroite,' " *PMLA*,
82 (1967), 640-648; rpt. Littlejohn, David, Ed. *Gide* . . . , 93-111.
Painter, George D. *André Gide* . . . , 86-90; rpt. with changes in his . . .
Critical Biography, 55-59.

Vandenriessche, Christian. "Structure d'un recit gidien: Le journal d'Alissa dans 'La porte étroite,' " *Revue des Sciences Humaines,* 137 (1970), 107-117.

"Theseus"
Cordle, Thomas. *Andrē Gide,* 157-161.
Ireland, G. W. *Andrē Gide . . . ,* 408-421.
Painter, George D. *Andrē Gide . . . ,* 179-183; rpt. with changes in his . . . *Critical Biography,* 127-129.

GEORGE GISSING

"House of Cobwebs"
Adams, Elsie B. "Gissing's Allegorical 'House of Cobwebs,' " *Stud Short Fiction,* 7 (1970), 324-326.
Ware, Thomas C. "Jerusalem Artichokes in Gissing's Garden: A Postscript to the Allegorical Reading of 'House of Cobwebs,' " *Stud Short Fiction,* 9 (1972), 86-89.

NIKOLAI GOGOL

"The Overcoat"
Schillinger, John. "Gogol's 'The Overcoat' as a Travesty of Hagiography," *Slavic & East European J,* 16 (1972), 36-41.

IVAN GONCHAROV

"A Cruel Illness"
Ehre, Milton. "Goncharov's Early Prose Fiction," *Slavonic & East European R,* 50 (1972), 365-368.

"A Happy Error"
Ehre, Milton. "Goncharov's Early Prose . . . ," 359-365.

CAROLINE GORDON

"All Lovers Love the Spring"
Alvis, John E. "The Idea of Nature and the Sexual Role in Caroline Gordon's Early Stories of Love," in Landess, Thomas H., Ed. . . . *Caroline Gordon . . . ,* 101-104.
Stuckey, W. J. *Caroline Gordon,* 119.

"The Brilliant Leaves"
   Alvis, John E. "The Idea of Nature . . . ," in Landess, Thomas H., Ed. . . .
      Caroline Gordon . . . , 98-101.
   Rocks, James E. "The Short Fiction of Caroline Gordon," *Tulane Stud
      Engl*, 18 (1970), 117-119.
   Stuckey, W. J. *Caroline Gordon*, 125-126.

"The Burning Eyes"
   Cowan, Louise. "Aleck Maury, Epic Hero and Pilgrim," in Landess,
      Thomas H., Ed. . . . *Caroline Gordon* . . . , 17-18.

"The Captive"
   Brown, Jane G. "Woman in Nature: A Study of Caroline Gordon's 'The
      Captive,' " in Landess, Thomas H., Ed. . . . *Caroline Gordon* . . . , 75-84.
   Rocks, James E. "The Short Fiction . . . ," 119-120.
   Stuckey, W. J. *Caroline Gordon*, 113-114.

"Emmanuele! Emmanuele!"
   Dupree, Robert S. "Caroline Gordon's 'Constants' of Fiction," in
      Landess, Thomas H., Ed. . . . *Caroline Gordon* . . . , 34-45.
   Rocks, James E. "The Short Fiction . . . ," 130-132.
   Stuckey, W. J. *Caroline Gordon*, 129-130.

"The Enemies"
   Stuckey, W. J. *Caroline Gordon*, 124-125.

"The Forest of the South"
   Bradford, M. E. "The High Cost of 'Union': Caroline Gordon's Civil War
      Stories," in Landess, Thomas H., Ed. . . . *Caroline Gordon* . . . , 115-120.
   Rocks, James E. "The Short Fiction . . . ," 120-121.

"Hear the Nightingale Sing"
   Bradford, M. E. " . . . Civil War Stories," in Landess, Thomas H., Ed. . . .
      Caroline Gordon . . . , 120-123.
   Rocks, James E. "The Short Fiction . . . ," 121.

"Her Quaint Honor"
   Landess, Thomas H. "Caroline Gordon's Ontological Stories," in
      Landess, Thomas H., Ed. . . . *Caroline Gordon* . . . , 68-73.

"The Ice House"
   Bradford, M. E. " . . . Civil War Stories," in Landess, Thomas H., Ed. . . .
      Caroline Gordon . . . , 124-126.
   Stuckey, W. J. *Caroline Gordon*, 119-124.

"The Last Day in the Field"
   Cowan, Louise. "Aleck Maury . . . ," in Landess, Thomas H., Ed. . . .
      Caroline Gordon . . . , 18-20.
   Rocks, James E. "The Short Fiction . . . ," 125-126.
   Stuckey, W. J. *Caroline Gordon,* 115-116.

"The Long Day"
   Landess, Thomas H. " . . . Ontological Stories," in Landess, Thomas H.,
      Ed. . . . *Caroline Gordon* . . . , 61-65.

"Mr. Powers"
   Landess, Thomas H. " . . . Ontological Stories," in Landess, Thomas H.,
      Ed. . . . *Caroline Gordon* . . . , 65-68.

"A Narrow Heart: The Portrait of a Woman"
   Rocks, James E. "The Short Fiction . . . ," 132-133.

"Old Red"
   Cowan, Louise. "Aleck Maury . . . ," in Landess, Thomas H., Ed. . . .
      Caroline Gordon . . . , 21-23.
   Rocks, James E. "The Short Fiction . . . ," 127-129.
   Stuckey, W. J. *Caroline Gordon,* 112-113.

"The Olive Garden"
   Dupree, Robert S. "Caroline Gordon's 'Constants' . . . ," in Landess,
      Thomas H., Ed. . . . *Caroline Gordon* . . . , 45-47.
   Rocks, James E. "The Short Fiction . . . ," 121-122.

"One Against Thebes" [complete reworking of "Summer Dust"]
   Alvis, John E. "The Idea of Nature . . . ," in Landess, Thomas H., Ed. . . .
      Caroline Gordon . . . , 92-93.
   Rocks, James E. "The Short Fiction . . . ," 134-135.
   Stuckey, W. J. *Caroline Gordon,* 133-134.

"One More Time"
   Cowan, Louise. "Aleck Maury . . . ," in Landess, Thomas H., Ed. . . .
      Caroline Gordon . . . , 24-26.
   Rocks, James E. "The Short Fiction . . . ," 126-127.
   Stuckey, W. J. *Caroline Gordon,* 116-117.

"Petrified Woman"
   Alvis, John E. "The Idea of Nature . . . ," in Landess, Thomas H., Ed.
      Caroline Gordon . . . , 93-98.

Rocks, James E. "The Short Fiction . . . ," 124-125.
Stuckey, W. J. *Caroline Gordon,* 132-133.

"The Presence"
    Cowan, Louise. "Aleck Maury . . . ," in Landess, Thomas H., Ed. . . .
        Caroline Gordon . . . , 24-26.
    Rocks, James E. "The Short Fiction . . . ," 129-130.
    Stuckey, W. J. *Caroline Gordon,* 130-132.

"Summer Dust" [rewritten as "One Against Thebes"]
    Rocks, James E. "The Short Fiction . . . ," 123-124.
    Stuckey, W. J. *Caroline Gordon,* 126-128.

"Tom Rivers"
    Landess, Thomas H. " . . . Ontological Stories," in Landess, Thomas H.,
        Ed. . . . *Caroline Gordon* . . . , 57-61.
    Stuckey, W. J. *Caroline Gordon,* 117-118.

"To Thy Chamber Window, Sweet"
    Cowan, Louise. "Aleck Maury . . . ," in Landess, Thomas H., Ed. . . .
        Caroline Gordon . . . , 20-21.

R. B. CUNNINGHAM GRAHAM

"The Grave of the Horseman"
    Smith, James S. "R. B. Cunningham Graham as a Writer of Short
        Fiction," *Engl Lit in Transition,* 12 (1969), 64-66.

GRAHAM GREENE

"The Hint of an Explanation"
    Coulthard, A. R. "Graham Greene's 'The Hint of an Explanation': A
        Reinterpretation," *Stud Short Fiction,* 8 (1971), 601-605.

WILL HARBEN

"Jim Trundle's Crisis"
    Skaggs, Merrill M. *The Folk* . . . , 65-66.

THOMAS HARDY

"The Fiddler of the Reels"
Miller, J. Hillis. *Thomas Hardy* . . . , 25-26.

"The Waiting Supper"
Miller, J. Hillis. *Thomas Hardy* . . . , 155-156.

FRANK HARRIS

"The Best Man in Garotte"
Pearsall, Robert B. *Frank Harris,* 40-41.

"Elder Conklin"
Pearsall, Robert B. *Frank Harris,* 42-46.

"First Love"
Pearsall, Robert B. *Frank Harris,* 59-61.

"A Fool's Paradise"
Pearsall, Robert B. *Frank Harris,* 112-114.

"A French Artist"
Pearsall, Robert B. *Frank Harris,* 111-112.

"Gulmore the Boss"
Pearsall, Robert B. *Frank Harris,* 46-47.

"The Interpreter"
Pearsall, Robert B. *Frank Harris,* 57-58.

"In the Vale of Tears"
Pearsall, Robert B. *Frank Harris,* 110-111.

"The Irony of Chance"
Pearsall, Robert B. *Frank Harris,* 91-92.

"Love Is My Sin"
Pearsall, Robert B. *Frank Harris,* 156-157.

"A Modern Idyll"
Pearsall, Robert B. *Frank Harris,* 48-51.

"Profit and Loss"
Pearsall, Robert B. *Frank Harris,* 58-59.

"The Sheriff and His Partner"
Pearsall, Robert B. *Frank Harris,* 41-42.

"The Yellow Ticket"
Pearsall, Robert B. *Frank Harris,* 107-108.

JOEL CHANDLER HARRIS

"Ananias"
Skaggs, Merrill M. *The Folk* . . . , 96-97.

"The Cause of the Difficulty"
Skaggs, Merrill M. *The Folk* . . . , 212-213.

"Free Joe and the Rest of the World"
Starke, Catherine J. *Black Portraiture* . . . , 53-54.

"Little Compton"
Skaggs, Merrill M. *The Folk* . . . , 134-135.

"Mingo"
Skaggs, Merrill M. *The Folk* . . . , 73-77.

"Mom Bi: Her Friends and Her Enemies"
Starke, Catherine J. *Black Portraiture* . . . , 129-130.

"Where's Duncan?"
Starke, Catherine J. *Black Portraiture* . . . , 96-97.

BRET HARTE

"The Luck of Roaring Camp"
Boggan, J. R. "The Regeneration of 'Roaring Camp,'" *Nineteenth Century Fiction,* 22 (1967), 271-280.
Folsom, James K. . . . *Western Novel,* 90-91.

JOHN HAWKES

"Charivari"
   Green, James L. "Nightmare and Fairy Tale in Hawkes's 'Charivari,' "
      Critique, 13, ii (1971), 83-95.

NATHANIEL HAWTHORNE

"Alice Doane's Appeal"
   Bell, Michael. *Hawthorne . . . Romance,* 68-76.
   Elias, Helen L. "Alice Doane's Innocence: The Wizard Absolved," *Engl
      Stud Q,* 62 (1971), 28-32.
   Fossum, Robert H. . . . *Problem of Time,* 13-22.

"The Ambitious Guest"
   Doubleday, Neal F. . . . *Early Tales,* 141-145.

"The Artist of the Beautiful"
   Cady, Edwin H. *The Light . . . ,* 26-31.
   Fossum, Robert H. . . . *Problem of Time,* 95-103.
   Malin, Irving. "The Compulsive Design," in Madden, David, Ed.
      American Dreams . . . , 64-65.
   Schriber, Mary S. "Emerson, Hawthorne, and 'The Artist of the
      Beautiful,' " *Stud Short Fiction,* 8 (1971), 607-616.
   Stubbs, John C. *The Pursuit . . . ,* 53-60.

"The Birthmark"
   Fossum, Robert H. . . . *Problem of Time,* 77-80.
   Horne, Lewis B. "The Heart, the Hand, and 'The Birthmark,' " *Am
      Transcendental Q,* 1 (1969), 38-41.
   Stubbs, John C. *The Pursuit . . . ,* 92-93.
   Van Winkle, Edward S. "Aminadab, the Unwitting 'Bad Anima,' " *Am
      Notes & Queries,* 8 (1970), 131-133.

"The Canterbury Pilgrims"
   Doubleday, Neal F. . . . *Early Tales,* 222-227.
   Fossum, Robert H. . . . *Problem of Time,* 69-71.
   Stubbs, John C. *The Pursuit . . . ,* 74-75.

"The Celestial Railroad"
   Fossum, Robert H. . . . *Problem of Time,* 76-77.

"The Christmas Banquet"
  Fossum, Robert H. . . . *Problem of Time*, 4-5.
  Stubbs, John C. *The Pursuit* . . . , 73-74.

"Dr. Heidegger's Experiment"
  Doubleday, Neal F. "Hawthorne's Use of Three Gothic Patterns," *Coll Engl*, 7 (1946), 260-261; rpt. in his . . . *Early Tales*, 178-182.

"Drowne's Wooden Image"
  Doubleday, Neal F. . . . *Early Tales*, 186-192.

"Earth's Holocaust"
  Fossum, Robert H. . . . *Problem of Time*, 73-76.

"Edward Randolph's Portrait"
  Doubleday, Neal F. . . . *Early Tales*, 123-128.
  Fossum, Robert H. . . . *Problem of Time*, 38-40.

"Endicott and the Red Cross"
  Bell, Michael. *Hawthorne . . . Romance*, 53-60.
  Bercovitch, Sacvan. "Diabolus in Salem," *Engl Lang Notes*, 6 (1969), 280-285.
  Doubleday, Neal F. . . . *Early Tales*, 101-108.
  Fossum, Robert H. . . . *Problem of Time*, 33-36.
  Halligan, John. "Hawthorne on Democracy: 'Endicott and the Red Cross,' " *Stud Short Fiction*, 8 (1971), 301-307.

"Ethan Brand"
  Dwight, Sheila. "Hawthorne and the Unpardonable Sin," *Stud Novel*, 2 (1970), 449-458.
  Fossum, Robert H. . . . *Problem of Time*, 92-93.
  Kelly, Richard. "Hawthorne's 'Ethan Brand,' " *Explicator*, 28 (1970), Item 47.
  McElroy, John. "The Brand Metaphor in 'Ethan Brand,' " *Am Lit*, 43 (1972), 633-637.
  Plank, Robert. "Heart Transplant Fiction," *Hartford Stud Lit*, 2 (1970), 102-112.
  Stubbs, John C. *The Pursuit* . . . , 92-93.

"Fancy's Show Box"
  Doubleday, Neal F. "The Theme of Hawthorne's 'Fancy's Show Box,' " *Am Lit*, 10 (1938), 341-343; rpt. in his . . . *Early Tales*, 155-159.
  Fossum, Robert H. . . . *Problem of Time*, 2-3.

"Feathertop"
Fossum, Robert H. . . . *Problem of Time*, 90-91.

"The Gentle Boy"
Bell, Michael. *Hawthorne . . . Romance*, 110-117.
Doubleday, Neal F. . . . *Early Tales*, 159-170.
Fossum, Robert H. . . . *Problem of Time*, 44-47.
Schneiderman, Lee. "Hawthorne and the Refuge of the Heart,"
   Connecticut R, 3 (April, 1970), 90-91.
Tremblay, William A. "A Reading of Hawthorne's 'The Gentle Boy,' "
   Massachusetts Stud Engl, 2 (Spring, 1970), 80-87.

"The Gray Champion"
Becker, John E. . . . *Historical Allegory . . .* , 30-39.
Bell, Michael. *Hawthorne . . . Romance*, 47-53.
Doubleday, Neal F. . . . *Early Tales*, 85-95.
Fossum, Robert H. . . . *Problem of Time*, 31-33.
Schneiderman, Lee. "Hawthorne . . . ," 91-92.

"The Great Carbuncle"
Doubleday, Neal F. . . . *Early Tales*, 145-151.

"The Hollow of the Three Hills"
Fossum, Robert H. . . . *Problem of Time*, 12-13.

"Howe's Masquerade"
Becker, John E. . . . *Historical Allegory . . .* , 43-49.
Fossum, Robert H. . . . *Problem of Time*, 36-38.

"Lady Eleanore's Mantle"
Becker, John E. . . . *Historical Allegory . . .* , 49-59.
Clayton, Lawrence. " 'Lady Eleanore's Mantle': A Metaphorical Key to
   Hawthorne's 'Legends of the Province House,' " *Engl Lang Notes*, 9
   (1971), 49-51.
Doubleday, Neal F. . . . *Early Tales*, 128-130.
Fossum, Robert H. . . . *Problem of Time*, 40-41.
Liebman, Sheldon W. "Ambiguity in 'Lady Eleanore's Mantle,' " *Engl
   Stud Q*, 58 (1970), 97-101.

"The Man of Adamant"
Doubleday, Neal F. . . . *Early Tales*, 218-222.
Dwight, Sheila. " . . . Unpardonable Sin," 449-458.
Fossum, Robert H. . . . *Problem of Time*, 66-68.

"The Maypole of Merry Mount"
   Becker, John E. . . . *Historical Allegory* . . . , 21-30.
   Bell, Michael. *Hawthorne . . . Romance*, 119-126.
   Doubleday, Neal F. . . . *Early Tales*, 92-101.
   Fossum, Robert H. . . . *Problem of Time*, 59-64.
   Sterne, Richard C. "Puritans at Merry Mount: Variations on a Theme,"
      Am Q, 22 (1970), 846-858.
   Stubbs, John C. *The Pursuit* . . . , 75-78.

"The Minister's Black Veil"
   Allen, John D. "Behind 'The Minister's Black Veil,' " in Burton, Thomas
      G., Ed. *Essays in Memory* . . . , 3-12.
   Bell, Michael. *Hawthorne . . . Romance*, 65-68.
   Benoit, Raymond. "Hawthorne's Psychology of Death," *Stud Short
      Fiction*, 8 (1971), 553-560.
   Doubleday, Neal F. . . . *Early Tales*, 170-178.
   Fossum, Robert H. . . . *Problem of Time*, 56-59.
   Santangelo, G. A. "The Absurdity of 'The Minister's Black Veil,' " *Pacific
      Coast Philol*, 5 (1970), 61-66.
   Schneiderman, Lee. "Hawthorne . . . ," 90.

"Mr. Higginbotham's Catastrophe"
   Mehte, R. N. " 'Mr. Higginbotham's Catastrophe': An Unusual
      Hawthorne Story," in Mukherjee, Sujit, and D. V. K.
      Raghavacharyulu, Eds. *Indian Essays* . . . , 113-119.

"My Kinsman, Major Molineux"
   Becker, John E. . . . *Historical Allegory* . . . , 7-13.
   Dennis, Carl. "How to Live in Hell: The Bleak Vision of Hawthorne's 'My
      Kinsman, Major Molineux,' " *Univ R*, 37 (1971), 250-258.
   Doubleday, Neal F. . . . *Native Land*, 87-88; rpt., expanded, in his . . . *Early
      Tales*, 227-238.
   England, A. B. "Robin Molineux and the Young Ben Franklin: A
      Reconsideration," *J Am Stud* (Cambridge), 6 (1972), 181-188.
   Fass, Barbara. "Rejection of Paternalism: Hawthorne's 'My Kinsman,
      Major Molineux,' " *Coll Lang Assoc J*, 14 (1971), 313-323.
   Fossum, Robert H. . . . *Problem of Time*, 26-31.

   Hoffman, Daniel G. "Yankee Bumpkin and Scapegoat King," *Sewanee R*,
      69 (1961), 48-60; rpt. in his *Form and Fable* . . . , 113-125; Galaxy Books
      ed., 113-125; Donohue, Agnes, Ed. . . . *the Hawthorne Question*, 62-71;
      Vickery, John B., and J'nan M. Sellery, Eds. *The Scapegoat* . . . , 132-
      142.

Houston, Neal B., and Fred A. Rodewald. " 'My Kinsman, Major Molineux': A Re-Evaluation," *Proceedings Conference Coll Teachers Engl* (Texas), 34 (1969), 18-22.

Lesser, Simon O. "The Image of the Father," *Partisan R,* 22 (1955), 372-380; rpt. in his *Fiction . . .* , 212-224; Phillips, William, Ed. *Art . . .* , 226-236; Meridian ed., 226-236; Malin, Irving, Ed. *Psychoanalysis . . .* , 87-98; rpt. in part Stallman, Robert W., and Arthur Waldhorn, Eds. *American Literature . . .* , 299-302.

Liebman, Sheldon W. "Robin's Conversion: The Design of 'My Kinsman, Major Molineux, ' " *Stud Short Fiction,* 8 (1971), 443-457.

Sharma, T. R. S. "Diabolic World and Naive Hero in 'My Kinsman, Major Molineux, ' " *Indiana J Am Stud,* 1, i (1969), 35-43.

Smith, Julien. "Historical Ambiguity in 'My Kinsman, Major Molineux,' " *Engl Lang Notes,* 8 (1970), 115-120.

Stubbs, John C. *The Pursuit . . .* , 67-71.

Thorpe, Dwayne. " 'My Kinsman, Major Molineux': The Identity of the Kinsman," *Topic,* 18 (1969), 53-63.

"Old Esther Dudley"
Bell, Michael. *Hawthorne . . . Romance,* 204-208.

Doubleday, Neal F. *. . . Early Tales,* 130-133.

Fossum, Robert H. *. . . Problem of Time,* 41-44.

"The Prophetic Pictures"
Doubleday, Neal F. *. . . Early Tales,* 109-117.

Fossum, Robert H. *. . . Problem of Time,* 91-95.

"Rappaccini's Daughter"
Alsen, Eberhard. "The Ambitious Experiment of Dr. Rappaccini," *Am Lit,* 43 (1971), 430-431.

Davis, Joe. "The Myth of the Garden: Nathaniel Hawthorne's 'Rappaccini's Daughter, ' " *Stud Literary Imagination,* 2, i (1969), 3-12.

Fossum, Robert H. *. . . Problem of Time,* 80-83.

Lyttle, David. " 'Giovanni! My Poor Giovanni!'," *Stud Short Fiction,* 9 (1972), 147-156.

Ross, Morton L. "What Happens in 'Rappaccini's Daughter'?" *Am Lit,* 43 (1971), 336-345.

Stubbs, John C. *The Pursuit . . .* , 60-65.

Uroff, M. D. "The Doctors in 'Rappaccini's Daughter, ' " *Nineteenth Century Fiction,* 27 (1972), 61-70.

Whelan, Robert E. " 'Rappaccini's Daughter' and Zenobia's Legend," *Research Stud,* 39 (1971), 47-52.

"Roger Malvin's Burial"
Doubleday, Neal F. *. . . Early Tales,* 192-200.

Erlich, Gloria C. "Guilt and Expiation in 'Roger Malvin's Burial,'"
  Nineteenth Century Fiction, 26 (1972), 377-389.
Fossum, Robert H. . . . *Problem of Time,* 5-12.
Schneiderman, Lee. "Hawthorne . . . ," 92.
Whelan, Robert E. "'Roger Malvin's Burial': The Burial of Reuben
  Bourne's Cowardice," *Research Stud,* 37 (1969), 112-121.

"The Seven Vagabonds"
Fossum, Robert H. . . . *Problem of Time,* 89-90.
Janssen, James G. "Hawthorne's Seventh Vagabond: 'The Outsetting
  Bard,'" *Emerson Soc Q,* 65 (Winter, 1971), 22-28.

"The Shaker Bridal"
Doubleday, Neal F. . . . *Early Tales,* 138-141.

"The Snow-Image"
Abel, Darrel. "A Vast Deal of Human Sympathy: Idea and Device in
  Hawthorne's 'The Snow-Image,'" *Criticism,* 12 (1970), 316-332.

"The Threefold Destiny"
Stubbs, John C. *The Pursuit . . . ,* 20-21.

"Wakefield"
Doubleday, Neal F. . . . *Early Tales,* 151-154.

"The Wives of the Dead"
Doubleday, Neal F. . . . *Early Tales,* 215-218.

"Young Goodman Brown"
Becker, John E. . . . *Historical Allegory . . . ,* 13-21.
Bell, Michael. *Hawthorne . . . Romance,* 76-81.
Campbell, Harry M. "Freudianism, Americanism, and 'Young Goodman
  Brown,'" *Coll Engl Assoc Critic,* 33 (March, 1971), 3-6.
Connolly, Thomas E. "Hawthorne's 'Young Goodman Brown': An
  Attack on Puritan Calvinism," *Am Lit,* 28 (1956), 370-375; rpt. in his *et
  al. Nathaniel Hawthorne . . . ,* 49-53; rpt. in part in Beebe, Maurice, Ed. .
  . . *Symbolism,* 107-111.
Cook, Reginald. "The Forest of Goodman Brown's Night: A Reading of
  Hawthorne's 'Young Goodman Brown,'" *New England Q,* 43 (1970),
  473-481.
Dickson, Wayne. "Hawthorne's 'Young Goodman Brown,'" *Explicator,*
  29 (1971), Item 44.
Doubleday, Neal F. " . . . Three Gothic Patterns," *Coll Engl,* 7 (1946), 255-
  256; rpt. in his . . . *Early Tales,* 200-212.

Ensor, Allison. " 'Whispers of the Bad Angel': A *Scarlet Letter* Passage As a Commentary on Hawthorne's 'Young Goodman Brown,' " *Stud Short Fiction,* 7 (1970), 467-469.

Fossum, Robert H. . . . *Problem of Time,* 52-56.

Paulits, Walter J. "Ambivalence in 'Young Goodman Brown,' " *Am Lit,* 41 (1970), 577-584.

Stubbs, John C. *The Pursuit* . . . , 71-73.

Whelan, Robert E. "Hawthorne Interprets 'Young Goodman Brown,' " *Engl Stud Q,* 62 (1971), 2-4.

JOHN HAY

"The Blood Seedling"

Monteiro, George. "John Hay's Short Fiction," *Stud Short Fiction,* 8 (1971), 550-552.

"The Foster-Brother"

Monteiro, George. ". . . Short Fiction," 546-548.

"Kane and Abel"

Monteiro, George. ". . . Short Fiction," 548-549.

"Shelby Cabell"

Monteiro, George. ". . . Short Fiction," 545-546.

ERNEST HEMINGWAY

"Big Two-Hearted River"

Anderson, Paul V. "Nick's Story in Hemingway's 'Big Two-Hearted River,' " *Stud Short Fiction,* 7 (1970), 564-572.

Gurko, Leo. *Ernest Hemingway* . . . , 201-203; Apollo ed., 201-203.

Howard, Daniel F. *Manual* . . . , 19-20.

Nahal, Chaman. *The Narrative Pattern* . . . , 101-108.

Twitchell, James. "The Swamp in Hemingway's 'Big Two-Hearted River, ' " *Stud Short Fiction,* 9 (1972), 275-276.

"The Butterfly and the Tank"

Smith, Julia. "Christ Times Four: Hemingway's Unknown Spanish Civil War Stories," *Arizona Q,* 25 (1969), 9-10.

"Cat in the Rain"

Srivastava, Ramesh. "Hemingway's 'Cat in the Rain': An Interpretation," *Literary Criterion,* 9 (Summer, 1970), 79-84.

"A Clean, Well-Lighted Place"
Bennett, Warren. "Character, Irony, and Resolution in 'A Clean, Well-Lighted Place, ' " *Am Lit,* 42 (1970), 70-79.
Lodge, David. "Hemingway's Clean, Well-Lighted, Puzzling Place," *Essays in Crit,* 21 (1971), 33-56.
May, Charles E. "Is Hemingway's 'Well-Lighted Place' Really Clean Now?" *Stud Short Fiction,* 8 (1971), 326-330.

"The Denunciation"
Smith, Julia. "Christ . . . ," 5-9.

"The Doctor and the Doctor's Wife"
Nahal, Chaman. *The Narrative Pattern* . . . , 90-93.

"The End of Something"
Barba, Harry. "The Three Levels of 'The End of Something, ' " *West Virginia Univ Bull Philol Papers,* 17 (1970), 76-80.

"Fifty Grand"
Martine, James J. "Hemingway's 'Fifty Grand': The Other Fight(s)," *J Mod Lit,* 2 (1971), 123-127.

"The Gambler, the Nun, and the Radio"
Mizener, Arthur. *A Handbook . . . "Modern Short Stories . . . Revised Edition,"* 68-73; rpt. *A Handbook . . . "Modern Short Stories . . . Third Edition,"* 70-75.
Rodgers, Paul C. "Levels of Irony in Hemingway's 'The Gambler, the Nun, and the Radio, ' " *Stud Short Fiction,* 7 (1970), 439-449.

"God Rest You Merry, Gentlemen"
Hays, Peter L. *The Limping Hero* . . . , 73-75.
Kruse, Horst. "Ernest Hemingways Kunst der Allegorie: Zeitgenössische, literarische und biblische Anspielungen in 'God Rest You Merry, Gentlemen, ' " *Jahrbuch für Amerikastudien,* 16 (1971), 128-150.
Smith, Julian. "Hemingway and the Thing Left Out," *J Mod Lit,* 1 (1970), 180-182.

"Hills Like White Elephants"
Maynard, Reid. "Leitmotif and Irony in Hemingway's 'Hills Like White Elephants, ' " *Univ R,* 37 (1971), 273-275.

"In Another Country"
Smith, Julian. "Hemingway . . . Left Out," 171-175.

"Indian Camp"
   Hays, Peter L. *The Limping Hero* . . . , 70-72.
   Nahal, Chaman. *The Narrative Pattern* . . . , 87-90.

"The Killers"
   Beards, Richard D. "Stereotyping in Modern American Fiction: Some
      Solitary Swedish Madmen," *Moderna Sprak,* 63 (1969), 329-337.
   Livingston, Howard. "Religious Instrusions in Hemingway's 'The
      Killers, ' " *Engl Record,* 21 (February, 1971), 42-45.
   Nahal, Chaman. *The Narrative Pattern* . . . , 93-94.
   Ward, J. A. " 'The Blue Hotel' and 'The Killers, ' " *Coll Engl Assoc Critic,*
      21 (1959), 1, 7-8; rpt. Katz, Joseph, Ed. *Stephen Crane* . . . , 68-70.

"The Light of the World"
   Bruccoli, Matthew J. " 'The Light of the World': Stan Ketchel as 'My
      Sweet Christ,' " in his *et al. Fitzgerald* . . . *1967,* 125-130.
   Martine, James J. "A Little Light on Hemingway's 'The Light of the
      World,' " *Stud Short Fiction,* 7 (1970), 465-467.
   Thomas, Peter. "A Lost Leader: Hemingway's 'The Light of the World, ' "
      Hum Assoc Bull, 21 (Fall, 1970), 14-19.

"Mr. and Mrs. Elliott"
   Shepherd, Allen. "Taking Apart 'Mr. and Mrs. Elliott, ' " *Markham R,* 2
      (September, 1969), 17-18.

"Night Before Battle"
   Smith, Julia. "Christ . . . ," 10-13.

"Now I Lay Me"
   Hovey, Richard B. "Hemingway's 'Now I Lay Me': A Psychological
      Interpretation," *Lit & Psych,* 15 (1965), 70-78; rpt. in his *Hemingway*
      . . . , 47-53.
   Johnston, Kenneth G. "The Great Awakening: Nick Adams and the
      Silkworms in 'Now I Lay Me, ' " *Hemingway Notes,* 1 (Fall, 1971), 7-9.
   Smith, Julian. "Hemingway . . . Left Out," 175-180.
   Young, Philip. *Ernest Hemingway,* 29-30; 2nd ed., 57-58; rpt. Browne,
      Ray B., and Martin Light, Eds. *Critical Approaches* . . . , II, 276-277.

"The Old Man and the Sea"
   Gahlot, Jai S. " 'The Old Man and the Sea': A Reading," in Maini,
      Darshan S., Ed. *Variations* . . . , 89-92.
   Hovey, Richard B. " 'The Old Man and the Sea'—A New Hemingway
      Hero," *Discourse,* 9 (1966), 283-294; rpt. in his *Hemingway* . . . , 191-
      203.

Johnston, Kenneth G. "The Star in Hemingway's 'The Old Ma.1 ind the Sea, ' " *Am Lit,* 42 (1970), 388-391.

Wylder, Delbert. *Hemingway's Heroes,* 199-222.

"Out of Season"

Johnston, Kenneth G. "Hemingway's 'Out of Season' and the Psychology of Error," *Lit & Psych,* 21 (1971), 41-49.

"The Revolutionist"

Groseclose, Barbara S. "Hemingway's 'The Revolutionist': An Aid to Interpretation," *Mod Fiction Stud,* 17 (1972), 565-570.

"The Sea Change"

Kobler, J. F. "Hemingway's 'The Sea Change': A Sympathetic View of Homosexuality," *Arizona Q,* 26 (1970), 318-324.

Wycherley, H. Alan. "Hemingway's 'The Sea Change, ' " *Am Notes & Queries,* 7 (1969), 67-68.

"The Short Happy Life of Francis Macomber"

Fleissner, R. F. "The Macomber Case: A Sherlockian Analysis," *Baker Street J,* 20 (1970), 154-156.

Gaillard, Theodore L. "The Critical Menagerie in 'The Short Happy Life of Francis Macomber, ' " *Engl J,* 60 (1971), 31-35.

Hill, John S. "Robert Wilson: Hemingway's Judge in 'Macomber, ' " *Univ R,* 35 (1968), 129-132.

Lewis, Clifford. " 'The Short Happy Life of Francis Macomber, ' " *Études Anglaises,* 23 (1970), 256-261.

Nahal, Chaman. *The Narrative Pattern . . . ,* 95-101.

Peirce, J. F. "The Car as Symbol in Hemingway's 'The Short Happy Life of Francis Macomber, ' " *So Central Bull,* 32 (1972), 230-232.

White, W. M. "The Crane-Hemingway Code: A Reevaluation," *Ball State Univ Forum,* 10 (Spring, 1969), 15-20.

"The Snows of Kilimanjaro"

Fisher, Marvin. "More Snow on Kilimanjaro," *Am Norwegia,* 2 (1968), 343-353.

Hays, Peter L. *The Limping Hero . . . ,* 76-77.

Howell, John M. "Hemingway's Riddle and Kilimanjaro's Reusch," *Stud Short Fiction,* 8 (1971), 469-470.

Nahal, Chaman. *The Narrative Pattern . . . ,* 109-118.

Tarbox, Raymond. "Blank Hallucination in the Fiction of Poe and Hemingway," *Am Imago,* 24 (1967), 335-343.

Thomaneck, Jurgen K. A. "Hemingway's Riddle of Kilimanjaro Once More," *Stud Short Fiction,* 7 (1970), 326-327.

Walz, Lawrence A. " 'The Snows of Kilimanjaro': A New Reading," in
Bruccoli, Matthew J., Ed. *Fitzgerald/Hemingway Annual, 1971,* 239-
245.

"Soldier's Home"
Lewis, Robert W. "Hemingway's Concept of Sport and 'Soldier's
Home, ' " *Rendezvous,* 5, ii (1970), 19-27.

"The Undefeated"
Nahal, Chaman. *The Narrative Pattern . . . ,* 95.

"Under the Ridge"
Smith, Julia. "Christ . . . ," 14-17.

HERMANN HESSE

"Journey to the East"
Field, G. W. *Hermann Hesse,* 142-148.

"Klein and Wagner"
Field, G. W. *Hermann Hesse,* 64-66.

"Klingsor's Last Summer"
Baumer, Franz. *Hermann Hesse,* 64-66.
Field, G. W. *Hermann Hesse,* 66-70.

"Siddhartha"
Field, G. W. *Hermann Hesse,* 71-85.

E. T. A. HOFFMANN

"The Gold Pot"
Lawson, Ursula D. *Subjective Time . . . , passim.*
Pikulik, Lothar. "Anselmus in der Flasche: Kontrast und Illusion in E. T.
A. Hoffmanns 'Der goldene Topf,' " *Euphorion,* 63 (1969), 341-370.

"The Story of Krespel"
Vitti-Maugher, Gisela. "Hoffmanns 'Rat Krespel' und der Schlafrock
Gottes," *Monatshefte,* 64 (1972), 51-57.

"The Story of the Lost Reflection"
Salamon, George. "In a Glass Darkly: The Morality of the Mirror in E. T.
A. Hoffmann and I. B. Singer," *Stud Short Fiction,* 7 (1970), 627-629.

LANGSTON HUGHES

"Berry"
Emanuel, James. *Langston Hughes,* 70-71.

"Big Meeting"
Emanuel, James. *Langston Hughes,* 97-101.

"Blessed Assurance"
Emanuel, James. *Langston Hughes,* 122-123.

"The Blues I'm Playing"
Emanuel, James. *Langston Hughes,* 140-141.

"Cora Unashamed"
Emanuel, James. *Langston Hughes,* 130-134.

"Father and Son"
Emanuel, James. *Langston Hughes,* 111-117.

"A Good Job Gone"
Emanuel, James. *Langston Hughes,* 120-121.

"Home" [originally "The Folks at Home"]
Emanuel, James. *Langston Hughes,* 102-107.

"Little Dog"
Emanuel, James. *Langston Hughes,* 123-125.

"Mother and Child"
Emanuel, James. *Langston Hughes,* 125-126.

"On the Road"
Emanuel, James. *Langston Hughes,* 92-96.

"On the Way Home"
Emanuel, James. *Langston Hughes,* 134-136.

"One Christmas Eve"
Emanuel, James. *Langston Hughes,* 73-74.

"Passing"
Emanuel, James. *Langston Hughes,* 161-162.

"Poor Little Black Fellow"
    Emanuel, James. *Langston Hughes,* 59-63.

"Powder-White Face"
    Emanuel, James. *Langston Hughes,* 83-84.

"Professor"
    Emanuel, James. *Langston Hughes,* 77-79.

"Red-Headed Baby"
    Emanuel, James. *Langston Hughes,* 122-123.

"Rejuvenation Through Joy"
    Emanuel, James. *Langston Hughes,* 63-66.

"Sailor Ashore"
    Emanuel, James. *Langston Hughes,* 74-76.

"Slave on the Block"
    Emanuel, James. *Langston Hughes,* 56-63.

"Slice Him Down"
    Emanuel, James. *Langston Hughes,* 160-161.

"Something in Common"
    Emanuel, James. *Langston Hughes,* 84-85.

" 'Tain't So"
    Emanuel, James. *Langston Hughes,* 85-86.

"Ways and Means"
    Chandler, G. Lewis. "Recreation and Reflection: 'Semple Speaks His
        Mind,' " *Phylon,* 12 (March, 1951), 94-95.
    Davis, Arthur P. "Jesse B. Semple: Negro American," *Phylon,* 15 (March,
        1954), 21-28.
    Jackson, Blyden. "A Word About Semple," *Coll Lang Assoc J,* 11 (1968),
        310-318.

"Who's Passing for Who?"
    Emanuel, James. *Langston Hughes,* 161-162.

ALDOUS HUXLEY

"A Country Walk"
  Firchow, Peter. *Aldous Huxley* . . . , 48-50.

"Cynthia"
  Holmes, Charles M. *Aldous Huxley* . . . , 20-21.

"The Farcical History of Richard Greenow"
  Firchow, Peter. *Aldous Huxley* . . . , 40-46.

"The Gioconda Smile"
  Holmes, Charles M. *Aldous Huxley* . . . , 33-34.
  Watt, Donald J. "The Absurdity of the Hedonist in Huxley's 'The Gioconda Smile,' " *Stud Short Fiction,* 7 (1970), 328-330.

"Nuns at Lunch"
  Holmes, Charles M. *Aldous Huxley* . . . , 34-36.

"Young Archimedes"
  Holmes, Charles M. *Aldous Huxley* . . . , 36-38.

WASHINGTON IRVING

"The Legend of Sleepy Hollow"
  Stone, Edward. *A Certain Morbidity* . . . , 101-120.

"The Pride of the Village"
  Monteiro, George. "Washington Irving: A Grace Note on 'The Pride of the Village,' " *Research Stud,* 36 (1968), 347-350.

SHIRLEY JACKSON

"The Witch"
  Kelly, Robert L. "Jackson's 'The Witch': A Satanic Gem," *Engl J,* 60 (1971), 1204-1208.

DAN JACOBSON

"Beggar My Neighbor"
  Mizener, Arthur. *A Handbook* . . . *"Modern Short Stories* . . . *Revised Edition,"* 83-86; rpt. *A Handbook* . . . *"Modern Short Stories* . . . *Third Edition,"* 89-92.

HENRY JAMES

"The Abasement of the Northmores"
  James, Henry. . . . *Critical Prefaces,* 234-235; pb. ed., 234-235; rpt. in his
  The Notebooks . . . , 286-287.

"Adina"
  Mackenzie, Manfred. "Communities of Knowledge: Secret Society in
  Henry James," *Engl Lit Hist,* 36 (1972), 148-152.

"The Altar of the Dead"
  James, Henry. . . . *Critical Prefaces,* 241-245; pb. ed., 241-245; rpt. in his
  The Notebooks . . . , 164-167.

"The Aspern Papers"
  Hux, Samuel. "Irony in 'The Aspern Papers': The Unreliable Symbolist,"
  Ball State Univ Forum, 10 (Winter, 1969), 60-65.
  James, Henry. . . . *Critical Prefaces,* 159-169; pb. ed., 159-169; rpt. Edel,
  Leon, Ed. *Henry James* . . . , 406-416; rpt. in part in James, Henry. *The
  Notebooks* . . . , 71-73.
  Segal, Ora. *The Lucid Reflector* . . . , 74-92.

"The Author of Beltraffio"
  James, Henry. . . . *Critical Prefaces,* 235-236; pb. ed., 235-236; rpt. in his
  The Notebooks . . . , 57-59.
  Segal, Ora. *The Lucid Reflector* . . . , 114-124.
  Stone, Donald D. *Novelists* . . . , 239-241.
  Stone, Edward. *A Certain Morbidity* . . . , 43-52.

"The Beast in the Jungle"
  Banta, Martha. . . . *the Occult,* 194-212.
  Beck, Ronald. "James's 'The Beast in the Jungle': Theme and Metaphor,"
  Markham R, 2 (February, 1970), 17-20.
  Cady, Edwin H. *The Light* . . . , 39-43.
  Conn, Peter J. "Seeing and Blindness in 'The Beast in the Jungle,' " *Stud
  Short Fiction,* 7 (1970), 472-475.
  Hansot, Elisabeth. "Imagination and Time in 'The Beast in the Jungle,' "
  in Tompkins, Jane P., Ed. . . . *"The Turn of the Screw,"* 88-94.
  James, Henry. *The Altar* . . . , ix-xiii; rpt. in his . . . *Critical Prefaces,* 245-
  248; pb. ed., 245-248; *The Notebooks* . . . , 311-312; Edel, Leon, Ed.
  Henry James . . . , 536-542; rpt. in part Stone, Edward, Ed. *Henry James*
  . . . , 242-243.
  Jefferson, Douglas W. *Henry James,* 76-78; Am. ed., 76-78.
  Kraft, James L. "A Perspective on 'The Beast in the Jungle,' " *Literatur in*

Wissenschaft und Unterricht, 2 (1969), 20-26; rpt. Tompkins, Jane P.,
Ed. . . . *"The Turn of the Screw,"* 95-98.
Segal, Ora. *The Lucid Reflector* . . . , 211-232.

"Benvolio"
Kraft, James. *The Early Tales* . . . , 81-82.

"The Birthplace"
Hartsock, Mildred. "The Conceivable Child: James and the Poet," *Stud
Short Fiction,* 8 (1971), 569-574.
James, Henry. . . . *Critical Prefaces,* 248-249; pb. ed., 248-249; rpt. in his
The Notebooks . . . , 306-307.

"Broken Wings"
James, Henry. . . . *Critical Prefaces,* 236-237; pb. ed., 236-237; rpt. in his
The Notebooks . . . , 282.

"Brooksmith"
James, Henry. . . . *Critical Prefaces,* 282-283; pb. ed., 282-283; rpt. in his
The Notebooks . . . , 64-65.

"A Bundle of Letters"
James, Henry. . . . *Critical Prefaces,* 212-213; pb. ed., 212-213; rpt. in his
The Notebooks . . . , 11-12.
Kraft, James. *The Early Tales* . . . , 110-116.

"The Chaperon"
James, Henry. . . . *Critical Prefaces,* 138-139; pb. ed., 138-139; rpt. in his
The Notebooks . . . , 106-109.

"Crawford's Consistency"
Kraft, James. *The Early Tales* . . . , 86-87.

"Daisy Miller"
Humma, John B. "The 'Engagement' of Daisy Miller," *Research Stud,* 39
(1971), 154-155.
James„ Henry. . . . *Critical Prefaces,* 267-270; pb. ed., 267-270; rpt. Edel,
Leon, Ed. *Henry James* . . . , 75-78.
————. "Letter to Mrs. Lynn Linton," in Layard, George S., Ed. *Mrs.
Lynn Linton,* 233-234; rpt. Stafford, William T., Ed. . . . *"Daisy Miller,"*
115-116.
Jefferson, Douglas. W. *Henry James,* 32-34; Am. ed., 32-34.
Kraft, James. *The Early Tales* . . . , 89-92.

"A Day of Days"
> Kraft, James. *The Early Tales . . . ,* 11-16.

"The Death of the Lion"
> James, Henry. . . . *Critical Prefaces,* 217-220; pb. ed., 217-220; rpt. in his *The Notebooks . . . ,* 147-150.
> Nicholas, Charles A. "A Second Glance at Henry James's 'The Death of the Lion, ' " *Stud Short Fiction,* 9 (1972), 143-146.

"De Grey: A Romance"
> Buitenhuis, Peter. *The Grasping Imagination . . . ,* 42-43.
> Kraft, James. *The Early Tales . . . ,* 20-21.

"The Diary of a Man of Fifty"
> Kraft, James. *The Early Tales . . . ,* 108-110.

"Eugene Pickering"
> Kraft, James. *The Early Tales . . . ,* 79-81.

"Europe"
> Buitenhuis, Peter. *The Grasping Imagination . . . ,* 173-174.
> Han, Pierre. "Organic Unity in 'Europe, ' " *So Atlantic Bull,* 35, iii (1970), 40-41.
> James, Henry. . . . *Critical Prefaces,* 238-240; pb. ed., 238-240; rpt. in his *The Notebooks . . . ,* 190-191.

"The Figure in the Carpet"
> Beattie, Munro. "The Many Marriages of Henry James," in LaFrance, Marston, Ed. *Patterns . . . ,* 96-97.
> Feidelson, Charles. "Art as Problem in 'The Figure in the Carpet' and 'The Madonna of the Future, ' " in Tompkins, Jane P., Ed. . . . *"The Turn of the Screw,"* 47-55.
> James, Henry. . . . *Critical Prefaces,* 227-229; pb. ed., 227-229; rpt. in his *The Notebooks . . . ,* 220-224.
> Lainoff, Seymour. "Henry James' 'The Figure in the Carpet': What Is Critical Responsiveness?" *Boston Univ Stud Engl,* 5 (1961), 122-128; rpt. Tompkins, Jane P., Ed. . . . *"The Turn of the Screw,"* 40-46.

"Flickerbridge"
> James, Henry. . . . *Critical Prefaces,* 284-285; pb. ed., 284-285; rpt. in his *The Notebooks . . . ,* 286-288.

"Four Meetings"
> Buitenhuis, Peter. *The Grasping Imagination . . . ,* 174-177.

Gurko, Leo. "The Missing Word in Henry James's 'Four Meetings, ' "
Stud Short Fiction, 7 (1970), 298-307.
Kraft, James. *The Early Tales . . . ,* 99-102.

"Gabrielle de Bergerac"
Kraft, James. *The Early Tales . . . ,* 51-52.
Powers, Lyall H. *Henry James . . . ,* 134-135.

"The Ghostly Rental"
Andreach, Robert J. "Literary Allusions as a Clue to Meaning: James's
'The Ghostly Rental' and Pascal's *Pensées," Comp Lit Stud,* 4 (1967),
299-306.
Banta, Martha. . . . *the Occult,* 106-111.
Buitenhuis, Peter. *The Grasping Imagination . . . ,* 85-88.
Kraft, James. *The Early Tales . . . ,* 86-89.

"Greville Fane"
James, Henry. . . . *Critical Prefaces,* 234; pb. ed., 234; rpt. in his *The
Notebooks . . . ,* 93-95.

"Guest's Confession"
Buitenhuis, Peter. *The Grasping Imagination . . . ,* 52-55.

"The Impressions of a Cousin"
Buitenhuis, Peter. *The Grasping Imagination . . . ,* 126-132.

"An International Episode"
Buitenhuis, Peter. *The Grasping Imagination . . . ,* 103-105.
Kraft, James. *The Early Tales . . . ,* 92-99.

"In the Cage"
Füger, Wilhelm. " 'In the Cage': Versuche zur Deutung einer umstrittenen
Henry James Novelle," *Die Neueren Sprachen,* 15 (1966), 506-513.
James, Henry. . . . *Critical Prefaces,* 154-158; pb. ed., 154-158.
Samuels, Charles T. *The Ambiguity . . . ,* 151-154.

"The Jolly Corner"
Banta, Martha. . . . *the Occult,* 136-142.
Buitenhuis, Peter. *The Grasping Imagination . . . ,* 210-221.
Freedman, William A. "Universality in 'The Jolly Corner,' " *Texas Stud
Lit & Lang,* 4 (1962), 12-15; rpt. Tompkins, Jane P., Ed. . . . *"The Turn
of the Screw,"* 106-109.
Geismar, Maxwell. *Henry James . . . ,* 355-364; rpt. Tompkins, Jane P.,
Ed. . . . *"The Turn of the Screw,"* 99-105.

James, Henry. *The Altar* . . . , xvii-xxiv; rpt. in his . . . *Critical Prefaces,*
252-258; pb. ed., 252-258; rpt. in part in Stone, Edward, Ed. *Henry
James* . . . , 292-293.
Mizener, Arthur. *A Handbook* . . . *"Modern Short Stories* . . . *Revised
Edition,"* 51-55; rpt. *A Handbook* . . . *"Modern Short Stories* . . . *Third
Edition, "* 53-57.

"Julia Bride"
Buitenhuis, Peter. *The Grasping Imagination* . . . , 225-233.
James, Henry. . . . *Critical Prefaces,* 262-266; pb. ed., 262-266.

"Lady Barberina"
James, Henry. . . . *Critical Prefaces,* 198-206; pb. ed., 198-206; rpt. in part
in his *The Notebooks* . . . , 49-51.
Powers, Lyall H. *Henry James* . . . , 73-75.
Segal, Ora. *The Lucid Reflector* . . . , 56-73.

"A Landscape Painter"
Buitenhuis, Peter. *The Grasping Imagination* . . . , 20-22.
Kraft, James. *The Early Tales* . . . , 16-17.

"The Lesson of the Master"
James, Henry. . . . *Critical Prefaces,* 223-226; pb. ed., 223-226; rpt. in part
in his *The Notebooks* . . . , 87.
Mizener, Arthur. *A Handbook* . . . *"Modern Short Stories* . . . *Revised
Edition,"* 57-59; rpt. *A Handbook* . . . *"Modern Short Stories* . . . *Third
Edition,"* 59-61.
Segal, Ora. *The Lucid Reflector* . . . , 125-143.
Smith, Charles R. " 'The Lesson of the Master': An Interpretive Note,"
Stud Short Fiction, 6 (1969), 654-658.

"The Liar"
James, Henry. . . . *Critical Prefaces,* 178-179; pb. ed., 178-179; rpt. in his
The Notebooks . . . , 61-62.
Segal, Ora. *The Lucid Reflector* . . . , 93-106.

"A Light Man"
Kraft, James. *The Early Tales* . . . , 44-47.

"A London Life"
Samuels, Charles T. *The Ambiguity* . . . , 159-161.
Stone, Donald D. *Novelists* . . . , 248-250.

"Louisa Pallant"
  Nicoloff, Philip L. "At the Bottom of All Things in Henry James's 'Louisa
    Pallant,' " *Stud Short Fiction,* 7 (1970), 409-420.

"Madame de Mauves"
  Bouraovi, H. A. "Henry James and the French Mind: The International
    Theme in 'Madame de Mauves,' " *Novel,* 3 (1970), 69-76.
  James, Henry. . . . *Critical Prefaces,* 196-197; pb. ed., 196-197.
  Jefferson, Douglas W. *Henry James,* 20-22; Am. ed., 20-22.
  Kirkham, E. Bruce. "A Study of Henry James's 'Madame de Mauves,' "
    Ball State Univ Forum, 12 (Spring, 1971), 63-69.
  Kraft, James. *The Early Tales* . . . , 53-69.
  Samuels, Charles T. *The Ambiguity* . . . , 155-159.
  Segal, Ora. *The Lucid Reflector* . . . , 15-32.

"The Madonna of the Future"
  Buitenhuis, Peter. *The Grasping Imagination* . . . , 69-70.
  Feidelson, Charles. "Art as Problem in 'The Figure in the Carpet' and 'The
    Madonna of the Future,' " in Tompkins, Jane P., Ed. . . . "*The Turn of
    the Screw,*" 47-55.
  Jefferson, Douglas W. *Henry James,* 14-15; Am. ed., 14-15.
  Kraft, James. *The Early Tales* . . . , 77-78.
  Winner, Viola H. *Henry James* . . . , 96-97.

"The Marriages"
  James, Henry. . . . *Critical Prefaces,* 281-282; pb. ed., 281-282; rpt. in his
    The Notebooks . . . , 70-71.

"Maud-Evelyn"
  D'Avanzo, Mario L. "James's 'Maud-Evelyn': Source, Allusion, and
    Meaning," *Iowa Engl Yearbook,* 13 (1968), 24-33.

"The Middle Years"
  James, Henry. . . . *Critical Prefaces,* 232-234; pb. ed., 232-234; rpt. in his
    The Notebooks . . . , 121-123.

"The Modern Warning"
  Buitenhuis, Peter. *The Grasping Imagination* . . . , 139-140.

"A Most Extraordinary Case"
  Kraft, James. *The Early Tales* . . . , 17-19.

"A New England Winter"
  Buitenhuis, Peter. *The Grasping Imagination* . . . , 133-138.

"The Next Time"
  James, Henry. . . . *Critical Prefaces,* 226-227; pb. ed., 226-227; rpt. in his
    The Notebooks . . . , 200-205.

"Owen Wingate"
  James, Henry. . . . *Critical Prefaces,* 258-260; pb. ed., 258-260; rpt. in his
    The Notebooks . . . , 118-121.

"Pandora"
  Buitenhuis, Peter. *The Grasping Imagination* . . . , 122-126.
  James, Henry. . . . *Critical Prefaces,* 270-274; pb. ed., 270-274; rpt. in his
    The Notebooks . . . , 56-57.

"A Passionate Pilgrim"
  Buitenhuis, Peter. *The Grasping Imagination* . . . , 58-61.
  James, Henry. . . . *Critical Prefaces,* 193-196; pb. ed., 193-196.
  Jefferson, Douglas W. *Henry James,* 13-14; Am. ed., 13-14.
  Kraft, James. *The Early Tales* . . . , 47-49.
  Segal, Ora. *The Lucid Reflector* . . . , 1-14.

"Paste"
  James, Henry. . . . *Critical Prefaces,* 237-238; pb. ed., 237-238; rpt. in his
    The Notebooks, 177-178; Matlaw, Myron, and Leonard Lief, Eds.
    Story and Critic, 330-331.
  Knieger, Bernard. "James's 'Paste,' " *Stud Short Fiction,* 8 (1971), 468-
    469.

"The Pension Beaurepas"
  James, Henry. . . . *Critical Prefaces,* 216; pb. ed., 216.
  Kraft, James. *The Early Tales* . . . , 103-104.

"The Point of View"
  Buitenhuis, Peter. *The Grasping Imagination* . . . , 130-140.
  James, Henry. . . . *Critical Prefaces,* 214-216; pb. ed., 214-216; rpt. in his
    The Notebooks . . . , 15.

"Poor Richard"
  Buitenhuis, Peter. *The Grasping Imagination* . . . , 31-33.
  Kraft, James. *The Early Tales* . . . , 5-11.

"The Private Life"
  James, Henry. . . . *Critical Prefaces,* 249-252; pb. ed., 249-252; rpt. in his
    The Notebooks . . . , 109-110.
  Jefferson, Douglas W. *Henry James,* 54-55; Am. ed., 54-55.

"Professor Fargo"
  Banta, Martha. . . . *the Occult,* 90-98.
  Buitenhuis, Peter. *The Grasping Imagination* . . . , 72-74.
  Kraft, James. *The Early Tales* . . . , 78-79.

"The Pupil"
  Cummins, Elizabeth. " 'The Playroom of Superstition': An Analysis of
    Henry James's 'The Pupil,' " *Markham R,* 2 (May, 1970), 13-16.
  Griffith, John. "James's 'The Pupil' As Whodunit: The Question of Moral
    Responsibility," *Stud Short Fiction,* 9 (1972), 257-268.
  Gross, Theodore L. *The Heroic Ideal* . . . , 78-79.
  James, Henry. *What Maisie Knew* . . . , xv-xviii; rpt. in his . . . *Critical
    Prefaces,* 150-154; pb. ed., 150-154; Edel, Leon, Ed. *Henry James* . . . ,
    476-480; rpt. in part in Stone, Edward, Ed. *Henry James* . . . , 183-185.
  Kenney, William. "The Death of Morgan in James's 'The Pupil,' " *Stud
    Short Fiction,* 8 (1971), 317-322.
  Martin, Terence. "James's 'The Pupil': The Art of Seeing Through," *Mod
    Fiction Stud,* 4 (1958), 335-345; rpt. Tompkins, Jane P., Ed. . . . *"The
    Turn of the Screw,"* 11-21; rpt. in part Stone, Edward, Ed. *Henry James*
    . . . , 187-191.

  Samuels, Charles T. *The Ambiguity* . . . , 180-184.
  Stein, William B. " 'The Pupil':The Education of a Prude," *Arizona Q,* 15
    (1959), 13-22; rpt. Tompkins, Jane P., Ed. . . . *"The Turn of the Screw,"*
    22-28; rpt. in part Stone, Edward, Ed. *Henry James* . . . , 193-198.

"The Real Thing"
  James, Henry. . . . *Critical Prefaces,* 283-284; pb. ed., 283-284; rpt. in his
    The Notebooks . . . , 102-105.
  Jefferson, Douglas W. *Henry James,* 52-54; Am. ed., 52-54.
  Labor, Earle. "James's 'The Real Thing': Three Levels of Meaning," *Coll
    Engl,* 23 (1962), 376-378; rpt. Browne, Ray B., and Martin Light, Eds.
    Critical Approaches . . . , II, 156-159; Tompkins, Jane P., Ed. . . . *"The
    Turn of the Screw,"* 29-32.
  Toor, David. "Narrative Irony in Henry James' 'The Real Thing,' " *Univ
    R,* 34 (1967), 95-99; rpt. Tompkins, Jane P., Ed. . . . *"The Turn of the
    Screw,"* 33-39.
  Uroff, M. D. "Perception in James's 'The Real Thing,' " *Stud Short
    Fiction,* 9 (1972), 41-46.
  Winner, Viola H. *Henry James* . . . , 108-112.

"The Romance of Certain Old Clothes"
  Buitenhuis, Peter. *The Grasping Imagination* . . . , 40-42.

"A Round of Visits"
Buitenhuis, Peter. *The Grasping Imagination* . . . , 233-237.

"The Siege of London"
Samuels, Charles T. *The Ambiguity* . . . , 138-141.

"Sir Edmund Orme"
Banta, Martha. . . . *the Occult,* 111-114.
James, Henry. . . . *Critical Prefaces,* 260-261; pb. ed., 260-261; rpt. in his
The Notebooks . . . , 9-10.

"The Story in It"
James, Henry. . . . *Critical Prefaces,* 285-286; pb. ed., 285-286; rpt. in his
The Notebooks . . . , 275-276.

"The Story of a Masterpiece"
Buitenhuis, Peter. *The Grasping Imagination* . . . , 39-40.
Kraft, James. *The Early Tales* . . . , 23-35.

"The Story of a Year"
Buitenhuis, Peter. *The Grasping Imagination* . . . , 17-20.

"The Tone of Time"
Mizener, Arthur. *A Handbook* . . . *"Modern Short Stories* . . . *Revised
Edition,"* 47-50; rpt. *A Handbook* . . . *"Modern Short Stories* . . . *Third
Edition,"* 49-52.

"The Tree of Knowledge"
James, Henry. . . . *Critical Prefaces,* 234-236; pb. ed., 234-236; rpt. in his
The Notebooks . . . , 289-290.

"The Turn of the Screw"
Ballorain, Rolande. " 'The Turn of the Screw': L'adulte et l'enfant ou les
deux regards," *Études Anglaises,* 22 (1969), 250-258.
Banta, Martha. . . . *the Occult,* 114-132.
Bontly, Thomas J. "Henry James's 'General Vision of Evil' in 'The Turn of
the Screw,' " *Stud Engl Lit, 1500-1900,* 9 (1969), 721-735.
Byers, John R. " 'The Turn of the Screw': A Hellish Point of View,"
Markham R, 2 (1971), 101-104.
Cranfill, Thomas M., and Robert L. Clark. "The Provocativeness of 'The
Turn of the Screw,' " *Texas Stud Lit & Lang,* 12 (1970), 93-100.
Goddard, Harold C. "A Pre-Freudian Reading of 'The Turn of the
Screw,'" *Nineteenth Century Fiction,* 12 (1957), 1-36; rpt. Willen,
Gerald, Ed. *A Casebook* . . . , 244-272; 2nd ed., 244-272; Kimbrough,

Robert, Ed. *The Turn of the Screw,* 181-209; Tompkins, Jane P., Ed....
"The Turn of the Screw," 60-87.

Guerin, Wilfred, *et al. Instructor's Manual* . . . , 101-103.

Heilman, Robert B. "Foreword," *Southern R,* 7 (1971), 6-8.

Kirby, David K. "Two Modern Versions of the Quest," *Southern Hum R,* 5 (1971), 392-394.

Lind, Sidney E. " 'The Turn of the Screw': The Torment of Critics," *Centennial R,* 14 (1970), 225-240.

Meldrum, Ronald M. "Three of Henry James's Dark Ladies," *Research Stud,* 37 (1969), 58-59.

Samuels, Charles T. *The Ambiguity* . . . , 11-22.

Siegel, Eli. *James* . . . , 3-149.

Tournadre, C. "Propositions pour une psychologie sociale de 'The Turn of the Screw,' " *Études Anglaises,* 22 (1969), 259-269.

Voegelin, Eric. "A Letter to Robert B. Heilman," *Southern R,* 7 (1971), 9-24.

————. "Postscript: On Paradise and Revolution," *Southern R,* 7 (1971), 25-48.

Zimmerman, Everett. "Literary Tradition and 'The Turn of the Screw,' " *Stud Short Fiction,* 7 (1970), 634-637.

"The Two Faces"

James, Henry. . . . *Critical Prefaces,* 177-179; pb. ed., 177-179; rpt. in his *The Notebooks* . . . , 284-286.

"The Velvet Glove"

Tintner, Adeline R. "James's Mock Epic:'The Velvet Glove,' Edith Wharton, and Other Late Tales," *Mod Fiction Stud,* 17 (1972), 483-499.

"Washington Square"

Beach, Joseph W. *The Method* . . . , 228-232; rpt. Willen, Gerald, Ed. *Washington Square,* 177-181.

Bowden, Edwin T. *The Themes* . . . , 40-44; rpt. Willen, Gerald, Ed. *Washington Square,* 190-198.

Buitenhuis, Peter. *The Grasping Imagination* . . . , 106-108.

Cambon, Glauco. "The Negative Gesture in Henry James," *Nineteenth Century Fiction,* 15 (1961), 335-340; rpt. Willen, Gerald, Ed. *Washington Square,* 221-230.

Canby, Henry S. *Turn West* . . . , 152-153; rpt. Willen, Gerald, Ed. *Washington Square,* 187-188.

Dupee, F. W. *Henry James,* 63-65; Anchor ed., 54-56; rpt. Current-García, Eugene, and Walton R. Patrick, Eds. *Realism and Romanticism* . . . , 387-389; Willen, Gerald, Ed. *Washington Square,* 188-190.

Edel, Leon. . . . *Conquest of London* . . . , 387-400; rpt. Willen, Gerald, Ed.
Washington Square, 215-218.

Geismar, Maxwell. *Henry James* . . . , 36-40; rpt. Willen, Gerald, Ed.
Washington Square, 218-221.

Gordon, David J. " 'Washington Square': A Psychological Perspective,"
in Willen, Gerald, Ed. *Washington Square,* 263-271.

Gurko, Leo. "The Dehumanizing Mind in 'Washington Square,' " in
Willen, Gerald, Ed. *Washington Square,* 230-243.

Kelley, Cornelia P. *The Early Development* . . . , 278-283; pb. ed., 278-283;
rpt. Willen, Gerald, Ed. *Washington Square,* 181-187.

Kenney, William. "Doctor Sloper's Double in 'Washington Square,' "
Univ R, 36 (1970), 301-306.

Matthiessen, F.O. *The American Novels* . . . , x-xi; rpt. in part Willen,
Gerald, Ed. *Washington Square,* 175-177.

Pendo, Mina. "Reason Under the Ailanthus," in Willen, Gerald, Ed.
Washington Square, 243-252.

Poirier, Richard. *The Comic Sense* . . . , 165-182; rpt. Willen, Gerald, Ed.
Washington Square, 196-215.

Roddman, Philip. "The Critical Sublime: A View of 'Washington
Square,' " in Willen, Gerald, Ed. *Washington Square,* 252-263.

Samuels, Charles T. *The Ambiguity* . . . , 141-149.

Stone, Donald D. *Novelists* . . . , 201-204.

RICHARD M. JOHNSON

"Old Friends and New"

Skaggs, Merrill M. *The Folk* . . . , 127-128.

JAMES JOYCE

"After the Race"

Adams, Robert M. *James Joyce* . . . , 64-68; rpt. Baker, James R., and
Thomas F. Staley, Eds. . . . *Critical Handbook,* 101-104.

Brandabur, Edward. . . . *Meanness* . . . , 82-88.

Torchiana, Donald T. "Joyce's 'After the Race,' the Races of Castlebar,
and Dun Laoghaire," *Eire,* 6 (1971), 119-128.

"Araby"

Brandabur, Edward. . . . *Meanness* . . . , 49-56.

Brooks, Cleanth, and Robert P. Warren. *Understanding Fiction,* 420-423;
2nd ed., 189-192; rpt. McCallum, John H., Ed. *Prose* . . . , 674-676;
Baker, James R., and Thomas F. Staley, Eds. . . . *Critical Handbook,*
93-96.

Brown, Homer O. . . . *Early Fiction* . . . , 28-29.

Freimarck, John. " 'Araby': A Quest for Meaning," *James Joyce Q*, 7 (1970), 366-368.

Mizener, Arthur. *A Handbook* . . . *"Modern Short Stories* . . . *Revised Edition,"* 118-119; rpt. *A Handbook* . . . *"Modern Short Stories* . . . *Third Edition,"* 138-139.

Turaj, Frank. " 'Araby' and *Portrait:* Stages of Pagan Conversion," *Engl Lang Notes,* 7 (1970), 209-213.

"The Boarding House"

Brandabur, Edward. . . . *Meanness* . . . , 31-32.

Tindall, William Y. *A Reader's Guide* . . . , 25-26; rpt. Baker, James R., and Thomas F. Staley, Eds. . . . *Critical Handbook,* 106-107.

"Clay"

Brandabur, Edward. . . . *Meanness* . . . , 67-73.

Brown, Homer O. . . . *Early Fiction* . . . , 28-29.

Carpenter, Richard, and Daniel Leary. "The Witch Maria," *James Joyce R,* 3 (1959), 3-7; rpt. Gullason, Thomas A., and Leonard Casper, Eds. . . . *Short Fiction,* 2nd ed., 598-602.

Cross, Richard K. *Flaubert* . . . , 26-29.

Easson, Angus. "Parody as Comment in James Joyce's 'Clay,' " *James Joyce Q,* 7 (1970), 75-81.

Henrietta, Sister M. "James Joyce's 'Clay,' " *Horizontes* (Puerto Rico), 24 (April, 1969), 59-62.

Magalaner, Marvin. "The Other Side of James Joyce," *Arizona Q,* 9 (1953), 7-16; rpt. Magalaner, Marvin, and Richard M. Kain. *Joyce* . . . , 84-91; Beebe, Maurice, Ed. . . . *Symbolism,* 119-125; Baker, James R., and Thomas F. Staley, Eds. . . . *Critical Handbook,* 124-130; Gullason, Thomas A., and Leonard Casper, Eds. . . . *Short Fiction,* 2nd ed., 586-594.

Noon, William T. "Joyce's 'Clay': An Interpretation," *Coll Engl,* 17 (1955), 93-95; rpt. Beebe, Maurice, Ed. . . . *Symbolism,* 125-129; Gullason, Thomas A., and Leonard Casper, Eds. . . . *Short Fiction,* 2nd ed., 595-598.

"Counterparts"

Brandabur, Edward. . . . *Meanness* . . . , 104-107.

Delaney, Paul. "Joyce's Political Development and the Aesthetic of *Dubliners,"* *Coll Engl,* 34 (1972), 261-262.

Hagopian, John V. "The Epiphany in Joyce's 'Counterparts,' " *Stud Short Fiction,* 1 (1964), 272-276; rpt. Hagopian, John V., and Martin Dolch, Eds. *Insight II* . . . , 201-206; Baker, James R., and Thomas F. Staley, Eds. . . . *Critical Handbook,* 120-124.

"The Dead"

Brandabur, Edward. . . . *Meanness* . . . , 115-129.

Brown, Homer O. . . . *Early Fiction* . . . , 85-103.

Cross, Richard K. *Flaubert* . . . , 29-32.

Delaney, Paul. "Joyce's Political Development . . . ," 263-264.

Gross, John. *James Joyce,* 35-37.

Howard, Daniel F. *Manual* . . . , 14-15.

Kennelly, Brendan. "The Irishness of 'The Dead' by James Joyce," *Moderna Sprak,* 61 (1967), 239-242.

Ludwig, Jack, and W. Richard Poirier, Eds. *Stories* . . . , 387-391; rpt. Baker, James R., and Thomas F. Staley, Eds. . . . *Critical Handbook,* 159-162.

Lytle, Andrew. "A Reading of Joyce's 'The Dead,' " *Sewanee R,* 77 (1969), 193-216.

McKenna, John P. "Joyce's 'The Dead,' " *Explicator,* 30 (1971), Item 1.

Robinson, Eleanor. "Gabriel Conroy's Cooked Goose," *Ball State Univ Forum,* 11 (Spring, 1970), 25.

Tate, Allen. "Three Commentaries: Poe, James, and Joyce," *Sewanee R,* 58 (1950), 10-15; rpt. Gordon, Caroline, and Allen Tate. *The House of Fiction,* 279-282; 2nd ed., 183-186; Scholes, Robert, and A. Walton Litz, Eds. *"Dubliners".* . . , 404-409.

Trilling, Lionel. . . . *Literature,* 652-655; rpt. Baker, James R., and Thomas F. Staley, Eds. . . . *Critical Handbook,* 155-159.

"An Encounter"

Brandabur, Edward. . . . *Meanness* . . . , 45-49.

Kaye, Julian B. "The Wings of Daedalus: Two Stories in *Dubliners," Mod Fiction Stud,* 4 (1958), 31-37; rpt. Baker, James R., and Thomas F. Staley, Eds. . . . *Critical Handbook,* 87-92.

Lachtman, Howard. "The Magic-Lantern Business: James Joyce's Ecclesiastical Satire in *Dubliners," James Joyce Q,* 7 (1970), 84-85.

"Eveline"

Brandabur, Edward. . . . *Meanness* . . . , 58-67.

Dolch, Martin. " 'Eveline,' " in Hagopian, John V., and Martin Dolch, Eds. *Insight II* . . . , 193-200; rpt. Baker, James R., and Thomas F. Staley, Eds. . . . *Critical Handbook,* 96-101.

Lachtman, Howard. "The Magic-Lantern . . . ," 86-87.

San Juan, Epifanio. " 'Eveline': Joyce's Affirmation of Ireland," *Eire,* 4 (Spring, 1969), 46-52.

"Grace"

Boyle, Robert. "Swiftian Allegory and Dantean Parody in Joyce's 'Grace,' " *James Joyce Q,* 7 (1969), 11-21.

Brown, Homer O. . . . *Early Fiction* . . . , 81-82.

Lachtman, Howard. "The Magic-Lantern . . . ," 88-90.

Niemeyer, Carl. " 'Grace' and Joyce's Method of Paradox," *Coll Engl,* 27 (1965), 196-201; rpt. Baker, Frank R., and Thomas F. Staley, Eds. . . . *Critical Handbook,* 148-154.

"Ivy Day in the Committee Room"

Blotner, Joseph L. " 'Ivy Day in the Committee Room': Death Without Resurrection," *Perspective,* 9 (1957), 201-217; rpt. Baker, James R., and Thomas F. Staley, Eds. . . . *Critical Handbook,* 138-146.

Brandabur, Edward. . . . *Meanness* . . . , 109-115.

Delaney, Paul. "Joyce's Political Development . . . ," 262-263.

Lachtman, Howard. "The Magic-Lantern . . . ," 87-88.

San Juan, E. "Form and Meaning in Joyce's 'Ivy Day in the Committee Room' " *Archiv Studium Neueren Sprachen und Literaturen,* 207 (1970), 185-191.

"A Little Cloud"

Brandabur, Edward. . . . *Meanness* . . . , 99-104.

Ruoff, James. " 'A Little Cloud': Joyce's Portrait of the Would-Be Artist," *Research Stud,* 25 (1957), 256-271; rpt. Baker, James R., and Thomas F. Staley, Eds. . . . *Critical Handbook,* 107-120.

Solomon, A. J. " 'The Celtic Note' in 'A Little Cloud,' " *Stud Short Fiction,* 9 (1972), 269-270.

"A Mother"

Collins, Ben L. "Joyce's Use of Yeats and of Irish History: A Reading of 'A Mother,' " *Eire,* 5, i (1970), 45-66.

Ghiselin, Brewster. "The Unity of Joyce's 'Dubliners,' " *Accent,* 16 (1956), 206; rpt. Garrett, Peter K., Ed. . . . *"Dubliners,"* 78-79.

Tindall, William Y. *A Reader's Guide* . . . , 36-38; rpt. Baker, James R., and Thomas F. Staley, Eds. . . . *Critical Handbook,* 146-148.

"A Painful Case"

Brandabur, Edward. . . . *Meanness* . . . , 73-82.

Brown, Homer O. . . . *Early Fiction* . . . , 79-81.

Corrington, John W. "Isolation as Motif in 'A Painful Case,' " *James Joyce Q,* 3 (1966), 182-191; rpt. Baker, James R., and Thomas F. Staley, Eds. . . . *Critical Handbook,* 130-139.

Sloan, Barbara L. "The D'Annunzian Narrator in 'A Painful Case': Silent, Exiled, and Cunning," *James Joyce Q,* 9 (1971), 26-36.

"The Sisters"

    Brandabur, Edward. . . . *Meanness* . . . , 35-45.

    Brown, Homer O. . . . *Early Fiction* . . . , 24-25.

    Connolly, Thomas E. "Joyce's 'The Sisters': A Pennyworth of Snuff," *Coll Engl,* 27 (1965), 189-195; rpt. Baker, James R., and Thomas F. Staley, Eds. . . . *Critical Handbook,* 79-86.

    Fischer, Theresa. "From Reliable to Unreliable Narrator: Rhetorical Changes in Joyce's 'The Sisters,' " *James Joyce Q,* 9 (1971), 85-92.

    Lachtman, Howard. "The Magic-Lantern . . . ," 83-84.

    San Juan, Epifanio. "Method and Meaning in Joyce's 'The Sisters,' " *Neueren Sprachen,* 20 (1971), 490-496.

    West, Michael. "Old Cotter and the Enigma of Joyce's 'The Sisters,' " *Mod Philol,* 67 (1970), 370-372.

"Two Gallants"

    Brandabur, Edward. . . . *Meanness* . . . , 88-99.

    Epstein, E. L. "Hidden Imagery in James Joyce's 'Two Gallants,' " *James Joyce Q,* 7 (1970), 369-370.

    Noon, William T. *Joyce and Aquinas,* 83-84; rpt. Baker, James R., and Thomas F. Staley, Eds. . . . *Critical Handbook,* 104-106.

FRANZ KAFKA

"Before the Law"

    Born, Jürgen. "Kafka's Parable 'Before the Law': Reflections Toward a Positive Interpretation," *Mosaic,* 3 (1970), 153-162.

    Deinert, Herbert. "Kafka's Parable 'Before the Law, ' " *Germanic R,* 39 (1964), 192-200.

"The Burrow"

    Fraiberg, Selma. "Dream and Creation in Kafka," *Partisan R,* 23 (1956), 57; rpt. Phillips, William, Ed. *Art* . . . , 31-32; Meridian ed., 31-32.

    Friedman, Maurice. *Problematic Rebel* . . . , 138-140; 2nd ed., 293-296.

    Weigand, Hermann J. "Franz Kafka's 'The Burrow' ('Der Bau'): An Analytical Essay," *PMLA,* 87 (1972), 152-166.

"A Country Doctor"

    Hatfield, Henry. *Crisis* . . . , 51-62.

    Minot, Stephen, and Robley Wilson. *Teacher's Manual* . . . , 29-30.

    Szanto, George H. *Narrative Consciousness* . . . , 50-52.

"Description of a Struggle"

    Greenberg, Martin. *The Terror* . . . , 29-36.

"The Great Wall of China"
  Friedman, Maurice. *Problematic Rebel* . . . , 154-157; 2nd ed., 309-312.

"A Hunger Artist"
  Friedman, Maurice. *Problematic Rebel* . . . , 150-152; 2nd ed., 305-308.
  Holtz, William. " 'The Hunger Artist': A Way In," *Coll Engl Assoc Critic*,
    29 (December, 1966), 3.
  Minot, Stephen, and Robley Wilson. *Teacher's Manual* . . . , 9-10.
  Neumarkt, Paul. "Kafka's 'A Hunger Artist': The Ego in Isolation," *Am
    Imago*, 27 (1970), 109-121.

"The Hunter Gracchus"
  Friedman, Maurice. *Problematic Rebel* . . . , 145-146; 2nd ed., 300-301.

"In the Gallery"
  Foulkes, A. P. " 'Auf der Galerie': Some Remarks Concerning Kafka's
    Concept and Portrayal of Reality," *Seminar*, 2, ii (1966), 34-42.

"In the Penal Colony"
  Fickert, Kurt J. "A Literal Interpretation of 'In the Penal Colony,' " *Mod
    Fiction Stud*, 17 (1971), 31-36.
  Globus, Gordon C., and Richard C. Pilliard. "Tausk's 'Influencing
    Machine' and Kafka's 'In the Penal Colony,' " *Am Imago*, 23 (1966),
    191-207.
  Greenberg, Martin. *The Terror* . . . , 104-112.
  Mendelsohn, Leonard R. "Kafka's 'In the Penal Colony' and the Paradox
    of Enforced Freedom," *Stud Short Fiction*, 8 (1971), 309-316.
  Sacharoff, Mark. "Pathological, Comic, and Tragic Elements in Kafka's
    'In the Penal Colony,' " *Genre*, 4 (1971), 392-411.

"Investigations of a Dog"
  Friedman, Maurice. *Problematic Rebel* . . . , 152-154; 2nd ed., 307-309.

"The Judgment"
  Fraiberg, Selma. "Dream . . . ," 58; rpt. Phillips, William, Ed. *Art* . . . , 33;
    Meridian ed., 33.
  Friedman, Maurice. *Problematic Rebel* . . . , 321-327; 2nd ed., 339-344.
  Greenberg, Martin. "The Literature of Truth: Kafka's 'Judgment,' "
    Salmagundi, 1, i (1966), 4-22; rpt. in his *The Terror* . . . , 48-67.
  Magny, Claude-Edmonde. "The Objective Depiction of Absurdity," *Q R
    Lit*, 2 (1945), 214-218; rpt. Flores, Angel, Ed. . . . *Problem*, 81-85;
    Gullason, Thomas A., and Leonard Casper, Eds. . . . *Short Fiction*, 2nd
    ed., 609-612.
  Neider, Charles. *The Frozen Sea* . . . , 73-76; rpt. Gullason, Thomas A.,

and Leonard Casper, Eds. . . . *Short Fiction,* 2nd ed., 612-614.

Politzer, Heinz. . . . *Paradox,* 53-65; rpt. Gullason, Thomas A., and Leonard Casper, Eds. . . . *Short Fiction,* 2nd ed., 614-625.

Pondrom, Cyrena N. "Coherence in Kafka's 'The Judgment': Georg's Perception of the World," *Stud Short Fiction,* 9 (1972), 59-76.

"The Married Couple"

Ware, Malcolm. "Catholic Ritual and the Meaning of Franz Kafka's 'Das Ehepaar, ' " *Symposium,* 19 (1965), 85-88.

"Memoirs of the Kalda Railroad"

Fraiberg, Selma. "Dream . . . ," 59-66; rpt. Phillips, William, Ed. *Art . . . ,* 42-49; Meridian ed., 42-49.

"The Merchant Messner"

Fraiberg, Selma. "Dream . . . ," 59-66; rpt. Phillips, William, Ed. *Art . . . ,* 42-49; Meridian ed., 42-49.

"Metamorphosis"

Corngold, Stanley. "Kafka's 'Die Verwandlung': Metamorphosis of the Metaphor," *Mosaic,* 3 (1970), 91-106.

Douglas, Kenneth, and John Hollander. "Masterpieces of Symbolism and the Modern School," in Mack, Maynard, *et al.,* Eds. *World Masterpieces,* II, 3rd. ed., 1363; Continental ed. rev., 1010-1011.

Friedman, Maurice. *Problematic Rebel . . . ,* 141-145; 2nd ed., 296-300.

Greenberg, Martin. *The Terror . . . ,* 69-91.

Hall, Calvin S., and Richard E. Lind. *Life . . . ,* 55-70.

Hamalian, Leo, and Edmond L. Volpe, Eds. *Eleven . . . Short Novels,* 2nd ed., 250-251.

MacAndrews, M. Elizabeth. "A Splacknuck and a Dung-Beetle: Realism and Probability in Swift and Kafka," *Coll Engl,* 31 (1970), 385-391.

Moss, Leonard. "A Key to the Door Image in 'The Metamorphosis, ' " *Mod Fiction Stud,* 17 (1971), 37-42.

Pearce, Richard. *Stages . . . ,* 19-25.

Szanto, George H. *Narrative Consciousness . . . ,* 37-39.

Witt, Mary A. "Confinement in 'Die Verwandlung' and *Les Sequestres d' Altona,*" *Comp Lit,* 23 (1971), 32-44.

"An Old Page [Manuscript]"

Bedwell, Carol B. "The Forces of Destruction in Kafka's 'Ein altes Blatt,' " *Monatshefte,* 58 (1966), 43-48.

"A Report to an Academy"

Friedman, Maurice. *Problematic Rebel . . . ,* 137-138; 2nd ed., 292-294.

HERMANN KASACK

"Fälschungen"
  Reinhardt, George W. "The Ordeal of Art: Hermann Kasack's
  'Fälschungen, ' " *Stud Short Fiction*, 9 (1972), 365-372.

BENEDICT KIELY

"A Ball of Malt and Madame Butterfly"
  Eckley, Grace. "The Fiction of Benedict Kiely," *Eire*, 3, iv (1968), 64-65.

"The Little Bishop"
  Eckley, Grace. "The Fiction . . . ," 59.

RUDYARD KIPLING

"The Arrest of Lieutenant Golightly"
  Gilbert, Elliot L. *The Good Kipling* . . . , 52-60.

"At the End of the Passage"
  Meyer, Jeffrey. " 'At the End of the Passage,' " *Kipling J*, 38 (June, 1971),
  20-22.

"The Bridge-Builders"
  Gilbert, Elliot L. *The Good Kipling* . . . , 126-157.

"The Bull That Thought"
  Gilbert, Elliot L. "The Aesthetics of Violence," *Engl Lit in Transition*, 7
  (1964), 212-216; rpt., expanded, in his *The Good Kipling* . . . , 168-187.

"Dayspring Mishandled"
  Beachcroft, T. O. *The Modern Art* . . . , 141-143.
  Gilbert, Elliot L. "The Aesthetics . . . ," 211-212; rpt. in his *The Good
  Kipling* . . . , 167-168.

"The Eye of Allah"
  Gilbert, Elliot L. "The Aesthetics . . . ," 211; rpt. in his *The Good Kipling*
  . . . , 166-167.

"The Gardener"
  Gilbert, Elliot L. "Kipling's 'The Gardener': Craft into Art," *Stud Short
  Fiction*, 7 (1970), 308-319; rpt. in his *The Good Kipling* . . . , 78-94.

Mizener, Arthur. *A Handbook . . . "Modern Short Stories . . . Revised Edition,"* 129-132; rpt. *A Handbook . . . "Modern Short Stories . . . Third Edition,"* 149-152.

"How Fear Came"
Gilbert, Elliot L. *The Good Kipling . . .* , 72-73.

"In the House of Suddhoo"
Gilbert, Elliot L. *The Good Kipling . . .* , 60-70.

"The Man Who Would Be King"
Hays, Peter L. *The Limping Hero . . .* , 137-140.

"Mrs. Bathurst"
Gilbert, Elliot L. "What Happens in 'Mrs. Bathurst'?" *PMLA,* 77 (1962), 450-458; rpt., expanded, in his *The Good Kipling . . .* , 94-117.

"The White Seal"
Gilbert, Elliot L. *The Good Kipling . . .* , 73-74.

"William the Conqueror"
Aykroyd, W. R. "Kipling and Famine," *Kipling J,* 38 (June, 1971), 12-17.

"Wireless"
Gilbert, Elliot L. "The Aesthetics . . . ," 210-211; rpt. in his *The Good Kipling . . .* , 164-167.

"Without Benefit of Clergy"
Gilbert, Elliot L. " 'Without Benefit of Clergy, ' " in Gilbert, Elliot L., Ed. *Kipling . . .* , 163-183; rpt. in his *The Good Kipling . . .* , 21-49.
Meyer, Jeffrey. "Thoughts on 'Without Benefit of Clergy, ' " *Kipling J,* 36 (December, 1969), 8-11.

HEINRICH VON KLEIST

"Die Heilige Cäcilie oder Die Gewalt der Musik"
Graf, Günther. "Der dramatische Aufbaustil der Legende Heinrich von Kleists 'Die heilige Cäcilie oder Die Gewalt der Musik': Ein Interpretationsversuch," *Études Germaniques,* 24 (1969), 346-359.

"The Marquise of O——"
Sokel, Walter. "Kleists 'Marquise von O——,' Kierkegaards 'Abraham' und Musils 'Tonka': Drei Stufen des Absurden in seiner Beziehung zum

Glauben," in Dinklage, Karl, Elizabeth Albertsen, and Karl Corino, Eds. *Robert Musil . . .* , 57-70.

"Michael Kohlhaas"
Cary, John R. "A Reading of Kleist's 'Michael Kohlhaas, ' " *PMLA*, 85 (1970), 212-218.
Ellis, John M. "Der Herr lässt regnen über Gerechte und Ungerechte: Kleists 'Michael Kohlhaas, ' " *Monatshefte*, 59 (1967), 35-40.
Müller, Richard. "Kleists 'Michael Kohlhaas, ' " *Deutsche Vierteljahrsschrift für literaturwissenschaft und Geistergeschichte*, 44 (1970), 101-119.

OLIVER La FARGE

"Captain Tom and Mother Carey's Chickens"
Pearce, T. M. *Oliver La Farge*, 30-31.

"Haunted Ground"
Pearce, T. M. *Oliver La Farge*, 94-95.

"North Is Black"
Pearce, T. M. *Oliver La Farge*, 88-89.

"Old Century River"
Pearce, T. M. *Oliver La Farge*, 90-91.

"La Spécialté de M. Duclos"
Pearce, T. M. *Oliver La Farge*, 92-94.

RING LARDNER

"Harmony"
Stein, Allen F. "This Unsporting Life: The Baseball Fiction of Ring Lardner," *Markham R*, 3 (1972), 31.

"Horseshoes"
Stein, Allen F. "This Unsporting Life . . . ," 30-31.

"Hurry Kane"
Stein, Allen F. "This Unsporting Life . . . ," 31-32.

D. H. LAWRENCE

"England, My England"
Vickery, John B. "Myth and Ritual in the Short Fiction of D. H. Lawrence," *Mod Fiction Stud,* 5 (1959), 71-76; rpt. Vickery, John B., and J'nan M. Sellery, Eds. *The Scapegoat* . . . , 178-184.

"The Fox"
Shields, E. F. "Broken Vision in Lawrence's 'The Fox,'" *Stud Short Fiction,* 9 (1972), 353-363.

"A Fragment of Stained Glass"
Baim, Joseph. "Past and Present in D. H. Lawrence's 'A Fragment of Stained Glass,'" *Stud Short Fiction,* 8 (1971), 323-326.

"The Horse Dealer's Daughter"
McCabe, Thomas H. "Rhythm as Form in Lawrence: 'The Horse Dealer's Daughter,'" *PMLA,* 87 (1972), 64-68.

"Odour of Chrysanthemums"
Amon, Frank. "D. H. Lawrence and the Short Story," in Hoffman, Frederick J., and Harry T. Moore, Eds. *The Achievement* . . . , 223-226; rpt. Consolo, Dominick, Ed. . . . *"The Rocking-Horse Winner,"* 85-87.
Douglas, Kenneth. "Masterpieces of the Modern World," in Mack, Maynard, *et al.,* Eds. *World Masterpieces,* II, 3rd ed., 1379-1380.
Howard, Daniel F. *Manual* . . . , 17-18.
Mizener, Arthur. *A Handbook* . . . *"Modern Short Stories* . . . *Revised Edition,"* 93-94; rpt. *A Handbook* . . *"Modern Short Stories* . . . *Third Edition,"* 109-110.

"The Prussian Officer"
Amon, Frank. "D. H. Lawrence . . . ," in Hoffman, Frederick J., and Harry T. Moore, Eds. *The Achievement* . . . , 226-231; rpt. Consolo, Dominick, Ed. . . . *"The Rocking-Horse Winner,"* 87-92.
Howard, Daniel F. *Manual* . . . , 16-17.

"The Rocking-Horse Winner"
Amon, Frank. "D. H. Lawrence . . . ," in Hoffman, Frederick J., and Harry T. Moore, Eds. *The Achievement* . . . , 231-233; rpt. Consolo, Dominick, Ed. . . . *"The Rocking-Horse Winner,"* 92-93.
Burroughs, William D. "No Defense for 'The Rocking-Horse Winner,'" *Coll Engl,* 24 (1963), 323; rpt. Consolo, Dominick, Ed. . . . *"The Rocking-Horse Winner,"* 55-56.
Davis, Robert G. *Instructor's Manual* . . . , 50; rpt. Consolo, Dominick,

Ed. . . . "*The Rocking-Horse Winner,*" 41-42.

Gordon, Caroline, and Allen Tate. *The House* . . . , 343-351; 2nd ed., 227-230; rpt. Consolo, Dominick, Ed. . . . "*The Rocking-Horse Winner,*" 37-40.

Hepburn, James G. "Disarming and Uncanny Visions: Freud's 'The Uncanny' with Regard to Form and Content in Stories by Sherwood Anderson and D. H. Lawrence," *Lit & Psych,* 9 (1959), 9-12; rpt. Consolo, Dominick, Ed. . . . "*The Rocking-Horse Winner,*" 60-68.

Lamson, Roy, *et al.,* Eds. *The Critical Reader,* 542-547; rpt. Consolo, Dominick, Ed. . . . "*The Rocking-Horse Winner,*" 47-51.

Lawrence, Robert G. "Further Notes on D. H. Lawrence's Rocking Horse," *Coll Engl,* 24 (1963), 324; rpt. Consolo, Dominick, Ed. . . . "*The Rocking-Horse Winner,*" 57.

Marks, W. S. "The Psychology of the Uncanny in Lawrence's 'The Rocking-Horse Winner,' " *Mod Fiction Stud,* 11 (1966), 381-392; rpt. Consolo, Dominick, Ed. . . . "*The Rocking-Horse Winner,*" 71-83.

Martin, W. R. "Fancy or Imagination? 'The Rocking-Horse Winner,' " *Coll Engl,* 24 (1962), 64-65; rpt. Consolo, Dominick, Ed. . . . "*The Rocking-Horse Winner,*" 52-54.

Moore, Harry T. . . . *D. H. Lawrence,* 277-279; rpt. Consolo, Dominick, Ed. . . . "*The Rocking-Horse Winner,*" 23-25.

O'Connor, Frank. *The Lonely Voice* . . . , 154-155; rpt. Consolo, Dominick, Ed. . . . "*The Rocking-Horse Winner,*" 58-59.

San Juan, Epifanio. "Theme Versus Imitation: D. H. Lawrence's 'The Rocking-Horse Winner,' " *D. H. Lawrence R,* 3 (1970), 136-140.

Snodgrass, W. D. "A Rocking-Horse: The Symbol, the Pattern, the Way to Live," *Hudson R,* 11 (1958), 191-200; rpt. Spilka, Mark, Ed. *D. H. Lawrence* . . . , 117-126; Albrecht, Robert C., Ed. . . . *Short Fiction,* 539-548; Consolo, Dominick, Ed. . . . "*The Rocking-Horse Winner,*" 26-36.

Tedlock, E. W. *D. H. Lawrence* . . . , 209-210; rpt. Consolo, Dominick, Ed. . . . "*The Rocking-Horse Winner,*" 69-70.

Turner, Frederick W. "Prancing in to a Purpose: Myths, Horses, and True Selfhood in Lawrence's 'The Rocking-Horse Winner,' " in Consolo, Dominick, Ed. . . . "*The Rocking-Horse Winner,*" 95-106.

Widmer, Kingsley. . . . *Perversity,* 92-95; rpt. Consolo, Dominick, Ed. . . . "*The Rocking-Horse Winner,*" 43-46.

"The Shadow in the Rose Garden"

Mizener, Arthur. *A Handbook* . . . "*Modern Short Stories* . . . *Revised Edition,*" 96-99; rpt. *A Handbook* . . "*Modern Short Stories* . . . *Third Edition,*" 112-115.

"Tickets, Please"

Lainoff, Seymour. "The Wartime Setting of Lawrence's 'Tickets, Please,' " *Stud Short Fiction,* 7 (1970), 649-651.

"The Undying Man"
  Zytaruk, George J. " 'The Undying Man': D. H. Lawrence's Yiddish
    Story," *D. H. Lawrence R,* 4 (1971), 20-27.

"The Virgin and the Gipsy"
  Meyers, Jeffrey. " 'The Voice of Water': Lawrence's 'The Virgin and the
    Gipsy,' " *Engl Miscellany,* 21 (1970), 199-207.

"The White Stocking"
  Mizener, Arthur. *A Handbook . . . "Modern Short Stories . . . Revised
    Edition,"* 100-105; rpt. *A Handbook . . . "Modern Short Stories . . .
    Third Edition,"* 116-121.

HENRY LAWSON

"The Babies in the Bush"
  Phillips, A. A. *Henry Lawson,* 91-92.

"Brighten's Sister-in-law"
  Phillips, A. A. *Henry Lawson,* 114-115.

"The Bush Undertaker"
  Matthews, Brian. " 'The Nurse and the Tutor of Eccentric Minds': Some
    Developments in Lawson's Treatment of Madness," *Australian Lit
    Stud,* 4 (1970), 251-253.

"A Double-Buggy at Lahey's Creek"
  Phillips, A. A. *Henry Lawson,* 117-119.

"The Drover's Wife"
  Matthews, Brian. " 'The Drover's Wife' Writ Large: One Measure of
    Lawson's Achievement," *Meanjin Q,* 27 (1968), 54-66.
  Moore, T. Inglis. *Social Patterns . . . ,* 24-27.
  Phillips, A. A. *Henry Lawson,* 72-73.

"A Hero in Dingo Scrubs"
  Phillips, A. A. *Henry Lawson,* 65-67.

"A Sketch of Mateship"
  Phillips, A. A. *Henry Lawson,* 77-78.

"Telling Mrs. Baker"
  Phillips, A. A. *Henry Lawson,* 67-68.

"The Union Buries Its Dead"
Matthews, Brian. "The Nurse . . . ," 253-254.
Phillips, A. A. *Henry Lawson,* 92-93.

"Water Them Geraniums"
Phillips, A. A. *Henry Lawson,* 115-117.

J. SHERIDAN LeFANU

"Carmilla"
Begnal, Michael H. . . . *LeFanu,* 43-45.

"Green Tea"
Begnal, Michael H. . . . *LeFanu,* 39-40.

"The Room in the Dragon Volant"
Begnal, Michael H. . . . *LeFanu,* 42-43.

DORIS LESSING

"The Day Stalin Died"
Mizener, Arthur. *A Handbook . . . "Modern Short Stories . . . Revised Edition,"* 38-39; rpt. *A Handbook . . . "Modern Short Stories . . . Third Edition,"* 44-45.

"The Nuisance"
Bloom, Edward A. and Lillian D., Eds. *The Variety . . . ,* 385-388.

WYNDHAM LEWIS

"Beau Séjour"
Materer, Timothy. "The Short Stories of Wyndham Lewis," *Stud Short Fiction,* 7 (1970), 618-619.

"Brotcotnaz"
Materer, Timothy. "The Short Stories . . . ," 622-623.

"The Cornac and His Wife"
Materer, Timothy. "The Short Stories . . . ," 621-622.

"The Death of Ankou"
  Materer, Timothy. "The Short Stories . . . ," 623-624.

OSMAN LINS

"The Betrothal"
  Rosenfeld, Anatol. "The Creative Narrative Process of Osman Lins,"
  Stud Short Fiction, 8 (1971), 239.

"A Dot in the Circle"
  Rosenfeld, Anatol. " . . . Narrative Process . . . ," 238-239.

JACK LONDON

"Batard"
  Labor, Earle. "Jack London's *Mondo Cane: The Call of the Wild* and
  White Fang," Jack London Newsletter, 1 (1967), 5-6.

"The Bones of Kahelili"
  McClintock, James I. "Jack London's Use of Carl Jung's *Psychology of
  the Unconscious," Am Lit,* 42 (1970), 344-345.

"The Call of the Wild"
  Labor, Earle. "Jack London's *Mondo Cane* . . . ," 6-11.
  Wilcox, Earl J. "Jack London's Naturalism: The Example of *The Call of
  the Wild," Jack London Newsletter,* 2 (1969), 91-101.

"The Chinago"
  Dhondt, Steven T. "Jack London's *When God Laughs:* Overman,
  Underdog and Satire," *Jack London Newsletter,* 2 (1969), 54-57.

"Like Argus of the Ancient Times"
  McClintock, James I. "Jack London's Use . . . ," 337-339.

"Shin Bones"
  McClintock, James I. "Jack London's Use . . . ," 343-344.

"The Tears of Ah Kim"
  McClintock, James I. "Jack London's Use . . . ," 339-341.

"To Build a Fire"
  Findley, Sue. "Naturalism in 'To Build a Fire,' " *Jack London Newsletter,*
  2 (1969), 45-50.

Jennings, Ann S. "London's Code of the Northland," *Alaska R,* 2 (Fall, 1964), 43-48.

Shevers, Alfred S. "The Romantic Jack London: Far Away Frozen Wilderness," *Alaska R,* 1 (Winter, 1963), 38-47.

"To the Man on Trail"
  Labor, Earle. " 'To the Man on Trail': Jack London's Christmas Carol," *Jack London Newsletter,* 3 (1970), 90-94.

"The Water Baby"
  McClintock, James I. "Jack London's Use . . . ," 341-343.

"When Alice Told Her Soul"
  McClintock, James I. "Jack London's Use . . . ," 339.

"When God Laughed"
  Dhondt, Steven T. "Jack London's *When God Laughed* . . . ," 51-54.

EDWARD LOOMIS

"Wounds"
  Gallagher, Edward J. "Edward Loomis's 'Wounds,' " *Stud Short Fiction,* 9 (1972), 247-256.

MALCOLM LOWRY

"The Bravest Boat"
  Dodson, Daniel B. *Malcolm Lowry,* 37-38.

"Elephant and Colosseum"
  Dodson, Daniel B. *Malcolm Lowry,* 39-40.

"The Forest Path to the Spring"
  Cross, Richard K. "Malcolm Lowry and the Columbian Eden," *Contemporary Lit,* 14 (Winter, 1973), 29-30.
  Dodson, Daniel B. *Malcolm Lowry,* 41-43.

"Gin and Goldenrod"
  Dodson, Daniel B. *Malcolm Lowry,* 40-41.

"The Last Address"
  Benham, David. "Lowry's Versions of 'Lunar Caustic, ' " *Canadian Lit,* 44 (1970), 29-34.

"The Present Estate of Pompeii"
Dodson, Daniel B. *Malcolm Lowry,* 40.

"Strange Comfort Afforded by the Professor"
Dodson, Daniel B. *Malcolm Lowry,* 38-39.

"Through the Panama"
Dodson, Daniel B. *Malcolm Lowry,* 36-37.
Durrant, Geoffrey. "Death in Life: Neo-Platonic Elements in 'Through the Panama, ' " *Canadian Lit,* 44 (1970), 13-27.

ANDREW LYTLE

"Alchemy"
Bradford, M. E. "Toward a Dark Shape: Lytle's 'Alchemy' and the Conquest of the New World," *Mississippi Q,* 23 (1970), 407-414.

"Jericho, Jericho, Jericho"
Landman, Sidney J. "The Walls of Mortality," *Mississippi Q,* 23 (1970), 415-423.

"The Mahogany Frame"
Krickel, Edward. "The Whole and the Parts: Initiation in 'The Mahogany Frame, ' " *Mississippi Q,* 23 (1970), 391-405.

"Mister McGregor"
Jones, Madison. "A Look at 'Mister McGregor, ' " *Mississippi Q,* 23 (1970); 363-370.
Mizener, Arthur. *A Handbook . . . "Modern Short Stories . . . Revised Edition,"* 166-170; rpt. *A Handbook . . . "Modern Short Stories . . . Third Edition,"* 186-190.

MARY McCARTHY

"Artists in Uniform"
Mizener, Arthur. *A Handbook . . . "Modern Short Stories . . . Revised Edition,"* 15-22; rpt. *A Handbook . . . "Modern Short Stories . . . Third Edition,"* 19-26.

CARSON McCULLERS

"The Ballad of the Sad Cafe"
Graver, Lawrence. *Carson McCullers,* 24-33.

Hamilton, Alice. "Loneliness and Alienation: The Life and Work of Carson McCullers," *Dalhousie R,* 50 (1970), 226-227.

Moore, Janice T. "McCullers' 'The Ballad of the Sad Cáfe,' " *Explicator,* 29 (1970), Item 27.

"Correspondence"
Edmonds, Dale. " 'Correspondence': A 'Forgotten' Carson McCullers Short Story," *Stud Short Fiction,* 9 (1972), 89-92.

"A Domestic Dilemma"
Grinnell, James W. "Delving 'A Domestic Dilemma,' " *Stud Short Fiction,* 9 (1972), 270-271.

JOAQUIM M. MACHADO DE ASSIS

"Un Esqueleto"
Dos Santos, María I. "El Celoso paranoico en Ciertas Historias de Machado de Assis," *R Iberoamericana,* 75 (1971), 442-443.

"El Mulher Prêto"
Dos Santos, María I. "El Celoso . . . ," 440.

"Sem Olhos"
Dos Santos, María I. "El Celoso . . . ," 443-445.

ARTHUR MACHEN

"The Angel of Mons"
Starrett, Vincent. "Arthur Machen and 'The Angel of Mons,' " *Open Court,* 32 (1918), 191.

JAMES A. McPHERSON

"Gold Coast"
Mizener, Arthur. *A Handbook . . . "Modern Short Stories . . . Third Edition,"* 81-84.

BERNARD MALAMUD

"Angel Levine"
Bluefarb, Sam. "Bernard Malamud: The Scope of Caricature," *Engl J,* 53

(1964), 322-324; rpt. Field, A. Leslie and Joyce W., Eds. . . . *Critics*, 143-146.

Goldman, Mark. "Bernard Malamud's Comic Vision and the Theme of Identity," *Critique*, 7 (1965), 97-98; rpt. Field, A. Leslie and Joyce W., Eds. . . . *Critics*, 156-157.

Howard, Daniel F. *Manual* . . . , 34-35.

Richman, Sidney. *Bernard Malamud*, 105-106; rpt. Field, A. Leslie and Joyce W., Eds. . . . *Critics*, 312-314.

"Behold the Key"
Richman, Sidney. *Bernard Malamud*, 113-114; rpt. Field, A. Leslie and Joyce W., Eds. . . . *Critics*, 321-322.

Siegel, Ben. "Victims in Motion: Bernard Malamud's Sad and Bitter Clowns," *Northwest R*, 5 (1962), 76; rpt. Waldmeir, Joseph J., Ed. . . . *Critical Views*, 210; Field, A. Leslie and Joyce W., Eds. . . . *Critics*, 131-132.

"The Bill"
Montague, Gene, and Marjorie Henshaw, Eds. . . . *Literature*, 9-16.
Richman, Sidney. *Bernard Malamud*, 107-109; rpt. Field, A. Leslie and Joyce W., Eds. . . . *Critics*, 314-316.

"The First Seven Years"
Richman, Sidney. *Bernard Malamud*, 102-104; rpt. Field, A. Leslie and Joyce W., Eds. . . . *Critics*, 309-311.

"The Girl of My Dreams"
Bluefarb, Sam. "Bernard Malamud . . . ," 321-322; rpt. Field, A. Leslie and Joyce W., Eds. . . . *Critics*, 141-143.
Richman, Sidney. *Bernard Malamud*, 111-112; rpt. Field, A. Leslie and Joyce W., Eds. . . . . *Critics*, 319-320.

"The Jewbird"
Bellman, Samuel I. "Women, Children, and Idiots First: The Transformation Psychology of Bernard Malamud," *Critique*, 7 (1965), 131-132; rpt. Field, A. Leslie and Joyce W., Eds. . . . *Critics*, 20-21.

"The Lady of the Lake"
Goldman, Mark. ". . . Theme of Identity," 98-100; rpt. Field, A. Leslie and Joyce W., Eds. . . . *Critics*, 157-160.
Richman, Sidney. *Bernard Malamud*, 114-115; rpt. Field, A. Leslie and Joyce W., Eds. . . . *Critics*, 322-323.

"The Last Mohican"
Goldman, Mark. " . . . Theme of Identity," 100-103; rpt. Field, A. Leslie

and Joyce W., Eds. . . . *Critics,* 160-163.

Richman, Sidney. *Bernard Malamud,* 115-118; rpt. Field, A. Leslie, and Joyce W., Eds. . . . *Critics,* 323-326.

Siegel, Ben. "Victims . . . ," 76; rpt. Waldmeir, Joseph J., Ed. . . . *Critical Views,* 210; Field, A. Leslie and Joyce W., Eds. . . . *Critics,* 132-133.

"The Loan"
May, Charles E. "The Bread of Tears: Malamud's 'The Loan,' " *Stud Short Fiction,* 7 (1970), 652-654.

Richman, Sidney. *Bernard Malamud,* 106-109; rpt. Field, A. Leslie and Joyce W., Eds. . . . *Critics,* 316-318.

"The Magic Barrel"
Bellman, Samuel I. "Women . . ," 128-129; rpt. Field, A. Leslie and Joyce W., Eds. . . . *Critics,* 16-18.

Bluefarb, Sam. "Bernard Malamud . . . ," 324-326; rpt. Field, A. Leslie and Joyce W., Eds. . . . *Critics,* 146-148.

Goldman, Mark. " . . . Theme of Identity," 96-97; rpt. Field, A. Leslie and Joyce W., Eds. . . . *Critics,* 155-156.

Hoyt, Charles A. "Bernard Malamud and the New Romanticism," in Moore, Harry T., Ed. . . . *Novelists,* 73-74; rpt. Field, A. Leslie and Joyce W., Eds. . . . *Critics,* 178-179.

Pinsker, Sanford. *The Schlemiel . . . ,* 89-93.

Richman, Sidney. *Bernard Malamud,* 118-123; rpt. Field, A. Leslie and Joyce W., Eds. . . . *Critics,* 326-331.

Rovit, Earl H. "Bernard Malamud and the Jewish Literary Tradition," *Critique,* 3 (1960), 6; rpt. Field, A. Leslie and Joyce W., Eds. . . . *Critics,* 6-7.

Siegel, Ben. "Victims . . . ," 76-77; rpt. Waldmeir, Joseph J., Ed. . . . *Critical Views,* 210-211; Field, A. Leslie and Joyce W., Eds. . . . *Critics,* 133-134.

"The Mourners"
Bluefarb, Sam. "Bernard Malamud . . ," 320-321; rpt. Field, A. Leslie and Joyce W., Eds. . . . *Critics,* 138-140.

Richman, Sidney. *Bernard Malamud,* 104-105; rpt. Field, A. Leslie and Joyce W., Eds. . . . *Critics,* 311-312.

"The Prison"
Wechsler, Diane. "An Analysis of 'The Prison,' by Bernard Malamud," *Engl J,* 59 (1970), 782-784.

"Take Pity"
Mizener, Arthur. *A Handbook . . . "Modern Short Stories . . . Revised Edition,"* 124-127; rpt. *A Handbook . . . "Modern Short Stories . . . Third Edition,"* 144-147.

THOMAS MANN

"At the Prophet's"
Feuerlicht, Ignace. *Thomas Mann,* 136-137.
Gross, Harvey. *The Contrived Corridor,* 156-158.

"The Black Swan"
Feuerlicht, Ignace. *Thomas Mann,* 146-149.

"Blood of the Walsungs"
Feuerlicht, Ignace. *Thomas Mann,* 140-141.

"Death in Venice"
Addison, Bill K. "Melville, Aschenbach, and We," *Conradiana,* 2 (Winter, 1970), 79-81.
Baron, Frank. "Sensuality and Morality in Thomas Mann's 'Tod in Venedig,' " *Germ R,* 45 (1970), 115-125.
Braverman, Albert, and Larry Nachman. "The Dialectic of Decadence: An Analysis of Thomas Mann's 'Death in Venice,' " *Germ R,* 45 (1970), 289-298.
Dyson, A. E. "The Stranger God: 'Death in Venice,' " *Critical Q,* 13 (1971), 5-20.
Egri, Peter. "The Function of Dreams and Visions in *A Portrait* and 'Death in Venice,' " *James Joyce Q,* 5 (1968), 86-102.
Feuerlicht, Ignace. *Thomas Mann,* 117-126.
Gross, Harvey. *The Contrived Corridor,* 164-167.
Lehnert, Herbert. "Notes on Mann's 'Der Tod in Venedig' and *The Odyssey,*" *PMLA,* 80 (1965), 306-307.
McWilliams, James R. "The Failure of a Repression: Thomas Mann's 'Tod in Venedig,' " *Germ Life & Letters,* 20 (1967), 233-241.
Slochower, Harry. "Thomas Mann's 'Death in Venice,' " *Am Imago,* 26 (1969), 99-122.
Stelzmann, Rainulf A. "Thomas Mann's 'Death in Venice': *Res et Imago,*" *Xavier Univ Stud,* 3 (1964), 160-167.
————. "Eine Ironisierung Nietzsches in Thomas Manns 'Der Tod in Venedig,' " *So Atlantic Bull,* 35 (May, 1970), 16-21.
Tarbox, Raymond. " 'Death in Venice': The Aesthetic Object as Dream Guide," *Am Imago,* 26 (1969), 123-144.
Woodward, Anthony. "The Figure of the Artist in Thomas Mann's 'Tonio Kröger' and 'Death in Venice,' " *Engl Stud Africa,* 9 (1966), 158-167.

"Disorder and Early Sorrow"
Feuerlicht, Ignace. *Thomas Mann,* 143-144.

"Gladius Dei"
Feuerlicht, Ignace. *Thomas Mann*, 133-135.
Gross, Harvey. *The Contrived Corridor*, 160-161.
Wolf, Ernest. "Savonarola in München: Eine Analyse von Thomas Manns 'Gladius Dei,' " *Euphorion*, 64 (1970), 85-96.

"The Infant Prodigy"
Feuerlicht, Ignace. *Thomas Mann*, 135-136.

"Little Herr Friedemann"
Feuerlicht, Ignace. *Thomas Mann*, 129-130.

"Little Lizzy"
Feuerlicht, Ignace. *Thomas Mann*, 131-132.

"A Man and His Dog"
Feuerlicht, Ignace. *Thomas Mann*, 141-142.

"Mario and the Magician"
Feuerlicht, Ignace. *Thomas Mann*, 126-129.
Hamalian, Leo, and Edmond L. Volpe, Eds. *Ten . . . . Short Novels*, 470-474; rpt. 2nd ed. (retitled *Eleven . . . Short Novels)*, 451-453.
Hays, Peter L. *The Limping Hero . . .* , 207-208.

"The Tables of the Law"
Feuerlicht, Ignace. *Thomas Mann*, 145-146.

"Tonio Kröger"
Feuerlicht, Ignace. *Thomas Mann*, 109-114.
Furst, Lillian R. "Thomas Mann's 'Tonio Kröger': A Critical Reconsideration," *Revue des langues vivantes* (Brussels), 27 (1961), 232-240.
McWilliams, James R. "Conflict and Compromise: Tonio Kröger's Paradox," *Revue des langues vivantes* (Brussels), 32 (1966), 376-383.
Swales, M. W. "Punctuation and the Narrative Mode: Some Remarks on 'Tonio Kröger,' " *Forum Mod Lang Stud*, 6 (1970), 235-242.
Woodward, Anthony. "The Figure . . . ," 158-167.

"The Transposed Heads"
Feuerlicht, Ignace. *Thomas Mann*, 144-145.

"Tristan"
Feuerlicht, Ignace. *Thomas Mann*, 114-117.

"The Wardrobe"
Feuerlicht, Ignace. *Thomas Mann,* 132-133.

"A Weary Hour"
Feuerlicht, Ignace. *Thomas Mann,* 139-140.

KATHERINE MANSFIELD

"At the Bay"
Magalaner, Marvin. . . . *Mansfield,* 38-45.

"Bliss"
Magalaner, Marvin. . . . *Mansfield,* 74-86.
Nebeker, Helen E. "The Pear Tree: Sexual Implications in Katherine
Mansfield's 'Bliss,' " *Mod Fiction Stud,* 18 (1973), 545-551.

"The Daughters of the Late Colonel"
Magalaner, Marvin. . . . *Mansfield,* 91-99.

"The Garden Party"
Iverson, Anders. "A Reading of Katherine Mansfield's 'The Garden
Party,' " *Orbis Litterarum,* 23 (1968), 5-34.
Magalaner, Marvin. . . . *Mansfield,* 110-119.

"Her First Ball"
Mizener, Arthur. *A Handbook . . . "Modern Short Stories . . . Revised
Edition,"* 121-123; rpt. *A Handbook . . ."Modern Short Stories . . .
Third Edition,"* 141-143.

"Je ne parle pas français"
Magalaner, Marvin. . . . *Mansfield,* 62-65.

"The Man Without a Temperament"
Magalaner, Marvin. . . . *Mansfield,* 65-73.

"Marriage à la Mode"
Magalaner, Marvin. . . . *Mansfield,* 86-91.

"Miss Brill"
Magalaner, Marvin. . . . *Mansfield,* 129-130.

"Prelude"
Magalaner, Marvin. . . . *Mansfield,* 26-38.

"Something Childish but Very Natural"
Magalaner, Marvin. . . . *Mansfield*, 53-62.

"The Stranger"
Magalaner, Marvin. . . . *Mansfield*, 99-106.

JOHN MARQUAND

"The End Game"
Birmingham, Stephen. . . . *John Marquand*, 185-188.

"Good Morning, Major"
Birmingham, Stephen. . . . *John Marquand*, 57-58.

GABRIEL MARQUEZ

"Los funerales de la Mamá Grande"
Goetzinger, Judith. "The Emergence of a Folk Myth in 'Los funerales de la Mamá Grande,' " *Revista de Estudios Hispánicos*, 2 (1972), 237-248.

GUY DE MAUPASSANT

"Moonlight"
Guerin, Wilfred L., *et al. Instructor's Manual . . . "Mandala" . . .*, 6-7.

FRANÇOIS MAURIAC

"Thérèse Desqueyroux"
Farrell, C. Frederick and Edith R. "The Multiple Murders of Thérèse Desqueyroux," *Hartford Stud Lit*, 2 (1970), 195-206.

E. K. MEANS

"The Late Figger Bush"
Starke, Catherine J. *Black Portraiture . . .*, 66-67.

HERMAN MELVILLE

"The Apple-Tree Table"
Browne, Ray B. *Melville's Drive* . . . , 271-279.
Fisher, Marvin. "Bug and Humbug in Melville's 'Apple-Tree Table, ' "
Stud Short Fiction, 8 (1971), 459-466.
Karcher, Carolyn L. "The 'Spiritual Lesson' of Melville's 'The Apple-Tree
Table, ' " *Am Q,* 23 (1971), 101-109.

"Bartleby the Scrivener"
Ayo, Nicholas. "Bartleby's Lawyer on Trial," *Arizona Q,* 28 (1972), 27-38.
Bigelow, Gordon E. "The Problem of Symbolist Form in Melville's
'Bartleby the Scrivener, ' " *Mod Lang Q,* 31 (1970), 345-358.
Bowen, James K. "Alienation and Withdrawal Are Not the Absurd:
Renunciation and Preference in 'Bartleby the Scrivener,' *Stud Short
Fiction,* 8 (1971), 633-635.
Browne, Ray B. "The Affirmation of 'Bartleby, ' " in Wilgus, D. K., Ed.
Folklore International . . . , 11-21; rpt. Browne, Ray B. *Melville's Drive*
. . . , 152-168.
Canzoneri, Robert, and Page Stegner, Eds. *Fiction* . . . , 28-31.
Colwell, J. L., and G. Spitzer. " 'Bartleby' and 'The Raven': Parallels of
the Irrational," *Georgia R,* 23 (1969), 37-43.
Fiene, Donald M. "Bartleby the Christ," *Am Transcendental Q,* 7 (Part II,
Summer, 1970), 18-23.
Friedman, Maurice. *Problematic Rebel* . . . , 93-95; 2nd ed., expanded, 82-
92.
Gross, Theodore L. *The Heroic Ideal* . . . , 45-46.
Guerin, Wilfred L., *et al. Instructor's Manual* . . . *"Mandala"* . . . , 97-98.
Knight, Karl F. "Melville's Variation of the Theme of Failure: 'Bartleby'
and 'Billy Budd, ' " *Arlington Q,* 2 (1969), 44-58.
Norman, Liane. "Bartleby and the Reader," *New England Q,* 44 (1971),
22-39.
Seelye, John. "The Contemporary 'Bartleby, ' " *Am Transcendental Q,*
No. 7, Part 1 (Summer, 1970), 12-18.
————. *Melville* . . . , 96-99.
Stone, Edward. *A Certain Morbidity* . . . , 32-42.
Widmer, Kingsley. "Melville's Radical Resistance: The Method and
Meaning of 'Bartleby, ' " *Stud Novel,* 1 (1969), 444-458; rpt., expanded,
in his . . . *Nihilism* . . . , 91-125.
Wright, Nathalia. "Melville and 'Old Burton' with 'Bartleby' as an
'Anatomy of Melancholy, ' " *Tenn Stud Lit,* 15 (1970), 1-13.
Zink, David D. "Bartleby and the Contemporary Search for Meaning,"
Forum (Houston), 8 (Summer, 1970), 46-50.

"The Bell Tower"
  Browne, Ray B. *Melville's Drive* . . . , 247-259.
  Morseberger, Robert E. "Melville's 'The Bell-Tower' and Benvenuto
    Cellini," *Am Lit,* 44 (1972), 459-462.
  Vernon, John. "Melville's 'The Bell-Tower, ' " *Stud Short Fiction,* 7
    (1970), 264-276.

"Benito Cereno"
  Browne, Ray B. "Political Symbolism in 'Benito Cereno, ' " in Browne,
    Ray B., and Martin Light, Eds. *Critical Approaches . . . ,* I, 309-325; rpt.
  Browne, Ray B. *Melville's Drive* . . . , 168-188.
  Forrey, Robert. "Herman Melville and the Negro Question,"
    Mainstream, 15 (February, 1962), 23-32.
  Gaillard, Theodore L. "Melville's Riddle for Our Time: 'Benito Cereno, ' "
    Engl J, 61 (1972), 479-487.
  Gross, Theodore L. *The Heroic Ideal* . . . , 43-45.
  Hays, Peter. "Slavery and 'Benito Cereno': An Aristotelian View," *Études
    Anglaises,* 23 (1970), 38-46.
  Lannon, Diedre. "A Note on Melville's 'Benito Cereno, ' " *Massachusetts
    Stud Engl,* 2 (Spring, 1970), 68-70.
  Lowance, Mason I. "Veils and Illusion in 'Benito Cereno, ' " *Arizona Q,* 26
    (1970), 113-126.
  Metzger, Charles R. "Melville's Saints: Allusion in 'Benito Cereno, ' "
    Emerson Soc Q, 58 (1970), 88-90.
  Nicol, Charles. "Iconography of Evil and Ideal in 'Benito Cereno, ' " *Am
    Transcendental Q,* No. 7, Part 2 (Summer, 1970), 25-31.
  Ray, Richard E. " 'Benito Cereno': Babo As Leader," *Am Transcendental
    Q,* No. 7, Part 2 (Summer, 1970), 31-37.
  Seelye, John. *Melville* . . . , 104-110.
  Starke, Catherine J. *Black Portraiture* . . . , 158-160.
  Swanson, Donald R. "The Exercise of Irony in 'Benito Cereno, ' " *Am
    Transcendental Q,* No. 7, Part 2 (Summer, 1970), 23-25.
  Widmer, Kingsley. "The Perplexity of Melville: 'Benito Cereno, ' " *Stud
    Short Fiction,* 5 (1968), 225-238; rpt., expanded, in his . . . *Nihilism* . . . ,
    59-90.
  Yellin, Jean F. "Black Masks: Melville's 'Benito Cereno, ' " *Am Q,* 12
    (1970), 678-689.

"Billy Budd"
  Auden, Wystan H. *The Enchafèd Flood* . . . , 144-149; rpt. Vincent,
    Howard P., Ed. . . . *"Billy Budd,"* 85-88; rpt. in part Stafford, William
    T., Ed. . . . *"Billy Budd"* . . . , 156-159.
  Berthoff, Warner. " 'Certain Phenomenal Men': The Example of 'Billy
    Budd, ' " *Engl Lit Hist,* 27 (1960), 334-351; rpt. in his *The Example* . . . ,

183-203; Vincent, Howard P., Ed. . . . *"Billy Budd,"* 67-81.

Bowen, Merlin. *The Long Encounter,* 216-233; rpt. Browne, Ray B., and Martin Light, Eds. *Critical Approaches* . . . , I, 326-339; Springer, Haskell S., Ed. *Studies* . . . , 90-105.

Brodtkorb, Paul. "The Definitive 'Billy Budd': 'But Aren't It All Sham?' " *PMLA,* 82 (1967), 602-612; rpt. in part Vincent, Howard P., Ed. . . . *"Billy Budd,"* 29-33.

Browne, Ray B. " 'Billy Budd': Gospel of Democracy," *Nineteenth Century Fiction,* 17 (1963), 321-337; rpt. in his *Melville's Drive* . . . , 370-394.

Chase, Richard. *Herman Melville* . . . , 258-277; rpt. in part Stafford, William T., Ed. . . . *"Billy Budd"* . . . , 112-119; Vincent, Howard P., Ed. . . . *"Billy Budd,"* 101-102.

————, Ed. *Selected Tales* . . . , xiii-xvi; rpt. Stafford, William T., Ed. . . . *"Billy Budd"* . . . , 143-145; Springer, Haskell S., Ed. *Studies* . . . , 32-35.

Dew, Marjorie. "The Prudent Captain Vere," *Am Transcendental Q,* No. 7, Part 2 (Summer, 1970), 81-85.

Fogle, Richard H. " 'Billy Budd'—Acceptance or Irony," *Tulane Stud Engl,* 8 (1958), 107-113; rpt. Gordon, Walter K., Ed. . . . *Critical Perspectives* . . . , 758-761; Vincent, Howard P., Ed. . . . *"Billy Budd,"* 41-47; rpt. in part Stafford, William T., Ed. . . . *"Billy Budd"* . . . , 146-149.

————. " 'Billy Budd': The Order of the Fall," *Nineteenth Century Fiction,* 15 (1960), 189-205; rpt. in part Springer, Haskell S., Ed. *Studies* . . . , 81-82.

Franklin, H. Bruce. *The Wake* . . . , 188-202; rpt. Springer, Haskell S., Ed. *Studies* . . . , 118-130.

Freeman, F. Barron. . . . *"Billy Budd,"* 62-126; rpt. in part Springer, Haskell S., Ed. *Studies* . . . , 21-22.

Friedman, Maurice. *Problematic Rebel* . . . , 285-290; 2nd ed., 136-142.

Fulwiler, Toby. "The Death of the Handsome Sailor: A Study of 'Billy Budd' and *The Red Badge of Courage,*" *Arizona Q,* 26 (1970), 101-112.

Glick, Wendell. "Expediency and Absolute Morality in 'Billy Budd, ' " *PMLA,* 68 (1953), 103-110; rpt. Stafford, William T., Ed. . . . *"Billy Budd"* . . . , 104-111; Springer, Haskell S., Ed. *Studies* . . . , 53-61.

Gross, Theodore L. *The Heroic Ideal* . . . , 48-50.

Hendrickson, John. " 'Billy Budd': Affirmation of Absurdity," *Re: Arts & Letters,* 2 (Spring, 1969), 30-37.

Hiner, James. "Only Catastrophe," *Minnesota R,* 10 (1970), 82-89.

Howard, Leon. . . . *Melville,* 42-44; rpt. Vincent, Howard P., Ed. . . . *"Billy Budd,"* 93-95.

Kenney, Blair G. "Melville's 'Billy Budd, ' " *Am Notes & Queries,* 9 (1971), 151-152.

Ketterer, David. "Some Co-ordinates in 'Billy Budd, ' " *J Am Stud,* 3 (1969), 221-237.

Kinnamon, Jon M. " 'Billy Budd': Political Philosophies in a Sea of Thought," *Arizona Q,* 26 (1970), 164-172.

Knight, Karl F. "Melville's Variation of the Theme of Failure: 'Bartleby' and 'Billy Budd, ' " *Arlington Q,* 2 (1969), 44-58.

Levin, Harry. *The Power of Blackness,* 194-197; Vintage ed., 194-197; rpt. Springer, Haskell S., Ed. *Studies . . . ,* 78-80.

Lewis, R. W. B. *The American Adam . . . ,* 147-152; rpt. Springer, Haskell S., Ed. *Studies . . . ,* 62-68.

McElderry, Bruce R. "Three Earlier Treatments of the 'Billy Budd' Theme," *Am Lit,* 27 (1955), 251-257; rpt. in part Springer, Haskell S., Ed. *Studies . . . ,* 69.

McNamara, Anne. "Melville's 'Billy Budd, ' " *Explicator,* 21 (1962), Item 11; rpt. Springer, Haskell S., Ed. *Studies . . . ,* 106-107.

Matthiessen, F. O. *American Renaissance,* 500-514; rpt. Chase, Richard, Ed. *Melville . . . ,* 156-168; rpt. in part Springer, Haskell S., Ed. *Studies . . . ,* 18-20.

Montale, Eugenio. "An Introduction to 'Billy Budd, ' " *Sewanee R,* 68 (1960), 419-422; rpt. Vincent, Howard P., Ed. . . . *"Billy Budd,"* 17-19.

Mumford, Lewis. *Herman Melville,* 353-356; rpt. in part Stafford, William T., Ed. . . . *"Billy Budd" . . . ,* 72-73; Springer, Haskell S., Ed. *Studies . . . ,* 10-11.

Nathanson, Leonard. "Melville's 'Billy Budd,' Chapter I," *Explicator,* 22 (1964), Item 75; rpt. Springer, Haskell S., Ed. *Studies . . . ,* 131-133.

Ortego, Philip D. "The Existential Roots of 'Billy Budd, ' " *Connecticut R,* 4 (October, 1970), 80-87.

Pearson, Norman H. "Billy Budd: 'The King's Yarn, ' " *Am Q,* 3 (1951), 99-114; Springer, Haskell S., Ed. *Studies . . . ,* 36-52.

Perry, Robert L. " 'Billy Budd': Melville's *Paradise Lost," Midwest Q,* 10 (1969), 173-185.

Reich, Charles A. "The Tragedy of Justice in 'Billy Budd, ' " *Yale R,* 56 (1967), 368-389; rpt. Vincent, Howard P., Ed. . . . *"Billy Budd,"* 56-66.

Rosenberry, Edward H. "The Problem of 'Billy Budd, ' " *PMLA,* 80 (1965), 489-498; rpt. Gordon, Walter K., Ed. . . . *Critical Perspectives . . . ,* 762-773; Vincent, Howard P., Ed. . . . *"Billy Budd,"* 48-55.

Rosenthal, Bernard. "Elegy for Jack Chase," *Stud Romanticism,* 10 (1971), 213-229.

Schiffman, Joseph. "Melville's Final Stage, Irony: A Re-examination of 'Billy Budd' Criticism," *Am Lit,* 22 (1950), 128-136; Springer, Haskell S., Ed. *Studies . . . ,* 23-31; rpt. in part Vincent, Howard P., Ed. . . . *"Billy Budd,"* 98-100.

Schroth, Evelyn. "Melville's Judgment on Captain Vere," *Midwest Q,* 10 (1969), 189-200.

Seelye, John. *Melville . . . ,* 161-172; rpt. Vincent, Howard P., Ed. . . . *"Billy Budd,"* 20-28.

Stitt, Peter. "Herman Melville's 'Billy Budd': Sympathy and Rebellion," *Arizona Q,* 28 (1972), 39-54.

Sutton, Walter. "Melville and the Great God Budd," *Prairie Schooner,* 34 (1960), 128-133; rpt. Springer, Haskell S., Ed. *Studies . . . ,* 83-89.

Thompson, Lawrance. *Melville's Quarrel . . . ,* 355-414; rpt. in part Stafford, William T., Ed. . . . *"Billy Budd" . . . ,* 140-141; Leavitt, Hart D., Ed. *Billy Budd . . . ,* 113-116; Vincent, Howard P., Ed. . . . *"Billy Budd,"* 100-101.

Tindall, William Y. "The Ceremony of Innocence," in MacIvor, R. M., Ed. *Great . . . Dilemmas . . . ,* 73-81; rpt. Gordon, Walter K., Ed. . . . *Critical Persepctives . . . ,* 719-723; Springer, Haskell S., Ed. *Studies . . . ,* 70-77; Vincent, Howard P., Ed. . . . *"Billy Budd,"* 34-40; rpt. in part Stafford, William T., Ed. . . . *"Billy Budd" . . . ,* 125-131.

Turnage, Maxine. "Melville's Concern with the Arts in 'Billy Budd, ' " *Arizona Q,* 28 (1972), 74-82.

Van Doren, Carl. "A Note of Confession," *Nation,* 127 (December 5, 1928), 622; rpt. Springer, Haskell S., Ed. *Studies . . . ,* 8-9.

Watson, E. L. Grant. "Melville's Testament of Acceptance," *New England Q,* 6 (1933), 319-327; rpt. Springer, Haskell S., Ed. *Studies . . . ,* 12-17; Vincent, Howard P., Ed. . . . *"Billy Budd,"* 11-16; rpt. in part Stafford, William T., Ed. . . . *"Billy Budd" . . . ,* 74-78.

Weaver, Raymond. *The Shorter Novels . . . ,* xlix-li; rpt. in part Stafford, William T., Ed. . . . *"Billy Budd" . . . ,* 71-72; Springer, Haskell S., Ed. *Studies . . . ,* 6-7.

West, Ray B. "The Unity of 'Billy Budd, ' " *Hudson R,* 5 (1952), 120-128; rpt. in part Stafford, William T., Ed. . . . *"Billy Budd' . . . ,* 119-125; Vincent, Howard P., Ed. . . . *"Billy Budd,"* 95-97.

Widmer, Kingsley. "The Perplexed Mythos of Melville: 'Billy Budd, ' " *Novel,* 2 (1968), 25-35; rpt., expanded, in his . . . *Nihilism . . . ,* 16-58.

Willett, Ralph W. "Nelson and Vere: Hero and Victim in 'Billy Budd, Sailor, ' " *PMLA,* 82 (1967), 370-376; rpt. Springer, Haskell S., Ed. *Studies . . . ,* 134-142.

Yoder, R. A. "Poetry and Science: 'Two Distinct Branches of Knowledge' in 'Billy Budd, ' " *Southern R* (Adelaide), 3 (1969), 223-239.

"Cock-A-Doodle-Doo"

Brack, Vida K. and O. M. "Weathering Cape Horn: Survivors in Melville's Minor Short Fiction," *Arizona Q,* 28 (1972), 64-65.

Browne, Ray B. *Melville's Drive . . . ,* 189-200.

"The Encantadas or Enchanted Isles"
Browne, Ray B. *Melville's Drive* . . . , 280-301.
Seelye, John. *Melville* . . . , 101-103.
Watson, Charles N. "Melville's Agatha and Hunilla: A Literary Reincarnation," *Engl Lang Notes,* 6 (1968), 114-118.

"The Fiddler"
Brack, Vida K. and O. M. "Weathering . . . ," 67-68.
Browne, Ray B. *Melville's Drive* . . . , 240-242.
Gupta, R. K. "Hautboy and Plinlimmon: A Reinterpretation of Melville's 'The Fiddler, ' " *Am Lit,* 43 (1971), 437-442.

"The Happy Failure"
Brack, Vida K. and O. M. "Weathering . . . ," 66.
Browne, Ray B. *Melville's Drive* . . . , 237-240.
Lynde, Richard D. "Melville's Success in 'The Happy Failure': A Story of the River Hudson," *Coll Lang Assoc J,* 13 (1969), 119-130.

"I and My Chimney"
Brack, Vida K. and O. M. "Weathering . . . ," 69-70.
Browne, Ray B. *Melville's Drive* . . . , 259-271.

"Jimmy Rose"
Brack, Vida K. and O. M. "Weathering . . . ," 66-67.
Browne, Ray B. *Melville's Drive* . . . , 242-247.

"The Lightning-Rod Man"
Brack, Vida K. and O. M. "Weathering . . . ," 68-69.
Browne, Ray B. *Melville's Drive* . . . , 229-237.
Fisher, Marvin. " 'The Lightning-Rod Man': Melville's Testament of Rejection," *Stud Short Fiction,* 7 (1970), 433-438.
Shusterman, Alan. "Melville's 'The Lightning-Rod Man': A Reading," *Stud Short Fiction,* 9 (1972), 165-174.

"The Paradise of Bachelors and the Tartarus of Maids"
Brack, Vida K. and O. M. "Weathering . . . ," 63-64.
Browne, Ray B. "Two Views of Commitment: 'The Paradise of Bachelors' and 'The Tartarus of Maids, ' " *Am Transcendental Q,* No. 7, Part 2 (Summer, 1970), 43-47.
————. *Melville's Drive* . . . , 219-229.
Fisher, Marvin. "Melville's 'Tartarus': The Deflowering of New England," *Am Q,* 23 (1971), 79-100.

"The Piazza"
  Donaldson, Scott. "The Dark Truth of *The Piazza Tales,*" *PMLA,* 85
    (1970), 1082-1083.

"Poor Man's Pudding and Rich Man's Crumbs"
  Brack, Vida K. and O. M. "Weathering . . . ," 63.
  Browne, Ray B. *Melville's Drive* . . . , 209-219.
  Rowland, Beryl. "Melville's Waterloo in 'Rich Man's Crumbs, '"
    Nineteenth Century Fiction, 25 (1970), 216-221.
  ————. "Sitting Up with a Corpse: Malthus According to Melville in
    'Poor Man's Pudding and Rich Man's Crumbs, '" *J Am Stud*
    (Cambridge), 6 (1972), 69-83.

"The Two Temples"
  Browne, Ray B. *Melville's Drive* . . . , 200-208.
  Fisher, Marvin. "Focus on Herman Melville's 'The Two Temples': The
    Denigration of the American Dream," in Madden, David, Ed.
    American Dreams . . . , 76-86.

W. S. MERWIN

"The Locker Room"
  Minot, Stephen, and Robley Wilson. *Teacher's Manual* . . . , 27.

CONRAD F. MEYER

"Das Amulett"
  Schimmelpfennig, Paul. "C. F. Meyer's Religion of the Heart: A
    Reevaluation of 'Das Amulett, '" *Germ R,* 47 (1972), 181-202.

"The Monk's Wedding"
  Jackson, D. A. "Dante the Dupe in C. F. Meyer's 'Die Hochzeit des
    Mönchs, '" 25 (1971), 5-15.

ARTHUR MILLER

"I Don't Need You Any More"
  Schraepen, Edmond. "Arthur Miller's Constancy: A Note on Miller as a
    Short Story Writer," *Revue des Langues Vivantes,* 36 (1970), 62-67.

"The Prophecy"
  Schraepen, Edmond. "Arthur Miller's Constancy . . . ," 67-71.

STEPHEN MINOT

"Journey to Ocean Grove"
Minot, Stephen, and Robley Wilson. *Teacher's Manual* . . . , 17-18.

YUKIO MISHIMA

"Patriotism"
Canzoneri, Robert, and Page Stegner, Eds. *Fiction* . . . , 255-257.

GEORGE MOORE

"A Clerk's Quest"
Beckson, Karl. "Moore's *The Untilled Fields* and Joyce's *Dubliners:* The Short Story's Intricate Maze," *Engl Lit in Transition,* 15 (1972), 299-300.

"The Exile"
Beckson, Karl. ". . . Intricate Maze," 295.

"Home Sickness"
Beckson, Karl. ". . . Intricate Maze," 296-297.

"In the Clay"
Beckson, Karl. ". . . Intricate Maze," 292-293.
Newell, Kenneth B. "The 'Artist' Stories in *The Untilled Fields,"* *Engl Lit in Transition,* 14 (1971), 123-128.

"Julia Cahill's Curse"
Beckson, Karl. ". . . Intricate Maze," 297-298.

"A Play-House in the Waste"
Beckson, Karl. ". . . Intricate Maze," 297.

"Some Parishioners"
Beckson, Karl. ". . . Intricate Maze," 293-295.
Cary, Meredith. "Saint Billy M'Hale," *Stud Short Fiction,* 6 (1969), 649-652.

"So on He Fares"
Beckson, Karl. ". . . Intricate Maze," 298-299.

"The Way Back"
  Beckson, Karl. ". . . Intricate Maze," 301-302.
  Newell, Kenneth B. "The 'Artist' Stories . . . ," 128-133.

"The Wild Goose"
  Beckson, Karl. ". . . Intricate Maze," 300-301.

ALBERTO MORAVIA

"Agostino"
  Hamalian, Leo, and Edmond L. Volpe, Eds. *Ten . . . Short Novels,* 717;
    rpt. 2nd ed. (retitled *Eleven . . . Short Novels),* 754.

"Automaton"
  Ross, Joan, and Donald Freed. . . . *Moravia,* 27-30.

"The Chimpanzee"
  Ross, Joan, and Donald Freed. . . . *Moravia,* 24-25.

"The Chinese Vase"
  Ross, Joan, and Donald Freed. . . . *Moravia,* 103-106.

"Crime at the Tennis Club."
  Ross, Joan, and Donald Freed. . . . *Moravia,* 102-103.

"In a Strange Land"
  Ross, Joan, and Donald Freed. . . . *Moravia,* 134-136.

"Mother's Boy"
  Ross, Joan, and Donald Freed. . . . *Moravia,* 96-100.

"Rain in May"
  Ross, Joan, and Donald Freed. . . . *Moravia,* 100-102.

SLAWOMER MROZEK

"Art"
  Guerin, Wilfred L., *et al. Instructor's Manual . . . "Mandala" . . . ,* 32-33.

MARY NOAILLES MURFREE
[pseud. CHARLES EGBERT CRADDOCK]

"A-Playin' of Old Sledge at the Settlemint"
Nilles, Mary. "Craddock's Girls: A Look at Some Unliberated Women,"
Markham R, 3 (1972), 75.

"The Dancin' Party at Harrison's Cove"
Nilles, Mary. "Craddock's Girls . . . ," 76-77.

"Drifting Down Lost Creek"
Nilles, Mary. "Craddock's Girls . . . ," 74-75.

"The Harnt That Walks Chilhowee"
Nilles, Mary. "Craddocks' Girls . . . ," 77.

"The Romance of Sunrise Rock"
Nilles, Mary. "Craddock's Girls . . . ," 76.

"Star in the Valley"
Nilles, Mary. "Craddock's Girls . . . ," 75-76.

ROBERT MUSIL

"The Portuguese Lady"
Boa, Elizabeth J. "Austrian Ironies in Musil's 'Drei Frauen,' " *Mod Lang R,* 63 (1968), 123-126.

"Tonka"
Sjögren, Christine O. "An Inquiry into the Psychological Condition of the Narrator in Musil's 'Tonka, ' " *Monatshefte,* 64 (1972), 153-161.
Sokel, Walter. "Kleists 'Marquise von O——,' Kierkegaards 'Abraham' und Musils 'Tonka': Drei Stufen des Absurden in seiner Beziehung zum Glauben," in Dinklage, Karl, Elizabeth Albertsen, and Karl Corino, Eds. *Robert Musil . . . ,* 57-70.

VLADIMIR NABOKOV

"Bend Sinister"
Hyman, Stanley E. "The Handle: *Invitation to a Beheading* and 'Bend Sinister, ' " in Appel, Alfred, and Charles Newman, Eds. *Nabokov . . . ,* 64-71.

"The Potato Elf"
Rowe, William W. *Nabokov's . . . World,* 76-78.

"Spring in Fialta"
Monter, Barbara H. " 'Spring in Fialta': The Choice That Mimics Chance," *Tri-Quarterly,* 17 (Winter, 1970), 128-135; concurrently in Appel, Alfred, and Charles Newman, Eds. *Nabokov . . . ,* 128-135.

RABBI BRATYLAV NAHAM

"A Story About a Clever Man and a Simple Man"
Wisse, Ruth R. *The Schlemiel . . . ,* 16-23.

R. K. NARAYAN

"A Breach of Promise"
Westbrook, Perry D. "The Short Stories of R. K. Narayan," *J Commonwealth Lit,* 5 (July, 1968), 44-46.

FLANNERY O'CONNOR

"The Artificial Nigger"
Byrd, Turner F. "Ironic Dimension in Flannery O'Connor's 'The Artificial Nigger,' " *Mississippi Q,* 21 (1968), 243-251.
Canzoneri, Robert, and Page Stegner, Eds. *Fiction . . . ,* 429-434.
Eggenschwiler, David. *The Christian Humanism . . . ,* 85-91.
Feeley, Kathleen. *Flannery O'Connor . . . ,* 120-124.
Malin, Irving. *New American Gothic,* 94; rpt. in his *Psychoanalysis . . . ,* 267-268.
————. "Flannery O'Connor and the Grotesque," in Friedman, Melvin J., and Lewis A. Lawson, Eds. *The Added Dimension . . . ,* 115-117.
Mizener, Arthur. *A Handbook . . . "Modern Short Stories . . . Revised Edition,"* 41-43.
Muller, Gilbert H. *Nightmare . . . ,* 71-75.
Nance, William L. "Flannery O'Connor: The Trouble with Being a Prophet," *Univ R,* 36 (1969), 104-106.
Orvell, Miles. *Invisible Parade . . . ,* 152-160.
Taylor, Henry. "The Halt Shall Be Gathered Together: Physical Deformity in the Fiction of Flannery O'Connor," *Western Hum R,* 22 (1968), 329-331.

"The Capture" [originally "The Turkey"]
  Driskell, Leon V., and Joan T. Brittain. . . . *Crossroads*, 34-35.
  Feeley, Kathleen. *Flannery O'Connor* . . . , 127-128.
  Orvell, Miles. *Invisible Parade* . . . , 70-72.

"A Circle in the Fire"
  Eggenschwiler, David. *The Christian Humanism* . . . , 34-40.
  Feeley, Kathleen. *Flannery O'Connor* . . . , 128-132.
  Frieling, Kenneth. "Flannery O'Connor's Vision: The Violence of
    Revelation," in French, Warren, Ed. *The Fifties* . . . , 119-120.

"The Comforts of Home"
  Eggenschwiler, David. *The Christian Humanism* . . . , 80-83.
  Feeley, Kathleen. *Flannery O'Connor* . . . , 32-38.
  Hendin, Josephine. *The World* . . . , 115-118.
  May, John R. "The Pruning Word: Flannery O'Connor's Judgment of
    Intellectuals," *Southern Hum R*, 4 (1970), 327-328.
  Pearce, Richard. *Stages* . . . , 67-69.

"The Displaced Person"
  Driskell, Leon V., and Joan T. Brittain. . . . *Crossroads*, 65-66.
  Eggenschwiler, David. *The Christian Humanism* . . . . , 78-80, 95-97.
  Feeley, Kathleen. *Flannery O'Connor* . . . , 172-176.
  Malin, Irving. *New American Gothic*, 95-97.
  ————. "Flannery O'Connor . . . ," in Friedman, Melvin J., and Lewis
    A. Lawson, Eds. *The Added Dimension* . . . , 117-118.
  Orvell, Miles. *Invisible Parade* . . . , 141-152.
  Taylor, Henry. "The Halt . . . ," 333-335.

"The Enduring Chill"
  Driskell, Leon V., and Joan T. Brittain. . . . *Crossroads*, 127-129.
  Eggenschwiler, David. *The Christian Humanism* . . . , 57-60.
  Feeley, Kathleen. *Flannery O'Connor* . . . , 38-45.
  Hendin, Josephine. *The World* . . . , 111-113.
  May, John R. "The Pruning Word . . . ," 332-334.
  Sullivan, Walter. "Flannery O'Connor, Sin, and Grace: *Everything That
    Rises Must Converge,*" *Hollins Critic*, 2 (September, 1965), 8-10; rpt. in
    his *Death* . . . , 32-33; Dillard, R. H. W., *et al.*, Eds. *The Sounder Few*
    . . . , 108-109.

"Everything That Rises Must Converge"
  Driskell, Leon V., and Joan T. Brittain. . . . *Crossroads*, 140-141.
  Feeley, Kathleen. *Flannery O'Connor* . . . , 101-105.
  Hendin, Josephine. *The World* . . . , 102-108.

Maida, Patricia D. " 'Convergence' in Flannery O'Connor's 'Everything
That Rises Must Converge,' " *Stud Short Fiction,* 7 (1970), 549-555.
May, John R. "The Pruning Word . . . ," 329-331.
Orvell, Miles. *Invisible Parade . . . ,* 6-10.

"The Geranium"
Feeley, Kathleen. *Flannery O'Connor . . . ,* 105-109.
Orvell, Miles. *Invisible Parade . . . ,* 180-187.

"Good Country People"
Eggenschwiler, David. *The Christian Humanism . . . ,* 52-57.
Feeley, Kathleen. *Flannery O'Connor . . . ,* 23-28.
Frieling, Kenneth. ". . . Revelation," 116-117.
Hendin, Josephine. *The World . . . ,* 69-75.
Howard, Daniel F. *Manual . . . ,* 48.
May, John R. "The Pruning Word . . . ," 328-329.
Nance, William L. "Flannery O'Connor . . . ," 103-104.
Orvell, Miles. *Invisible Parade . . . ,* 136-141.
Sullivan, Walter. "Flannery O'Connor . . . ," 5-6; rpt. in his *Death . . . ,* 29;
Dillard, R. H. W., *et al.,* Eds. *The Sounder Few . . . ,* 105-106.
Taylor, Henry. "The Halt . . . ," 327-329.

"A Good Man Is Hard To Find"
Eggenschwiler, David. *The Christian Humanism . . . ,* 46-52.
Feeley, Kathleen. *Flannery O'Connor . . . ,* 68-76.
Frieling, Kenneth. " . . . Revelation," 114-115.
Hendin, Josephine. *The World . . . ,* 148-151.
Malin, Irving. *New American Gothic,* 120-121; rpt. in his *Psychoanalysis*
. . . , 266-267.
————. "Flannery O'Connor . . . ," in Friedman, Melvin J., and Lewis
A. Lawson, Eds. *The Added Dimension . . . ,* 113-115.
Montgomery, Marion. "Flannery O'Connor's 'Leaden Tract Against
Complacency and Contraception,' " *Arizona Q,* 24 (1968), 133-142.
Orvell, Miles. *Invisible Parade . . . ,* 130-136.
Pearce, Richard. *Stages . . . ,* 69-71.
Sullivan, Walter. "Flannery O'Connor . . . ," 4-5; rpt. in his *Death . . . ,* 26-
27; Dillard, R. H. W., *et al.,* Eds. *The Sounder Few . . . ,* 104-105.

"Greenleaf"
Eggenschwiler, David. *The Christian Humanism . . . ,* 60-66.
Feeley, Kathleen. *Flannery O'Connor . . . ,* 94-99.
Hendin, Josephine. *The World . . . ,* 113-115.
Muller, Gilbert H. *Nightmare . . . ,* 82-84.
Orvell, Miles. *Invisible Parade . . . ,* 23-27.

"Judgment Day"
  Feeley, Kathleen. *Flannery O'Connor* . . . , 105-111.
  Orvell, Miles. *Invisible Parade* . . . , 180-188.

"The Lame Shall Enter First"
  Asals, Frederick. "Flannery O'Connor's 'The Lame Shall Enter First, ' "
    Mississippi Q, 23 (1970), 103-120.
  Feeley, Kathleen. *Flannery O'Connor* . . . , 79-84.
  Hays, Peter L. *The Limping Hero* . . . , 96-98.
  Orvell, Miles. *Invisible Parade* . . . , 177-179.
  Sullivan, Walter. "Flannery O'Connor . . . ," 6-8; rpt. in his *Death* . . . , 30-
    32; Dillard, R. H. W., *et al.,* Eds. *The Sounder Few* . . . , 106-108.
  Taylor, Henry. "The Halt . . . ," 331-333.
  Feeley, Kathleen. *Flannery O'Connor* . . . , 92-94.

"A Late Encounter with the Enemy"
  Orvell, Miles. *Invisible Parade* . . . , 10-12.

"The Life You Save May Be Your Own"
  Feeley, Kathleen. *Flannery O'Connor* . . . , 28-31.
  Hendin, Josephine. *The World* . . . , 62-69.
  Orvell, Miles. *Invisible Parade* . . . , 134-136.
  Taylor, Henry. "The Halt . . . ," 326-327.

"Parker's Back"
  Eggenschwiler, David. *The Christian Humanism* . . . , 74-78.
  Feeley, Kathleen. *Flannery O'Connor* . . . , 145-150.
  Hendin, Josephine. *The World* . . . , 154-155.
  Taylor, Henry. "The Halt . . . ," 329-331.

"The Partridge Festival"
  Feeley, Kathleen. *Flannery O'Connor* . . . , 45-51.
  May, John R. "The Pruning Word . . . ," 331-332.

"Revelation"
  Eggenschwiler, David. *The Christian Humanism* . . . , 41-45.
  Hendin, Josephine. *The World* . . . , 119-130.
  May, John R. "The Pruning Word . . . ," 334-335.
  Nance, William L. "Flannery O'Connor . . . ," 104-105.
  Skaggs, Merrill M. *The Folk* . . . , 256-258.
  Sullivan, Walter. "Flannery O'Connor . . . ," 10; rpt. in his *Death* . . . , 34-
    35; Dillard, R. H. W., *et al.,* Eds. *The Sounder Few* . . . , 109-110.

"The River"
  Eggenschwiler, David. *The Christian Humanism* . . . , 66-67.

Frieling, Kenneth. " . . . Revelation," 117.
Muller, Gilbert H. *Nightmare* . . . , 57-60.
Pearce, Richard. *Stages* . . . , 71-72.

"A Stroke of Good Fortune" [originally "Woman on the Straits"]
Orvell, Miles. *Invisible Parade* . . . , 72-73.

"A Temple of the Holy Ghost"
Eggenschwiler, David. *The Christian Humanism* . . . , 20-24.
Feeley, Kathleen. *Flannery O'Connor* . . . , 135-138.
Frieling, Kenneth. " . . . Revelation," 118.
Hendin, Josephine. *The World* . . . , 75-95.
Orvell, Miles. *Invisible Parade* . . . , 46-47.
Quinn, M. Bernetta. "View from the Rock: The Fiction of Flannery
O'Connor and J. F. Powers," *Critique,* 2 (Fall, 1958), 25.
————. "Flannery O'Connor, A Realist of Distances," in Friedman,
Melvin J., and Lewis A. Lawson, Eds. *The Added Dimension* . . . , 163.

"The Train" [revised to become chapter in *Wise Blood*]
Orvell, Miles. *Invisible Parade* . . . , 76-77.

"A View of the Woods"
Eggenschwiler, David. *The Christian Humanism* . . . , 68-70.
Feeley, Kathleen. *Flannery O'Connor* . . . , 124-127.
Hendin, Josephine. *The World* . . . , 108-111.
Orvell, Miles. *Invisible Parade* . . . , 13-16.

FRANK O'CONNOR

"The Cheapjack"
Averill, Deborah. "Human Contact in the Short Stories," in Sheehy,
Maurice, Ed. *Michael* . . . , 33.

"My Oedipus Complex"
Mizener, Arthur. *A Handbook* . . . *"Modern Short Stories . . . Revised
Edition,"* 26-28; rpt. *A Handbook* . . . *"Modern Short Stories . . . Third
Edition,"* 32-35.

"The Study of History"
Averill, Deborah. "Human Contact . . . ," in Sheehy, Maurice, Ed.
Michael . . . , 31-32.

SEAN O'FAOLAIN

"Lovers of the Lake"
    Harmon, Maurice. "Sean O'Faolain: 'I have nobody to vote for,' " *Stud: Irish Q,* 56 (1967), 58-59.

O. HENRY [WILLIAM SYDNEY PORTER]

"The Atavism of John Tom Little Bear"
    Gallegly, Joseph. *From Alamo Plaza* . . . , 122-125.

"The Caballero's Way"
    Gallegly, Joseph. *From Alamo Plaza* . . . , 155-158.

"The Chair of Philanthromathematics"
    Gallegly, Joseph. *From Alamo Plaza* . . . , 72-74.

"A Chaparral Christmas Gift"
    Gallegly, Joseph. *From Alamo Plaza* . . . , 158-160.

"The Handbook of Hymen"
    Gallegly, Joseph. *From Alamo Plaza* . . . , 90-92.

"The Lonesome Road"
    Gallegly, Joseph. *From Alamo Plaza* . . . , 113-115.

"A Municipal Report"
    Starke, Catherine J. *Black Portraiture* . . . , 59-61.

"The Passing of Black Eagle"
    Gallegly, Joseph. *From Alamo Plaza* . . . , 131-135.

SEUMAS O'KELLY

"The Building"
    Grennan, Eamon. "Figures in a Landscape: The Short Stories of Seumas O'Kelly," *Stud: Irish Q,* 56 (1967), 289-290.

"The Prodigal Daughter"
    Grennan, Eamon. "Figures . . . ," 291-292.

"The Weaver's Grave"
    Grennan, Eamon. "Figures . . . ," 292-294.

Ro₁ e, Marilyn G. "An Irish Widow of Ephesus: Seumas O'Kelly's 'The Weaver's Grave,' " *Eire,* 2 (Spring, 1967), 58-62.

IURII OLESHA

"The Chain"
Beaujour, Elizabeth K. *The Invisible Land . . .* , 99-101.

"In Summer"
Beaujour, Elizabeth K. *The Invisible Land . . .* , 123-125.

"Love"
Beaujour, Elizabeth K. *The Invisible Land . . .* , 72-77.

DIANE OLIVER

"Neighbor"
Mizener, Arthur. *A Handbook . . . "Modern Short Stories . . . Third Edition,"* 28-30.

JUAN CARLOS ONETTI

"Dreaded Hell"
Deredita, John F. "The Short Stories of Juan Carlos Onetti," *Stud Short Fiction,* 8 (1971), 117.

"A Dream Come True"
Deredita, John F. "The Short Stories . . . ," 114-115.

"Esbjerg, on the Coast"
Deredita, John F. "The Short Stories . . . ," 115-116.

"The Face of Misfortune"
Deredita, John F. "The Short Stories . . . ," 116-117.

"The House in the Sand"
Deredita, John F. "The Short Stories . . . ," 120.

"Masquerade"
Deredita, John F. "The Short Stories . . . ," 115.

"The Nameless Tomb"
    Deredita, John F. "The Short Stories . . . ," 121.

"Welcome, Bob"
    Deredita, John F. "The Short Stories . . . ," 114.

GEORGE ORWELL

"Animal Farm"
    Lief, Ruth A. *Homage to Oceania* . . . , 55-56.
    Smyer, Richard I. " ' Animal Farm': The Burden of Consciousness," *Engl Lang Notes*, 9 (1971), 55-59.
    Williams, Raymond. *George Orwell*, 69-75.

THOMAS PAGE

"Marse Chan"
    Gross, Theodore L. *The Heroic Ideal* . . . , 106-111.

GRACE PALEY

"Goodbye and Good Luck"
    Wisse, Ruth R. *The Schlemiel* . . . , 82-85.

WALTER PATER

"Apollo in Picardy"
    Frazier, Sloane. "Two Pagan Studies: Pater's 'Denys L'Auxerrois' and 'Apollo in Picardy,' " *Folklore*, 81 (1970), 280-285.

"Denys L'Auxerrois"
    Frazier, Sloane. "Two Pagan Studies . . . ," *Folklore*, 81 (1970), 280-285.

GEORGE PATTULO

"The More Abundant Life"
    Folsom, James K. . . . *Western Novel*, 192-193.

118 GUDRUN PAUSEWANG

GUDRUN PAUSEWANG

"Der Weg nach Tongay"
  Glenn, Jerry. "Gudrun Pausewang and'Der Weg nach Tongay,' " *Stud Short Fiction,* 7 (1970), 556-563.

JULIA PETERKIN

"Ashes"
  Starke, Catherine J. *Black Portraiture . . .* , 130-131.

EDGAR ALLAN POE

"The Balloon Hoax"
  Levine, Stuart. *Edgar Poe . . .* , 129-133.

"Berenice"
  Levine, Stuart. *Edgar Poe . . ..* , 26-27.

"The Black Cat"
  Gargano, James W. " 'The Black Cat': Perverseness Reconsidered," *Texas Stud Lit & Lang,* 2 (1960), 172-178; rpt. Howarth, William L., Ed. . . . *Poe's Tales,* 87-93.
  Levine, Stuart. *Edgar Poe . . .* , 89-90.
  Shulman, Robert. "Poe and the Power of the Mind," *J Engl Lit Hist,* 37 (1970), 256-259.

"The Cask of Amontillado"
  Broussard, Louis. *The Measure of Poe,* 97-98.
  Henninger, F.J. "The Bouquet of Poe's Amontillado," *So Atlantic Bull,* 35 (March, 1970), 35-40.
  Levine, Stuart. *Edgar Poe . . .* , 80-92.

"The Colloquy of Monos and Una"
  Levine, Stuart. *Edgar Poe . . .* , 154-162.

"A Descent into the Maelstrom"
  Levine, Stuart. *Edgar Poe . . .* , 18-26.

  Shulman, Robert. ". . . Power of the Mind," 253-254.

"The Domain of Arnheim, or The Landscape Garden"

Levine, Stuart. *Edgar Poe* . . . , 11-14.

"Eleonora"
 Pollin, Burton R. "Poe's Use of the Name *Ermengarde* in 'Eleonora,' "
  Notes & Queries, 17 (1970), 332-333.

"The Facts in the Case of M. Valdemar"
 Levine, Stuart. *Edgar Poe* . . . , 142-150.

"The Fall of the House of Usher"
 Cox, James R. "Edgar Poe: Style as Pose," *Virginia Q R,* 44 (1968), 80-81.
 Davidson, Edward H. *Poe* . . . , 196-198; rpt. Feidelson, Charles, and Paul
  Brodtkorb, Eds. *Interpretations* . . . , 74-76; Woodson, Thomas, Ed. . . .
  "The Fall of the House of Usher," 96-98.
 Garmon, Gerald M. "Roderick Usher: Portrait of the Madman as an
  Artist," *Poe Stud,* 5 (June, 1972), 11-14.
 Goldhurst, William. "Edgar Allan Poe and the Conquest of Death," *New
  Orleans R,* 1 (1969), 317.
 Hill, John S. "The Dual Hallucination in 'The Fall of the House of
  Usher,' " *Southwest R,* 48 (1963), 396-402; rpt. Howarth, William L.,
  Ed. . . . *Poe's Tales,* 55-62.
 Levine, Stuart. *Edgar Poe* . . . , 38-41.
 Marsh, John L. "The Psycho-Sexual Reading of 'The Fall of the House of
  Usher,' " *Poe Stud,* 5 (June, 1972), 8-9.
 Martindale, Colin. "Archetype and Reality in 'The Fall of the House of
  Usher,' " *Poe Stud,* 5 (June, 1972), 9-11.
 Phillips, H. Wells. "Poe's Usher: Precursor of Abstract Art," *Poe Stud,* 5
  (June, 1972), 14-16.
 St. Armand, Barton L. "Usher Unveiled: Poe and the Metaphysic of
  Gnosticism," *Poe Stud,* 5 (June, 1972), 1-8.
 Schwaber, Paul. "On Reading Poe," *Lit & Psych,* 21 (1971), 83-86.
 Seelye, John. "Edgar Allan Poe: *Tales of the Grotesque and Arabesque,*"
  in Cohen, Hennig, Ed. *Landmarks* . . . , 107-110.
 Thompson, G.R. "The Face in the Pool: Reflections on the Doppelgänger
  Motif in 'The Fall of the House of Usher,' " *Poe Stud,* 5 (June, 1972),
  16-21.
 Walker, I.M. "The 'Legitimate Sources' of Terror in 'The Fall of the
  House of Usher,' " *Mod Lang R,* 61 (1966), 585-592; rpt. Howarth,
  William L., Ed. . . . *Poe's Tales,* 47-54.
 Wilbur, Richard. "The House of Poe," in Carlson, Eric W., Ed. . . . *Edgar
  Allan Poe,* 264-268; rpt. Regan, Robert, Ed. *Poe* . . . , 104-111.

"The Gold Bug"
 Goldhurst, William. ". . . Conquest of Death," 317-319.

St. Armand, Barton L. "Poe's 'Sober Mystification': The Uses of Alchemy in 'The Gold Bug,' " *Poe Stud,* 4 (1971), 1-7.

"Hop-Frog"
Levine, Stuart. *Edgar Poe . . . ,* 71-75.
Shulman, Robert. ". . . Power of the Mind," 252-253.

"The Imp of the Perverse"
Kanjo, Eugene R. " ' The Imp of the Perverse': Poe's Dark Comedy of Art and Death," *Poe Newsletter,* 2 (1969), 41-44.
Levine, Stuart. *Edgar Poe . . . ,* 203-212.

"Ligeia"
Broussard, Louis. *The Measure of Poe,* 92-95.
Cox, James R. "Edgar Poe . . . ," 78-80.
Engelberg, Edward. *The Unknown Distance . . . ,* 120-121.
Garrett, Walter. "The 'Moral' of 'Ligeia' Reconsidered," *Poe Stud,* 4 (1971), 19-20.
Garrison, Joseph M. "The Irony of 'Ligeia,' " *Engl Stud Q,* No. 60 (1970), 13-17.
Goldhurst, William. ". . . Conquest of Death," 316-317.
Griffith, Clark. "Poe's 'Ligeia' and the English Romantics," *Univ Toronto Q,* 24 (1954), 8-25; rpt. Howarth, William L., Ed. . . . *Poe's Tales,* 63-72.
Lauder, John. " 'Ligeia' and Its Critics: A Plea for Literalism," *Stud Short Fiction,* 4 (1966), 28-32; rpt. Howarth, William L., Ed. . . . *Poe's Tales,* 73-77.
Levine, Stuart. *Edgar Poe. . . ,* 26-37.
Ramakrishna, D. "Poe's 'Ligeia,' " *Explicator,* 25 (1966), Item 19.
————. "The Conclusion of Poe's 'Ligeia,' " *Emerson Soc Q,* No. 47 (Second Quarter, 1967), 69-70.
Rea, J. "Classicism and Romanticism in Poe's 'Ligeia,' " *Ball State Univ Forum,* 8, i (1967), 25-29.
Reed, Kenneth T. " 'Ligeia': The Story as Sermon," *Poe Stud,* 4 (1971), 20.
Stauffer, Donald B. "Style and Meaning in 'Ligeia' and 'William Wilson,' " *Stud Short Fiction,* 2 (1965), 318-324; rpt. Howarth, William L., Ed. . . . *Poe's Tales,* 78-82.

"The Man of the Crowd"
Levine, Stuart. *Edgar Poe . . . ,* 224-237.

"The Masque of the Red Death"
Broussard, Louis. *The Measure of Poe,* 98-100.
Levine, Stuart. *Edgar Poe . . . ,* 198-203.

Shulman, Robert. ". . . Power of the Mind," 247-249.
Vanderbilt, Kermit. "Art and Nature in 'The Masque of the Red Death,'"
Nineteenth Century Fiction, 22 (1968), 379-389.

"Mellonta Tauta"
Pollin, Burton R. "Politics and History in Poe's 'Mellonta Tauta': Two
Allusions Explained," *Stud Short Fiction,* 8 (1971), 627-631.

"Metzengerstein"
Fisher, Benjamin F. "Poe's 'Metzengerstein': Not a Hoax," *Am Lit,* 42
(1971), 487-494.

"Morella"
Broussard, Louis. *The Measure of Poe,* 94-95.
Richmond, Lee J. "Edgar Allan Poe's 'Morella': Vampire of Volition,"
Stud Short Fiction, 9 (1972), 93-94.

"MS. Found in a Bottle"
Tarbox, Raymond. "Blank Hallucinations in the Fiction of Poe and
Hemingway," *Am Imago,* 24 (1967), 318-322.

"The Murders in the Rue Morgue"
Levine, Stuart. *Edgar Poe . . . ,* 162-168.
Schwaker, Paul. "On Reading Poe," 92-98.

"The Narrative of Arthur Gordon Pym"
Campbell, Josie P. "Deceit and Violence: Motifs in 'The Narrative of
Arthur Gordon Pym,'" *Engl J,* 59 (1970), 206-212.
Cox, James R. "Edgar Poe . . . ," 72-77.
Levine, Richard A. "The Downward Journey of Purgation: Notes on an
Imagistic Leitmotif in 'The Narrative of Arthur Gordon Pym,'" *Poe
Newsletter,* 2 (1969), 29-31.
Levine, Stuart. *Edgar Poe . . . ,* 237-252.
Moldenhauer, Joseph J. "Imagination and Perversity in 'The Narrative of
Arthur Gordon Pym,'" *Texas Stud Lit & Lang,* 13 (1971), 267-280.
O'Donnell, Charles. "From Earth to Ether: Poe's Flight into Space,"
PMLA, 77 (1962), 87-91; rpt. Howarth, William L., Ed. . . . *Poe's Tales,*
39-46.
Quinn, Patrick. "Le voyage imaginaire de Poe," *Le Revue des Lettres
Modernes,* Nos. 193-198 (1969), 147-189.
Ridgely, J. V. "The Continuing Puzzle of 'Arthur Gordon Pym,'" *Poe
Newsletter,* 3 (1970), 5-7.
Sheehan, Peter J. "Dirk Peters: A New Look at Poe's *Pym,*" *Laurel R,* 9
(1969), 60-67.

Tarbox, Raymond. "Blank Hallucinations . . . ," 322-335.

"Never Bet the Devil Your Head"
  Glassheim, Eliot. "A Dogged Interpretation of 'Never Bet the Devil Your
    Head,' " *Poe Newsletter,* 2 (1969), 44-45.

"The Oblong Box"
  Levine, Stuart. *Edgar Poe . . . ,* 68-70.

"The Oval Portrait"
  Thompson, G. R. "Dramatic Irony in 'The Oval Portrait': A
    Reconsideration of Poe's Revisions," *Engl Lang Notes,* 6 (1968), 107-
    114.

"The Pit and the Pendulum"
  Engelberg, Edward. *The Unknown Distance . . . ,* 124-125.

"The Power of Words"
  Levine, Stuart. *Edgar Poe . . . ,* 155-162.
  Shulman, Robert. ". . . Power of the Mind," 254-256.

"A Predicament"
  Levine, Stuart. *Edgar Poe . . . ,* 42-43.

"The Premature Burial"
  Levine, Stuart. *Edgar Poe . . . ,* 246-247.

"The Purloined Letter"
  Levine, Stuart. *Edgar Poe . . . ,* 162-168.

"Shadow—A Parable"
  Levine, Stuart. *Edgar Poe . . . ,* 154-155.

"Silence—A Fable"
  Claudel, Alice M. "What Has Poe's 'Silence' to Say?" *Ball State Univ
    Forum,* 10 (Winter, 1969), 66-70.
  Levine, Stuart. *Edgar Poe . . . ,* 154-155.

"The Sphinx"
  Levine, Stuart. *Edgar Poe . . . ,* 82-85.

"A Tale of the Ragged Mountains"
  Levine, Stuart. *Edgar Poe . . . ,* 133-142.

"The Tell-Tale Heart"
  Canario, John W. "The Dream in 'The Tell-Tale Heart,' " *Engl Lang Notes*, 7 (1970), 194-197.
  Reilly, John E. "The Lesser Death-Watch and 'The Tell-Tale Heart,' " *Am Transcendental Q*, 2 (2nd Quarter, 1969), 3-9.
  Robinson, E. Arthur. "Poe's 'The Tell-Tale Heart,' " *Nineteenth Century Fiction*, 19 (1965), 369-378; rpt. Howarth, William L., Ed. . . . *Poe's Tales*, 94-102.
  Shulman, Robert. ". . . Power of the Mind," 259-261.

"The Unparalleled Adventures of One Hans Pfaall"
  Greer, H. Allen. "Poe's 'Hans Pfaall' and the Political Scene," *Engl Stud Q*, No. 60 (1970), 67-73.
  Ketterer, David. "Poe's Usage of the Hoax and the Unity of 'Hans Pfaall,' " *Criticism*, 13 (1971), 377-385.
  Levine, Stuart. *Edgar Poe* . . . , 123-133.

"William Wilson"
  Cox, James R. "Edgar Poe . . . ," 81-83.
  Engelberg, Edward. *The Unknown Distance* . . . , 122-123.
  Freese, Peter. "Das Motiv des Doppelgänger in Truman Capotes 'Shut a Final Door' und Edgar Allan Poes 'William Wilson,' " *Literatur in Wissenschaft & Unterricht*, 1 (1968), 41-49.
  Gargano, James W. "Art and Irony in 'William Wilson,' " *Engl Stud Q*, No. 60 (1970), 18-22.
  Levine, Stuart. *Edgar Poe* . . . , 184-193.
  Stauffer, Donald B. "Style and Meaning . . . ," 324-330; rpt. Howarth, William L., Ed. . . . *Poe's Tales*, 82-86.

HAL PORTER

"Say to Me Ronald"
  Lord, Mary. "Hal Porter's Comic Mode," *Australian Lit Stud*, 4 (1970), 371-382.

KATHERINE ANNE PORTER

"The Circus"
  Schwartz, Edward G. "The Fiction of Memory," *Southwest R*, 45 (1960), 204-207; rpt. Hartley, Lodwick, and George Core, Eds. *Katherine Anne Porter* . . . , 69-70.

"The Cracked Looking-Glass"

Wiesenfarth, Brother Joseph. "Illusion and Allusion: Reflections in 'The Cracked Looking-Glass,' " *Four Quarters,* 12 (November, 1962), 30-37; rpt. Hartley, Lodwick, and George Core, Eds. *Katherine Anne Porter* . . . , 139-148.

"Flowering Judas"
Gross, Beverly. "The Poetic Narrative: A Reading of 'Flowering Judas,' " *Style,* 2 (1968), 129-139.
Liberman, M.M. . . . *Porter's Fiction,* 70-79.
Madden, David. "The Charged Image in Katherine Anne Porter's 'Flowering Judas,' " *Stud Short Fiction,* 7 (1970), 277-289.
Partridge, Colin. " 'My Familiar Country': An Image of Mexico in the Works of Katherine Anne Porter," *Stud Short Fiction,* 7 (1970), 607-610.
West; Ray B. "Katherine Anne Porter: Symbol and Theme in 'Flowering Judas,' " *Accent,* 7 (1947), 182-188; rpt. West, Ray B., and Robert W. Stallman, Eds. *The Art* . . . , 287-292; Aldridge, John, Ed. *Critiques* . . . , 217-230; Hartley, Lodwick, and George Core, Eds. *Katherine Anne Porter* . . . , 121-128; rpt. in part Stallman, Robert W., and Arthur Waldhorn, Eds. *American Literature* . . . , 767-770.

"The Grave"
Brooks, Cleanth. "On 'The Grave,' " *Yale R,* 55 (1966), 275-279; rpt. Hartley, Lodwick, and George Core, Eds. *Katherine Anne Porter* . . . , 115-119.
Guerin, Wilfred L., *et al. Instructor's Manual* . . . *"Mandala"* . . . , 22-23.
Mizener, Arthur. *A Handbook* . . . *"Modern Short Stories* . . . *Revised Edition,"* 30-32; rpt. *A Handbook* . . . *"Modern Short Stories* . . . *Third Edition,"* 36-38.
Schwartz, Edward G. "The Fiction . . . ," 214-215; rpt. Hartley, Lodwick, and George Core, Eds. *Katherine Anne Porter* . . . , 80-82.

"Hacienda"
Johnson, James W. "Another Look . . . ," 606; rpt. Hartley, Lodwick, and George Core, Eds. *Katherine Anne Porter* . . . , 90.
Partridge, Colin. " 'My Familiar Country' . . . ," 610-613.

"He"
Liberman, M.M. . . . *Porter's Fiction,* 87-91.

"Holiday"
Core, George. "The *Best* Residuum of Truth," *Georgia R,* 20 (1966), 280-285; rpt., expanded and retitled " 'Holiday': A Version of Pastoral," Hartley, Lodwick, and George Core, Eds. *Katherine Anne Porter* . . . ,

149-158.
Liberman, M. M. . . . *Porter's Fiction,* 80-87.

"The Jilting of Granny Weatherall"
Barnes, Daniel R. and Madeline T. "The Secret Sin of Granny
Weatherall," *Renascence,* 21 (1969), 162-165.
Wiesenfarth, Joseph. "Internal Opposition in Porter's 'Granny
Weatherall,' " *Critique,* 11, ii (1969), 47-55.

"The Leaning Tower"
Johnson, James W. "Another Look . . . ," 603; rpt. Hartley, Lodwick, and
George Core, Eds. *Katherine Anne Porter . . . ,* 87-88.

"Maria Concepción"
Johnson, James W. "Another Look . . . ," 605-608; rpt.. Hartley, Lodwick,
and George Core, Eds. *Katherine Anne Porter . . . ,* 92-93.
Partridge, Colin. " ' My Familiar Country' . . . ," 600-602.

"The Martyrs"
Partridge, Colin. " 'My Familiar Country' . . . ," 602-603.

"Noon Wine"
Beards, Richard D. "Stereotyping in Modern American Fiction: Some
Solitary Swedish Madmen," *Moderna Sprak,* 63 (1969), 329-337.
Hoffman, Frederick J. "Katherine Anne Porter's 'Noon Wine,' " *Coll
Engl Assoc Critic,* 18 (1956), 1,6-7; rpt. with changes in his *The Art . . . ,*
44-47.
Johnson, James W. "Another Look . . . ," 605; rpt. Hartley, Lodwick, and
George Core, Eds. *Katherine Anne Porter . . . ,* 90-91.
Liberman, M.M. . . . *Porter's Fiction,* 91-94.
Wescott, Glenway. "Praise," *Southern R,* 5 (1939), 161-173; rpt. in his
Images of Truth . . . , 38-44; rpt. in part Current-García, Eugene, and
Walton R. Patrick, Eds. *Realism . . . ,* 487-490; Hartley, Lodwick, and
George Core, Eds. *Katherine Anne Porter . . . ,* 38-40.

"Old Mortality"
Liberman, M.M. . . . *Porter's Fiction,* 37-51.
Warren, Robert P. "Irony with a Center: Katherine Anne Porter,"
Kenyon R, 4 (1942), 35-40; rpt. in his *Selected Essays,* 149-154; Knoll,
Robert E., Ed. *Contrasts,* 2nd ed., 497-501; Guth, Hans P., Ed.
Literature, 2nd ed., 278-281; *Katherine Anne Porter . . . ,* 51-66.

"The Old Order"
Pinkerton, Jan. "Katherine Anne Porter's Portrayal of Black
Resentment," *Univ R,* 36 (1970), 315-317.

"Pale Horse, Pale Rider"
   Johnson, James W. "Another Look . . . ," 604; rpt. Hartley, Lodwick, and
      George Core, Eds. *Katherine Anne Porter . . . ,* 88-89.
   Youngblood, Sarah. "Structure and Imagery in Katherine Anne Porter's
      'Pale Horse, Pale Rider,' " *Mod Fiction Stud,* 5 (1959), 344-352; rpt.
      Hartley, Lodwick, and George Core, Eds. *Katherine Anne Porter . . . ,*
      129-138.

"Virgin Violeta"
   Partridge, Colin. " ' My Familiar Country' . . . ," 603-604.

J. F. POWERS

"The Forks"
   Kelly, Richard. "Father Eudex, the Judge and the Judged: An Analysis of
      J. F. Powers' 'The Forks,' " *Univ R,* 35 (1969), 316-318.

"A Losing Game"
   Mizener, Arthur. *A Handbook . . . "Modern Short Stories . . . Revised
      Edition,"* 79-82; rpt. *A Handbook . . . "Modern Short Stories . . . Third
      Edition,"* 85-88.

"The Valiant Woman"
   Burgess, C.F. "The Case of the Hen-Pecked Priest in J.F. Powers' 'The
      Valiant Woman,' " *Cithara,* 9, i (1969), 67-71.

V. S. PRITCHETT

"The Scapegoat"
   Sellery, J'nan M., and John B. Vickery. "Ritual in the Streets: A Study of
      Pritchett's 'The Scapegoat,' "*Psychological Perspectives,* 1 (Spring,
      1970), 7-68; rpt. in their *The Scapegoat . . . ,* 226-237.

JAMES PURDY

"Don't Call Me by My Right Name"
   Schwarzschild, Bettina. . . . *James Purdy,* 15-18.

"63: Dream Palace"
   Schwarzschild, Bettina. . . . *James Purdy,* 6-13.

THOMAS PYNCHEON

"Entropy"
    Mizener, Arthur. *A Handbook . . . "Modern Short Stories . . . Third Edition,"* 94-101.

EUGENE MANLOVE RHODES

"Beyond the Desert"
    Folsom, James K. . . . *Western Novel,* 128-129.

JULIO RIBEYRO

"Una aventura nocturna"
    Aldrich, Earl M. "Recent Trends in the Peruvian Short Story," *Stud Short Fiction,* 8 (1971), 28.

"De color modesto"
    Aldrich, Earl M. "Recent Trends . . . ," 27-28.

"La piel de un indio no cuesta cara"
    Aldrich, Earl M. "Recent Trends . . . ," 27.

ISAAC ROSENFELD

"The Hand That Fed Me"
    Wisse, Ruth R. *The Schlemiel . . . ,* 85-87.

SINCLAIR ROSS

"Circus in Town"
    Frazer, Keath. "Futility at the Pump: The Short Stories of Sinclair Ross," *Queens Q,* 77 (1970), 73-74.

"Cornet at Night"
    Frazer, Keath. "Futility at the Pump . . . ," 74-75.

"Not by Rain Alone"
    Frazer, Keath. "Futility at the Pump . . . ," 75-77.

"The Painted Door"
  Frazer, Keath. "Futility at the Pump . . . ," 78-79.
  McCourt, Edward A. *The Canadian West* . . . , 97-99.

PHILIP ROTH

"Defender of the Faith"
  Mizener, Arthur. *A Handbook* . . . *"Modern Short Stories* . . . *Revised Edition,"* 75-78; rpt. *A Handbook* . . . *"Modern Short Stories* . . . *Third Edition,"* 77-80.

JUAN RULFO

"Luvina"
  Leal, Luis. "The New Mexican Short Story," *Stud Short Fiction,* 8 (1971), 16-17.

SAKI [H. H. MUNRO]

"The Achievement of the Cat"
  Gillen, Charles H. *H.H. Munro,* 80-81.

"The Forbidden Buzzards"
  Gillen, Charles H. *H.H. Munro,* 82-83.

"The Music on the Hill"
  Gillen, Charles H. *H.H. Munro,* 83-84.

"The Occasional Garden"
  Gillen, Charles H. *H.H. Munro,* 73-74.

"Sredni Vashtar"
  Gillen, Charles H. *H.H. Munro,* 86-87.

"Tea"
  Gillen, Charles H. *H.H. Munro,* 78-79.

"The Treasure Ship"
  Gillen, Charles H. *H.H. Munro,* 75-76.

J. D. SALINGER

"De Daumier-Smith's Blue Period"
Goldstein, Bernice and Sanford. "Zen and *Nine Stories,*" *Renascence,* 22 (1970), 178-181.
Stone, Edward. *A Certain Morbidity . . . ,* 121-139.

"For Esmé—With Love and Squalor"
Deer, Irving, and John H. Randall. "J.D. Salinger and the Reality Beyond Words," *Lock Haven R,* 6 (1964), 17-18.
Goldstein, Bernice and Sanford. "Zen . . . ," 177-178.

"Franny"
Deer, Irving, and John H. Randall. "J.D. Salinger . . . ," 14-15.
Goldstein, Bernice and Sanford. "Bunnies and Cobras: Zen Enlightenment in Salinger," *Discourse,* 13 (1970), 98-106.

"Hapworth 16, 1924"
Quagliano, Anthony. " 'Hapworth 16, 1924': A Problem in Hagiography," *Univ Dayton R,* 8 (Fall, 1971), 35-43.

"The Laughing Man"
Deer, Irving, and John H. Randall. "J.D. Salinger . . . ," 18-19.
Goldstein, Bernice and Sanford. "Zen . . . ," 173-175.

"A Perfect Day for Bananafish"
Goldstein, Bernice and Sanford. "Zen . . . ," 175-177.
Metcalf, Frank. "The Suicide of Salinger's Seymour Glass," *Stud Short Fiction,* 9 (1972), 243-246.

"Seymour: An Introduction"
Goldstein, Bernice and Sanford. "Bunnies and Cobras . . . ," 98-106.
—————." 'Seymour: An Introduction'—Writing As Discovery," *Stud Short Fiction,* 7 (1970), 248-257.
Schulz, Max F. "Epilogue to 'Seymour: An Introduction': Salinger and the Crisis of Consciousness," *Stud Short Fiction,* 5 (1968), 128-138; rpt. with changes in his *Radical Sophistication . . . ,* 204-211.

"Teddy"
Goldstein, Bernice and Sanford. "Zen . . . ," 181-182.

"Uncle Wiggily in Connecticut"
Goldstein, Bernice and Sanford. "Zen . . . , 172-173.

"Zooey"
   Goldstein, Bernice and Sanford. "Bunnies and Cobras . . . ," 98-106.

JEAN PAUL SARTRE

"Chambre"
   Greenlee, James "Sartre's 'Chambre': The Story of Eve," *Mod Fiction Stud,* 16 (1970), 77-84.

"The Childhood of a Leader"
   Kern, Edith. *Existential Thought . . . ,* 140-142.

"Erostratus"
   Kern, Edith. *Existential Thought . . . ,* 138.

"The Room"
   Boros, Marie-Denise. *Un séquestré . . . ,* 23-25.
   Greenlee, James. "Sartre's 'Chambre' . . . ," 77-84.
   Kern, Edith. *Existential Thought . . . ,* 138-139.
   Magny, Claude-Edmonde. *Les Sandales . . . ,* 120-131.
   Simon, John K. "Madness in Sartre: Sequestration and the Room," *Yale French Stud,* 30 (1964), 63-67.
   ————. "Sartre's Room," *Mod Lang Notes,* 79 (1964), 526-538.

"Intimacy"
   Kern, Edith. *Existential Thought . . . ,* 139.

"The Wall"
   Kern, Edith. *Existential Thought . . . ,* 139-140.

ARTHUR SCHNITZLER

"Frau Berta Garlan"
   Alexander, Theodor W. "From the Scientific to the Supernatural in Schnitzler," *So Central Bull,* 31 (1971), 165.

"Fräulein Else"
   Alexander, Theodor W. "From the Scientific . . . ," 165-166.

"Leutnant Gustl"
   Alexander, Theodor W. and Beatrice W. "Schnitzler's 'Leutnant Gustl' and Dujardin's *Les Lauriers sont coupés,*" *Mod Austrian Lit,* 2, ii (1969), 7-15.

"Spiel im Morgengrauen"
  Lindken, Hans-Ulrich. "Arthur Schnitzler: 'Spiel im Morgengrauen,' "
  Österreich in Geschichte und Literatur, 13 (1969), 407-426.

"Die Weissagung"
  Alexander, Theodor W. "From the Scientific . . . ," 166-167.

IRWIN SHAW

"The Girls in Their Summer Dresses"
  Berke, Jacqueline. "Further Observations on 'A Shaw Story and Brooks
  and Warren,' " Coll Engl Assoc Critic, 33 (November, 1970), 28-29.

ALAN SILLITOE

"Noah's Ark"
  Penner, Allen R. "Illusory Deluge: Sillitoe's 'Noah's Ark,' " Coll Lang
  Assoc J, 12 (1968), 134-141.

"The Ragman's Daughter"
  Beachcroft, T. O. The Modern Art . . . , 224-225.

"To Be Collected"
  Beachcroft, T. O. The Modern Art . . . , 225-226.

ISAAC BASHEVIS SINGER

"The Black Wedding"
  Malin, Irving. Isaac Bashevis Singer, 82-84.

"Blood"
  Malin, Irving. Isaac Bashevis Singer, 86-89.

"Caricature"
  Mintz, Samuel I. "Spinoza and Spinozism in Singer's Short Fiction," in
  Malin, Irving, Ed. . . . Isaac Bashevis Singer, 215-216.

"Cockadoodledoo"
  Malin, Irving. Isaac Bashevis Singer, 98-101.

"The Gentleman from Cracow"
Malin, Irving. *Isaac Bashevis Singer,* 72-75.

"Gimpel the Fool"
Malin, Irving. *Isaac Bashevis Singer,* 70-72.
Pinsker, Sanford. *The Schlemiel . . . ,* 62-70.
Siegel, Ben. *Isaac Bashevis Singer,* 18-19.
Wisse, Ruth R. *The Schlemiel . . . ,*60-65.

"The Last Demon"
Malin, Irving. *Isaac Bashevis Singer,* 89-91.

"The Little Shoemaker"
Malin, Irving. *Isaac Bashevis Singer,* 75-78.

"The Man Who Came Back"
Malin, Irving. *Isaac Bashevis Singer,* 84-86.

"The Mirror"
Salamon, George. "In a Glass Darkly: The Morality of the Mirror in E. T.
A. Hoffman and I. B. Singer," *Stud Short Fiction,* 7 (1970), 630-632.

"The Séance"
Malin, Irving. *Isaac Bashevis Singer,* 93-96.

"The Shadow of a Crib"
Mintz, Samuel I. "Spinoza . . . ," in Malin, Irving, Ed. . . . *Isaac Bashevis
Singer,* 214-215.

"Shiddah and Kuziba"
Malin, Irving. *Isaac Bashevis Singer,* 80-82.

"Short Friday"
Malin, Irving. *Isaac Bashevis Singer,* 91-93.

"The Slaughterer"
Malin, Irving. *Isaac Bashevis Singer,* 96-98.
Siegel, Ben. *Isaac Bashevis Singer,* 40-41.

"The Spinoza of Market Street"
Malin, Irving. *Isaac Bashevis Singer,* 78-80.
Mintz, Samuel I. "Spinoza . . . ," in Malin, Irving, Ed. . . . *Isaac Bashevis
Singer,* 207-214.

WILLIAM JOSEPH SNELLING

"The Bois Brulé"
  Folsom, James K. . . . *Western Novel*, 168-169.

ALEXANDER SOLZHENITSYN

"Matryona's House"
  Douglas, Kenneth. "Masterpieces of the Modern World," in Mack,
  Maynard, *et al.*, Eds. *World Masterpieces*, II, 3rd ed., 1393-1394.

WILBUR DANIEL STEELE

"Always Summer"
  Bucco, Martin. *Wilbur Daniel Steele*, 58-59.

"An American Comedy"
  Bucco, Martin. *Wilbur Daniel Steele*, 133-134.

"The Anglo-Saxon"
  Bucco, Martin. *Wilbur Daniel Steele*, 60-61.

" 'Arab Stuff' "
  Bucco, Martin. *Wilbur Daniel Steele*, 64.

"At Two-in-the-Bush"
  Bucco, Martin. *Wilbur Daniel Steele*, 59-60.

"Autumn Bloom"
  Bucco, Martin. *Wilbur Daniel Steele*, 95.

"A Bath in the Sea"
  Bucco, Martin. *Wilbur Daniel Steele*, 132-133.

"The Black Road"
  Bucco, Martin. *Wilbur Daniel Steele*, 142-143.

"Blue Murder"
  Bucco, Martin. *Wilbur Daniel Steele*, 91-93.

"The Body of the Crime"
  Bucco, Martin. *Wilbur Daniel Steele*, 131-132.

"Both Judge and Jury"
Bucco, Martin. *Wilbur Daniel Steele,* 58.

"Brother's Keeper"
Bucco, Martin. *Wilbur Daniel Steele,* 150-151.

"Bubbles"
Bucco, Martin. *Wilbur Daniel Steele,* 89-90.

"By Appointment"
Bucco, Martin. *Wilbur Daniel Steele,* 148-149.

"Can't Cross Jordan by Myself"
Bucco, Martin. *Wilbur Daniel Steele,* 128-129.

"Ching, Ching, Chinaman"
Bucco, Martin. *Wilbur Daniel Steele,* 75-76.

"Conjuh"
Bucco, Martin. *Wilbur Daniel Steele,* 129-130.

"Crocuses"
Bucco, Martin. *Wilbur Daniel Steele,* 78-79.

"The Dark Hour"
Bucco, Martin. *Wilbur Daniel Steele,* 124-125.

"A Devil of a Fellow"
Bucco, Martin. *Wilbur Daniel Steele,* 45-46.

"Down on Their Knees"
Bucco, Martin. *Wilbur Daniel Steele,* 43-44.

"A Drink of Water"
Bucco, Martin. *Wilbur Daniel Steele,* 95-97.

"Due North"
Bucco, Martin. *Wilbur Daniel Steele,* 134-136.

"Fe-Fi-Fo-Fum"
Bucco, Martin. *Wilbur Daniel Steele,* 98.

"Footfalls"
Bucco, Martin. *Wilbur Daniel Steele,* 111-112.

"The Mad"
Bucco, Martin. *Wilbur Daniel Steele,* 110-111.

"Man and Boy" [originally "Man Without a God"]
Bucco, Martin. *Wilbur Daniel Steele,* 145-146.

"A Man's a Fool"
Bucco, Martin. *Wilbur Daniel Steele,* 47.

"The Man Who Sat"
Bucco, Martin. *Wilbur Daniel Steele,* 64-65.

"The Man Who Saw Through Heaven"
Bucco, Martin. *Wilbur Daniel Steele,* 85-87.

"The Marriage Kairwan"
Bucco, Martin. *Wilbur Daniel Steele,* 61-62.

"Mary Drake and Will Todd"
Bucco, Martin. *Wilbur Daniel Steele,* 106-107.

"Never Anything That Fades . . ."
Bucco, Martin. *Wilbur Daniel Steele,* 112-113.

"Out of Exile"
Bucco, Martin. *Wilbur Daniel Steele,* 77-78.

"Out of the Wind"
Bucco, Martin. *Wilbur Daniel Steele,* 82-83.

"Renegade"
Bucco, Martin. *Wilbur Daniel Steele,* 144-145.

" 'Romance' "
Bucco, Martin. *Wilbur Daniel Steele,* 49.

"Sailor! Sailor!"
Bucco, Martin. *Wilbur Daniel Steele,* 88-89.

"The Shame Dance"
Bucco, Martin. *Wilbur Daniel Steele,* 55-56.

"Six Dollars"
Bucco, Martiln. *Wilbur Daniel Steele,* 80-82.

"Sooth"
Bucco, Martin. *Wilbur Daniel Steele,* 87-88.

"Survivor"
Bucco, Martin. *Wilbur Daniel Steele,* 137-138.

"The Thinker"
Bucco, Martin. *Wilbur Daniel Steele,* 97-98.

"Tower of Sand"
Bucco, Martin. *Wilbur Daniel Steele,* 103-104.

"Two Seconds"
Bucco, Martin. *Wilbur Daniel Steele,* 149-150.

"The Wages of Sin"
Bucco, Martin. *Wilbur Daniel Steele,* 76-77.

"A Way with Women"
Bucco, Martin. *Wilbur Daniel Steele,* 143.

"What Do You Mean—American?"
Bucco, Martin. *Wilbur Daniel Steele,* 67-68.

"When Hell Froze"
Bucco, Martin. *Wilbur Daniel Steele,* 93-94.

"White Hands"
Bucco, Martin. *Wilbur Daniel Steele,* 75.

"White Horse Winter"
Bucco, Martin. *Wilbur Daniel Steele,* 42-43.

"The White Man"
Bucco, Martin. *Wilbur Daniel Steele,* 56-57.

"The Woman at Seven Brothers"
Bucco, Martin. *Wilbur Daniel Steele,* 42.

"The Yellow Cat"
Bucco, Martin. *Wilbur Daniel Steele,* 46-47.

WALLACE STEGNER

"A View from the Balcony"
  Flora, Joseph M. "A View from the Balcony," *Western Am Lit,* 5 (1970),
    121-128.

GERTRUDE STEIN

"Melanctha"
  Starke, Catherine J. *Black Portraiture* . . . , 183-186.

JOHN STEINBECK

"The Gift"
  Goldsmith, Arnold L. "Thematic Rhythm in *The Red Pony,*" *Coll Engl,*
    26 (1965), 391-394; rpt. Davis, Robert M., Ed. *Steinbeck* . . . , 70-74.
  Levant, Howard. "John Steinbeck's *The Red Pony:* A Study in Narrative
    Technique," *J Narrative Technique,* 1 (May, 1971), 77-85.
  Shuman, R. Baird. "Initiation in Steinbeck's *The Red Pony,*" *Engl J,* 59
    (1970), 1252-1255.

"The Great Mountain"
  Goldsmith, Arnold L. "Thematic Rhythm . . . ," 391-394; rpt. Davis,
    Robert M., Ed. *Steinbeck* . . . , 70-74.
  Levant, Howard. ". . . Narrative Technique," 77-85.
  Shuman, R. Baird. "Initiation . . . ," 1252-1255.

"The Leader of the People"
  Goldsmith, Arnold L. "Thematic Rhythm . . . ," 391-394; rpt. Davis,
    Robert M., Ed. *Steinbeck* . . . , 70-74.
  Houghton, Donald E. "Westering in 'Leader of the People,' " *Western
    Am Lit,* 4 (1969), 117-124.
  Martin, Bruce K. " 'The Leader of the People': Reëxamined," *Stud Short
    Fiction,* 8 (1971), 423-432.

"The Promise"
  Goldsmith, Arnold L. "Thematic Rhythm . . . ," 391-394; rpt. Davis,
    Robert M., Ed. *Steinbeck* . . . , 70-74.
  Levant, Howard. " . . . Narrative Technique," 77-85.
  Shuman, R. Baird. "Initiation . . . ," 1252-1255.

"The Snake"
Guerin, Wilfred L., *et al. Instructor's Manual . . . "Mandala" . . .* , 31-32.

STENDAL [MARIE HENRI BEYLE]

"Ernestine"
Tillett, Margaret. *Stendal . . . ,* 75-77.

ROBERT LOUIS STEVENSON

"The Body-Snatcher"
Egan, Joseph J. "Grave Sites and Moral Death: A Re-examination of Stevenson's 'The Body-Snatcher,' " *Engl Lit in Transition,* 13 (1970), 9-15.

"A Lodging for the Night"
Egan, Joseph J. "Dark in the Poet's Corner: Stevenson's 'A Lodging for the Night,' " *Stud Short Fiction,* 7 (1970), 402-408.

"Providence and the Guitar"
Warner, Fred B. "The Significance of Stevenson's 'Providence and the Guitar,' " *Engl Lit in Transition,* 14 (1971), 103-114.

"The Strange Case of Dr. Jekyll and Mr. Hyde"
Philmus, Robert M. *Into the Unknown . . . ,* 90-99.
Stone, Donald D. *Novelists . . . ,* 55-56.

"Thrawn Janet"
Beachcroft, T.O. *The Modern Art . . . ,* 110-111.
Warner, Fred B. "Stevenson's First Scottish Story," *Nineteenth Century Fiction,* 24 (1969), 335-344.

ADALBERT STIFTER

"Abdias"
Lachinger, Johann. "Adalbert Stifters 'Abdias': Eine Interpretation," *Adalbert Stifter Institut des Landes Oberösterreich: Vierteljahrsschrift,* 18 (1969), 97-114.

"Brigitta"
Hahns, Walther L. "Zu Stifters Konzept der Schönheit: 'Brigitta,' "

Adalbert Stifter Institut des Landes Oberösterreich: Vierteljahrsschrift,
19 (1970), 149-159.

RUTH McENERY STUART

"Uncle Mingo's 'Speculations' "
  Skaggs, Merrill M. *The Folk* . . . , 12-16.

WILLIAM STYRON

"The Enormous Window" [originally "Autumn"]
  Ratner, Marc L. *William Styron,* 24-25.

"The Long March"
  Hays, Peter L. *The Limping Hero* . . ., 166-171.
  Nigro, August. "*The Long March:* The Expansive Hero in a Closed
    World," *Critique,* 9, iii (1967), 103-112.
  Ratner, Marc L. "The Rebel Purged: Styron's 'The Long March,' "
    Arlington Q, 2 (1969), 27-42; rpt. in his *William Styron,* 57-69.

ALLEN TATE

"The Immortal Woman"
  Squires, Radcliffe. "Allen Tate's *The Fathers," Virginia Q R,* 46 (1970),
    633-635.

"The Migration"
  Squires, Radcliffe. "Allen Tate's *The Fathers,"* 632-633.

PETER TAYLOR

"Allegiance"
  Griffith, Albert J. *Peter Taylor,* 40-43.

"At the Drugstore"
  Griffith, Albert J. *Peter Taylor,* 140-143.

"Bad Dreams"
  Griffith, Albert J. *Peter Taylor,* 93-94.

"A Cheerful Disposition"
Griffith, Albert J. *Peter Taylor,* 153-154.

"Cookie"
Griffith, Albert J. *Peter Taylor,* 80-81.

"The Dark Walk"
Griffith, Albert J. *Peter Taylor,* 75-79.

"The End of the Play"
Griffith, Albert J. *Peter Taylor,* 151-152.

"The Fancy Woman"
Griffith, Albert J. *Peter Taylor,* 46-51.

"Friend and Protector"
Griffith, Albert J. *Peter Taylor,* 117-120.

"Guests"
Griffith, Albert J. *Peter Taylor,* 120-123.

"Heads of Houses"
Griffith, Albert J. *Peter Taylor,* 123-124.

"Je Suis Perdu"
Griffith, Albert J. *Peter Taylor,* 114-116.

"The Lady Is Civilized"
Griffith, Albert J. *Peter Taylor,* 143-144.

"A Long Fourth"
Griffith, Albert J. *Peter Taylor,* 51-56.

"Miss Leonora When Last Seen"
Griffith, Albert J. *Peter Taylor,* 137-140.

"Mrs. Billingsby Wine"
Griffith, Albert J. *Peter Taylor,* 147-148.

"Nerves"
Griffith, Albert J. *Peter Taylor,* 146-147.

"1939"
Griffith, Albert J. *Peter Taylor,* 107-113.

"Two Pilgrims"
Griffith, Albert J. *Peter Taylor,* 136-137.

"Uncles"
Griffith, Albert J. *Peter Taylor,* 145-146.

"Venus, Cupid, Folly and Time"
Griffith, Albert J. *Peter Taylor,* 125-128.

"A Walled Garden"
Griffith, Albert J. *Peter Taylor,* 116-117.

"What You Hear from 'Em?"
Griffith, Albert J. *Peter Taylor,* 83-86.
Mizener, Arthur. *A Handbook* . . . *"Modern Short Stories* . . . *Revised Edition,"* 171-174; rpt. *A Handbook* . . . *"Modern Short Stories* . . . *Third Edition,"* 191-194.

"A Wife of Nashville"
Griffith, Albert J. *Peter Taylor,* 81-83.

DYLAN THOMAS

"An Adventure from a Work in Progress"
Pratt, Annis. *Dylan Thomas* . . . , 74-76.

"Adventures in the Skin Trade"
Pratt, Annis. *Dylan Thomas* . . . , 154-157.

"After the Fair"
Tritschler, Donald. "The Stories in Dylan Thomas' Red Notebook," *J Mod Lit,* 2 (1971), 39-40.

"Anagram" [originally entitled "Mr. Tritas on the Rocks"]
Tritschler, Donald. "The Stories . . . ," 51-54.

"Ballad of the Long-legged Bait"
Pratt, Annis. *Dylan Thomas* . . . , 159-160.

"The Burning Baby"
Pratt, Annis. *Dylan Thomas* . . . , 37-38.
Tritschler, Donald. "The Stories . . . ," 50-51.

"The Dress"
Tritschler, Donald. "The Stories . . . ," 42-43.

"The Enemies"
Tritschler, Donald. "The Stories . . . ," 40-41.

"The Followers"
Bloom, Edward A. and Lillian D., Eds. *The Variety* . . . , 245-248.

"Gaspar, Melchior, Balthasar"
Tritschler, Donald. "The Stories . . . ," 48-50.

"The Holy Six"
Pratt, Annis. *Dylan Thomas* . . . , 114-116.
Tritschler, Donald. "The Stories . . . ," 41.

"The Horse's Ha"
Pratt, Annis. *Dylan Thomas* . . . , 122-123.

"In the Direction of the Beginning"
Pratt, Annis. *Dylan Thomas* . . . , 72-74.

"The Lemon"
Pratt, Annis. *Dylan Thomas* . . . , 132-136.

"The Map of Love"
Pratt, Annis. *Dylan Thomas* . . . , 66-70.

"The Mouse and the Woman"
Pratt, Annis. *Dylan Thomas* . . . , 142-146.

"The Orchard"
Pratt, Annis. *Dylan Thomas* . . . , 136-138.

"A Prospect of the Sea"
Pratt, Annis. *Dylan Thomas* . . . , 170-172.

"The School for Witches"
Pratt, Annis. *Dylan Thomas* . . . , 120-121.

"The Tree"
Pratt, Annis. *Dylan Thomas* . . . , 98-101.
Tritschler, Donald. "The Stories . . . ," 36-38.

"The True Story"
    Tritschler, Donald. "The Stories . . . ," 38-39.

"The Vest"
    Tritschler, Donald. "The Stories . . . ," 46-48.

"The Visitor"
    Pratt, Annis. *Dylan Thomas* . . . , 92-95.
    Tritschler, Donald. "The Stories . . . ," 43-46.

THOMAS THORPE

"The Big Bear of Arkansas"
    Hauck, Richard B. *A Cheerful Nihilism* . . . , 204-207.

JAMES THURBER

"The Beast in the Dingle"
    Tobias, Richard C. . . . *James Thurber,* 98-101.

"The Breaking Up of the Winships"
    Tobias, Richard C. . . . *James Thurber,* 75-79.

"The Catbird Seat"
    Dias, Earl J. "The Upside-Down World of Thurber's 'The Catbird Seat,'"
        Coll Engl Assoc Critic, 30 (February, 1968), 6-7.
    Kane, Thomas S. "A Note on the Chronology of 'The Catbird Seat,'" *Coll
        Engl Assoc Critic,* 30 (April, 1968), 8-9.
    Tobias, Richard C. . . . *James Thurber,* 91-93.

"A Couple of Hamburgers"
    Mizener, Arthur, Ed. *Modern Short Stories* . . . , rev. ed., 201-206; rpt. 3rd
        ed., 205-208.

"The Secret Life of Walter Mitty"
    Guerin, Wilfred L., *et al. Instructor's Manual* . . . *"Mandala"* . . . , 23-24.

LEO TOLSTOY

"A Captive in the Caucasus"
    Christian, R. F. *Tolstoy* . . . , 265-266.

"The Death of Ivan Ilych"
Christian, R. F. *Tolstoy* . . . , 236-238.
Hamalian, Leo, and Edmond L. Volpe, Eds. *Ten . . . Short Novels*, 59-60;
rpt. 2nd ed. (retitled *Eleven . . . Short Novels)*, 60-61.
Simmons, Ernest J. *Introduction* . . . , 148-150.
Speirs, Logan. *Tolstoy and Chekhov*, 141-146.
Wellek, Renê. "Masterpieces of Realism and Naturalism," in Mack,
Maynard, *et al.*, Eds. *World Masterpieces*, II, 1717-1718; 3rd ed., 732-
733; Continental ed., 1434-1438; Continental ed. rev., 510-512.

"Family Happiness"
Christian, R. F. *Tolstoy* . . . , 90-93.

"Hadji Murad"
Christian, R. F. *Tolstoy* . . . , 240-246.
Speirs, Logan. *Tolstoy and Chekhov*, 132-134.

"The Kreutzer Sonata"
Christian, R. F. *Tolstoy* . . . , 230-234.

"Sevastopol in August"
Christian, R. F. *Tolstoy* . . . , 66-67.

"Sevastopol in December, 1854"
Christian, R. F. *Tolstoy* . . . , 58-60.

"Sevastopol in May"
Christian, R. F. *Tolstoy* . . . , 60-67.

"Three Deaths"
Christian, R. F. *Tolstoy* . . . , 88-90.

"The Wood-felling"
Christian, R. F. *Tolstoy* . . . , 54-58.

JEAN TOOMER

"Avey"
Lieber, Todd. "Design and Movement in *Cane*," *Coll Lang Assoc J*, 13
(1969), 44.

"Blood-Burning Moon"
  Lieber, Todd. "Design . . . ," 42-43.
  Starke, Catherine J. *Black Portraiture* . . . , 101-102.

"Box Seat"
  Ackley, Donald G. "Theme and Vision in Jean Toomer's *Cane*," *Stud Black Lit*, 1, i (1970), 56-58.
  Lieber, Todd. "Design . . . ," 45-46.

"Esther"
  Waldron, Edward E. "The Search for Identity in Jean Toomer's 'Esther,' " *Coll Lang Assoc J*, 14 (1971), 277-280.

"Fern"
  Westerfield, Hargis. "Jean Toomer's 'Fern,' " *Coll Lang Assoc J*, 14 (1971), 274-276.

"Kabnis"
  Ackley, Donald G. "Theme and Vision . . . ," 58-62.
  Lieber, Todd. "Design . . . ," 47-49.
  McKeever, Benjamin F. "*Cane* as Blues," *Negro Am Lit Forum*, 4 (1970), 61-63.
  Turner, Darwin T. "Jean Toomer's *Cane*," *Black World*, 18 (1969), 58-60; rpt. in his *In a Minor Chord* . . . , 23-25.

"Mr. Costyve Duditch"
  Turner, Darwin T. *In a Minor Chord* . . . , 44-46.

"Theater"
  Lieber, Todd. "Design . . . ," 42-43.

B. TRAVEN

"The Night Visitor"
  Warner, John M. "Tragic Vision in B. Traven's 'The Night Visitor,' " *Stud Short Fiction*, 7 (1970), 377-384.

IVAN TURGENEV

"First Love"
  Mills, Judith O. "Theme and Symbol in 'First Love,' " *Slavic & East European J*, 15 (1971), 433-440.

MARK TWAIN [SAMUEL LANGHORNE CLEMENS]

"Baker's Blue-Jay Yarn"
Hauck, Richard B. *A Cheerful Nihilism* . . . , 54-56.

"The Great Dark"
Hauck, Richard B. *A Cheerful Nihilism* . . . , 157-163.

"The Man That Corrupted Hadleyburg"
Geismar, Maxwell. *Mark Twain* . . . , 183-199.
Nebeker, Helen E. "The Great Corrupter or Satan Rehabilitated," *Stud Short Fiction,* 8 (1971), 635-637.
Werge, Thomas. "Mark Twain and the Fall of Adam," *Mark Twain J,* 15 (Summer, 1970), 10-13.

"The Mysterious Stranger"
Giesmar, Maxwell. *Mark Twain* . . . , 331-359.

Gervais, Ronald J. " 'The Mysterious Stranger': The Fall As Salvation," *Pacific Coast Philol,* 5 (1970), 24-33.
Hauck, Richard B. *A Cheerful Nihilism* . . . , 163-164.
May, John R. "The Gospel According to Philip Traum: Structural Unity in 'The Mysterious Stranger,' " *Stud Short Fiction,* 8 (1971), 411-422.
Parsons, Coleman O. "The Background of 'The Mysterious Stranger,' " *Am Lit,* 32 (1960), 55-74.
Spengermann, William C. *Mark Twain* . . . , 120-129.

MIGUEL DE UNAMUNO

"Abel Sanchez"
Hamalian, Leo, and Edmond L. Volpe, Eds. *Ten* . . . *Short Novels,* 371-372; rpt. 2nd ed. (retitled *Eleven* . . . *Short Novels*) , 349-350.

JOHN UPDIKE

"A & P"
Burchard, Rachael C. *John Updike* . . . , 139-140.
Fisher, Richard E. "John Updike: Theme and Form in the Garden of Epiphanies," *Moderna Sprak,* 56 (1962), 255-260.

"Archangel"
Burchard, Rachael C. *John Updike* . . . 140-141.

"The Astronomer"
    Burchard, Rachael C. *John Updike . . .* , 145.
    Sykes, Robert H. "A Commentary on Updike's Astronomer," *Stud Short
        Fiction* , 8 (1971), 575-579.

"The Bulgarian Poetess"
    Taylor, Larry E. *Pastoral . . .* , 132-133.

"Churchgoing"
    Burchard, Rachael C. *John Updike . . .* , 146-147.

"The Crow in the Woods"
    Burchard, Rachael C. *John Updike . . .* , 143-144.

"The Doctor's Wife"
    Howard, Daniel F. *Manual . . .* , 57-58.

"A Dying Cat"
    Burchard, Rachael C. *John Updike . . .* , 145-146.

"The Family Meadow"
    Taylor, Larry E. *Pastoral . . .* , 118.

"Flight"
    Burchard, Rachael C. *John Updike . . .* , 142.

"A Gift from the City"
    Burchard, Rachael C. *John Updike . . .* , 136-137.

"The Happiest I've Been"
    Burchard, Rachael C. *John Updike . . .* , 141-142.

"The Hermit"
    Burchard, Rachael C. *John Updike . . .* , 154-159.
    Taylor, Larry E. *Pastoral . . .* , 118-121.

"His Finest Hour"
    Burchard, Rachael C. *John Updike . . .* , 137-138.

"In Football Season"
    Taylor, Larry E. *Pastoral . . .* , 113-116.

"Leaves"
    Burchard, Rachael C. *John Updike . . .* , 154.

"Lifeguard"
   Burchard, Rachael C. *John Updike* . . . , 142-143.

"The Music School"
   Burchard, Rachael C. *John Updike* . . . , 153-154.
   Taylor, Larry E. *Pastoral* . . . , 116-118.

"Pigeon Feathers"
   Burchard, Rachael C. *John Updike* . . . , 147-152.

"A Sense of Shelter"
   Edwards, A.S.G. "Updike's 'A Sense of Shelter,' " *Stud Short Fiction*, 8
      (1971), 467-468.
   Minot, Stephen, and Robley Wilson. *Teacher's Manual* . . . , 2-3.
   Mizener, Arthur. *A Handbook* . . *"Modern Short Stories* . . *Revised
      Edition,"* 34-37; rpt. *A Handbook* . . . *"Modern Short Stories* . . . *Third
      Edition,"* 467-469.
   Reising, R.W. "Updike's 'A Sense of Shelter,' " *Stud Short Fiction*, 7
      (1970), 651-652.

ALFRED DE VIGNY

"La Veillée de Vincennes"
   Doolittle, James. *Alfred de Vigny*, 118-119.

KURT VONNEGUT

"EPICAC"
   Minot, Stephen, and Robley Wilson. *Teacher's Manual* . . . , 16-17.

ROBERT PENN WARREN

"When the Light Gets Green"
   Mizener, Arthur. *A Handbook* . . . *"Modern Short Stories* . . . *Revised
      Edition,"* 151-156; rpt. *A Handbook* . . . *"Modern Short Stories* . . .
      Third Edition," 171-176.

DENTON WELCH

"At Sea"
   Phillips, Robert. *"Brave and Cruel*: The Short Stories of Denton Welch,"
      Stud Short Fiction, 7 (1970), 364-366.

"The Barn"
Phillips, Robert. "*Brave and Cruel* . . . ," 362-363.

"Brave and Cruel"
Phillips, Robert. "*Brave and Cruel* . . . ," 372-373.

"The Coffin on the Hill"
Phillips, Robert. "*Brave and Cruel* . . . ," 359-361.

"The Fire in the Wood"
Phillips, Robert. "*Brave and Cruel* . . . ," 374-375.

"The Judas Tree"
Phillips, Robert. "*Brave and Cruel* . . . ," 368-369.

"Narcissus Bay"
Joad, C. E. M. *Decadence* . . . , 291-293; Am. ed., 291-293.
Phillips, Robert. "*Brave and Cruel* . . . ," 363-364.

"The Trout Stream"
Phillips, Robert. "*Brave and Cruel* . . . ," 369-371.

"When I Was Thirteen"
Phillips, Robert. "*Brave and Cruel* . . . ," 366-368.

H. G. WELLS

"The Country of the Blind"
Steinmann, Theo. "The Second Death of Nunez in 'The Country of the Blind,' " *Stud Short Fiction,* 9 (1972), 157-163.

"The Door in the Wall"
Bergonzi, Bernard. . . . *H. G. Wells* . . . , 84-88.

"The Empire of Ants"
Philmus, Robert M. *Into the Unknown* . . . , 144-146.

"The Flowering of the Strange Orchid"
Bergonzi, Bernard. . . . *H. G. Wells* . . . , 67-68.

"The Lord of the Dynamos"
Bergonzi, Bernard. . . . *H. G. Wells* . . . , 68-71.
Borello, Alfred. *H. G. Wells* . . . , 74-75.

"The Plattner Story"
Bergonzi, Bernard. . . . *H. G. Wells* . . . , 71-72.

"The Remarkable Case of Davidson's Eyes"
Bergonzi, Bernard. . . . *H. G. Wells* . . . , 63-65.

"A Slip Under the Microscope"
Borello, Alfred. *H. G. Wells* . . . , 73-74.

"The Star"
Bergonzi, Bernard. . . . *H. G. Wells* . . . , 74-76.
Borello, Alfred. *H. G. Wells* . . . , 76-77.

"The Stolen Body"
Borello, Alfred. *H. G. Wells* . . . , 75-76.

"The Time Machine"
Bergonzi, Bernard. . . . *H. G. Wells* . . . , 46-61.

"The Triumph of a Taxidermist"
Borello, Alfred. *H. G. Wells* . . . , 72-73.

EUDORA WELTY

"The Bride of the Innisfallen"
Jones, Alun. "A Frail Travelling Coincidence: Three Late Stories of
Eudora Welty," *Shenandoah,* 20 (1969), 47-49.

"The Burning"
Howell, Elmo. "Eudora Welty's Civil War Story," *Notes on Mississippi
Writers,* 2 (1969), 3-12.

"Death of a Traveling Salesman"
McFarland, Ronald E. "Vision and Perception in the Works of Eudora
Welty," *Markham R,* 2 (1971), 96-97.

"Delta Wedding"
Prenshaw, Peggy. "Cultural Patterns in Eudora Welty's 'Delta Wedding'
and 'The Demonstrators,'" *Notes on Mississippi Writers,* 3 (Fall, 1970),
51-70.

"The Demonstrators"
Prenshaw, Peggy. "Cultural Patterns . . . ," 51-70.

"First Love"
McFarland, Ronald E. "Vision . . . ." 95-96.

"Going to Naples"
Jones, Alun. "A Frail . . . Coincidence . . . ," 49-51.

"Keela, the Outcast Indian Maiden"
McFarland, Ronald E. "Vision . . . ," 97-99.
May, Charles E. "'Le Roi Mehaigne' in Welty's 'Keela, the Outcast Indian Maiden,' " *Mod Fiction Stud,* 18 (1973), 559-566.

"Kin"
Isaacs, Neil D. "Four Notes on Eudora Welty," *Notes on Mississippi Writers,* 2 (Fall, 1969), 44-45.
Skaggs, Merrill M. *The Folk . . . ,* 237-240.

"No Place for You, My Love"
Jones, Alun. "A Frail . . . Coincidence . . . ," 45-47.

"The Optimist's Daughter"
Price, Reynolds. "The Onlooker, Smiling: An Early Reading of 'The Optimist's Daughter,' " *Shenandoah,* 20 (Spring, 1969), 59-73.

"Petrified Man"
Kraus, W. Keith. "Welty's 'Petrified Man,' " *Explicator,* 29 (1971), Item 63.

"Powerhouse"
Canzoneri, Robert, and Page Stegner, Eds. *Fiction . . . ,* 191-193.
Kirkpatrick, Smith. "The Anointed Powerhouse," *Sewanee R,* 77 (1969), 94-108.

"A Visit of Charity"
May, Charles E. "The Difficulty of Loving in 'A Visit of Charity,' " *Stud Short Fiction,* 6 (1969), 338-341.

"The Whistle"
McDonald, W. U. "Welty's 'Social Consciousness': Revisions of 'The Whistle,' " *Mod Fiction Stud,* 16 (1970), 193-198.

"A Worn Path"
Howell, Elmo. "Eudora Welty's Negroes: A Note on 'A Worn Path,' " *Xavier Univ Stud,* 9 (1970), 28-32.
Mizener, Arthur. *A Handbook . . . "Modern Short Stories . . . Revised Edition,"* 163-165; rpt. *A Handbook . . . "Modern Short Stories . . . Third Edition,"* 178-180.

GLENWAY WESCOTT

"Adolescence"
Johnson, Ira. *Glenway Wescott* . . . , 90.

"The Babe's Bed"
Johnson, Ira. *Glenway Wescott* . . . , 104-107.

"The Dove Came Down"
Johnson, Ira. *Glenway Wescott* . . . , 94-95.

"A Guilty Woman"
Johnson, Ira. *Glenway Wescott* . . . , 92-94.

"Hurt Feelings"
Johnson, Ira. *Glenway Wescott* . . . , 108-109.

"In a Thicket"
Johnson, Ira. *Glenway Wescott* . . . , 89-90.

"Like a Lover"
Johnson, Ira. *Glenway Wescott* . . . , 90-91.

"The Pilgrim Hawk"
Johnson, Ira. *Glenway Wescott* . . . , 113-142.

"Prohibition"
Johnson, Ira. *Glenway Wescott* . . . , 88-89.

"The Rescuer"
Johnson, Ira. *Glenway Wescott* . . . , 109-110.

"The Runaway"
Johnson, Ira. *Glenway Wescott* . . . , 83-84.

"The Sailor"
Johnson, Ira. *Glenway Wescott* . . . , 84-85.

"The Sight of a Dead Body"
Johnson, Ira. *Glenway Wescott* . . . , 110-111.

"The Wedding March"
Johnson, Ira. *Glenway Wescott* . . . , 95-96.

"The Whistling Swan"
 Johnson, Ira. *Glenway Wescott* . . . , 85-86.

NATHANAEL WEST

"A Cool Million"
 Cramer, Carter M. "The World of Nathanael West: A Critical
  Interpretation," *Emporia State Research Stud,* 19 (June, 1971), 27-38.
 Galloway, David D. "A Picaresque Apprenticeship: Nathanael West's
  'The Dream Life of Balso Snell' and 'A Cool Million,'" *Wisconsin Stud
  Contemp Lit,* 5 (1964), 118-126; rpt. Martin, Jay, Ed. *Nathanael West*
  . . . , 40-47.
 Malin, Irving. *Nathanael West's Novels,* 67-83.
 Petrullo, Helen B. "Clichés and Three Political Satires of the Thirties,"
  Satire Newsletter, 8 (1971), 109-112.
 Steiner, T. R. "West's Lemuel and the American Dream," *Southern R,* 7
  (1971), 994-1006.

"The Dream Life of Balso Snell"
 Cramer, Carter M. "The World of Nathanael West . . ," 10-26.
 Galloway, David D. "A Picaresque Apprenticeship . . . ," 110-118; rpt.
  Martin, Jay, Ed. *Nathanael West* . . . , 32-40.
 Malin, Irving. *Nathanael West's Novels,* 11-30.

"Miss Lonelyhearts"
 Andreach, Robert J. "Nathanael West's 'Miss Lonelyhearts' Between the
  Dead Pan and the Unborn Christ," *Mod Fiction Stud,* 12 (1966), 251-
  260; rpt. Jackson, Thomas H., Ed. *Twentieth Century* . . . , 49-60.
 Cohen, Arthur. "Nathanael West's Holy Fool," *Commonweal,* 64 (1956),
  276-278; rpt. Jackson, Thomas H., Ed. *Twentieth Century* . . . , 46-48.
 Cramer, Carter M. "The World of Nathanael West . . . ," 39-71.
 Edenbaum, Robert I. "To Kill God and Build a Church: Nathanael West's
  'Miss Lonelyhearts,'" *Coll Engl Assoc Critic,* 29 (June, 1967), 5-7, 11;
  rpt. Jackson, Thomas H., Ed. *Twentieth Century* . . . , 61-69.
 Geha, Richard. " 'Miss Lonelyhearts': A Dual Mission of Mercy,"
  Hartford Stud Lit, 3 (1971), 116-131.
 Herbst, Josephine. " 'Miss Lonelyhearts': An Allegory," *Contempo,* 3
  (July 25, 1933), 11; rpt. Jackson, Thomas H., Ed. *Twentieth Century*
  . . . , 97-98; Martin, Jay, Ed. *Nathanael West* . . . , 69-70.
 Hyman, Stanley E. *Nathanael West,* 16-28; rpt. O'Connor, William V.,
  Ed. *Seven* . . . *Novelists,* 235-246; Jackson, Thomas H., Ed. *Twentieth
  Century* . . . , 70-80.

Light, James F. *Nathanael West* . . . , 74-101; rpt. Jackson, Thomas H.,
   Ed. *Twentieth Century* . . . , 19-38.
Malin, Irving. *Nathanael West's Novels,* 31-66.
Ratner, Marc L. " 'Anywhere Out of This World': Baudelaire and
   Nathanael West," *Am Lit,* 31 (1960), 456-463; rpt. Martin, Jay, Ed.
   Nathanael West . . . , 102-109.
Reid, Randall. *The Fiction* . . . , 41-105; rpt. in part Jackson, Thomas H.,
   Ed. *Twentieth Century* . . . , 93-96.
Smith, Marcus. "Religious Experience in 'Miss Lonelyhearts,'" *Contemp
   Lit,* 9 (1968), 172-188; rpt. Martin, Jay, Ed. *Nathanael West* . . . , 74-90.
Volpe, Edmond L. "The Waste Land of Nathanael West," *Renascence,* 13
   (1961), 69-77, 112; rpt. Jackson, Thomas H., Ed. *Twentieth Century*
   . . . , 81-92; Martin, Jay, Ed. *Nathanael West* . . . , 91-101.

EDITH WHARTON

"After Holbein"
   Walton, Geoffrey. *Edith Wharton* . . . , 158-159.

"All Souls"
   McDowell, Margaret B. "Edith Wharton's Ghost Stories," *Criticism,* 12
   (1970), 144-145.

"Autres Temps"
   Walton, Geoffrey. *Edith Wharton* . . . , 104-105.

"Bewitched"
   McDowell, Margaret B. " . . . Ghost Stories," 145-151.

"The Blond Beast"
   Walton, Geoffrey. *Edith Wharton* . . . , 101-102.

"Ethan Frome"
   Hays, Peter L. *The Limping Hero* . . . , 145-148.
   Shuman, R. Baird. "The Continued Popularity of 'Ethan Frome,'" *Revue
   des Langues Vivantes,* 37 (1971), 257-263.
   Walton, Geoffrey. *Edith Wharton* . . . , 78-83.

"His Father's Son"
   Walton, Geoffrey. *Edith Wharton* . . . , 100-101.

"Kerfol"
   McDowell, Margaret B. " . . . Ghost Stories," 140-141.

"The Letters"
Walton, Geoffrey. *Edith Wharton* . . . , 102-103.

"The Long Run"
Walton, Geoffrey. *Edith Wharton* . . . , 103-104.

"Miss Mary Pask"
McDowell, Margaret B. " . . . Ghost Stories," 138-139.

"Mrs. Manstey's View"
Walton, Geoffrey. *Edith Wharton* . . . , 72.

"Pomegranate Seed"
McDowell, Margaret B. " . . . Ghost Stories," 139-140.

"The Pot-Boiler"
Walton, Geoffrey. *Edith Wharton* . . . , 99-100.

"Roman Fever"
Mizener, Arthur. *A Handbook* . . . "*Modern Short Stories* . . . *Revised Edition*," 61-66; rpt. *A Handbook* . . . "*Modern Short Stories* . . . *Third Edition*," 63-68.
Walton, Geoffrey. *Edith Wharton* . . . , 159-160.

"Summer"
Walton, Geoffrey. *Edith Wharton* . . . , 83-92.

"The Triumph of Night"
McDowell, Margaret B. " . . . Ghost Stories," 141-143.

"Xingu"
Walton, Geoffrey. *Edith Wharton* . . . , 105-106.

OSCAR WILDE

"The Portrait of Mr. W. H."
Poteet, Lewis J. "Romantic Aesthetics in Oscar Wilde's 'Mr. W. H.,' " *Stud Short Fiction* , 7 (1970), 458-464.

TENNESSEE WILLIAMS

"The Kingdom of Earth"
Reck, Tom S. "The Short Stories of Tennessee Williams: Nucleus for His Drama," *Tennessee Stud Lit* , 16 (1971), 150-152.

"Man Bring This Up Road"
    Reck, Tom S. "The Short Stories . . . ," 148-150.

"The Night of the Iguana"
    Reck, Tom S. "The Short Stories . . . ," 147-148.

"Portrait of a Girl in Glass"
    Reck, Tom S. "The Short Stories . . . ," 142-143.

"Three Players of a Summer Game"
    Reck, Tom S. "The Short Stories . . . ," 145-147.

"The Yellow Bird"
    Reck, Tom S. "The Short Stories . . . ," 344-345.

WILLIAM CARLOS WILLIAMS

"Comedy Entombed"
    Whitaker, Thomas R. *William Carlos Williams*, 105-106.

"A Face of Stone"
    Breslin, James E. *William Carlos Williams* . . . , 156-158.
    Whitaker, Thomas R. *William Carlos Williams*, 102-104.

"The Girl with a Pimply Face"
    Breslin, James E. *William Carlos Williams* . . . , 152-153.

"Jean Beicke"
    Breslin, James E. *William Carlos Williams* . . . , 150-152.
    Whitaker, Thomas R. *William Carlos Williams*, 102.

"A Night in June"
    Breslin, James E. *William Carlos Williams* . . . , 158-160.
    Whitaker, Thomas R. *William Carlos Williams*, 101.

"Old Doc Rivers"
    Breslin, James E. *William Carlos Williams* . . . , 146-149.
    Whitaker, Thomas R. *William Carlos Williams*, 98-100.

"The Use of Force"
    Breslin, James E. *William Carlos Williams* . . . , 155-156.
    Minot, Stephen, and Robley Wilson. *Teacher's Manual* . . . , 5-6.

ROBLEY WILSON

"The Apple"
Minot, Stephen, and Robley Wilson. *Teacher's Manual* . . . , 18-19.

OWEN WISTER

"The Gift Horse"
Folsom, James K. . . . *Western Novel,* 120-121.

"Hank's Woman"
Lambert, Neal. "Owen Wister's 'Hank's Woman': The Writer and His Comment," *Western Am Lit,* 4 (1969), 39-50.

VIRGINIA WOOLF

"A Haunted House"
Baldeschwiler, Eileen. "The Lyric Short Story: A Sketch of History," *Stud Short Fiction,* 6 (1969), 443-453.
Beja, Morris. *Epiphany* . . . , 111-114.
Chapman, R.T. "*The Lady in the Looking-Glass:* Modes of Perception in a Short Story by Virginia Woolf," *Mod Fiction Stud,* 18 (1972), 331-337.

"The Mark on the Wall"
Marder, Herbert. *Feminism* . . . , 130-133.

"The String Quartet"
Bloom, Edward A. and Lillian D., Eds. *The Variety* . . . , 340-346.

CONSTANCE FENIMORE WOOLSON

"The South Devil"
Skaggs, Merrill M. *The Folk.* . . , 206-207.

RICHARD WRIGHT

"Big Black Good Man"
Brignano, Russell C. *Richard Wright* . . . , 170-171.
Margolies, Edward. *The Art* . . . , 87-89.

"Big Boy Leaves Home"
  Jackson, Blyden. "Richard Wright in a Moment of Truth," *Southern Lit J,* 3 (1971), 3-17.
  Kinnamon, Keneth. *The Emergence* . . . , 82-87.
  Margolies, Edward. *The Art* . . . , 61-63.
  Mizener, Arthur. *A Handbook* . . . *"Modern Short Stories* . . . *Third Edition,"* 134-137.

"Bright and Morning Star"
  Brignano, Russell C. *Richard Wright* . . . , 63-66.
  Kinnamon, Keneth. *The Emergence* . . . , 112-116.
  Margolies, Edward. *The Art* . . . , 70-72.

"Down by the Riverside"
  Brignano, Russell C. *Richard Wright* . . . , 17-19.
  Kinnamon, Keneth. *The Emergence* . . . , 87-94.
  Margolies, Edward. *The Art* . . . , 63-65.

"Fire and Cloud"
  Brignano, Russell C. *Richard Wright* . . . , 19-20.
  Kinnamon, Keneth. *The Emergence* . . . , 100-106.
  Margolies, Edward. *The Art* . . . , 67-69.

"Long Black Song"
  Brignano, Russell C. *Richard Wright* . . . , 16-17, 61-62.
  Kinnamon, Keneth. *The Emergence* . . . , 94-100.
  Margolies, Edward. *The Art* . . . , 65-67.
  Timmerman, John. "Symbolism As Syndectic Device in Wright's 'Long Black Song,' " *Coll Lang Assoc J,* 14 (1971), 291-297.

"Man of All Work"
  Brignano, Russell C. *Richard Wright* . . . , 41-42.
  Margolies, Edward. *The Art* . . . , 83-85.

"Man, God Ain't Like That"
  Brignano, Russell C. *Richard Wright* . . . , 169-170.
  Margolies, Edward. *The Art* . . . , 85-87.

"The Man Who Killed a Shadow"
  Brignano, Russell C. *Richard Wright* . . . , 40-41.
  Margolies, Edward. *The Art* . . . , 81-82.

"The Man Who Lived Underground"
  Bakish, David. "Underground in an American Dreamworld," *Stud Black*

Lit, 2 (1971), 18-23.

Brignano, Russell C. *Richard Wright . . .* , 148-154.

Fabre, Michel. "Richard Wright: 'The Man Who Lived Underground,' "
   Stud Novel, 3 (1971), 165-179.

Hamalian, Leo, and Edmond L. Volpe, Eds. *Eleven . . . Short Novels,* 2nd
   ed., 672-673.

Howard, Daniel F. *Manual . . .* , 32-33.

Margolies, Edward. *The Art . . .* , 76-81.

Meyer, Shirley. "The Identity of 'The Man Who Lived Underground,' "
   Negro Am Lit Forum, 3 (1969), 52-55.

"The Man Who Was Almost a Man"

Margolies, Edward. *The Art . . .* , 75-76.

CHECK LIST OF BOOKS USED

Adams, Robert M. *James Joyce: Common Sense and Beyond.* New York: Random House, 1966.

Albrecht, Robert C., Ed. *The World of Short Fiction.* New York: Free Press, 1969.

Aldridge, John, Ed. *Essays in Modern Fiction, 1920-1951.* New York: Ronald, 1952.

Andreach, Robert J. *The Slain and Resurrected God: Conrad, Ford, and the Christian Myth.* New York: New York Univ. Press, 1970.

Appel, Alfred, and Charles Newman, Eds. *Nabokov: Criticism, Reminiscences, Translations and Tributes.* Evanston: Northwestern Univ. Press, 1970.

Auden, Wystan H. *The Enchafèd Flood, or The Romantic Iconography of the Sea.* New York: Random House, 1950.

Backman, Melvin. *Faulkner: The Major Years.* Bloomington: Indiana Univ. Press, 1966.

Baker, James R., and Thomas F. Staley, Eds. *James Joyce's "Dubliners": A Critical Handbook.* Belmont: Wadsworth, 1969.

Band, Arnold J. *Nostalgia and Nightmare: A Study in the Fiction of S.Y. Agnon.* Berkeley: Univ. of California Press, 1968.

Banta, Martha. *Henry James and the Occult: The Great Extension.* Bloomington: Indiana Univ. Press, 1972.

Basler, Roy P. *Sex, Symbolism and Psychology in Literature.* New Brunswick: Rutgers Univ. Press, 1948.

Bassan, Maurice, Ed. *Stephen Crane's "Maggie": Text and Context.* Belmont: Wadsworth, 1966.

————, Ed. *Stephen Crane: A Collection of Critical Essays.* Englewood Cliffs: Prentice-Hall, 1967.

Baumer, Franz. *Hermann Hesse,* trans. John Conway. New York: Ungar, 1969.

Beach, Joseph W. *The Method of Henry James,* rev. ed. New Haven: Yale Univ. Press, 1918.

Beachcroft, T.O. *The Modern Art: A Survey of the Short Story in English.* London: Oxford Univ. Press, 1968.

Beaujour, Elizabeth K. *The Invisible Land: A Study of the Artistic Imagination of Iurii Olesha.* New York: Columbia Univ. Press, 1970.

Becker, John E. *Hawthorne's Historical Allegory: An Examination of the American Conscience.* Port Washington: Kennikat, 1971.

Beebe, Maurice, Ed. *Literary Symbolism.* San Francisco: Wadsworth, 1960.

Begnal, Michael H. *Joseph Sheridan LeFanu.* Cranbury: Bucknell Univ. Press, 1971.

Beja, Morris. *Epiphany in the Modern Novel.* Seattle: Univ. of Washington Press, 1971.

Bell, Michael D. *Hawthorne and the Historical Romance of New England.* Princeton: Princeton Univ. Press, 1971.

Bergonzi, Bernard. *The Early H. G. Wells: A Study of the Scientific Romances.* Toronto: Univ. of Toronto Press, 1961.

Berryman, John. *Stephen Crane.* New York: William Sloane, 1950; Meridian ed. Cleveland: World, 1962.

Berthoff, Warner. *The Example of Melville.* Princeton: Princeton Univ. Press, 1962.

Birmingham, Stephen. *The Late John Marquand.* Philadelphia: Lippincott, 1972.

Bloom, Edward A. and Lillian B., Eds. *The Varieties of Fiction.* New York: Odyssey, 1969.

Borello, Alfred. *H. G. Wells: Author in Agony.* Carbondale: Southern Illinois Univ. Press, 1972.

Boros, Marie-Denise. *Un séquestré: l'homme sartrien.* Paris: Nizet, 1968.

Bowden, Edwin T. *The Themes of Henry James.* New Haven: Yale Univ. Press, 1956.

Bowen, Merlin. *The Long Encounter.* Chicago: Univ. of Chicago Press, 1960.

Brandabur, Edward. *A Scrupulous Meanness: A Study of Joyce's Early Work.* Urbana: Univ. of Illinois Press, 1971.

Breslin, James E. *William Carlos Williams: An American Artist.* New York: Oxford Univ. Press, 1970.

Brignano, Russell Carl. *Richard Wright: An Introduction to the Man and His Works.* Pittsburgh: Univ. of Pittsburgh Press, 1970.

Brooks, Cleanth, and Robert P. Warren. *Understanding Fiction.* New York: Crofts, 1943; 2nd ed. New York: Appleton-Century-Crofts, 1959.

Broussard, Louis. *The Measure of Poe.* Norman: Univ. of Oklahoma Press, 1969.

Brown, Homer O. *James Joyce's Early Fiction: The Biography of a Form.* Cleveland: Case Western Reserve Univ. Press, 1973.

Browne, Ray B. *Melville's Drive to Humanism.* Lafayette: Purdue University, 1971.

Browne, Ray B., and Martin Light, Eds. *Critical Approaches to American Literature,* 2 vols. New York: Crowell, 1965.

Bruccoli, Matthew J., Ed. *Fitzgerald/Hemingway Annual, 1969.* Washington: National Cash Register, 1969.

————. *Fitzgerald/Hemingway Annual, 1971.* Washington: National Cash Register, 1971.

Bucco, Martin. *Wilbur Daniel Steele.* New York: Twayne, 1972.

Buitenhuis, Peter. *The Grasping Imagination: The American Writings of Henry James.* Toronto: Univ. of Toronto Press, 1970.

Burchard, Rachael C. *John Updike: Yea Saying.* Carbondale: Southern Illinois Univ. Press, 1971.

Burton, Thomas G., Ed. *Essays in Memory of Christine Burgleson in Language and Literature by Former Colleagues and Students.* Johnson City: East Tennessee State Univ., 1969.

Cady, Edwin H. *Stephen Crane.* New York: Twayne, 1962; *The Light of* 813.4 *Common Day: Realism in American Fiction.* Bloomington: Indiana C819c Univ. Press, 1971.

Campbell, Harry M., and Ruel E. Foster. *William Faulkner: A Critical Appraisal.* Norman: Univ. of Oklahoma Press, 1951.

Canby, Henry S. *Turn West, Turn East: Mark Twain and Henry James.* Boston: Houghton Mifflin, 1951.

Canzoneri, Robert, and Page Stegner, Eds. *Fiction and Analysis: Seven Major Themes.* Glenview: Scott, Foresman, 1970.

Carden, Patricia. *The Art of Isaac Babel.* Ithaca: Cornell Univ. Press, 1972.

Champigny, Robert J. *A Pagan Hero: An Interpretation of Meursault in Camus' "The Stranger,"* trans. Rowe Portis. Philadelphia: Univ. of Pennsylvania Press, 1970.

————. *Sur un héros païen.* Paris: Librairie Gallimard, 1959.

Chase, Richard. *Herman Melville: A Critical Study.* New York: Macmillan, 1949.

————, Ed. *Selected Tales and Poems of Herman Melville.* New York: Rinehart, 1950.

————, Ed. *Melville: A Collection of Critical Essays.* Englewood Cliffs: 818.3 Prentice-Hall, 1962. M53/c

Christian, R. F. *Tolstoy: A Critical Introduction.* Cambridge: Cambridge Univ. Press, 1969.

Cohen, Hennig, Ed. *Landmarks of American Writing.* New York: Basic Books, 1969.

Consolo, Dominick, Ed. *D. H. Lawrence: "The Rocking-Horse Winner."* Columbus: Merrill, 1969.

Cordle, Thomas. *Andre Gide.* New York: Twayne, 1969.

Cormier, Raymond J., and Urban T. Holmes, Eds. *Essays in Honor of Louis Francis Solano.* Chapel Hill: Univ. of North Carolina Press, 1970.

Cowan, James C. *D. H. Lawrence's American Journey: A Study in Literature and Myth.* Cleveland: Press of Case Western Reserve Univ., 1970.

Cross, K. G. W. *F. Scott Fitzgerald.* Edinburgh: Oliver & Boyd, 1964; Am. ed. New York: Putnam, 1971.

Cross, Richard K. *Flaubert and Joyce.* Princeton: Princeton Univ. Press, 1971.

Current-Garcia, Eugene, and Walton R. Patrick, Eds. *Realism and Romanticism in Fiction.* Chicago: Scott, Foresman, 1962.

Davidson, Edward H. *Poe: A Critical Study*. Cambridge: Harvard Univ. Press, 1957.

Davis, Robert G. *Instructor's Manual for "Ten Modern Masters: An Anthology of the Short Story."* New York: Harcourt, Brace, 1953.

Davis, Robert M., Ed. *Steinbeck: A Collection of Critical Essays*. Englewood Cliffs: Prentice-Hall, 1972.

Dillard, R. H. W., George Garrett, and John R. Moore, Eds. *The Sounder Few: Essays from the "Hollins Critic."* Athens: Univ. of Georgia Press, 1971.

Dinklage, Karl, Elisabeth Albertsen, and Karl Corino, Eds. *Robert Musil: Studien zu seinem Werk*. Hamburg: Rowohlt, 1970.

Dodson, Daniel B. *Malcolm Lowry*. New York: Columbia Univ. Press, 1970.

Donohue, Agnes, Ed. *A Casebook on the Hawthorne Question*. New York: Crowell, 1963.

Doolittle, James. *Alfred de Vigny*. New York: Twayne, 1967.

Doubleday, Neal F. *Hawthorne's Early Tales, A Critical Study*. Durham: Duke Univ. Press, 1972.

————, Ed. *Hawthorne: Tales of His Native Land*. Boston: Heath, 1962.

Dowden, Wilfred S. *Joseph Conrad: The Imaged Style*. Nashville: Vanderbilt Univ. Press, 1970.

Driskell, Leon V., and Joan T. Brittain. *The Eternal Crossroads*. Lexington: Univ. of Kentucky Press, 1971.

Dupee, F. W. *Henry James*. New York: William Sloane, 1951; Anchor ed. Garden City: Doubleday, 1956.

Dutton, Robert R. *Saul Bellow*, New York: Twayne, 1971.

Edel, Leon. *Henry James: The Conquest of London, 1870-1881*. Philadelphia: Lippincott, 1962.

————, Ed. *Henry James: Selected Fiction*. New York: Dutton, 1953.

Eggenschwiler, David. *The Christian Humanism of Flannery O'Connor*. Detroit: Wayne State Univ. Press, 1972.

Emanuel, James. *Langston Hughes*. New York: Twayne, 1967.

Engelberg, Edward. *The Unknown Distance, From Consciousness to Conscience: Goethe to Camus*. Cambridge: Harvard Univ. Press, 1972.

Erling, Larsen. *James Agee*. Minneapolis: Univ. of Minnesota Press, 1971.

Feeley, Kathleen. *Flannery O'Connor: Voice of the Peacock*. New Brunswick: Rutgers Univ. Press, 1972.

Feidelson, Charles, and Paul Brodtkorb, Eds. *Interpretations of American Literature*. New York: Oxford Univ. Press, 1959.

Feuerlicht, Ignace. *Thomas Mann*. New York: Twayne, 1968.

Field, A. Leslie and Joyce W., Eds. *Bernard Malamud and the Critics*. New York: New York Univ. Press, 1970.

Field, G. W. *Hermann Hesse*. New York: Twayne, 1970.

Firchow, Peter. *Aldous Huxley, Satirist and Novelist.* Minneapolis: Univ. of
Minnesota Press, 1972.

Flores, Angel, Ed. *The Kafka Problem.* New York: New Directions, 1946.

Folsom, James K. *The American Western Novel.* New Haven: College &
Univ. Press, 1966.

Fossum, Robert H. *Hawthorne's Inviolable Circle: The Problem of Time.*
Deland: Everett/Edwards, 1972.

Frakes, James, and Isadore Traschen, Eds. *Short Fiction: A Critical
Collection.* Englewood Cliffs: Prentice Hall, 1959.

Franklin, H. Bruce. *The Wake of the Gods: Melville's Mythology.* Stanford:
Stanford Univ. Press, 1963.

Freeman, F. Barron, Ed. *Herman Melville's "Billy Budd."* Cambridge:
Harvard Univ. Press, 1948.

French, Warren, Ed. *The Fifties: Fiction, Poetry, Drama.* Deland: Everett/
Edwards, 1970.

Friedman, Maurice. *Problematic Rebel: An Image of Modern Man.* New
York: Random House, 1963; 2nd ed. retitled *Problematic Rebel: Melville, Dostoievsky, Kafka, Camus.* Chicago: Univ. of Chicago Press, 1970.

Friedman, Melvin J., Ed. *Samuel Beckett Now.* Chicago: Univ. of Chicago
Press, 1970.

Gallegly, Joseph. *From Alamo Plaza to Jack Harris's Saloon: O. Henry and
the Southwest He Knew.* The Hague: Mouton, 1970.

Garrett, Peter K. *Scene and Symbol from George Eliot to James Joyce.* New
Haven: Yale Univ. Press, 1969.

————, Ed. *Twentieth Century Interpretations of "Dubliners."*
Englewood Cliffs: Prentice-Hall, 1968.

Garzilli, Enrico. *Circle Without Center.* Cambridge: Harvard Univ. Press,
1972.

Geismar, Maxwell. *Rebels and Ancestors: The American Novel, 1890-1915.*
Boston: Houghton Mifflin, 1953.

————. *Henry James and the Jacobites.* Boston: Houghton Mifflin, 1963.

————. *Mark Twain: An American Prophet.* Boston: Houghton Mifflin,
1970.

Gibson, Donald B. *The Fiction of Stephen Crane.* Carbondale: Southern
Illinois Univ. Press, 1966. 1968

Gilbert, Elliot L. *The Good Kipling: Studies in the Short Story.* Athens:
Ohio Univ. Press, 1970.

————, Ed. *Kipling and the Critics.* New York: New York Univ. Press,
1965.

Gillen, Charles H. *H. H. Munro.* New York: Twayne, 1969.

Gordon, Caroline, and Allen Tate. *The House of Fiction.* New York:
Scribner, 1950; 2nd ed., 1960.

Gordon, Walter K., Ed. *Literature in Critical Perspectives: An Anthology.*
New York: Appleton-Century-Crofts, 1969.

Graver, Lawrence. *Carson McCullers*. Minneapolis: Univ. of Minnesota Press, 1969.

Greenberg, Martin. *The Terror of Art: Kafka and Modern Literature*. New York: Basic Books, 1968.

Grenander, Mary E. *Ambrose Bierce*. New York: Twayne, 1971.

Griffith, Albert J. *Peter Taylor*. New York: Twayne, 1970.

Gross, Harvey. *The Contrived Corridor*. Ann Arbor: Univ. of Michigan Press, 1971.

Gross, John. *James Joyce*. New York: Viking, 1971.

— Gross, Theodore L. *The Heroic Ideal in American Literature*. New York: Free Press, 1971.

Guerin, Wilfred L., Earle Labor, Lee Morgan, and John R. Willingham. *Instructor's Manual to Accompany "Mandala: Literature for Critical Analysis."* New York: Harper & Row, 1970.

Gullason, Thomas A., Ed. *Stephen Crane's Career: Perspectives and Evaluations*. New York: New York Univ. Press, 1972.

Gullason, Thomas A., and Leonard Casper, Eds. *The World of Short Fiction*, 2nd ed. New York: Harper & Row, 1971.

Gurko, Leo. *Ernest Hemingway and the Pursuit of Heroism*. New York: Crowell, 1968; Apollo pb. ed., 1969.

Guth, Hans P., Ed. *Literature*, 2nd ed. Belmont: Wadsworth, 1968.

Guttmann, Allen. *The Jewish Writer in America: Assimilation and the Crisis of Identity*. New York: Oxford Univ. Press, 1971.

Hagopian, John V., and Martin Dolch, Eds. *Insight I: Analyses of American Literature*. Frankfurt: Hirschgraben, 1962.

————. *Insight II: Analyses of British Literature*. Frankfurt: Hirschgraben, 1964.

Hall, Calvin S., and Richard E. Lind. *Dream, Life, and Literature: A Study of Franz Kafka*. Chapel Hill: Univ. of North Carolina Press, 1970.

Hamalian, Leo, and Edmund Volpe, Eds. *Eleven Modern Short Novels*. New York: Putnam, 1970.

Hartley, Lodwick, and George Core, Eds. *Katherine Anne Porter: A Critical Symposium*. Athens: University of Georgia Press, 1969.

Hatfield, Henry. *Crisis and Continuity in Modern German Fiction*. Ithaca: Cornell Univ. Press, 1969.

Hauck, Richard B. *A Cheerful Nihilism: Confidence and "The Absurd" in American Humorous Fiction*. Bloomington: Indiana Univ. Press, 1971.

Hays, Peter L. *The Limping Hero: Grotesques in Literature*. New York: New York Univ. Press, 1971.

Hendin, Josephine. *The World of Flannery O'Connor*. Bloomington: Indiana Univ. Press, 1970.

Hochman, Baruch. *The Fiction of S. Y. Agnon*. Ithaca: Cornell Univ. Press, 1970.

Hoffman, Daniel G. *Form and Fable in American Fiction.* New York: Oxford Univ. Press, 1961; Galaxy Books ed., 1965.

Hoffman, Frederick J. *The Art of Southern Fiction: The Study of Some Modern Novels.* Carbondale: Southern Illinois Univ. Press, 1967.

Hoffman, Frederick J., and Olga W. Vickery, Eds. *William Faulkner: Two Decades of Criticism.* East Lansing: Michigan State College Press, 1951.

Hoffman, Frederick J., and Harry T. Moore, Eds. *The Achievement of D. H. Lawrence.* Norman: Univ. of Oklahoma Press, 1953.

Holmes, Charles M. *Aldous Huxley and the Way to Reality.* Bloomington: Indiana Univ. Press, 1970.

Holton, Milne. *Cylinders of Vision: The Fiction and Journalistic Writing of Stephen Crane.* Baton Rouge: Louisiana State Univ. Press, 1972.

Hovey, Richard B. *Hemingway: The Inward Terrain.* Seattle: Univ. of Washington Press, 1968.

Howard, Daniel F. *Manual to Accompany "The Modern Tradition: An Anthology of Short Stories, Second Edition."* Boston: Little, Brown, 1972.

Howard, Leon. *Herman Melville.* Minneapolis: Univ. of Minnesota Press, 1961.

Howarth, William L., Ed. *Twentieth Century Interpretations of Poe's Tales: A Collection of Critical Essays.* Englewood Cliffs: Prentice-Hall, 1971.

Howe, Irving. *William Faulkner: A Critical Study.* New York: Random House, 1952; 2nd ed. New York: Vintage, 1962.

Hyman, Stanley Edgar. *Nathanael West.* Minneapolis: Univ. of Minnesota Press, 1962.

Inge, M. Thomas, Ed. *William Faulkner: "A Rose for Emily."* Columbus: Charles E. Merrill, 1970.

Ireland, G. W. *André Gide: A Study of His Creative Writings.* Oxford: Oxford Univ. Press, 1970.

Jackson, Thomas H., Ed. *Twentieth Century Interpretations of "Miss Lonelyhearts."* Englewood Cliffs: Prentice-Hall, 1970.

James, Henry. *The Altar of the Dead and Other Tales.* New York: Scribner, 1908.

————. *What Maisie Knew and Other Tales.* New York: Scribner, 1908.

————. *The Art of the Novel: Critical Prefaces,* ed. R. P. Blackmur. New York: Scribner, 1934; pb. ed., 1946.

————. *The Notebooks of Henry James,* ed. F. O. Matthiessen and Kenneth B. Murdoch. New York: Oxford Univ. Press, 1947.

Jefferson, Douglas W. *Henry James.* Edinburgh: Oliver & Boyd, 1960; Am. ed. New York: Putnam, 1971.

Joad, C. E. M. *Decadence: A Philosophical Inquiry.* London: Faber, 1948; Am. ed. New York: Philosophical Library, 1949.

Johnson, Bruce. *Conrad's Modes of Mind.* Minneapolis: Univ. of Minnesota Press, 1971.

Johnson, Ira. *Glenway Wescott: The Paradox of Voice.* Port Washington, N. Y.: Kennikat Press, 1971.

Katz, Joseph, Ed. *Stephen Crane: "The Blue Hotel."* Columbus: Charles E. Merrill, 1969.

Kelley, Cornelia. *The Early Development of Henry James.* Urbana: Univ. of Illinois Press, 1930; pb. ed., 1965.

Kempton, Kenneth P. *The Short Story.* Cambridge: Harvard Univ. Press, 1947.

Kimbrough, Robert, Ed. *The Turn of the Screw.* New York: Norton, 1966.

Kinnamon, Keneth. *The Emergence of Richard Wright.* Urbana: Univ. of Illinois Press, 1972.

Knoll, Robert E., Ed. *Contrasts,* 2nd ed. New York: Harcourt, Brace, 1959.

Kraft, James. *The Early Tales of Henry James.* Carbondale: Southern Illinois Univ. Press, 1969.

Kramer, Karl D. *The Chameleon and the Dream: The Image of Reality in Čexov's Stories.* The Hague: Mouton, 1970.

LaFrance, Marston. *Patterns of Commitment in American Literature.* Toronto: Univ. of Toronto Press, 1967.

————. *A Reading of Stephen Crane.* New York: Oxford Univ. Press, 1971.

Lamson, Roy, Hallett Smith, Hugh Maclean, and Wallace W. Douglas, Eds. *The Critical Reader,* rev. ed. New York: Norton, 1962.

Landess, Thomas H., Ed. *The Short Fiction of Caroline Gordon: A Critical Symposium.* Dallas: Univ. of Dallas Press, 1972.

Lawson, Ursula D. *Subjective Time in E. T. A. Hoffmann's "Der goldne Topf."* Athens: Ohio Univ. Modern Language Department, 1968.

Layard, George S., Ed. *Mrs. Lynn Linton.* London: Methuen, 1901.

Leavitt, Hart D., Ed. *Billy Budd, Foretopman.* New York: Bantam, 1965.

Lesser, Simon O. *Fiction and the Unconscious.* Boston: Beacon, 1957.

Levin, Harry. *The Power of Blackness.* New York: Knopf, 1958; 2nd ed., 1960.

Levine, Stuart. *Edgar Poe: Seer and Craftsman.* Deland: Everett/Edwards, 1972.

Lewis, R. W. B. *The American Adam: Innocence, Tragedy, and Tradition in the Nineteenth Century.* Chicago: Univ. of Chicago Press, 1955.

————. *The Picaresque Saint.* Philadelphia: Lippincott, 1959; Keystone pb. ed., 1961.

Liberman, M. M. *Katherine Anne Porter's Fiction.* Detroit: Wayne State Univ. Press, 1971.

Lid, Richard W. *Instructor's Manual for "Grooving the Symbol."* New York: Free Press, 1970.

Lief, Ruth Ann. *Homage to Oceania: The Prophetic Vision of George Orwell.* Columbus: Ohio State Univ. Press, 1969.

Light, James F. *Nathanael West: An Interpretative Study.* Evanston:

Northwestern Univ. Press, 1961.

848.9 Littlejohn, David, Ed. *Gide: A Collection of Critical Essays*. Englewood
G453R Cliffs: Prentice-Hall, 1970.

Locke, Louis, William Gibson, and George Arms, Eds. *An Introduction to Literature*. New York: Rinehart, 1948; 2nd ed., 1952; 3rd ed., 1957.

Lord, Robert. *Dostoevsky: Essays and Perspectives*. Berkeley: Univ. of California Press, 1970.

Ludwig, Jack, and W. Richard Poirier, Eds. *Stories: British and American*. Boston: Houghton Mifflin, 1953.

McCallum, John H., Ed. *Prose and Criticism*. New York: Harcourt, Brace & World, 1966.

McCourt, Edward A. *The Canadian West in Fiction*. Toronto: Ryerson Press, 1949.

McDowell, Frederick P. W. *E. M. Forster*. New York: Twayne, 1969.

MacIvor, R. M., Ed. *Great Moral Dilemmas in Literature, Past and Present*. New York: Harper, 1956.

Mack, Maynard, *et al.*, Eds. *World Masterpieces*, 2 vols. New York: Norton, 1956; 2nd ed., 1965; 3rd ed., 1973; Continental ed., 1962; Continental ed. rev., 1966.

Madden, David, Ed. *American Dreams, American Nightmares*. Carbondale: Southern Illinois Univ. Press, 1970.

Magalaner, Marvin. *The Fiction of Katherine Mansfield*. Carbondale: Southern Illinois Univ. Press, 1971.

Magalaner, Marvin, and Richard M. Kain. *Joyce: The Man, The Work, The Reputation*. New York: New York Univ. Press, 1956.

Magalaner, Marvin, and Edmond L. Volpe. *Teachers' Manual to Accompany "Twelve Short Stories."* New York: Macmillan, 1961.

Magny, Claude-Edmonde. *Les Sandales d'Empédocle*. Neuchâtel: Editions de la Baconnière, 1945.

Maini, Darshan S., Ed. *Variations on American Literature*. New Delhi: U. S. Educational Foundation in India, 1968.

Malin, Irving. *New American Gothic*. Carbondale: Southern Illinois Univ. Press, 1962.

————. *Isaac Bashevis Singer*. New York: Ungar, 1972.

————. *Nathanael West's Novels*. Carbondale: Southern Illinois Univ. Press, 1972.

————. Ed. *Psychoanalysis and American Fiction*. New York: Dutton, 1965.

————. Ed. *Critical Views of Isaac Bashevis Singer*. New York: New York Univ. Press, 1969.

Marder, Herbert. *Feminism and Art: A Study of Virginia Woolf*. Chicago: Univ. of Chicago Press, 1968.

O.P. Margolies, Edward. *The Art of Richard Wright*. Carbondale: Southern Illinois Univ. Press, 1967.

Martin, Jay. *Harvests of Change: American Literature, 1865-1914.* Englewood Cliffs: Prentice-Hall, 1967.

——, Ed. *Nathanael West: A Collection of Critical Essays.* Englewood Cliffs: Prentice-Hall, 1971.

Matlaw, Myron, and Leonard Lief, Eds. *Story and Critic.* New York: Harper & Row, 1963.

Matthiessen, F. O. *American Renaissance.* New York: Oxford Univ. Press, 1941.

——, Ed. *The American Novels and Stories of Henry James.* New York: Knopf, 1947.

Mews, Siegfried, Ed. *Studies in German Literature of the Nineteenth and Twentieth Centuries: Festschrift for Frederic E. Coenen.* Chapel Hill: Univ. of North Carolina Press, 1970.

Miller, J. Hillis. *Thomas Hardy: Distance and Desire.* Cambridge: Harvard Univ. Press, 1970.

Millgate, Michael. *William Faulkner.* Edinburgh: Oliver & Boyd, 1961; Am. ed. New York: Grove, 1961; New York: Putnam, 1971.

Minot, Stephen, and Robley Wilson. *Teacher's Manual[for] Three Stances of Modern Fiction."* Cambridge: Winthrop, 1972.

Mizener, Arthur. *A Handbook for Use with "Modern Short Stories: The Uses of Imagination, Revised Edition."* New York: Norton, 1966; 3rd ed., 1971.

————, Ed. *Modern Short Stories: The Uses of Imagination,* 3rd ed. New York: Norton, 1971.

Montague, Gene, and Marjorie Henshaw, Eds. *The Experience of Literature.* Englewood Cliffs: Prentice-Hall, 1966.

Moore, Harry T. *The Life and Works of D. H. Lawrence.* New York: Twayne, 1951.

————, Ed. *Contemporary American Novelists.* Carbondale: Southern Illinois Univ. Press, 1964.

Moore, T. Inglis. *Social Patterns in Australian Literature.* Berkeley: Univ. of California Press, 1971.

Mukherjee, Sujit, and D. V. K. Raghavacharyulu, Eds. *Indian Essays in American Literature: Papers in Honor of Robert E. Spiller.* Bombay: Popular Prakashan, 1969.

Muller, Gilbert H. *Nightmare and Vision: Flannery O'Connor and the Catholic Grotesque.* Athens: Univ. of Georgia Press, 1972.

Mumford, Lewis. *Herman Melville.* New York: Harcourt, Brace, 1929.

Munson, Gorham. *Style and Form in American Prose.* New York: Doubleday, 1929.

Nahal, Chaman. *The Narrative Pattern in Ernest Hemingway's Fiction.* Cranbury: Fairleigh Dickinson Univ. Press, 1971.

Nance, William L. *The World of Truman Capote.* New York: Stein & Day, 1970.

Neider, Charles. *The Frozen Sea: A Study of Franz Kafka.* New York: Oxford Univ. Press, 1948.

Noon, William T. *Joyce and Aquinas.* New Haven: Yale Univ. Press, 1957.

O'Brien, Conor C. *Albert Camus of Europe and Africa.* New York: Viking, 1970.

O'Connor, Frank. *The Lonely Voice: A Study of the Short Story.* Cleveland: World, 1963.

O'Connor, William V., Ed. *Seven Modern American Novelists.* Minneapolis: Univ. of Minnesota Press, 1964.

Ohlin, Peter H. *Agee.* New York: Obolensky, 1966.

Onimus, Jean. *Albert Camus and Christianity,* trans. Emmett Parker. University: Univ. of Alabama Press, 1970.

Orvell, Miles. *Invisible Parade: The Fiction of Flannery O'Connor.* Philadelphia: Temple Univ. Press, 1972.

Page, Sally R. *Faulkner's Women: Characterization and Meaning.* Deland: Everett/Edwards, 1972.

Painter, George D. *André Gide: A Critical and Biographical Study.* New York: Roy, 1951; rev. ed. retitled *André Gide: A Critical Biography.* New York: Atheneum, 1968.

Peace, Richard. *Dostoyevsky: An Examination of the Major Novels.* Cambridge: Cambridge Univ. Press, 1971.

Pearce, Richard. *Stages of the Clown: Perspectives on Modern Fiction from Dostoyevsky to Beckett.* Carbondale: Southern Illinois Univ. Press, 1970.

Pearce, T. M. *Oliver La Farge.* New York: Twayne, 1972.

Pearsall, Robert B. *Frank Harris.* New York: Twayne, 1970.

Phillips, A. A. *Henry Lawson.* New York: Twayne, 1970.

Phillips, William, Ed. *Art and Psychoanalysis.* New York: Criterion, 1957; pb. ed. Cleveland: World, 1963.

Philmus, Robert M. *Into the Unknown: The Evolution of Science Fiction from Francis Godwin to H. G. Wells.* Berkeley: Univ. of California Press, 1970.

Pinsker, Sanford. *The Schlemiel As Metaphor: Studies in the Yiddish and American Jewish Novel.* Carbondale: Southern Illinois Univ. Press, 1971.

Pizer, Donald. *Realism and Naturalism in Nineteenth-Century American Literature.* Carbondale: Southern Illinois Univ. Press, 1966.

Poirier, Richard. *The Comic Sense of Henry James: A Study of the Early Novels.* London: Chatto & Windus, 1960; Am. ed. New York: Oxford Univ. Press, 1967.

Powers, Lyall H. *Henry James and the Naturalist Movement.* East Lansing: Michigan State Univ. Press, 1971.

Pratt, Annis. *Dylan Thomas' Early Prose: A Study in Creative Mythology.* Pittsburgh: Univ. of Pittsburgh Press, 1970.

Ratner, Marc L. *William Styron.* New York: Twayne, 1972.

Regan, Robert, Ed. *Poe: A Collection of Critical Essays*. Englewood Cliffs: Prentice-Hall, 1967.

Reid, Randall. *The Fiction of Nathanael West*. Chicago: Univ. of Chicago Press, 1967.

Reiss, Edmund, Ed. *"The Mysterious Stranger" and Other Tales*. New York: New American Library, 1962.

Richman, Sidney. *Bernard Malamud*. New York: Twayne, 1966.

Robinson, Michael. *The Long Sonata of the Dead: A Study of Samuel Beckett*. New York: Grove, 1969.

Ross, Danforth. *The American Short Story*. Minneapolis: Univ. of Minnesota Press, 1961.

Ross, Joan, and Donald Freed. *The Existentialism of Alberto Moravia*. Carbondale: Southern Illinois Univ. Press, 1972.

Roussel, Royal. *The Metaphysics of Darkness: A Study in the Unity and Development of Conrad's Fiction*. Baltimore: Johns Hopkins Press, 1971.

Rowe, William W. *Nabokov's Deceptive World*. New York: New York Univ. Press, 1971.

Ryf, Robert S. *Joseph Conrad*. New York: Columbia Univ. Press, 1970.

Rysten, Felix S. A. *False Prophets in the Fiction of Camus, Dostoevsky, Melville, and Others*. Coral Gables: Univ. of Miami Press, 1972.

Samuels, Charles T. *The Ambiguity of Henry James*. Urbana: Univ. of Illinois Press, 1971.

Saul, George B. *Withdrawn in Gold*. The Hague: Mouton, 1970.

Scheer-Schäzler, Brigitte. *Saul Bellow*. New York: Ungar, 1972.

Schmitter, Dean M., Ed. *William Faulkner: A Collection of Criticism*. New York: McGraw-Hill, 1973.

Scholes, Robert, and A. Walton Litz, Eds. *"Dubliners": Text, Criticism, and Notes*. New York: Viking, 1969.

Schwarzschild, Bettina. *The Not-Right House: Essays on James Purdy*. Columbia: Univ. of Missouri Press, 1968.

Seelye, John. *Melville: The Ironic Diagram*. Evanston: Northwestern Univ. Press, 1970.

Segal, Ora. *The Lucid Reflector: The Observer in Henry James' Fiction*. New Haven: Yale Univ. Press, 1969.

Sheehy, Maurice, Ed. *Michael/Frank: Studies on Frank O'Connor*. New York: Knopf, 1969.

Siegel, Ben. *Isaac Bashevis Singer*. Minneapolis: Univ. of Minnesota Press, 1969.

Siegel, Eli. *James and the Children: A Consideration of Henry James's "The Turn of the Screw."* New York: Definition Press, 1963.

Simmons, Ernest J. *Introduction to Tolstoy's Writings*. Chicago: Univ. of Chicago Press, 1968.

Skaggs, Merrill M. *The Folk of Southern Fiction: A Study in Local Color Tradition*. Athens: Univ. of Georgia Press, 1972.

Snell, George. *The Shapers of American Fiction.* New York: Dutton, 1947. *801.9 S67/a*

Solomon, Eric. *Stephen Crane: From Parody to Realism.* Cambridge: Harvard Univ. Press, 1966.

Speirs, Logan. *Tolstoy and Chekhov.* Cambridge: Cambridge University, 1971.

Spengermann, William C. *Mark Twain and the Backwoods Angel.* Kent: Kent State Univ. Press, 1966.

Spilka, Mark, Ed. *D. H. Lawrence: A Collection of Critical Essays.* *828.912*
Englewood Cliffs: Prentice-Hall, 1963.   *L419a*

Sprague, Rosemary. *George Eliot: A Biography.* Philadelphia: Chilton, 1968.

Springer, Haskell S., Ed. *Studies in "Billy Budd."* Columbus: Merrill, 1970.

Stabb, Martin S. *Jorge Luis Borges.* New York: Twayne, 1970.

Stafford, William T., Ed. *Melville's "Billy Budd" and the Critics.* San Francisco: Wadsworth, 1961.

————, Ed. *James's "Daisy Miller."* New York: Scribner, 1963.

Stallman, Robert W. *Stephen Crane: An Omnibus.* New York: Knopf, 1952.

————. *The Houses That James Built and Other Literary Studies.* East Lansing: Michigan Univ. Press, 1961.

Stallman, Robert W., and Arthur Waldhorn, Eds. *American Literature: Readings and Critiques.* New York: Putnam, 1961.

Stallman, Robert W., and R. E. Watters, Eds. *The Creative Reader.* New York: Ronald, 1954.

Stanford, Donald E., Ed. *Nine Essays on Modern Literature.* Baton Rouge: Louisiana State Univ. Press, 1965.

Starke, Catherine J. *Black Portraiture in American Fiction.* New York: Basic Books, 1971.

Stone, Donald D. *Novelists in a Changing World: Meredith, James, and the Transformation of English Fiction in the 1880's.* Cambridge: Harvard Univ. Press, 1972.

Stone, Edward. *A Certain Morbidity: A View of American Literature.* Carbondale: Southern Illinois Univ. Press, 1969.

————, Ed. *Henry James: Seven Stories and Studies.* New York: Appleton-Century-Crofts, 1961.

Stubbs, John C. *The Pursuit of Form: A Study of Hawthorne and the Romance.* Urbana: Univ. of Illinois Press, 1970.

Stuckey, W. J. *Caroline Gordon.* New York: Twayne, 1972.

Sullivan, Walter. *Death by Melancholy: Essays on Modern Southern Fiction.* Baton Rouge: Louisiana State Univ. Press, 1972.

Szanto, George H. *Narrative Consciousness: Structure and Perception in the Fiction of Kafka, Beckett, and Robbe-Grillet.* Austin: Univ. of Texas Press, 1972.

Taylor, Larry E. *Pastoral and Anti-Pastoral Patterns in John Updike's Fiction.* Carbondale: Southern Illinois Univ. Press, 1971.

Tedlock, E. W. *D. H. Lawrence: Artist and Rebel.* Albuquerque: Univ. of New Mexico Press, 1963.

Thompson, Lawrance. *Melville's Quarrel with God.* Princeton: Princeton Univ. Press, 1952.

Tillett, Margaret. *Stendhal: The Background to the Novels.* New York: Oxford Univ. Press, 1971.

Tindall, William Y. *A Reader's Guide to James Joyce.* New York: Noonday, 1959.

Tobias, Richard C. *The Art of James Thurber.* Athens: Ohio Univ. Press, 1969.

Tompkins, Jane P., Ed. *Twentieth Century Interpretations of "The Turn of the Screw" and Other Tales.* Englewood Cliffs: Prentice-Hall, 1970.

Trilling, Lionel. *The Experience of Literature.* New York: Holt, Rinehart & Winston, 1967.

Turner, Darwin T. *In a Minor Chord: Three Afro-American Writers and Their Search for Identity.* Carbondale: Southern Illinois Univ. Press, 1971.

Utley, Francis L., Lynn Z. Bloom, and Arthur F. Kinney, Eds. *Bear, Man, and God: Seven Approaches to William Faulkner's "The Bear."* New York: Random House, 1964; 2nd ed., retitled . . . *Eight Approaches.* . . . New York: Random House, 1971.

Vickery, John B., Ed. *Myth and Literature: Contemporary Theory and Practice.* Lincoln: Univ. of Nebraska Press, 1966.

Vickery, John B., and J'nan M. Sellery, Eds. *The Scapegoat: Ritual and Literature.* Boston: Houghton Mifflin, 1972.

Vickery, Olga W. *The Novels of William Faulkner: A Critical Interpretation.* Baton Rouge: Louisiana State Univ. Press, 1959.

Vincent, Howard P., Ed. *Twentieth Century Interpretations of "Billy Budd."* Englewood Cliffs: Prentice-Hall, 1971.

Walcutt, Charles. *American Literary Naturalism: A Divided Stream.* Minneapolis: Univ. of Minnesota Press, 1956.

Waldmeir, Joseph J., Ed. *Recent American Fiction: Some Critical Views.* Boston: Houghton Mifflin, 1963.

Walton, Geoffrey. *Edith Wharton: A Critical Interpretation.* Cranbury: Fairleigh Dickinson Univ. Press, 1970.

Warren, Robert P. *Selected Essays.* New York: Random House, 1958.

———, Ed. *Faulkner: A Collection of Critical Essays.* Englewood Cliffs: Prentice-Hall, 1966.

Weaver, Raymond, Ed. *The Shorter Novels of Herman Melville.* New York: Liveright, 1928.

Webb, Eugene. *Samuel Beckett: A Study of His Novels.* Seattle: Univ. of Washington Press, 1970.

Wertheim, Stanley, Ed. *Studies in "Maggie" and "George's Mother."* Columbus: Charles E. Merrill, 1970.

Wescott, Glenway. *Images of Truth: Remembrances and Criticism.* New York: Harper & Row, 1962.

West, Ray B. *The Art of Writing Fiction.* New York: Crowell, 1968.

West, Ray B., and Robert W. Stallman, Eds. *The Art of Modern Fiction.* New York: Rinehart, 1949.

Westbrook, Max. *Walter Van Tilburg Clark.* New York: Twayne, 1969.

Whitaker, Thomas R. *William Carlos Williams.* New York: Twayne, 1968.

Widmer, Kingsley. *The Art of Perversity.* Seattle: Univ. of Washington Press, 1962.

————. *The Ways of Nihilism: A Study of Melville's Short Novels.* Los Angeles: California State Colleges, 1970.

Wilgus, D. K., Ed. *Folklore International: Essays in Traditional Literature, Belief, and Custom in Honor of Wayland Debs Hand.* Hatboro: Folklore Associates, 1967.

Willen, Gerald, Ed. *A Casebook on Henry James's "The Turn of the Screw."* New York: Crowell, 1960; 2nd ed. 1969.

————, Ed. *Washington Square.* New York: Crowell, 1970.

Williams, Raymond. *George Orwell.* New York: Viking, 1971.

Winner, Viola H. *Henry James and the Visual Arts.* Charlottesville: Univ. Press of Virginia, 1970.

Wisse, Ruth R. *The Schlemiel As Modern Hero.* Chicago: Univ. of Chicago Press, 1971.

Woodress, James. *Willa Cather: Her Life and Art.* New York: Pegasus, 1970.

Woodson, Thomas, Ed. *Twentieth Century Interpretations of "The Fall of the House of Usher."* Englewood Cliffs: Prentice-Hall, 1969.

Wylder, Delbert. *Hemingway's Heroes.* Albuquerque: Univ. of New Mexico Press, 1969.

Young, Philip. *Ernest Hemingway.* New York: Rinehart, 1952; 2nd ed. University Park: Pennsylvania State Univ. Press, 1966.

INDEX OF SHORT STORY WRITERS

WHEN LAMBS
CRY

BY
LINDA JACKSON

Copyright ©2008 by Linda Jackson

Library of Congress Control Number: 20079412567

ISBN 978-0971644267

Printed in the U.S.A.
Jackson Publishing
Southaven, Mississippi 38672

Cover art design by Olivia Jackson

www.jacksonbooks.com

For Jeff, Olivia, Chloe, and Benjamin

...always

CONTENTS

SPOILED CITY KID

The dingy water kept Joshua Tanner from seeing the face belonging to the rough hands that held a grip around his throat. Another set of evil hands held his body in place. That face, too, was nameless. Joshua struggled with all his might, but his fight was futile. The strength of his ten-year-old body was no match for the powers that held him under the murky waters of the pond. His muscles wanted to give up, but his mind said no.

"Somebody, save me!" his mind cried out. When he could no longer hold his breath, the water began to seep into his nostrils. With one final breath of strength, Joshua swung his right arm as high as he could. His hand hit the face of the monster holding him by the throat. The hands let go, and Joshua sprang up out of the water.

Joshua found himself sitting straight up with his legs level. He focused his eyes, and his enemies were gone. He was no longer in the dark waters of the pond. He was home in bed, yet he was still soaked to the skin. He looked around, feeling shaky. The room was still dark, but he could see the first pink light of the morning pressing against the mini-blinds.

He had had that awful dream again, thanks to his little brother Caleb. Since Caleb had come down from Chicago and had been sleeping in Joshua's bed, Joshua had had that recurring nightmare. Joshua took the pillow that Caleb had obviously thrown over his head and tossed it angrily against the wall. Caleb threw his arm on Joshua's side of the bed, and Joshua knew instantly why he had dreamed of someone choking him.

Joshua threw the wet sheets off his legs and bundled them over Caleb. "Drown in your own wet sheets, you little stinkin' bed-wetter," he muttered.

He got up and grabbed a set of clothes from the dresser drawer. As he took the three steps from his bedroom to the bathroom, he could hear that his grandmother was snoring contentedly as usual. "Must be nice to have a dry bed!" he yelled toward her room as he entered the bathroom.

"I'm sick of that little baby wettin' my bed," Joshua mumbled as he peeled off his wet clothes. He took Caleb's Spider Man towel from the rack and dried himself with it. He then took the towel and wrapped it around the bundle of wet clothes, squeezing as much of the wetness out of the clothes and into the towel as possible. He hung the towel back in its place. "You should smell real fresh after your bath, little brother," he said scornfully. "That'll teach you for wettin' my bed."

After Joshua changed, he decided to finish out his morning on the sofa. It was only a week into summer vacation, and Joshua was looking forward to sleeping late, watching a few cartoons, then heading out with his best friend Marvin. But all that had changed in the last month.

Joshua and his grandmother Sadie Belle had not heard

from Joshua's mother since the night she dumped Joshua into Sadie Belle's lap and caught a Greyhound to Chicago. So when she phoned and said she would be coming to Mississippi, Joshua had mixed feelings of happiness and hatred. Secretly, he still wanted to go to Chicago and live with his mother, in spite of how much he loved his grandmother. But, his darker secret was that he still resented her for having abandoned him for so long in the first place.

His anxiety was unwarranted, however. He never got the opportunity to see his mother. She came while he was in school, dumped his seven-year-old brother Caleb and everything he ever owned at Sadie Belle's door, then caught the Greyhound back to Chicago.   Joshua had been too excited to concentrate at school the whole day, only to come home and find a newly acquired brother, rather than his mother, waiting for him.

Joshua's mind wouldn't allow him to sleep, so he lay on the sofa and looked around the living room, resenting its transformation. Before last month, his picture had dominated the walls and the tables. Now Caleb's pictures were everywhere.

"How can you just love him like that, Grandma" Joshua mumbled. "How can you just put his pictures all over the place like he's been here all the time," he muttered as he buried his face into a cushion.

He thought about all that had happened to him over the last few years, since the time he had almost been killed at the pond. Everybody had called him a hero when he remembered who had murdered Sandy Cassin. His picture had been in the paper, and he had been on the news. He had been famous, for a while.

And, of course, everybody felt sorry for him because they thought Marsha Hopkins had tried to kidnap him. He became popular at school, and he could get away with almost anything with the teachers. Everybody seemed to feel sorry for him and pamper him except his mother. Joshua was sure she had somehow heard about him through the news and would come running down to get him. But she never did. She just traumatized him more by bringing that spoiled little bed-wetter into his life.

Joshua awoke to the smell of Sadie Belle's coffee brewing and biscuits baking. He looked into the hallway and saw that the bathroom door was closed. The bed-wetter was up. The bathroom door opened, and Caleb came out, proudly displaying his Spider Man towel wrapped snugly around his body. Joshua smiled.

"Joshua, go pull the sheets from your bed, and let the mattress air out," Sadie Belle called from the kitchen.

"What!" Joshua answered, sitting up suddenly. "Caleb wet the bed. How come he can't take the sheets off?"

"You know Caleb ain't old enough to go down to the laundry mat and wash sheets," answered Sadie Belle.

"I got to wash 'em too!" Joshua yelled as he jumped from the sofa. "Ughhh!" he moaned and stamped his foot.

"Caleeeb! Pull the sheets off the bed!" Joshua ordered.

"Granny told you!" Caleb yelled back.

Joshua stormed toward the bedroom and found the door locked. He kicked the door with his barefoot and yelled at Caleb again because he had hurt his toe. When Caleb opened the door, Joshua pushed him to the floor as he walked toward the bed. He yanked the wet sheets off the bed and threw them

over Caleb's head.

"Lay off the liquids, you big baby!" he yelled.

Caleb jumped from under the wet sheets. "I'm not a baby!" he yelled back.

Joshua kicked at the sheets. "You think you're special 'cause you been in Chicago, don't you? If you was so special, you wouldn't be wettin' my bed every night."

"I don't wet the bed every night for your information," Caleb answered. "It's only when I drink Coke."

"Coke?" Joshua laughed. "We ain't even had Coke this week, you little snot nose. You couldn't hold water even if you was a brand new bucket!" he said, laughing in Caleb's face.

"At least I can talk right, country bumpkin!" Caleb said as he quickly ran from the room before Joshua could say another word. He knew that Joshua wouldn't dare taunt him in Sadie Belle's presence.

In Sadie Belle's eyes, Caleb was worse off than Joshua. She felt that it was far worse for a child to have thought he had his mother's love, then be abandoned, than to have never known what her love felt like at all.

"I fixed you some biscuits and grits this morning," Sadie Belle called to Caleb who had parked himself cross-legged on the floor in front of the TV.

"Thank you, Granny," Caleb replied. "Can I eat them in here while I watch cartoons?"

Sadie Belle hesitated for a moment. She had always adhered to a strict rule of sitting at the table while eating.

"I promise not to drop anything," Caleb reassured her.

"You never let me eat in front of the TV," Joshua quickly pointed out as he entered the living room.

"He's just a baby, Joshua," Sadie Belle answered, "just like you were when you were seven."

"Is that why he's still wettin' the bed?" Joshua taunted as he dropped the wet sheets into a pillow case.

"You can eat in the living room, Caleb" said Sadie Belle.

"That ain't fair!" Joshua exclaimed. "Grandma, Caleb is just tryin' to make a fool out of you. He ain't as sweet and innocent as he pretends to be. Ask him what he used to do in Chicago."

"You better watch your mouth, Joshua Tanner!" Sadie Belle answered back. "I know full well what this boy went through in Chicago. You think I don't?"

Joshua turned his face from Sadie Belle's. He was sick of her feeling sorry for Caleb. All she could think of was how their mother had moved Caleb from one roach-infested apartment to the next, trying to stay ahead of the police and drug dealers. She didn't seem to notice what a spoiled brat he was. She didn't seem to notice that he had enough clothes to outfit every kid in the neighborhood. She didn't seem to notice how chubby he was from all the fast food he had been eating. So much for being neglected. Caleb was nothing more than a spoiled city kid who had been picking pockets for his mother since the age of three.

"You need to worry about getting them sheets washed, Mr. Know-it-all," said Sadie Belle. "Go on put 'em in the washer and get back here and eat."

Joshua walked out, taking his chances by slamming the door behind him. As soon as he was done with breakfast and washing Caleb's stinky sheets, he would get with Marvin and come up with a plan to make the spoiled city kid pay for messing up his life.

The Preacher's Kid

"I think the verse you're looking for is Romans 3:23, 'For all have sinned and fall short of the glory of God'. That's the New King James Version," came the taunting voice from the back of the room.

Terrence McGee didn't have to look up from his Bible. He knew the voice all too well. He knew it was Basil, the preacher's kid. He never failed to make Terrence look inept during Bible study.

Since coming to the Youth Correctional Facility, Terrence McGee had been diligent in studying the Bible given to him by his social worker, Mrs. Greenwald. Although he had memorized a lot of scripture and had been leading one of the morning group studies for several months, he still found himself no match for the heckling Basil Jamerson III, wayward son of the Reverend Basil Jamerson II, Senior Pastor of the 4000-member Living Waters Christian Center. His grandfather, the Reverend Basil Jamerson I, had been the founder of the Living Waters Christian Center. Basil, the Third, thought they should rename the church, the Jamerson Center. Every Jamerson living within a 60-mile radius of the

city was a member, and head of this committee or that committee. Basil reasoned he would rather be in prison than to be doomed to be their next Senior Pastor.

Terrence knew that Basil was not interested in the group studies. He simply came to win favor with the chaplain, who, in turn, could win him favor with the guards. Basil had observed how Terrence had gone from being the mistrusted foster kid from the projects to being a trusted role model for the other boys by applying himself to his Bible studies and anger management sessions. He also knew that Basil's only interest in attending the studies was to earn the privilege of participating in an offsite work duty.

"Thank you, Brother Basil," Terrence replied with all the humility he could muster.

"No problem, Brother Preacher," said Basil. "It was my pleasure," he added, as he nudged Ron in the side. "I could see you were struggling a bit. Just wanted to help a brother out."

The other twelve boys gathered around the three tables in the recreation room began to laugh. Unlike Terrence, they seemed to enjoy Basil's attempt at comedy. Most of them also saw Bible study as a way to impress the guards rather than a way to transform their lives.

"Romans 3:23, 'For all have sinned, and *come* short of the glory of God'," Terrence repeated over the laughter. "*Old King James Version,*" he added, without turning a page of his Bible. "When the apostle Paul wrote this letter-"

"That's 'a-po-sel'," Basil interrupted.

"Excuse me," said Terrence.

"The 't' is silent," said Basil. "You said 'a-pos-tle'."

"Basil!" came the stern voice of the guard on duty. "You

have five minutes left in this room. Be quiet and let Terrence finish the study."

Basil waved his hands innocently. "My apologies to the Preacher," he said. "I just don't want the people misled. I've seen enough of that in my lifetime."

"In light of our limited time," said Terrence. "We'll go ahead and close with a word of prayer. Before our next study, please read the first chapter of the book of James."

After Terrence's prayer, the fourteen juvenile offenders filed out of the room, led and followed by guards.

"You better lay off Terrence a bit," Ron whispered to Basil as they headed to their morning carpentry class. Each inmate was required to choose a career path and take the required courses, in hopes that when they were released they would have a useful skill to contribute to society. Both Ron and Basil had chosen carpentry, not because they enjoyed building, but because they were both continually trying to come up with a plan to escape. Basil had been using most of his free time in the library, secretly reading any articles he could find on prison escapes. He had concluded that the ones who managed an escape were skilled at fashioning tools which they had used in their escape.

"Keep that up, and the guards will know you're not really interested in Bible study," Ron said under his breath.

"I can't help it," Basil whispered back. "Terrence McGee is an idiot. He doesn't know the Bible from a Mother Goose rhyme. He reminds me of my daddy, always trying to be perfect. Preach, preach, preach. That's all they do," he said, scornfully. "Heads in the clouds. Need to come back to earth. Come back to reality. There's more to life than quoting the Bible."

"Yeah, like gettin' outta this joint," Ron said as he raised his hand for a high-five.

"I hear ya', bro'," said Basil, slapping Ron's hand.

"There ain't no way y'all gettin' outta here," Allen Smith interrupted as he poked his head between their shoulders. He was also on his way to the carpentry class. Like Ron and Terrence, Allen was serving time for the murder of Sandy Cassin. They had all held on to the idea that since they were juveniles, they would not be tried and sentenced as adults. They had held on to their motto of "one for all and all for one". They all found themselves serving life sentences, with the first years at a correctional facility for juveniles until they reached the age of 21.

After the sentencing, Allen had tried to convince the judge that he and Terrence were innocent, that Ron and Jay had done the killing, that they were just at the scene. But by that time, the confessions and been made and recorded. There was no turning back.

"They got too many cameras up in here," Allen said. "A fly couldn't get out without being detected."

"I don't know about Ron, but I think I'm smarter than a fly," Basil whispered back.

"Yeah, that's how you got locked up in the first place," said Allen.

"I'm in here for the same reason you claim to be," said Basil. "Being in the wrong place at the wrong time, hanging with a bunch of losers like you."

TELLING SECRETS

From behind thick-lensed glasses, Marvin Carter squinted at his best friend Joshua. "What took you so long?" he asked as he looked up at the nearly noonday sun. "It's almost twelve."

Joshua nodded toward Caleb. "I had to wash sheets this morning." He stared at Caleb, trying hard to intimidate him. "I wish he'd get lost. I'm tired of him following me."

Marvin shrugged. "You wanna go to the gravel pit?"

"I don't care," Joshua replied. "My shadow's gonna follow me everywhere anyway."

"The gravel pit's dangerous," Caleb interjected. "Granny told you not to go there. I heard her."

"Shut up!" Joshua yelled. He gave Caleb's shoulder a hard punch.

"Leave me alone before I tell Marvin what you do every night," Caleb threatened.

"Be quiet before I bust your nose, you big baby," Joshua said.

"At least I don't kiss the mirror every night and pretend

it's a girl!" Caleb said, rolling his eyes and sticking his tongue out.

"You liar!" Joshua screamed as he reached for the collar of Caleb's T-shirt. Caleb pulled away and ran back toward the apartment. Joshua chased him, but Caleb reached the apartment door before Joshua caught him. He stuck out his tongue one last time and rushed inside.

"I haaate him," Joshua moaned as he returned to Marvin.

Marvin thought he saw tears forming in Joshua's eyes. "We don't have to go to the gravel pit right now if you don't want to. We can go play PlayStation or watch TV or something."

"I don't care," Joshua shrugged. "I wish I didn't ever have to see that little punk again," he groaned. He stopped walking and sat on the edge of the sidewalk and stretched his legs out along the speed bump in front of him. "How come my crack head mama didn't just keep him in Chicago?"

Marvin sat down on the hot sidewalk. "I didn't believe what he said about you kissing the mirror."

Joshua pulled a weed growing out of the sidewalk and angrily threw it into the street. "I hate her too. I hate her more than I hate him. And wherever my daddy is, I hate him too."

"Sometimes I feel that way about my daddy too," said Marvin. "I only get to see him on some weekends."

"Grandma thinks Caleb is all that. But he ain't. He didn't tell her how he used to steal for his mama. That's how she got her drug money."

"My daddy drinks beer," said Marvin. "He drinks it while he's driving too. He got pulled over one day and got a DUI."

"If I could just get that little punk one good time,"

Joshua pondered. He stared blankly into the direction of the woods. "One good time," he repeated absent-mindedly.

Marvin looked toward the woods. He made no more comments.

A WEEK AWAY FROM PRISON

Basil leaned over on his stool to whisper to Allen while the carpentry instructor had his back turned for a moment. He wasn't too concerned about the armed guard who stood at the door; everyone had heard how he never paid much attention to his surroundings. His mind was always thousands of miles away in Iraq where his wife was at war.

"You see," Basil whispered to Allen, "I did something dumb. I got myself locked in this place like a brainless fly, but I won't be wandering around like one, looking for a way out. I have motivation. I'm only a week away from prison."

"You turn twenty-one next week?" Allen asked with shock.

Basil nodded.

Allen nudged Ron. "Basil will be twenty-one next week," he whispered.

The carpentry instructor began again, and Basil sat up to attention. Allen nudged him on the arm and held up two fin-

gers on one hand and one finger on the other. His face still held a questioning look. Basil nodded and mouthed the words, "State pen. I've got to get out."

Skyscrapers, Six flags, and Secret Places

Sadie Belle had called for Joshua to come home shortly after one o'clock because Caleb was bored and needed someone to play with. He didn't want to go to outside because he said it was too hot. Joshua had suggested they play the quiet game in his room since Sadie Belle was watching soap operas. Caleb would start talking just ten seconds after Joshua would give the "go" signal, so Joshua knew the game was pointless. Joshua fumed as he sat on the floor of his bedroom listening to Caleb rattle on and on about Chicago and *his mom*. Caleb sat on the floor, right next to the door, probably to make an easy escape in case Joshua decided to take a swing at him again.

"You ever seen the Sears Tower?" Caleb asked. "It's the tallest building in the whole world."

Joshua rolled his eyes. He didn't know that Sears even had a tower. As a matter of fact, he had never been inside a Sears store. The tallest building he had ever seen was a hos-

pital in Jackson when he was with Joe and Marsha.

"They call it a skyscraper because it can almost touch the sky," Caleb continued. "If we stacked up this apartment a hundred times, we still couldn't reach the top of it."

"What about the rat trap you and your mama lived in?" Joshua snapped. "Did it scrape the sky too?"

"I'm telling Granny you're teasing me," Caleb said, placing his hand on the door knob.

"I was just kidding," Joshua added quickly. "You don't have to go running to Grandma all the time. Nobody likes a tattletale."

The two sat quietly for a few moments, then Joshua asked, "What other tall buildings they got in Chicago?"

Caleb released his grip on the doorknob. He scratched his head as if in thought. He didn't know of any other tall buildings in Chicago. Truthfully, he had never seen the Sears Tower either; he had only heard about it. But, he would never let Joshua know that. He could never let Joshua know that the only tall buildings he had seen in Chicago were the tenement housing projects where he and he mother moved about all too frequently. He wished that for once, just once, he could have gone downtown and seen the Sears Tower and all the other things his mother would promise him when her mind was sober. All he ever saw were tall buildings with busted-out, boarded-up windows.

"There's a big store in Chicago called Macy's," Caleb said. "That's where Mom bought all my clothes."

Joshua grunted and rolled his eyes. Fred's Dollar Store was where Sadie Belle bought all his clothes.

"That's where I got these Jordan's," Caleb added, extending his right foot so that Joshua could admire his barely-

worn shoes. Just a week prior to getting his prized shoes, Caleb had narrowly escaped after stealing a wallet from a teenager, who was loitering with his friends outside a convenience store. Caleb had approached the group of teens under the pretense that he needed a few dollars to buy milk for his baby sister. When the teen took out his wallet, Caleb grabbed it and ran as fast as he could. He was probably the fastest kid in Chicago. His mother had promised she would use some of the money to buy him something special as his reward. Caleb had told her he wanted a pair of shoes. His mother bought him a pair dirt cheap from a street hustler who sold stolen items from Macy's.

"Chicago got Six Flags?" Joshua asked.

"Of course we got Six Flags," Caleb smugly assured him. "I've been lots a times. Everybody's been to Six Flags."

Joshua hadn't. He slumped lower on the floor. He thought about how close he had come to seeing Disney World, if only Marsha hadn't messed up. Then he despised Caleb even more.

"We got something better than Six Flags. You wanna go play there with me and Marvin this evening when it's not too hot?" Joshua asked.

"Where? The gravel pit?" Caleb asked.

"Nope, we got somewhere even better," answered Joshua.

"Where?"

"It's a secret place."

"Tell me," pleaded Caleb. "I won't tell Granny."

"Do you wanna go or not?"

"Yes," Caleb answered, his eyes rounding with excitement.

"Then you just have to wait and find out, and you can't even tell Grandma nothing about it, not even that we're going. Okay?"

"Okay," Caleb replied.

"Now, you wait right here while I go to Grandma's room and call Marvin."

"Okay," said Caleb.

"And don't tell Grandma nothing, or the deal is off. You hear?"

"I hear," Caleb answer.

Joshua sneaked right past Sadie Belle, whose eyes were glued to the TV. He hastily dialed Marvin's number. Marvin answered after the first ring. Joshua announced, "It's time to ditch the snitch."

THE LIE THAT BINDS

"I know you ain't writin' that loser again," Allen teased
as he leaned over Terrence's shoulder.

Terrence looked up from his yellow notepad and held his
pen still for a moment. He had not been aware that the shade
from the tree under which he sat had shifted to the other side
and left him exposed to the afternoon sun. He sat cross-
legged on the ground with his notepad in his lap, which is
how he spent most of what was mockingly known as free
time in the correctional facility.

"No, I'm not writing a loser," Terrence answered. "I'm
writing Jay."

"Why? He'll just pretend he can't read it, so he can stay
locked up in the crazy house and not have to do time like the
rest of us."

"Ms. Rita can read it to him," Terrence answered, as he
observed a group of inmates playing three-on-three basketball.

"Tell him I got something for him the next time I see
him," Allen said sarcastically.

"Seeing that you're serving a life sentence, I don't think

Jay has anything to worry about."

Allen replied, "Just wait. One day somebody'll be smart enough to figure out that Jay ain't crazy. The rest of us are just foolish enough to serve time for his crime."

"We're all guilty," Terrence said.   .

"Yeah, yeah, yeah, I know all about that stuff you talked about this morning, about all people have sinned," Allen answered with a short temper. He leaned against the tree, crossed his arms, and looked up at the sky. "Basil and Ron say they're gonna escape." Terrence didn't respond. "If they find a way, I should go with them," Allen continued. He waited a few seconds for a response from Terrence, but Terrence was still silent. "I mean, I didn't really do nothing, you know. Ron helped Jay kill Sandy."

Terrence placed his notepad and pen on the ground and stood next to Allen. "Whose idea was it to shut Sandy up? Who wanted to scare her?"

Allen didn't answer. That had been his idea, he suddenly remembered. Of the foursome, he and Jay had been best friends. Jay seemed to understand Allen's pain when Allen's father was killed in a car accident. They were both being raised by hard-working single mothers who did their best, but always seemed to fall short somewhere. Maybe Terrence was right about that thing about all have sinned and fall short, Allen thought.

When Sandy Cassin was mocking Jay and torturing him about the drug money he owed her boyfriend, Allen had become even more irate than Jay. He remembered that he had always tried to be Jay's protector. He remembered how weak and troubled Jay had been even before that dreadful day at the pond.

"They say he's a paranoid schizophrenic," Allen said matter-of-factly.

"Yeah, that's what Ms. Rita said," Terrence replied. "They don't know if he'll ever get better after what happened." Terrence shook his head. "I wouldn't want to be him."

Allen grunted. "Him? Man, I don't wanna be *me*." He stuffed his hands in the back pockets of his pants. "I wish I'd of been smart like my little brother, Timmy. Made all A's last year. At least Mama got one son she can be proud of."

Terrence stared silently at the ground.

"He won't even come see me," Allen added, as he stared at the ground too. "He tells his friends that he doesn't have a brother."

Allen stubbed a piece of grass into the ground with his foot. It reminded him of when he would sneak and smoke cigarettes with Ron, and they would smash the butts on the sidewalk. At the time it made him feel cool. Now, it just made him feel stupid.

"At least your mama comes to see you," Terrence said. "I haven't heard from my folks in ten years, since they left when I was seven."

"What about that guy, Jesse, your foster pop?"

Terrence shrugged. "You know that clown got locked up. Robbed somebody."

"Yeah. I forgot."

"But I still got Ms. Greenwald," Terrence added. "If it wasn't for her, I'd probably be worse off than I am."

"How can you be worse off, bro'? You're in prison!"

"I could be without hope," Terrence answered.

"Hope in what? Gettin' outta here?"

"Naw, man, hope in Jesus."

Allen rolled his eyes and threw up his hands. "Aw! Here we go again!" he exclaimed. "Do you have to bring God into everything?"

"God *is* everything," Terrence answered.

"Then how come he didn't keep your butt from gettin' locked up?"

"Because I'm guilty."

"You didn't kill anybody."

"I was there. I knew about it. I didn't try to stop anybody. I helped cover up the crimes. I'm guilty."

"Well I ain't," Allen answered with strong conviction. "I didn't do nothing to deserve being locked up."

Terrence shook his head. "The lie that binds, man. The lie that binds."

"The lie was pleading guilty when I wasn't," Allen said. "I should've plea bargained or something."

Terrence shook his head and laughed. "Naw, Allen. The lie was believing we could fix things ourselves. Jay should-n've been foolish enough to think anybody could get his brothers out of prison. He saw where dealing drugs got them, then he turned around and did the same thing." Terrence shook his head again. "That was dumb, man."

Allen slumped back on the ground and stared at his prison garb. It seemed only a short time ago that he had hounded his mom for name-brand clothes, begging her not to get him anything from Goodwill. He had burdened her in vain, he now realized. Here he was in a place where every-body wore the same thing, bright orange pants and a bright orange shirt, every day.

"Can you say a prayer for me?" he asked, almost mum-

bling, without looking up at Terrence.

"Sure," Terrence answered as he joined Allen and sat cross-legged on the ground.

"Pray that Timmy will keep his head on straight. Keep his head in his books and don't give my mama any trouble."

"Yeah, we can pray right now," said Terrence.

"Naw, dawg," answered Allen with a chuckle. "You pray in your cell or something. I don't want everybody thinking I lost my mind, out here praying and junk, looking like some Jesus freak."

"Yeah, I can see I need to throw in a good word for you too," said Terrence.

"That's cool," Allen shrugged. "Say a prayer for my mama too."

"I got your whole family covered," Terrence answered, "even your old racist granddaddy."

"Man, leave my granddaddy alone. He don't know no better. He was born and raised a hater, and he gone die a hater."

Terrence shrugged. "That's what I thought about me 'til I learned to put my trust in Jesus."

Allen let out a long, exasperated sigh. He rolled his eyes and crossed his arms. "Just say the prayers that I asked you, okay?"

"Okay," Terrence said, throwing up his hands as if in defense.

"You need to finish your letter," Allen said. "I'm gonna use my last few minutes to shoot some hoops. And don't waste any praying time on my granddaddy," he added, as he rushed away toward the basketball court.

MISCHIEF AND MAYHEM

The scent of Sadie Belle's neighborhood-famous corn-bread and candied yams filled the apartment. But even the temptation of crispy cornbread and syrupy sweet potatoes couldn't keep Joshua from carrying out his afternoon plan of mischief and mayhem. He wasn't worried that Caleb would be tempted by the mouth-watering Southern cuisine. His stomach still craved the junk his mother had fed him in Chicago. Besides, Caleb was too excited about the secret expedition that Joshua had planned for them to care about food.

"Has the sun cooled off yet?" Caleb had asked Joshua every five minutes.

"I told you it'll be time when *Oprah* goes off," Joshua would answer in a whisper, reminding Caleb to keep quiet. Caleb would then proceed to ask Sadie Belle whether *Oprah* was on yet.

"I never saw a little boy that likes *Oprah* so much," Sadie Belle replied. "I'll let you know when it's on."

Caleb was still not satisfied. He continued to rotate between Joshua and Sadie Belle, asking the same two questions.

When *Oprah* finally came on, Caleb fidgeted while Joshua watched his favorite show. During the last commercial break, Joshua called Marvin. "Meet us at the path at five after five," he said.

"Grandma, me and Caleb going out to play," Joshua yelled into the kitchen. "We know to be back before dark, so you don't have to call for us."

"Where y'all going, Joshua?" Sadie Belle asked.

At first Joshua thought to answer, "to play at Marvin's", but he remembered Sadie Belle's habit of calling to check on him. "Down by the basketball goal," he answered, knowing Sadie Belle would never walk that far to check on them.

"Y'all stay away from them big boys, Joshua," Sadie Belle admonished. "They keep up too much mess."

"Yes, ma'am," Joshua answered.

"And don't be gone too long and let your supper get cold," Sadie Belle added.

"I like my food cold!" Joshua yelled as he and Caleb escaped from the apartment.

At exactly five after five, Joshua and Caleb met Marvin at the path that led into the woods. Joshua and Marvin looked as adventurous as Tom Sawyer and Huck Finn in their cut-off blue jeans and battered gym shoes, while Caleb sported a pair of khaki shorts and Jordans, looking much like the spoiled city kid which Joshua had taken him to be.

"The woods!" Caleb exclaimed with disdain. "Is that the big surprise? You think this is better than Six Flags?"

Marvin gave Joshua a puzzled look.

Joshua shook his head. "It's a long story," he said to

Marvin. "Look, lil' bro'," he said, "which would you rather do, watch the news with Grandma or go look for buried treasure in the woods?"

Marvin squinted at Joshua.

"What kind of buried treasure?" Caleb asked with suspicion. "Like in the movies?"

"Better," answered Joshua.

"How?" asked Caleb.

"This treasure was hid by a slave a long time ago," Joshua answered, nudging Marvin with his elbow.

"Slaves didn't have money!" exclaimed Caleb.

"This slave did," replied Joshua.

"How?"

"Here's the scoop," answered Joshua. "Over a hundred years ago, this whole place was a big cotton plantation, except the woods, you see. This slave named Arthur stole a big bag of money from the master's house one day. Then he hid it in these here woods, you see."

Caleb crossed his arms and stared at Joshua. "You're just lying!" he yelled. "They didn't name people Arthur in slavery times."

Joshua rolled his eyes. Marvin stifled a laugh.

"Well, that's the name Grandma told me," Joshua replied. "His name might've been Kunta Kinte. But that ain't the point. The point is that he buried his treasure 'cause he planned to escape on the Underground Railroad the next day."

Caleb shook his head. "I didn't see a railroad anywhere around here."

Joshua groaned. "It's not a real railroad, little dumb one. They just called it that. Didn't they teach you anything in

Chicago?"

"Can we get back to the story?" Marvin asked. His eyes had grown large with interest.

"But, that night, the master knew somebody had stole some money. Arthur, or Kunta Kinte, was the only man slave who worked in the house. He was like the butler, and the butler is always the first one suspected.

But, when the master questioned him, he said, 'I don' know 'nuddin 'bout no money, Suh,' so the master beat him 'cause he knew he was lying. The master kept beatin' him trying to get him to confess. But, by the time Ar-, I mean Kunta Kinte, confessed, the master had beat him to death. So he couldn't show nobody where the treasure was. They searched the woods but never found the treasure."

Caleb stared at Joshua and shook his head.

"The treasure's still out there," Joshua said.

"If it is, the money is all crumbled up by now," said Caleb.

"It was in coins, not dollar bills, silly" said Joshua. "And if I'm lyin', I'm dyin'," he said, crossing his heart.

"I don't believe you, but I'll go anyway," Caleb said.

"How we gonna dig it up?" asked Marvin. "We don't have a shovel."

Joshua punched Marvin hard on the shoulder.

"I knew it!" Caleb cried. "I knew you were lying all the time!"

"Whatever, chump!" Joshua said angrily. "I don't care if you don't go, you big baby. Go on back and watch the news with Grandma for all I care."

"You can't tell me what to do," answered Caleb. "You're not the boss of me. I can go to the woods if I want."

"Not if we don't let you," Joshua said.

"You can't stop me," said Caleb, as he brushed past Joshua and headed toward the path.

Joshua smiled victoriously at Marvin. Marvin shrugged his shoulders and looked confused. "What now?" he whispered.

"Plan Ditch the Snitch is now in action," Joshua announced.

"So what's all this about a buried treasure?" Marvin asked in a hushed tone as he and Joshua followed Caleb along the path. "I thought we were just gonna play hide and go seek."

Joshua watched Caleb walk cautiously along the path, shoving overgrown vines out of his way as he pushed through. "That was just because little dumb one didn't want to come. I had to think of something to get him in here."

"He didn't believe you any way," said Marvin as he fanned pesky bugs away from his arms and legs. "Who would believe a crazy story like that any way?"

"You did!" Joshua exclaimed, laughing and pointing a finger at Marvin. "You thought it was true, didn't you?"

"Naw, I knew you were lying too," Marvin replied. "Slaves didn't live on this land anyway. The house would still be here if it had been a plantation a long time ago."

"It got burned down in the Civil War," Joshua said. "I guess you don't know nothing about history either."

Marvin shook his head. "You lie entirely too much, Joshua Tanner."

"I don't lie," Joshua replied. "I just have a good imagination."

Caleb stopped and turned around to face Joshua and

Marvin. He crossed his arms defiantly. "So what we plan to do in these boring old woods anyway?" he asked. "And don't say look for buried treasure either."

"Play hide and go seek," Marvin answered.

"Hide and seek!" Caleb shrieked. "That baby game!"

"When you play in the woods, it ain't a baby game," Marvin replied. "Being in the woods makes it harder to find people."

"Yeah, Caleb," Joshua chimed in. "Being in the woods makes it harder 'cause you gotta look out for snakes and stuff too while you try to find us."

"While *I* try to find *you*?" Caleb asked. "Why do I have to be it? I want to go hide."

"Me and Marvin already know these woods, and we would find you in a minute," Joshua answered. "It'll be better if we hide and you seek."

Marvin nodded in approval. Caleb gave them both a skeptical look, but agreed to be the seeker.

"You know how to play, don't you?" Joshua asked.

"Anybody can play hide and seek," replied Caleb. "You stand at the base, close your eyes, and count to ten."

"That may be the Chicago way, but here in Mississippi we count to a hundred," Joshua said with a devilish grin.

"A hundred! That'll take too long!" Caleb retorted.

Joshua waved his arms around. "Look at all these trees, lil' bro'," he said. "You think we can hide in ten seconds?"

"You said you already know these woods," Caleb answered.

"Well, we can't hide right around the next tree from where you countin', can we?" Joshua asked. "You'd find us in a second. What kinda fun is that?"

"Okaaay," Caleb said with a groan. "I'll count to one hundred."

"And you gotta sing the hide and go seek song," Marvin added.

"What song?" asked Caleb.

"You know, 'Last night, night before, twenty-four robbers at my door. I got up and let 'em in. Hit 'em in the head with a rollin' pin.'," Marvin sang.

"Yeah, you gotta sing the song too," Joshua chimed in.

"I'll be *it* forever if I have to sing that dumb song and count to a hundred," Caleb said with a long sigh.

"Okay, you can count to fifty," said Marvin.

"Noooo!" exclaimed Joshua. "A hundred. He gotta count to a hundred," he said to Marvin with a wink.

"Oh, yeah, I forgot," Marvin responded. "You gotta count to a hundred."

"Whatever!" Caleb shouted. "Let's just play before it gets dark, and we have to go home."

Joshua and Marvin smiled contentedly.

"But I won't sing that song," Caleb added.

The three boys went deeper into the woods to find a tree to use as the base. When the perfect tree was found, Caleb leaned against it, resting his face on his arm, and began counting. Joshua and Marvin snickered as they scampered hastily away, listening to Caleb's counting slowly fade.

"Now, let's see if that little corn flake brain can find his way home," Joshua announced to Marvin once they were out of hearing distance from Caleb.

Marvin stopped walking and turned to the direction where they had left Caleb counting. "You sure we oughta do this?" he asked. "By the time he gets to a hundred, he might

not remember how to get back."

Joshua shook his head in disbelief. "That's the whole point. We want him to get lost. Ditch the snitch, remember?"

Marvin looked scared. "I thought we were gonna hide somewhere and watch him wander around the woods a lil' bit."

"Is that what I told you?" Joshua asked with a laugh.

"Yes!" Marvin exclaimed. "You didn't say nothing about leaving him out here."

"Well, that's what I meant," Joshua sneered. He brushed past Marvin and headed back in the direction of the path.

"Wait, Josh!" Marvin called. "That's your little brother," he said almost tearfully.

Joshua stopped and turned around, stuffing his hands into the pockets of his cut-off jeans. "So," he shrugged. "It'll teach him to stop braggin' all the time."

"What if he can't find his way out?" asked Marvin. "How long we gon' leave him out here?"

"Forever, for all I care," Joshua answered.

Marvin turned around and headed back into the thick of the woods. "Where you goin'!" Joshua yelled.

"To get Caleb," Marvin answered without looking back.

"Ugggh!" Joshua screamed. He turned around and began stomping toward the path. He was now even more determined to pay Caleb back.

THE OUTSIDE WORLD

Not another announcement, Basil thought, as he and four other juvenile offenders sat in what was referred to as a conference room. Ron was there also, so Basil wondered what kind of trouble they must have been in. He had been good about keeping himself out of bad situations since his arrival at the correctional facility, but his friend Ron seemed to attract trouble like flowers attract bees.

"Act like you're good," he had told Ron, "and no one will ever suspect that escape is on your mind."

Basil hoped he didn't sound too much like his constantly preaching father, "Don't be misled: 'Bad company corrupts good character'," is what his father had quoted repeatedly from the Bible. There was never a conversation that didn't lead to a sermon. Basil Jamerson, the Second, couldn't open his mouth without preaching. Even when he whispered, which was rare, his voice boomed.

Basil hoped they were all proud of the product the Jamerson dynasty had produced. Of the "bad company" his father warned him about, he was the only one locked away in a juvenile correctional facility, awaiting shipment to the state pen

after his twenty-first birthday.

"You know what this is about?" Ron leaned over and asked Basil as the five of them assembled themselves around one of the tables in the conference room.

Basil shrugged. "Beats me," he answered. "You're here, so it can't be good news."

"Yeah, but Nerd Man is here too, so it can't be that bad," Ron replied. He was referring to a sixteen-year-old boy named Alden, who had once been a straight-A student, who went psycho on his parents, killing his father and critically injuring his mother, when they punished him for neglecting to study hard enough and failing a science test.

No one at the facility could understand how a boy as well-mannered as Alden could harm another person. He wouldn't even kill the roaches that sometimes crawled up the walls of his cell. He dutifully attended extra courses in addition to his required anger management and life skills courses. He ate the horrible cafeteria food without complaining; he never griped about the hot water running out after 30 seconds in the shower; nor did he ever grumble about the mandatory 5 A.M. physical training sessions four days a week, even though he was never able to complete the required 125 push-ups.

Some speculated that the pressure his parents had put on him to be perfect had driven him to insanity. Yet, the judge didn't buy his insanity plea. There he was, locked up with the rest of the juvenile delinquents who could have cared less about their grades or any other achievements in school. The judge had told him that he had had a choice to think before he acted, then sentenced him to life in prison.

Alden wrote his mother every day to tell her how sorry

he was. She never wrote back.

"Congratulations," the officer in charge of the meeting announced, "you five have been selected for an offsite work assignment."

Basil looked around the table. "Was this some kind of joke?" he thought. Sure, they had all put on a good show, but every one of them around the table was locked up for life, and three of them on murder charges.

"A church needs some repairs done, and the five of you were chosen," the officer continued.

Basil wanted badly to raise his hand and ask why, but he knew that would be foolish. This was just too good to be true - a trip to the outside world. He pinched Ron to make sure he wasn't dreaming.

"Ouw!" Ron moaned under his breath.

"You got something to say, young man?" asked the officer.

"No, Sir," Ron answered, rubbing his arm. He cut his eyes toward Basil, who was smiling. It wasn't a dream. He had earned the privilege of going offsite. That meant he must be looking as good as the Nerd Man, or even Terrence. If he had learned nothing else from his father, he had learned how to put on a good show.

VENGEANCE IS MINE

Joshua was bored silly. Sadie Belle had allowed Caleb to dominate the TV in the living room, so Joshua couldn't watch his favorite shows. The TV in Sadie Belle's bedroom displayed only the bottom half of the screen, so it was pointless to watch. Joshua hated reading, so that was out of the question. He wasn't talking to Marvin because he had double-crossed him in the woods the day before, so he couldn't go over and play video games. There was absolutely nothing to do except sit in his room, on the floor, and fume.

To make matters worse, he could hear Caleb singing dumb songs from the cartoon he was watching. For such a tough city kid, he sure did act like a big baby, Joshua thought. He could hear Sadie Belle going from room to room hurriedly cleaning before it was time for her to settle down with her afternoon soap operas. Everybody seemed to have a place except him.

He thought about Chicago. Though he had never been, he imagined that a life of pick-pocketing for his mother had to be more exciting than sitting around all summer with nothing to do. Joshua smiled wickedly when he thought about

how Caleb believed he was only visiting for the summer and would be heading back to Chicago when school started. "Big Dummy!" he said out loud. "She ain't never comin' back to get you!" he said, as he took his gym shoe from under his bed and threw it at the door.

Joshua got up and walked over to his window. "Grandma needs to dust," he grumbled as he opened the blinds. He saw Marvin throwing a football with another boy their age. Marvin had been his best friend since he could remember having a best friend. They had always covered for each other when necessary, with Marvin doing more covering than Joshua, since Joshua seemed to get into trouble more often.

Fortunately for Joshua, he and Marvin had been in the same class each year. Marvin loved to read, and he made good grades, all A's, as a matter of fact. Joshua, on the other hand, preferred TV and video games over books, and he had the grades to prove it. Joshua wondered whether he would even be going into fifth grade if Marvin had not been helping him do his homework since first grade.

"Traitor!" Joshua yelled, as he angrily closed the blinds. Marvin should have been on his side in the woods, he reasoned. He should understand what a pest Caleb is. If he wanted to get Caleb back he knew he would have to do it himself; he couldn't rely on Marvin for help.

"I'll get him back," Joshua grumbled under his breath. "I'll take him back out there myself, when it's almost dark, and leave him there," he said as he slumped back on the floor and crossed his arms over his chest. "Vengeance is mine," he whispered wickedly.

TICKET TO FREEDOM

Ruth Jones was not the ugliest baby born in 1990, but she came in close at second place. And, as she grew, she continued the winning streak in her elementary school, middle school, and high school.

Her mother, who had been crowned homecoming queen many years ago, searched diligently through the family albums to try to figure out where Ruth got her unfortunate looks. Ruth's father's family had been what society would call beautiful people as well, and even her two sisters, one older and one younger, were both gorgeous.

Ruth's older sister blamed her unattractiveness on what she termed "the curse of the middle child". She had read somewhere that the middle child suffered from some kind of syndrome, and she was convinced that Ruth's syndrome showed on her face. And, Diana's words seemed to have some merit. Ruth did have issues, starting with her name. Unlike Diana, who was named after her grandmother's favorite singer from a long time ago, and Ruth's younger sister Whitney, who was named after her mother's favorite singer from a long time ago, Ruth had been named by her aunt, after

her favorite Bible character.

Secondly, there was aptitude. Diana, although not necessarily the brightest light bulb in the box, did manage to maintain a low "B" average while being captain of her dance team and secretary of the student council. Whitney, a near genius, never ceased to amaze her parents with her almost perfect score in every class.

Then there was poor Ruth. Her grades resembled the weather predictions of a Canadian winter. Regardless of how hard she worked, she never seemed to measure up to the high academic standards which her sisters had set.

And, of course, the most obvious distinction among the three sisters was their looks. "Beauty is only skin deep," Ruth's aunt would tell her.

"Don't believe that lie," Whitney would, in turn, whisper in Ruth's ear.

Neither Diana or Whitney ever worried about a date for a dance. Their biggest problem had been which boy to turn down and which dress made them look the most flattering.

So, it was no wonder Ruth was so easily flattered when the charming young man from the Youth Correctional Facility told her she had beautiful eyes. She had never heard a compliment like that before. As a matter of fact, she had never heard a compliment, unless she considered, "Hey, aren't you Diana's sister?" a compliment.

Ruth was a receptionist at the same church where Basil, Ron, the Nerd Man, and two other young men from the correctional facility had been assigned to do repairs. She happened to be working the desk alone when the two armed security guards and the five prisoners entered the foyer of the church building.

Basil had gotten close enough to Ruth to stare into her eyes for a moment and tell her how beautiful they were. For Ruth, it was love at first sight. For Basil, he knew that this gullible-looking, plain Jane could be his ticket to freedom.

He had seen plenty of girls like Ruth, girls who never got a date, and could easily be swindled into a quick romance, if one could call it that. Basil was smart and smooth. He knew not to ask her name or say something lame like, "Drop me your seven digits." Those lines didn't work on even the gullible girls. He knew it was best to pay her a sincere sounding compliment, then leave her wondering for a while. Later he would steal a look at her, let her catch him looking, then quickly look away. That one always worked.

"Beautiful eyes?" Ron whispered as they walked toward the church's fellowship hall where the repairs were to be made. "Man, you better not mess up trying to hit on a church girl."

"Who knows church girls better than I do?" Basil asked in a whisper. "I've been around them all my life. I know how to handle them," he said. He leaned closer to Ron. "I've got a plan."

"A plan? What kinda plan?"

"A plan to get out of here," answered Basil.

Ron rolled his eyes. "How you gon' get outta here, fool? Try to run and get shot in the back?"

Basil shook his head. "Forget all that other stuff I told you about escaping. We don't need tools. I think that girl at the desk will be able to help us out real good."

Basil saw one of the guards looking his way. He stopped talking and gave Ron the be-quiet signal. Thanks to the church's old air conditioning system, the guards really could-

n't tell they were talking unless they looked at them and saw their mouths moving. The air conditioning system clanked so loudly that it drowned out their whispered voices. Still, they walked in silence down a darkened hallway that held classrooms. The hallway ended at the fellowship hall. An old man wearing wire-rimmed glasses was inside painting a wall. He stopped painting and came over and introduced himself to the guards. He was a deacon. He told the guards what repairs they wanted done, and the guards made assignments. Ron and Basil found themselves conveniently paired together. They would be building shelves in a closet.

A guard sat nearby. He was reading a magazine and drinking 7-Up from a bottle. He looked up periodically to check on his prisoners.

"I just read last week about an inmate who sweet-talked a woman who helped him escape," Basil said as he stretched a measuring tape from one corner of the walk-in closet to the other.

"And I guess you think you can do the same?" Ron asked.

"You don't know the whole story," said Basil. "See, this evangelistic team of men and women were coming to the prison to have church services on Sunday."

"Hold up," said Ron. "What's an evangelistic team?"

Basil shook his head. "I forgot I was talking to the unchurched. An evangelistic team is a group of crazy church folks who go out trying to save lost souls like yours."

"Like the people who come waking you up on Saturday morning," Ron sneered.

"Anyway," Basil sighed, "old prison dude starting showing interest in this weak-looking chick. The articles I

read called her a spinster."

Ron gave Basil a blank look.

"Dawg, a spinster is a woman who's getting up in age and still hadn't found a husband, like that chick at the front desk is gonna be one day."

Ron nodded in agreement.

"To make a long story short, the lady started writing between visits. Next thing you know, they're talking about marriage and all that junk when he gets out. But, dude was serving a life sentence and wasn't about to get out."

"So the chick gave him wings?" Ron interrupted.

"Let me tell the story, okay?"

Ron shrugged, took a peek at the guard, and went back to sanding the shelf he had cut.

"Anyway, he told the woman to go on and marry somebody else since he wasn't getting out any time soon. But the woman was so desperate that she sold everything she owned and took the money and arranged for the two of them to go to Mexico or somewhere like that."

"All that was in the paper?" asked Ron.

"Nah, the internet, CNN."

Ron shrugged.

"The next Sunday when the evangelistic team went to the prison, the chick insisted she needed to drive her own car. She said she had somewhere to go afterward. An hour after the church services, the prison noticed the old dude was missing."

"Dawg! Stop lying!" Ron cried.

The guard put down his magazine and looked up at Ron.

"My bad," Ron apologized.

"I swear on my grandmama's grave. It's the truth," said

Basil.

"So how you gon' get this girl to fall in love with you?" asked Ron.

"I already have," answered Basil.

AM I MY BROTHER'S KEEPER?

"Joshua!" Sadie Belle called through the door. "This sink is full of dishes!"

"Wash them!" is what Joshua wanted to yell back, but he knew better. "Yes ma'am," he said instead.

He had been flipping through a book that his fourth-grade teacher had given him to read over the summer. It was supposed to get him interested in reading. It was something about a magic library card. Who would want to read about a library card, Joshua wondered. He tossed the book back among the dust bunnies under his bed. Reading was for losers like Marvin.

Joshua reluctantly got up from his usual spot on the floor between his bed and his dresser and headed to the dirty dishes awaiting him.

"Great!" he thought to himself when he saw the sink. He remembered that Sadie Belle had cooked eggs, which were not her specialty. The word scrambled never crossed her mind when she prepared them, but the words "fried hard and stuck to the skillet" did.

Sadie Belle had already run water in the sink. "I don't want you using up all my dishwashing soap," she said repeatedly. Joshua took the bottle of no-brand liquid and squeezed a few extra drops into the sud-barren water just the same. As he worked the water into a mountain of suds, he cringed as he pulled up a handful of eggs.

"Caleeeb! You need to clean your stinkin' plate before you put it in the sink, you little rodent!"

"Be quiet! I'm watching TV!" Caleb yelled back from across the living room.

"Don't tell me to be quiet!" Joshua retaliated. "You shut up yourself!"

"Granny! Joshua's saying bad words again!" Caleb yelled towards Sadie Belle's room.

"No I didn't! You know you didn't hear me say a bad word!"

Sadie Belle stormed out of the bedroom and planted herself halfway between the living room-kitchen combo. As usual, she wore one of her old-fashioned house dresses that was covered with faded flowers and buttoned down the front. She stuck her hands into the front pockets. She tapped one foot, her beat-up house shoe silently hitting the floor.

"Joshua, I don't know what's got into you, but you better get it out real fast. You been acting like you lost your mind since the day this boy came here. I ain't seen him do nothing to deserve all your meanness."

"But, Grandma," Joshua pleaded. "He be picking on me."

"Hush, boy! You should be glad you have a brother. Instead, you sittin' around acting like Cain. After all you both been through, you could be nicer to him."

"But, Grandma, he ain't nice to me!" Joshua protested. "He don't even wanna do work around the house. Just wanna sit around and watch TV all day and make fun of people."

"I don't make fun of anybody!" Caleb shot back, his eyes pleading with Sadie Belle for sympathy. "I'm just glad I have a brother."

Joshua mumbled something under his breath.

"What did you say!" demanded Sadie Belle.

"He said, 'A bunch of crap'," Caleb answered.

"No I didn't!" Joshua cried.

"Did too!" yelled Caleb.

"Did not!"

"Then what did you say, Joshua?" asked Sadie Belle.

"I said, 'Oh, snap'," Joshua mumbled.

"Liar!" yelled Caleb.

"Y'all gone drive an old woman to an early grave," Sadie Belle said as she turned toward the hallway. "Caleb, get over there and help Joshua clean up that kitchen," she ordered as she headed back to her bedroom, where she continued to try to figure out how she could make the money outlast the month.

INNOCENT INMATES

"Hello," Basil heard a tender voice call from behind him. He had been holding an aluminum level in place to determine whether Ron was placing a shelf in straight. Startled, he dropped the level on Ron's foot and turned to see the eyes he had once called beautiful staring at him.

"Uh, hi," he stumbled. He had not expected that the girl from the front desk would respond to his wooing so soon. Gullible.

"I'm Ruth," she said, and quickly diverted her beautiful eyes to the floor.

"Basil," responded Basil, extending his hand for a shake.

"Like the stuff you put in spaghetti?" asked Ruth. She had a shy look.

Basil nodded. "Yep, Basil, just like the spice."

Ruth smiled. Basil could tell she had worn braces, although they hadn't done her much good. Straight teeth or not, she was still homely. But her eyes really were kind of beautiful, Basil thought. Or at least different from anyone else's he knew. They were dark and small and round like a little inno-

cent animal. Basil almost felt sorry for her, but he couldn't let emotions ruin his plans.

"He let you in here?" Basil asked, nodding toward the guard.

Ruth shrugged. "I came in through the other door. Besides, nobody cares if I come in here. My pastor said y'all aren't dangerous."

"Don't believe everything a pastor tells you," Basil replied.

Ron chuckled as he placed the level back into Basil's hand. "Of course, we're not dangerous," he said. "They don't let dangerous criminals come work on a church building, do they, Basil?"

Basil shook his head. "Nope. They keep the dangerous ones locked up at all times. Maximum security."

"What y'all in for?" Ruth asked.

"For crimes we didn't commit," answered Ron.

"Like what?"

"I stole a shovel," said Ron.

Ruth looked puzzled. "A shovel?" she asked.

"Yeah," Ron answered. "Me and some of my buddies stole a shovel so we could dig a hole out in the woods. Next thing we know, we off to juvie."

"That doesn't seem fair," said Ruth.

"It ain't."

Basil crossed his arms and glared at Ron.

"My bro', Basil, here got locked up for kidnapping his neighbor's dog," Ron said.

Basil coughed into his fist to keep from laughing.

"I didn't know you could go to prison for kidnapping a dog," Ruth said.

"You can if you torture the dog and cut off his front legs," said Ron.

Ruth gasped. Basil shook his head. No wonder she has strange eyes he thought. Her brain was leaking through them.

"Ron's actually a murderer," Basil interrupted.

Ruth gasped again and stepped back a bit.

"Quit lying," said Ron. "You're scaring her." He looked at Ruth with pleading eyes. "Don't believe him, sweetheart. I didn't kill anybody. Would they let me come here if I had?"

Ruth shook her head. "I guess not," she said with uncertainty. "That would be crazy."

In his mind, Basil agreed with Ruth. It was crazy to allow convicted murderers on an off-site work assignment. But that Bible study and good behavior stuff obviously worked. Truthfully, Basil wasn't sure what his actual crime had been - murder or stupidity. All he remembered from that dreadful night was having a fight with Basil, the second, about another one of his dumb ministries he wanted him to spearhead. His father was always dreaming up new ministries. Then he would expect Basil to carry them out. Basil told him no, and all the demons in Hades broke loose.

That same night, Basil's friend Donnell called and asked him to go for a ride with him and his boys. Basil had been more than happy to leave the holy haven he called home. He remembered hating his father to the core as Donnell's Grand Am sped down the street. Basil recalled how Donnell and the other two guys had had enough weed with them to get a whole football team high.

The next morning Basil was awakened by the police. He had been lying on the far end of the back parking lot of his father's church. He had no clue how he got there. The police

had a warrant for his arrest.

A family of six had been murdered, or rather executed, the night before. A neighbor had called the police to report a disturbance. The neighbor had gotten the license number on Donnell's car as well as described the four teenage boys he had seen running from the house.

When the police arrived, they found a father, a mother, two teenage girls, a six-year-old boy, and a two-year-old girl, side by side, lying face-down in a pool of their own blood. They each had bullet holes in the backs of their heads and one in the middle of their backs. The gun used to kill the six-year-old and the two-year-old had been found in Basil's pocket. His prints were the only ones on it.

One of the teenage girls had been Donnell's girlfriend, and the two-year-old was their daughter. Donnell was seeking revenge because the girl had broken up with him and refused to allow him to see their daughter. Basil couldn't remember a thing from that night, except riding around with Donnell and the boys and smoking weed. He couldn't even make a statement in his own defense. He was found guilty based on the testimony of one of the other boys. He was sentenced to life in prison.

"You okay?" Ruth asked as she touched Basil on the shoulder, then quickly snatched her hand back. Basil hadn't been aware of how his face had twisted into anger as he recalled that nightmarish night.

"Yeah. Sure. I'm alright," he answered. He glanced over at the guard. The guard was glaring back. "I think you probably should leave," he told Ruth. "I don't think you're supposed to be over here with us."

"It's okay. Pastor said y'all aren't dangerous," Ruth said.

Basil wasn't so sure about that. "Don't believe everything the pastor tells you," he said again.

THE ROD OF CORRECTION

"Just go back to your stupid cartoon," Joshua ordered Caleb. Caleb had splashed more water on the counter and the floor than on the dishes he was supposed to be rinsing.

"I'm telling Granny you keep using bad words," Caleb retaliated. "She said not to say 'stupid' in her house."

"Bad words!" Joshua exclaimed. "What about that little filthy mouth you brought from Chicago? Huh? What did she say about that, chump?"

"I stopped saying bad words," Caleb answered as he dried his hands on his shirt. "I do what Granny tells me."

"Yeah, right, dog breath," Joshua said. He threw a mixing bowl into the rinse side of the sink, splashing more water on Caleb. "Rinse that bowl!" he barked.

"You told me to leave," Caleb said. "I'm going back to my cartoon like you said."

Caleb tried to walk away, but Joshua grabbed the back of his shirt and yanked him back toward the sink. Caleb slipped on the wet floor then let out a wail.

"I'm sorry, Caleb," Joshua lied as he frantically tried to

help Caleb off the floor. "I didn't mean to make you fall." He said this loudly enough for Sadie Belle to hear.

"Yes you did!" Caleb screamed as he kicked at Joshua and refused his assistance.

"Now what's going on?" Sadie Belle asked, throwing her hands into the air. Her face looked older and more tired than what Joshua was accustomed to. Or had he just never noticed before?

"Joshua threw me down!" cried Caleb. He began to cry louder.

"Grandma, he slipped!" Joshua exclaimed. "Look at all that water he splashed on the floor," he said, motioning around the kitchen.

"You pulled my shirt! You made me fall!"

"No I didn't! You slipped!" Joshua's voice had turned whiny. He was trying to win Sadie Belle's affection.

Sadie Belle turned and walked away. Caleb, still on the floor, kicked Joshua on the shin. Joshua kicked him back. Sadie Belle returned to the kitchen. She had a long, black leather belt in her right hand. Joshua had not seen that belt in quite a while. Both he and Caleb fell totally silent.

"Turn around and touch the counter," Sadie Belle ordered.

Joshua did as ordered.

"You too, Caleb," said Sadie Belle.

"But, Granny, he hurt me," Caleb answered.

"Touch the counter, Caleb," Sadie Belle said calmly. "Somebody is lying, and I'm too tired to try to figure out who."

Sadie Belle gave them each three whacks across their bottoms. Caleb cried. Joshua didn't. Sadie Belle made Joshua

finish cleaning the kitchen. She gave Caleb a dust cloth and ordered him to dust everything in the apartment that was made of wood or even looked like wood. Then she settled on the sofa and waited for her favorite soap opera to start.

With the dishes finished and the floor dried, Joshua now sat on the steps outside their apartment. Needless to say, the afternoon sun poured a bucket of heat on his head. But what did Joshua care? He would rather scorch in the sun than be inside with Caleb, running around looking for wood to dust, trying to win back Sadie Belle's favor.

Joshua heard the door open to the apartment next door. It was the teenage girl named JaLisa. Sadie Belle had called her fast, not because she was a good runner, but because she was only fifteen and had a baby.

JaLisa waved at Joshua and closed the door before he could wave back. Joshua didn't bother waving at the closed door.

Joshua looked across the street and thought about Marvin. He was probably playing his Playstation or reading that dumb book the teacher had given him, something about a boy and his stupid dog named Skip. Sounded dumb, just like Marvin. He was just a plain nerd. Joshua reasoned that maybe he should start hanging with boys as cool as he and not losers like Marvin, a straight-A teacher's pet. If it hadn't been for Marvin wimping out on him, he could have had the pleasure of Caleb being lost in the woods. And, with any luck, he might've wandered onto the highway and gotten picked up by a lunatic named Marsha.

"I'll get him real good this evening," Joshua mumbled. "I'll scare him so bad that he won't have to wait til tonight to

wet his pants."

Joshua leaned back on the hot steps, resting his head on the top step and his elbows on the next. He closed his eyes and let the sun melt away his worries. He would pay Caleb back for all his teasing and thinking he was such a big-city big shot. He would make him confess to Sadie Belle that he was just a big fat liar and that he was a pick-pocketing thief. Then Sadie Belle would quit thinking that Caleb was all that, and Joshua would be her favorite grandson again.

TRUTH OR DARE

"I think the justice system is so unfair," Ruth said as she leaned back against the wall. "I mean, y'all didn't really do anything bad, and y'all had to go to prison. You got people out selling drugs and robbing people and stuff, and they're still walking around free every day."

Ron had to turn his head to conceal his smirking face.

"Well, we'll get out one day," Basil said with a long exasperated sigh.

"When?" asked Ruth.

"When we're sixty-five," Ron said over his shoulder. "You know, sort of like retirement."

"How old are you now?" Ruth asked.

"Twenty, almost twenty-one," said Basil. "Ron's seventeen."

"So that's like," Ruth looked up at the ceiling as if in deep thought. "That's like forty-five years for you," she said to Basil.

She did her blank look again and calculated Ron's time. "And like forty-eight for you," she said to Ron.

Neither Basil nor Ron had ever really thought of their

sentences in terms of how many years of their lives would be spent caged up like animals.

"There should be like an activist group or something to help people like you. I mean, you didn't really do anything bad," Ruth said, shaking her head. "I can't imagine how long you would've got if you killed somebody."

"I can," Ron said sarcastically.

"I think I'll talk to the pastor and see if he knows anything we could do."

"Don't bother. Don't waste your time," Basil said quickly. "My own daddy is a pastor, and he couldn't do anything to help me. Not that he cared anyway."

"Your dad is a pastor?"

"By definition. You can call him that. He keeps watch over his flock," said Basil.

"He just couldn't keep his eye on his dog-napping son," Ron commented with a devilish wink.

"How could your own dad let that happen?" asked Ruth, her hands gesturing in the direction of her own pastor's office. "There is no way my pastor would ever let that happen to me."

Ruth paused for a moment, then shrugged. "My own daddy might let me go to prison, just so he wouldn't have to have me around anymore," she said.

"Join the reject-club," Ron said. "Mine was happy to see me go. Less trouble for him. One less mouth to feed."

"Your daddy a preacher too?" Ruth asked.

"My daddy never set foot in a church in his whole life," Ron said, rolling his eyes. "Creep," he added with a grunt.

"All mine ever wanted from me was a miniature copy of himself," said Basil. "He came from a long line of preachers,

and I was supposed to fall right in line with them."

"You didn't want to be a preacher?" Ruth asked.

"Nobody in their right mind would want to be a preacher," Basil answered. "Living under a microscope all the time. Everybody expecting you to be perfect, never making any mistakes. They love you as long as you live up to their expectations. You fall one time, and they throw you away like trash.

"Folks giving you nice cars, then other folks gettin' mad at you for driving 'em. If you live in a small house, they say you must not be real cause God ain't blessin' you. If you live in a big house, they say you're stealing from the church. Why would anybody want to live like that?"

"Because they love people and want to see them saved," Ruth answered.

"Yeah, my daddy loved alright. He loved everybody except me and Mama," Basil said. "He was so busy taking care of his flock that he forgot about his family. Life was always a sermon with him," Basil said. He slammed his fist against the door frame of the closet. "Whenever I needed to talk, he had to weave in a Bible story. We couldn't just sit down like normal people. You know, just go to McDonald's or something, eat a burger and talk, laugh, have a good time. I would've given anything to have just one conversation with my dad that didn't include a scripture."

Ruth interrupted. "Doesn't the Bible tell parents to teach the Bible to their children all the time, when you sit at home, when you walk along the rode, all that stuff?"

"Deuteronomy, chapter six, sweetheart" said Basil.

"So your dad was just doing what the Bible says to do," said Ruth.

Basil shook his head. "He was trying to cram religion down my throat," he said angrily. "You can't make anybody love church or love God by preaching all the time. You have to show 'em. There was nothing about his life that I wanted to imitate. I didn't want his god."

Ron interrupted. "If you know so much, how come you ended up in prison?"

"I've been going to church since before I was born, and I've been reading the Bible since I was four. I know church folks. Church ain't nothing but a big social club for most of them."

Ruth decided to change the subject. "So, why did you kidnap a dog?" she asked.

Basil laughed as he fiddled with a measuring tape. "I didn't kidnap a dog," he answered. "Ron was just kidding."

"Then what did you do?" Ruth asked.

Basil snapped the measuring tape in and out. "I didn't do anything. Some guys that I thought were my friends set me up," he said, extending the tape along the wall, trying to avoid Ruth's stare.

"How? What happened? Ruth asked.

"They killed somebody and made it look like I did it," answered Basil.

"Oh," Ruth answered blankly as she stared at the floor and shuffled her feet.

"Honestly," Basil added when he noticed Ruth's uneasiness. He turned to Ron. "Your turn," he said. "Fess up."

Ron rolled his eyes at Basil. He was ruining whatever chance he thought he had to use Ruth as a way of escape. "I already told you what I did," Ron answered. "I stole a shovel."

"Come on, Ron, tell the truth, man," Basil urged.

"I just did. I told you. My only crime was stealing a shovel." Ron turned his back to Basil and Ruth and went back to his work. He had made a promise to himself that he would never confess to that stupid crime again. Terrence had compelled him to confess, convincing him that they would not go to prison. What a fool he had been. He never even meant to kill anybody. It was an accident, except that nosey little kid. He really did want to kill him, but he lived anyway.

"Yep," Ron began, "I'm here installing dumb shelves in a closet that nobody will probably ever use, just because I stole a shovel."

"Liar," said Basil. "Tell her how you used to deal drugs in your little town."

"I didn't deal drugs," replied Ron.

"My bad," said Basil. "I forgot. You deal cards; you sell drugs."

Ruth looked from face to face, searching for answers, as the two inmates exchanged words. She remained silent.

"My friend sold drugs," Ron corrected. "I was trying to keep him out of trouble," Ron said, looking at Ruth.

"And?" Basil motioned his right hand in a circle. "Tell the rest."

"Why you trippin', Baze?" Ron replied with a nervous laugh.

"Just tell the lady what you did."

Ruth waved her hands as if to say no. She looked at her watch. "I've got to go," she said. "I need to get back to the front desk."

"What's your problem?" Ron asked heatedly after Ruth

was out of earshot. "You just ruined everything."

Basil shrugged. "What chance did we have anyway. You think her pastor doesn't know what we did?"

Ron didn't answer. He just rolled his eyes at Basil and mouthed something profane.

"Dude, the girl's elevator stopped short of the first floor. She was going to her pastor to try to get him to help us. She thinks we're innocent."

"I am innocent," said Ron.

"Yeah, I know. Until proven guilty, which you have been. You killed somebody. End of story."

"Accidentally."

"You tried to kill a seven-year-old boy."

"That was his fault."

"You stole a shovel to bury the bodies."

"Who made you judge and jury?" Ron spat. "You killed two little innocent kids."

"I was demon-possessed," answered Basil.

"You mean drug-possessed."

"Same thing."

"You shouldn't have told her what we did," said Ron.

Basil shook his head. "They already know. Everybody knows. We're on Google, dawg. Just type in your name and hometown. Everything we did is on the World Wide Web for the whole wide world to read," Basil said with a worried laugh. "We're scarred for life."

Ron squinted his eyes. "You think that's funny?"

"No," Basil answered, shaking his head and still laughing. "I actually think it's pretty scary, but I laugh to keep from crying."

BROTHERLY LOVE

"Yo! Caleb!" Joshua called from the doorway. "Come outside for a sec'."

"I can't. I'm dusting," Caleb called back.

"There ain't that much wood in Mississippi. You should be done by now," said Joshua. "What you doing? Dusting plastic too?"

"What do you want?" Caleb asked abruptly, poking his head through the doorway.

"Come outside for a minute," Joshua said, motioning his hand.

"I don't have time," Caleb answered. He tried to close the door.

Joshua grabbed the door. "Wait," he said, "I want to make peace with you."

Caleb gave him a sideways glance. "What do you mean, 'make peace'?"

"You know, shake hands, be friends, be brothers," answered Joshua.

Caleb tried to close the door again, but Joshua held it tightly. "We shouldn't fight like this. It makes Grandma's

blood pressure go up."

"Then you stop fighting," Caleb said as he yanked the door shut.

Joshua followed him into the apartment. "Where's Grandma?" he whispered.

"She's in the bathroom. Didn't you just hear the toilet flush. You think we got ghosts or something?"

"Put down your little dust rag and come back outside for a minute," Joshua said. "I gotta tell you something."

"You can tell me right here," Caleb replied.

"I can't," Joshua whispered. "It's a secret."

"I don't want to hear anymore of your dumb secrets, okay?"

Joshua grabbed Caleb by the wrist. "Come on," he said as he pulled him quickly toward the door. "This is important." He pulled Caleb outside before he could protest again.

"Ouch! You hurt me!" Caleb yelled as he rubbed his dusting arm.

"Sorry, lil' bro', I didn't mean to," Joshua replied.

"That's what you always say. And you're always lying," said Caleb.

"No, I really didn't mean to hurt you," Joshua replied, reaching for Caleb's arm. "I don't mean to be mean. I hate being such a lousy big brother. I keep trying to do better."

"Liar," said Caleb. "What do you want?"

"Nothing. I mean, I just want to be a better brother. That's all."

"You're a big fat liar. You don't even like me," Caleb replied. "Why should I believe you anyway?"

"Cause I cross my heart and hope to die," said Joshua as he motioned a cross on his chest with one hand and pointed

toward the sky with his other. "I really am sorry that I've been mean to you."

"Yeah, right," said Caleb.

"No, for real," said Joshua. "See, at first I was mad cause you came, and I didn't get to see my mama. But when I saw how much I hurt Grandma, I felt bad about it."

"Yeah, right," Caleb grumbled, still rubbing his arm.

"I'm for real. I do feel bad. I want to make it up to you."

Caleb crossed his arms and stared at Joshua for a moment. "How?" he asked, unable to resist the temptation.

With his voice down to a whisper, Joshua asked, "Do you like to swim?"

FIRE ESCAPE

All was quiet. Ron was too angry at Basil to talk to him anymore. Basil was tired of making small talk, and Ron not answering back. The guard was lost in another magazine, looking up occasionally to ensure that Ron and Basil were still with him.

The guard suddenly screamed. Ron and Basil looked towards him and saw that a fire sprinkler was gushing water straight down on him. Two other sprinklers were also drenching the room. The guard, who had been knocked out of his chair, was scrambling to his feet. He had thrown his magazine in one direction and his drink in another. A fire alarm was also screeching loudly throughout the entire building.

A wild-eyed Ruth came bolting through the door where the miffed guard had finally gotten his footing and moved out of the path of the spraying water.

"What the-?" was all he managed to scream over the sound of the fire alarm before Ruth yelled something about a fire down the hall and the other guard needing help.

As the confused guard scrambled past Ruth and out of

the room, Ruth hurried in the direction of Ron and Basil. "Quick!" she motioned for them to follow her. "This is the best way out."

"What's going on?" Ron asked.

Ruth didn't answer. She just kept running down a back hallway toward an exit marked "Emergency Only". Ron and Basil, their eyes now as wild as Ruth's, followed her. Ruth hit the handle on the emergency exit with a bang. She no longer needed to motion for the two inmates to follow her. They were right on her heals, anxious to save themselves from the screaming fire alarm and the gushing sprinklers.

Once outside, Ron and Basil found themselves in a parking lot behind the building. A blue Ford Conversion Van was the sole vehicle in the lot.

"Get in the back and stay down!" Ruth yelled.

The van screeched out of the parking lot.

~ ~ ~ ~ ~

By the time the guard realized he had left Ron and Basil alone, it was too late.

"Why did you do a stupid thing like that!" the other guard screamed.

"That girl said you needed me."

The other guard shook his head and let out an exasperated moan. "You know what this means, don't you?"

Before the first guard could answer, the pastor and a fire

fighter rushed to the scene. The entire church was in chaos. The building was drenched from the sprinklers. Fire fighters were trampling all over the place. And everyone was asking what had happened.

"A fire was set in a garbage can," the fire fighter said. "That's what set off the alarm and the sprinklers."

"Could one of your boys have done it?" the pastor asked.

"They never left our sight," the guard said as he rolled his eyes at the guard who had been watching Ron and Basil.

"Maybe that girl set the fire," the other guard said in defense.

"Ruth?" the pastor inquired.

"The one who was at the front desk," the guard replied.

"Why would Ruth set a fire?" asked the pastor.

The guard shrugged. "She's the one who came and got me and said that Officer Scott needed my help. When I got back, my two boys were gone, and your girl is no where in sight either."

"Go get Ruth," the pastor told the church secretary, who had just walked into the room.

"Two of our boys are missing," the guard told the pastor.

"What do you mean by missing?" the pastor asked.

"They're not here, Reverend," the guard answered, his voice sarcastic.

"Where are they?" asked the pastor. His voice held a hint of panic.

The guard threw up his hands. "We don't know," he said.

"Have you searched the building?" the fire fighter asked.

The guard shook his head. "They're not in the building. They're gone." He looked at the pastor. "That girl set this up. She helped them escape."

With worry covering his face, the pastor shook his head and replied, "Ruth wouldn't do that."

The secretary ran into the room. Her look was panicked. "I can't find Ruth," she announced. "And my van is gone."

A Safe Town

"Where we goin', Bonnie?" Ron called from the back-seat.

Ruth didn't answer. A few cars were in the area, and she didn't want to call attention to herself. She was flattered that Ron had called her Bonnie. She had seen the movie *Bonnie and Clyde* with her aunt. Being compared to someone so bold made her feel special, even though the character was a criminal.

"Don't talk to me unless I talk to you first," Ruth said when there were no other cars on the street. "We're going to my house. We can get clothes and money," she said. "I need you two to just stay down and don't make a sound. If you do, you'll blow everything."

Basil circled his finger around his head to make the psycho symbol. Ron nodded in agreement. Ruth kept to the back roads until she was near her neighborhood. Then she turned onto a main street, being careful to obey all traffic laws and not to call any attention to herself. She called her home phone to make sure no one was home before she turned on to her street.

As she headed down her street, she could see that the old man who lived across from her was outside washing his truck. The truck had been a gift from his daughter, who died a week later in a car accident. It seemed to Ruth that the old man washed the truck every day regardless of the weather.

Ruth again warned Basil and Ron to stay down. She waved at her neighbor like she always did as she pulled into the driveway. "Don't move an inch!" she warned. "Don't make a sound!"

Ruth hurried into the house and did a quick run through to make sure no one was home. Everyone was at work like they were supposed to be, except Ruth. She was busy rescuing helpless criminals.

Ruth ran to her room and grabbed a gym bag. She threw in a few personal items. Then she went to her parents' room. She got some of her dad's clothes that she knew he wouldn't miss. Then she hit the family's emergency cash fund.

Diana and Whitney always managed their money well and never needed to take anything from the emergency fund. It seemed as if Ruth was always pulling out money; she never seemed to be able to manage what she had. She cleared out the fire-proof box of all the cash. Nobody else ever used it anyway, she reasoned. She didn't bother counting it; she would worry about that later.

Money and clothes were all she had planned to get, but Ruth thought about one more thing she knew her daddy kept around the house. She went back to her parents' closet. She reached into the far right corner of the top shelf. She fished around until she felt the metal security box. She carefully pulled the box out of the closet. She knew the box wasn't locked because her mother had accidentally thrown away the

key while cleaning one day. Her dad had never gotten around to replacing it.

Ruth opened the metal box and took out the gun. Her hand trembled as she held it. She checked to see whether it was loaded. It was. Her father always kept it loaded, but locked. He had shown them all how to use it. He never wanted to take a chance on someone breaking in and his family not be protected.

Ruth unloaded the gun and put the bullets in her pocket. She didn't know why. She just felt as if she should. She didn't really know why she was taking the gun either. She threw the gun in the bag with the rest of her stolen goods and rushed back out to the van. Her neighbor, Mr. Clean, was still in the yard. He looked straight at Ruth and smiled. Ruth didn't smile back; she just hurried to the van.

Ruth hastily took the clothes out of the gym bag and tossed them into the back of the van. "Put those on," she said.

"Your phone was ringing," Ron said.

Ruth grabbed the phone from the seat where she had left it. She checked the missed calls. "Dog!" she exclaimed. "It was Ms. Goins from church; they know I'm missing."

"Duh!" cried Ron.

Ruth hurriedly, but carefully, got out of her neighborhood. She hoped that Ron and Basil had stayed down like she told them, and Mr. Clean hadn't see them. She just knew he'd tell her parents that he saw her come home and that she was driving a blue van. She knew she was in big trouble. She felt a sharp pain shoot across her stomach. It was the same feeling she got when they had family gatherings and she had to listen to everyone brag about how wonderful Diana and Whitney were, while they acted as if she didn't exist.

Ruth drove along methodically, obeying traffic laws, being careful not to drive too fast or too slow. Her mind was spinning. She could turn around and go back and say that Ron and Basil forced her. But that wouldn't work. How could she explain the fact that they allowed her to take them back. Or, she could go back and apologize, look stupid, lose her job, become an even bigger ridicule, and be sent to prison to top it all off. Better yet, she could just keep driving, get out of town, find a spot where no one would suspect them, and start a new life.

Now that was a dream! Start a new life. She could become somebody else. She would no longer have to be Ruth, sandwiched between Diana and Whitney. Nobody would know her. She could be the person she's always wanted to be without the worry of criticism, without worrying that people would think she was imitating her sisters.

Ruth shook her head. Stupid daydreaming, she thought. She had a bad habit of living in a fantasy world; a world where she was the star, where she was prettier than Diana and smarter than Whitney. A world where she wore the right clothes and had the jewelry to match. A world where she said the right things, and everybody laughed. A world where she could even have a cute boyfriend like Basil. It would be a world where everyone would approve of her, and she would be loved.

"Can we get up now?" Basil called from the backseat.

"No!" Ruth yelled back. She had been so lost in her thoughts that she had almost forgotten her backseat cargo. "We still have a ways to go before we get out of traffic."

"Where you taking us?" Basil asked.

Ruth fumbled with her thoughts, and her words came out

jumbled and confused with a bunch of "Uh's" and "I's".

"You don't even know, do you?" Basil asked. His voice sounded distressed.

"I-I--" Ruth started.

"You realize you just caused us more trouble than we already had!" Basil yelled. "We thought you were trying to keep us from getting cooked in a fire and you order us into the back of a van."

Ruth looked straight ahead. She didn't answer.

"You got us scrunched up in the back of this van like sardines. We're riding around, don't know where we're going, nothing, just waiting to get shot at by the police," Basil said with contempt. "Just take us back to the church and turn yourself in." Then he hissed, "Stupid!" under his breath.

"I'm not stupid," Ruth said. "I know what I'm doing, and I know where I'm going."

"Then where we going?" asked Basil.

"Do either of you know how to hot wire a car?" Ruth asked.

"Of course," answered Ron. "My uncle showed me how when I was about five." Basil gave him the "you liar" look.

"It's almost four o'clock. The shift just changed at the chicken plant," said Ruth. "We need to ditch this van and get a car at the plant. Nobody is watching the lot, and half the people leave their doors unlocked or their windows cracked."

"So we're stealing a car?" Basil asked.

"Yep," Ruth answered with assurance.

"Girl, you've lost it," Basil said, shaking his head. But he knew he was stuck with this lunatic. All he had wanted for the last two years was to escape from prison. He was finally getting his big break and couldn't appreciate it. He hated not

being in control of the situation. He was strictly at Ruth's mercy. There he was hunched in the back of a stolen van, changing into ill-fitting clothes, heading to a chicken plant to steal a car, all at the command of some lunatic chick that he was supposed to take advantage of. He guessed his dad had been right; he was under some kind of curse.

"We're at the plant," Ruth announced.

"What's your plan?" Basil asked sharply.

Ruth ignored him. "What's the easiest car to hot wire?" she asked Ron.

"You see a Camry or a Honda Accord?"

"Every ten feet," Ruth answered.

"Just pick one with a window cracked, and we're home free," said Ron.

"What's your plan?" Basil asked again.

"I see one, a Camry," said Ruth. "Can you drive?" she asked Ron.

"Course I can drive," Ron answered with a smug laugh. "Learned that too when I was five."

"I'll let you out at the car, and I'll drive back to the end of the lot," Ruth said. "You get the car and come to the end of the lot and get us. Deal?"

"You sure there's nobody out here," said Ron.

"I am absolutely, positively sure," Ruth replied. "My cousin works second shift. They go in at three. They don't get a break til seven. They take smoke breaks on the back. Nobody comes to the parking lot this time of day. No deliveries, nobody applying for jobs, nothing. Look around. Do you see anybody?"

"What about security cameras, Smarty?" Basil asked.

"This is a safe town," Ruth answered curtly. "We don't

need security cameras."

THIN LINE BETWEEN LOVE AND HATE

"Hurry up!" Joshua ordered Caleb as they trekked along the path to the pond. Joshua smiled inwardly. He wasn't really in a hurry; he just enjoyed bossing Caleb.

"Thought you were going to be nice to me from now on," Caleb said.

"I am being nice. I'm taking you to the pond," said Joshua. "I'm gonna teach you how to swim."

"Granny says you don't even know how to swim," said Caleb. "She said you almost drowned."

"Oh, you talking 'bout that summer? That was an accident," said Joshua.

"When those boys tried to drown you?" Caleb asked.

"Grandma tell you that?"

Caleb shook his head. "My mama told me."

Joshua stopped walking.

"Why are you stopping?" asked Caleb. He stopped too and stared at Joshua.

Joshua shook his head. "Nothing, never mind," he mumbled, then started walking again.

"Weird," Caleb said with a shrug. "Mama said you saw some boys kill a girl," Caleb said casually. He stopped and broke off a low-lying limb. Joshua stopped again too. "She said they tried to kill you," Caleb added as he began making marks in the dirt with the tree limb.

"When did she tell you this?" asked Joshua.

Caleb shrugged. He continued scratching in the dirt. "She told me when I was still little, I think. When I was like four or something."

"So you knew about me?"

"That was the first time she said something about you," Caleb answered. "I never heard of you before that. I just wanted to know why she was crying."

"She was crying?"

"Yeah, she was like just sitting on the couch crying with her hands all over her face, like this," Caleb said, demonstrating. "She was crying real hard, so I thought the police had been by or something, or we were getting ready to move again. She always cried when we had to move. Like one time she cried four whole days. That was when they changed the lock on our apartment, and we couldn't get in to get our stuff. Then they called the police on Mama because she kept screaming at them. It was real cold that day too."

"What did she tell you?" Joshua asked.

"What I just told you," Caleb answered.

"I know that, but just tell me the whole thing, okay?"

Caleb groaned impatiently. "She said, 'Your brother almost died.' Then I said, 'What brother?' Then she said, 'Your older brother, Joshua.' And she was all sniffling and stuff, too, like this," Caleb said, demonstrating again.

"What else?" Joshua demanded.

"Then I think I said, 'My brother?' And she nodded. Then I said, 'I didn't know I had a brother.' Then she told me how she left you in Mississippi and came to Chicago because she was young and scared and didn't know how to take care of a baby."

Joshua slumped to the ground. He sat cross-legged with his face buried in his palms.

"You about to start crying, too?" asked Caleb.

"I was just thinking," Joshua answered.

"Okay," Caleb said with a shrug. He started walking along the path again, dragging his tree limb behind him. "Aren't you coming?" he called back to Joshua.

Joshua got up and followed Caleb to the pond. He hated him more now than ever before.

Breaking News

With most of her work done for the day and those two bickering grandsons outside playing, Sadie Belle made herself a cup of tea and sat down to enjoy it while she watched *Oprah*. She wished Oprah would do a show on grandmothers raising their grandchildren. She needed all the advice she could get. She simply did not know how she could continue taking care of those boys on her meager income and her aging nerves. This is not how she had pictured her retirement years.

Oprah was interviewing a celebrity on her show. Sadie Belle didn't care much for celebrity interviews. She thought about folding laundry instead, but she had already made her tea and didn't want to waste a good relaxing break. So she changed the channel, and a Breaking News Bulletin caught her attention.

"Officials are looking for two inmates who escaped from a juvenile correctional facility in south Mississippi while on an offsite

work assignment at a church," the news reporter announced. "Twenty-year-old Basil
Earl Jamerson, III, and seventeen-year-old
Ronald Lee Anderson are believed to have
escaped with seventeen-year-old Ruth Jones.
Authorities do not know whether Ms. Jones is
an accomplice or whether she was forced and
kidnapped by the two inmates."

The reporter continued with descriptions of Basil, Ron,
and Ruth, the van used in the escape, and the nature of the
escape. Then Sadie Belle's blood ran cold. The name and description of Ron had not rung a bell, but his photo did. Although his face had matured slightly and he had obviously
gained a bit of weight, Sadie Belle recognized the face of the
delinquent who had tried to murder her grandson three years
ago.

"Oh, Lord!" she cried. She bolted from her chair and ran
to the door. "Joshua!" she yelled as she stepped outside.
"Caleb!" She looked around but didn't see either of her
grandsons. She megaphoned her hands to her mouth and
yelled again. "Joshua!"

JaLisa, the girl next door, opened the door and looked
out. She held her four-month-old son in her arms.

"Have you seen my boys?" Sadie Belle asked her.

"I saw them going toward the woods a little while ago,"
JaLisa answered, nodding in the direction of the woods as she
gently patted her son's back.

"Lord, I told them boys not to be going to that pond!
Joshua is so hard-headed!" Sadie Belle said as she wiped
sweat from her face. "Did you see the news?" she asked.

JaLisa shook her head. "No, ma'am," she answered. "I don't watch the news."

"That boy escaped. The one named Ron. I got to get my boys home," said Sadie Belle.

"Ron wasn't locked up nowhere close by here, was he?" JaLisa asked.

"Nah, I think he was down there somewhere 'round Jackson," Sadie Belle answered.

"You don't think he'd come back here, do you?" JaLisa asked.

"I don't know, chil'," said Sadie Belle. "Never can tell. I need to send somebody to go get them boys for me. And they ain't gonna never set foot outside this apartment again."

UTOPIA

The red Camry zoomed out of the parking lot, leaving the big blue conversion van behind. Cool is the only word to describe how Ruth felt. For the first time, since she was old enough to reason, the word stupid didn't enter her mind.

Ron and Basil had changed into Ruth's dad's clothes and the baseball caps she had brought them. Ron sat up front with Ruth so they wouldn't look suspicious with both he and Basil sitting in the backseat.

"How do you know this car won't have problems?" the cynical Basil called from the backseat.

"Stop asking stupid questions. We'll get another one, bro'," said Ron. "Hotwiring this puppy was a piece of cake, like taking candy from a baby."

"Uh, that's not so easy to do," said Ruth. "I've tried it."

She and Ron laughed; Basil didn't think it was funny. He figured Ron had lost his mind just like Ruth. This was not how they were supposed to escape. They were sure to get caught, running without a plan. From what he had read, every prisoner that actually got away had a plan. Everyone that didn't have a plan got caught within a day or so. They would-

n't last that long. He just hoped he wouldn't get shot.

"Hey!" he yelled at Ruth. "Turn this car around. I'm turning myself in."

Ron and Ruth laughed again.

"Funny, man," Ron said.

"I wasn't being funny," said Basil. "Look, dawg, we can't just escape like this. We need a plan. I read--"

"See, that's your problem. You read too much," said Ron. "We just wanna escape. I don't care whose plan we use. I don't care if we use your grandmama's plan. I'm out. I'm gettin' away. And I'm stayin' away." Then he high-fived Ruth.

Basil shook his head. "Man!" he yelled as he slapped the seat. He felt as if he were always being controlled by somebody else. He had only escaped from one prison to another - first his father, then to drugs, then to prison, now this.

"Okay, I tell you what," said Ruth. "I'll pull over and let you out. You can walk back."

"You crazy?" Ron asked. "He ain't going no where 'cause we'll get caught."

"Come on, Baze," Ron pleaded as he leaned over the back of the seat. "Be cool. It's gon' be a'ight. Think about it. You on the verge of twenty-one. You get sent to the state pen, the real deal, dude. No more juvenile correctional facility.

"See, right now, you the man, the big dog - ruling over a bunch of thirteen and fourteen-year-old boys. They respect you, dawg. They fear you. You go to the state, all that changes. They got dudes been in their twenty, thirty years, just waitin' for some fresh meat like you. That what you want?"

Basil slumped in his seat and angrily crossed his arms over his chest. Steam shot from his ears as he stared out of

the window. It had been two years since he had ridden in the backseat of anything other than a police car. And he had to admit that it felt good.

He looked at the houses they passed along the highway. How he longed for a family. Everything looked serene in the well-maintained subdivisions, but Basil knew from experience that the inside of those homes could tell another story.

If they made a clean getaway, he could start over. He could change his identity, and go to college and study elementary education like he always wanted to. He wouldn't have to worry about his father mocking him with his "real men don't teach elementary school" look.

He could find a wife, and he wouldn't drive her insane like his father did his mother. He would treat her like his equal. She would never have to hide her feelings around him. She wouldn't have to keep her thoughts secret because he would value every word that came out of her mouth. He would be her companion, not her competition.

They would have a son, a daughter, and a dog named Benji, just like the movie. Basil smiled when he recalled that when he was a little boy he would tell his mother that he wanted three children when he grew up - a boy, a girl, and a little baby. Those were happier days.

"Basil? You with us?" Ron asked.

Basil smiled. "Yeah, dawg, I'm with you."

Ron turned on the radio. "We need to listen for the news," he said. The station was set on an AM gospel station.

"You gonna have to change that," said Basil. "I've heard enough of that to last me a lifetime. Find some rap."

"I don't like rap," Ruth replied.

"Well, we can't listen to gospel, not while I'm in the car,"

said Basil. "Just turn it off."

"We gotta have it on, so we can hear the news," said Ron.

"Put it on public radio or something," said Basil. "Anything but that."

"Then we might as well listen to rap!" Ruth cried. She had suffered enough public radio with her brainiac sister listening to it every day after school. She quickly changed the station to a local FM one that played rap.

"Oh, yeah," said Ron, as he began snapping and bopping. "Now that's what I'm talkin' 'bout."

FREE FRIDAY

Fridays are always eventful at the juvenile correctional facility, with possible off-site work assignments, and extra-curricular activities such as art and music, but no one was prepared for one of the most celebrated events among inmates - the escape of one of their own. Terrence had just returned from his work assignment when he heard the news from a sixteen-year-old inmate called Big Baby, who was over six-feet tall but still had a baby face.

Terrence found Allen in the activity room, where inmates were allowed to read, talk, or do some other activity while they waited for dinner time. Allen was sitting on the floor near a bookcase. He had a letter in his hand.

"Hey, look at this, man," he told Terrence. He held up a portion of the letter, which was from his mom. "Look at Timmy's report card."

Terrence took the report card from Allen. "You ever seen anything like that?" Allen asked. "All A's and a 100 average in math. Man, how you get a 100 average in math? That's like never getting a problem wrong the whole year. Can you believe it? My little brother."

Terrence showed his agreement by giving Allen five.

"He's gonna be something, you know?" Allen said, his grin stretching across his face. "He was supposed to go to some summer program at Duke for smart kids this summer, but my mom didn't have a way to go to North Carolina."

Allen noticed that Terrence's smile had vanished and had been replaced by a worried look. "What's up, dawg? Why the long face?"

Terrence shook his head. "Ron and Basil escaped."

LUNATICS AND LOSERS

Ruth kept looking at the gas hand. Any minute now the little light would come on and remind her that she needed gas. It was Friday; she should have known that any car she picked would be low in gas. Everybody knew that people at the plant filled their tanks on Saturday, after payday. And most of them only put in enough gas to get them through another week.

"We've gotta stop for gas," Ruth announced.

"How far have we gone?" Ron asked.

"We're almost at I-55," Ruth answered. "There's a station at the next exit."

"Great!" Ron yelled. "How we gon' stop for gas?"

Basil felt a weight drop in his stomach. Stopping for gas was sure to get them caught.

"Y'all just be cool," said Ruth. "Remember the cops are looking for a blue van. They don't know that it's sitting in the parking lot at the plant. They won't be looking for this car until well after eleven o'clock tonight when the second shift is over. We'll be long gone by then."

"You think you're so smart, don't you?" Basil asked. "How do you know there won't be a road block up ahead? What you gonna do then, sistah?"

"You know, I'm kinda sorry I rescued you," Ruth said, glancing back and forth at Basil through the rearview mirror.

"Rescued me? You didn't rescue me!" Basil yelled. "If I had known what you were up to, I would've stayed where I was. I don't need you. I had my own plans."

Ron started laughing. "You always got a plan," he said. "You been planning your escape for two years. You finally get it, and your ego is too big to accept it."

"Why you doing this anyway?" Basil asked Ruth, diverting attention away from himself. "No one with good sense would help two convicts escape for no reason, but then I don't figure you're someone with good sense anyway."

Ruth didn't answer.

"What's in it for you?" asked Basil.

Ruth still didn't answer. Ron stared at Ruth, waiting for an answer. Ruth looked straight ahead, eyes intent on the road, her only motion was a twitch in her eye.

"What's up, sistah?" Basil urged. "That big mouth of yours on vacation?"

"Why don't you chill, Baze?" Ron interrupted. He hunched his shoulders smugly and rubbed his chin as he grinned. "I'm just glad to be out. I ain't complaining."

"You're not out, fool," Basil replied. "You're just on the run with a lunatic for a minute. We'll be caught before we reach that gas station at the next exit."

"I'm not a lunatic," Ruth answered softly. She briefly made eye contact with Basil in the rearview mirror before he quickly looked out the window. "All I was doing was trying to help," Ruth said. "You said you were innocent, and I believe you."

"Why?" Basil asked sharply.

Ruth shrugged. "I don't know. I just do, okay?"

"Don't believe all you feel, girl," Basil answered harshly.

"Every gut feeling is not a good feeling."

"Hey, I don't need a lecture from you!" snapped Ruth. "If you're so smart, why are you in prison?"

Basil crossed his arms and stared hard at Ruth through the rearview mirror. Then very slowly and clearly he answered, "I'm in prison for getting higher than cloud nine and blowing the brains out of two little innocent children."

A hush fell over the car. The voices on the radio seemed so far away as Ruth's heart nearly stopped.

"And my buddy Ron killed a girl," Basil added. "She was about your age, wasn't she, Ron?"

Ron looked straight ahead, not making a sound, not moving a muscle.

"He said it was an accident," Basil continued. "But then he tried to drown a seven-year-old boy to keep him from talking. Oh, and I forgot, he stabbed his own friend, too, scared he might talk. Ain't that true, Ron?"

Ruth gripped the steering wheel so hard that her knuckles ashened.

"Still feeling smart, Bright Eyes?" Basil taunted. "You just helped two convicted murderers escape from prison. Your daddy's gonna be so proud."

Ruth began to cry.

"Dawg, Basil! Why you gotta get all stupid!" Ron exclaimed.

"I'm not the stupid one. Your girl up there is," replied Basil.

"I'm not stupid!" Ruth screamed.

Basil made eye contact with Ruth, then he grinned smugly.

"You wanna see stupid?" Ruth asked calmly. Then,

without warning, she floored the Camry. The odometer flew from 70 to 80 in a couple of seconds, then to 90 before Ron or Basil could blink. An SUV was ahead of them, about a half a mile away. The Camry was coming upon it fast.

"You're gonna kill us!" Ron cried.

"What difference does it make?" Ruth asked, her eyes focused on the SUV in front of them. "We're all losers anyway. We might as well end it all right here." Then she slammed on the brakes, snapping everyone's neck in the process. The car slowed to 70, just feet away from the car in front of them. Ruth then swirved into the other lane, barely missing the SUV. "Don't ever call me stupid again," she said with a trembling voice.

Ron sighed and slumped down into the seat. The fun and games were over. Basil, with crossed arms and a frowning face, silently stared out the window again. He was now convinced that Ruth was a lunatic, and he had to somehow get control of that car.

DINNER IS SERVED

It was almost dinner time at the correctional facility, and Terrence could smell the grease coming through the vents. It was something fried, but he wasn't sure what. His guess was the usual steak fingers, along with the greasiest fries in Mississippi. Terrence smiled to himself when he thought about the steak fingers. Who ever heard of a cow with fingers? That would make a good joke one day when he wasn't locked up behind bars.

Not much was funny in the life of a prisoner. Terrence couldn't find the words to describe how he felt about being disconnected from the outside world except through television and computer screens. He could only look at all the places he had hoped to visit someday. Maybe if he changed his life while imprisoned, the system would have mercy on him and let him go before he was a useless, old man.

Allen had put his letter aside and was rushing from person to person, inquiring about Ron's and Basil's escape. Terrence admitted, but only to himself, that he was a little jealous. Although he knew he was where he belonged, it was

only human to long to be free.

"How did Ron get so lucky, man?" a boy named Enrique asked, interrupting Terrence's thoughts.

Terrence shrugged. "You think they're lucky?"

"Yeah!" Enrique exclaimed, his eyes wild with excitement. "Nerd Man says a girl helped them escape. They got it made, man."

"They'll be back," said Terrence.

"Don't wish trouble on 'em, man" Enrique said, talking with his hands. "I wish I was with 'em. I know some guys who can give 'em the hook up."

"The same guys that gave you the hook up?" Terrence asked.

"Nah, nah, man," Enrique said, laughing. "This is legit, man. My cousin Angel has a real business, man. He got real jobs waiting for guys like us."

"Yeah, sure," Terrence said, shrugging. Everybody in the facility knew someone on the outside who had a legitimate hook-up waiting for them. They could have saved the state a bunch of money, Terrence thought, if they had pursued those legitimate hook-ups in the first place. There would be no need for juvenile correctional facilities.

Terrence saw Allen's excitement over the escape and felt sorry for him. He didn't have the sense to realize that things had just gone from bad to worse for Ron. A loud buzzer sounded, indicating that the prisoners' deep-fried meal was done, and it was time to go enjoy it. How Terrence longed for a Big Mac or even a regular old cheeseburger would do. Jesse had not been much of a cook and neither had Terrence, but even that had been better than prison grub every day.

GOT GAS?

Ron could feel his heart racing out of control. Now he knew how Joshua Tanner must have felt when he faced death at the pond that summer day.

"Ding! Ding!" he heard the alert on the car ring out to notify them that the gas was low.

"I hope you know that your little stunt caused a lot of gas," Basil said to Ruth. "We might not make it to the station."

At that moment they passed a sign that showed the gas station was in one mile. Ruth caught a glance at Basil in the rearview mirror. She wanted to smirk, but decided differently. The murder of two innocent kids rang in her head like an alarm clock. This guy that appeared so innocent, so cute, only hours ago now looked like the devil to her.

And what about the one seated next to her? Neither one of them was so cute anymore. Ruth's mind was spinning with a plan to go back and turn herself in when she was suddenly jolted by her ringing cell phone. All three of them looked in the direction of the phone. Ruth looked at the caller id. It

was her mother, who undoubtedly had heard the news by now.

"Don't even think about answering it!" Basil barked. Ruth kept both hands on the wheel and let the phone ring until voice mail picked up.

"Turn it off," Basil ordered. Ruth began adjusting the volume to vibrate.

"What part of 'off' don't you understand?" asked Basil.

Ruth turned the phone off as she felt hopelessly isolated from the world.

Ron breathed a sigh of relief when they finally reached the exit. The gas station was right off the highway.

"You pump," Basil said to Ron. "I'll go pay for it."

Basil unfastened his seat belt and reached over the seat. "Give me the money," he said harshly to Ruth. "And hop in the backseat. I'll be driving from now on."

Ruth handed Basil a twenty dollar bill.

"You think we don't have TV's in prison?" Basil asked. "Twenty dollars won't fill up a tank, baby. I need at least forty."

Ruth pulled seven one-dollar bills from her purse. "That's all I have," she told Basil.

Basil snatched the purse from Ruth and dumped the contents onto the backseat. A bunch of personal hygiene items and pennies flew everywhere. Basil didn't bother putting the items back into the purse. He got out and went to pay for the gas. Ruth didn't tell him about the money she had taken from home. She kept it safely in her pocket.

Basil looked rushed when he came out of the store. "Hurry up and pump the gas," he told Ron. "Something's not

right about this place."

Ron took the pump out of the cradle and placed it into the tank. "I can only move as fast as the gas," he replied.

Basil looked around nervously. "I'll wait in the car," he said as he gave one quick look around the station. No other customers were pumping gas, but a few cars were parked at the store.

Ron got back into the car as the gas pumped. "What's the matter with you?" he asked, seeing Basil still looking anxiously around and tapping on the wheel.

"There's an old dude at the register. Kept asking me questions about where I was from. Said I looked familiar," Basil answered, looking back at the store. "He asked me who my folks were and junk like that."

"What did you tell him?"

"What do you think I told him? I told him I was just passing through." Basil looked down at his clothes. For the first time he noticed how ridiculously old-fashioned they were. He didn't look familiar. He looked suspicious. He thought about the TV he had seen behind the counter too. The old man probably knew something. "Stop the pump," he ordered Ron. "Let's get out of here."

WIC AND WELFARE

Joshua hurried back through the woods from the pond. He decided not to run, only to walk quickly. Running always interrupted his thoughts, and right now he needed to think. One side of his mind was telling him to love Caleb because none of his problems was his fault. But there seemed to be another side of him that just couldn't resist hating him. The thought conquered his mind, blocking any positive thoughts about Caleb from entering.

Despite how hard he tried, Joshua couldn't stop the jealousy. He felt it was his right, his duty even, to hate Caleb. After all, Caleb had spent seven years with their mother, and he had spent none. It didn't matter that they were running from the police and drug dealers most of the time, Joshua would've given anything to spend just one day with the woman known as his mother.

What made Caleb different, Joshua wondered. Why hadn't he too been dumped as a baby? Why now, at seven? Joshua wondered if Caleb had ever met his father. He himself felt about as worthless as Sadie Belle's old TV that only

showed half the screen. He had a mother, and he guessed a father somewhere, but neither of them cared a thing about him.

Joshua, completely wrapped up in his thoughts and walking at lightning speed, walked right into his neighbor JaLisa without ever missing a beat.

"Hey!" Joshua yelled. "What you doing out here!"

"I was looking for you and your little brother," JaLisa answered. "Ms. Sadie sent me to get y'all."

Joshua brushed past JaLisa, intentionally bumping her in the side with his shoulder. "I don't have a little brother," he answered. "So there ain't no 'y'all'."

"Where's Caleb, Joshua?" JaLisa asked sternly, as she placed herself firmly in front of Joshua, blocking his way.

Joshua crossed his arms and glared back at JaLisa. "You're not my boss," he said, fearlessy. "You're stupid just like my mama, having a baby and can't even take care of yourself." He then pushed his way past JaLisa and headed down the path.

JaLisa had heard that condemnation a thousand times before, and she wasn't about to stand there and take it from a ten-year-old boy. She grabbed Joshua by the wrist and snapped him around to face her.

"I'm nothing like your mama!" she yelled directly into Joshua's face. "I take care of my son, you here?"

Joshua snatched his arm away. "Yeah, with WIC and Welfare!" he smarted back.

"And who do you think takes care of you, chump?" JaLisa asked.

Joshua rolled his eyes and turned and began to walk away.

"Where is Caleb?" JaLisa demanded again.

Joshua shrugged angrily. "I don't know!" he yelled, waving his arms. "Do my pockets look big enough to hold him?"

"He came out here with you. You should know where he is."

"Grandma tell you that?"

"Look, boy, I saw you come out here, okay?" JaLisa answered impatiently. "Now where is Caleb?"

"He ain't out here," Joshua answered, then walked away. He stopped and turned back to JaLisa. "Since you're so nosey, you should've seen him when he went home," he said smugly.

"Home?" JaLisa asked with raised brows.

"Did I stutter?"

"When did he go home?" JaLisa asked, her tone serious.

"Who are you supposed to be, the gatekeeper to the woods? He went home a little bit after we got out here. Said he was hot," Joshua answered with an unconcerned shrug.

"Then why did Ms. Sadie ask me if I had seen y'all?"

"'Cause Grandma's as blind as a bat in dark shades. Caleb could've been right under her nose, and she wouldn't have saw him."

"Quit fooling around, Joshua Tanner. You know Ms. Sadie ain't blind. If Caleb was at home, she would've seen him."

"He might've been sleep. You ever think of that?" Joshua asked, crossing his arms and nodding his head as if he'd just won a fight. "I bet Grandma didn't even look."

Against her better judgement, JaLisa felt she had no choice but to believe that Caleb was at home, even though she knew that Joshua was a notorious liar. She felt sorry for

him, always feeling as if he had to lie his way out of everything. She had been that way once herself.

She remembered how her mother had warned her again and again to be careful with boys. "No matter how wonderful they might seem, most of them have only one thought constantly on their minds," was what her mother had said.

JaLisa's mother had also been a teenage mother, having had JaLisa when she was only 13. Still JaLisa found it hard to believe that it could happen to her. Her mother just hadn't been very smart, she reasoned. Besides, she didn't even like boys that much at age 13, and having a boyfriend was the farthest thing from her mind. All she wanted was an education and to move from the housing project.

Nonetheless, by age fourteen, she found herself falling, what she thought was in love, with a boy named Kevin Duncan, who happened to be the best player on the basketball team. When her best friend Denise told her that Kevin liked her, something changed in JaLisa. Almost overnight, she went from not being interested in boys to practicing writing her name as Mrs. Kevin Duncan. It didn't help either that Kevin was cool, cute, and lived on the right side of town.

JaLisa finally convinced her mother to allow her to go on group dates with Kevin and other friends. Yet, she failed to mention the fact that she and Kevin often separated themselves from the group. Regardless of how much her mother tried to get her to be open with her about Kevin, JaLisa felt too ashamed of herself to tell her anything. When she finally got the nerve to talk, it was too late. A baby was on the way. Consequently, Kevin called JaLisa a string of bad names and dumped her.

But there was one thing that JaLisa was sure of, and that

was that Joshua was wrong about her. She loved her son and took good care of him. Even though it was hard having to get up at night and change diapers and fix bottles, JaLisa knew it wasn't the baby's fault, but her own. Every time her son woke up screaming in the middle of the night, right after she had just dozed off again, JaLisa thought about a girl at her school who had placed a pillow over her baby's head because she didn't want her parents to hear the baby crying and make her get up and take care of him. The next morning, the baby was dead.

JaLisa couldn't imagine allowing anything like that to happen to her baby. She would make whatever sacrifices necessary to finish school and go to college. She wanted a better life for herself and her son, and she knew that an education was her ticket to get there.

would wear this junk? Like we came straight off Soul Train."
Basil threw a quick glance at Ruth. "Didn't your daddy have
anything better to wear?"

"Whatever," Ruth mumbled.

"Come on, Basil," said Ron. "Don't get started with her
again."

"Don't worry. I got more important things on my mind
anyway," said Basil.

"Like gas, I hope."

Basil shrugged.

"We didn't even get a half a tank," said Ron. "And we
used all the money. You sure that's all you got?" he asked
Ruth.

"That's it," Ruth answered, keeping her hand over her
pocket.

"So what we do when we run out?" Ron asked Basil.

"In the words of my infamous father, 'We'll cross that
bridge when we get there'," said Basil.

But, Basil couldn't take his mind off the gas station and
the old man behind the counter.

"You look familiar," the old man had said.

Basil had ignored the old man's staring and told him he
wanted $27 in gas. After making a comment about how he
remembered when $27 filled up two tanks, the old man again
squinted his eyes and commented that Basil looked familiar.

"Who your folks?" he asked.

"I'm not from around here," Basil answered.

The old man looked toward the pumps. "I see," he said.
"Not a local tag."

"Scott county," the old man remarked. "I got folks down
there. You know any Johnsons?"

MEET ME IN SAINT LOUIS

Ron was concerned about all the anxiety Basil had shown at the gas station. Even now that they were back on the highway, Basil still appeared overly anxious.

"What up, dawg?" Ron asked. "Why we scat like a cat without filling up the tank?"

Basil rubbed the back of his neck and kept his eyes focused on the road. Worry lines covered his forehead. "I told you," he answered, "that old dude was asking too many questions."

"All he asked was who your folks were," Ron replied. "You know how country people are. That's one of their favorite questions."

Basil shook his head. "No, it wasn't just that," he said. "He was suspicious."

"Suspicious? Of what? You just went in to pay for gas like anybody else, right?"

Basil took his eyes off the road long enough to give Ron a sideways glance. "Look at these clothes. What dude my age

Basil shook his head. "You set the pump?" he asked.

"All set at $27," the man answered. "That might get you a half-tank."

Basil hurried out of the store without bothering with a thank-you.

Even now that he was back on the road, he was still angry at the old man for staring at him and taking note of the tag. "We've gotta stop and get another car," he told Ron.

Ron nodded in agreement. "And I know just the place," he said.

"Where?" asked Basil.

"My hometown. We need to make a little stop there any way."

"You're not still thinking about getting even with that kid, are you?" asked Basil.

Ron shook his head. "Even better," he said, smiling. "I didn't want to tell you this before 'cause I didn't know if we'd get this far. But I got money stashed away."

"Money?"

"You heard me," said Ron. "Money."

"Where?"

"Hidden."

"Don't play, man" said Basil.

"Who's playing?" asked Ron. "The money's a little secret stash I kept back from my dealing days."

"I thought you didn't deal drugs," Ruth boldly proclaimed from the back seat.

"Mind your own business," said Ron. "I didn't deal drugs. I was helping out a friend."

"And you kept some of the money?" Ruth asked, in a condescending tone.

"My uncle always said, 'Pay yourself first'," Ron said.

"How do you know the money's still there?" Basil asked.

"Because I hid it where no one would ever find it."

"How much is it?" Basil asked. "I mean, is it worth risking a stop for?"

"How does around $5000 sound to you?"

"You got that much money?"

Ron nodded.

"Sounds like music to my ears," Basil replied.

"I thought it would," said Ron.

"What about a car?" asked Basil.

"We'll swipe one from my daddy's shop after dark."

"So we go pick up some hidden cash then steal a car from your daddy's shop," Basil said, giving Ron a look of unbelief.

"You got it."

"You sure you got money?"

"I'm positive I got money," answered Ron. "Nobody knows about it but me. And it's buried so good that I might not be able to dig it up. What do we have to lose?"

"Time."

"Money is more important than time," said Ron.

"You sound like my dad," Basil said with a grunt, "and you're both wrong."

"Okay, so time is more important than money, but you gotta admit we need money. We're broke, dawg. You see, we make the quick stop. We get the money and the car. Jet to Saint Louis, and my Uncle Floyd can hook us up."

"Saint Louis? Who said anything about Saint Louis?" Basil asked as he passed an eighteen-wheeler and tried to keep and eye on Ruth at the same time to make sure she didn't try anything funny like she had a few miles back.

"Saint Louis is big enough to get lost in," said Ron. "We go there. Fit right in with the rest of them thugs."

"Hold up," said Basil. "I'm not a thug," he said pointing to himself. "And I don't plan on living like one either."

"My bad. I didn't mean you were a thug," said Ron. "I just meant we wouldn't look suspicious right off. We go to my old hood, and we look like everybody else."

"And what about this Uncle Floyd? What kind of 'hook up' are we talking about? Is it legal?"

"Depends on what you call legal," replied Ron.

"Anything that I don't have to hide from the police," answered Basil. "Look, man, I'm looking for a fresh start. A new identity. A new life."

"Uncle Floyd can get you that."

"Get me what?"

"Whatever you want. A fresh start. A new identity. A new life. He can get you a new face if you want."

"I don't need a new face. I just need a new name," said Basil.

"And my uncle can get you that," said Ron. "See, that's why we need the money. Uncle Floyd can get us all the stuff we need on paper - social security card, birth certificate, whatever. Then we can get a job and an apartment and all that junk with the rest of the money."

Basil frowned at the idea, although there was nothing more that he wanted than to start over. But Ron didn't seem to be one who could be trusted. The last thing he needed was to get into something illegal. Maybe he could just go to Saint Louis and get the papers from Ron's uncle, convince Ron to give him half the money, then get a fresh start somewhere else, far away from Ron.

"So, we going to Saint Louis?" Ron asked.

"Uh, yeah, sure," Basil answered, half-heartedly. He would go to Saint Louis and get his new identity, but after that he hoped to never see Ron again.

UNDER COVER

Joshua had run ahead of JaLisa and left her in the woods. The last thing he needed was a nosey girl getting into his business. Who did she think she was, coming to the woods to get him. Since when did she become the neighborhood baby-sitter?

Joshua came to the edge of the woods, which was also known as the Rosewood Dump. Shortly after Joshua had almost drowned in the pond, the city decided to put a chain-linked fence around the back of the apartment complex to keep little kids from going to the woods. Unfortunately, the older kids cut an opening through the fence because they got tired of climbing over it. Then it wasn't long before residents began to find it easier to dump unwanted items over the fence than to wait to place them on the curb on trash day. So the once peaceful woods had now become littered with broken chairs, bikes, mattresses, even TV's. Joshua wished he were strong enough to carry the one in Sadie Belle's bedroom. He would gladly dump it over the fence.

As Joshua passed the back row of apartments, he waved

at a few of the old people. A scrawny old man called Mr. Popeye, not because he liked spinach, but because his eyes seemed to sit right on top of his face, asked Joshua how Sadie Belle was doing.

"Fine," Joshua called back as he kept walking, not having time for chit chat. He had business to take care of at home. Sadie Belle would be asking about Caleb. Joshua had to hurry home and cover his tracks.

~~~~~

Joshua hurried to the back of the apartment where he had left his bedroom window unlocked. He looked around to make sure nosey JaLisa wasn't watching. Then he carefully, but quickly, raised the window and climbed into the room. He looked around. All was clear. He hurriedly grabbed his winter bedding from the closet and stuffed them under the sheets on his bed. Perfect. They looked just like Caleb.

Joshua sneaked back out of the window.

FIGHT! FIGHT!

"Yo, Preacher Man!" Terrence heard a voice call from the table behind him. Terrence turned around cautiously to the familiar voice of a big, clumsy thug nicknamed Grill. Terrence found it amusing that everyone called him Grill when he was actually nearly toothless. The story was that he had once had a grill until after he tripped over his own shoe-laces and fell across a bicycle rack, knocking out all his front teeth.

"Preacher Man," Grill repeated. "Why didn't you tell me your buddy Basil was escaping?"

Terrence turned back around, dipped a greasy fry into a glob of ketchup, and tried to ignore Grill. Then a steak finger came sailing past him and landed in his chocolate milk. Terrence ignored the incident despite all the "ooh's" coming from the crowd.

"Punk!" Terrence heard Grill call out. Everyone around them laughed, including Allen.

"I can do all things through Christ who-"

But before Terrence could say, "strengthens me", Grill

threw another steak finger. Again, it went "plunk" into Terrence's milk. More ooh's came from the crowd.

"Resist the devil," Terrence said through clenched teeth.

"Who you calling a devil, punk!" Grill growled as he noisily got up from his seat. He pushed Terrence hard on the back of the head. "I said, 'Who you calling a devil'?"

Terrence felt his hands curl into fists, but he hurriedly pushed his arms to his sides to resist retaliation. Then Grill snatched a fry off Terrence's plate, stuck it in his own nose, then stuck the fry into Terrence's ketchup. The crowd howled again, including Allen.

"Fight! Fight!" someone began chanting. Several others joined in and began banging on the tables. "Fight! Fight!" they cried, until the chanting quickly filled the room.

A guard tried to hurry to the scene while the other guards tried to calm the crowd. But before he could intervene, Terrence had picked up his tray and slammed it into Grill's toothless face. Grill tried to retaliate by reaching for his own tray, but Terrence hit him again and knocked him to the floor.

"Number 3428!" the guard yelled. "Break it up!"

Grill got up and took a swing at Terrence. He missed and hit Allen in the face. Allen got up and tried to hit Grill back, but he slipped on the food Terrence had spilled on the floor.

Terrence, like a madman, hit Grill several more times before Grill was able to take a good swing at him and knock him to the table. And just before Grill grabbed Terrence by the collar, the guard ended the fight with a billy club.

THE EXORCIST

Terrence sat in the chaplain's office and waited for him to return from the restroom. Terrence clenched his fists tight, as he felt a familiar twitch in his eye. He could feel the old Terrence returning.

He had so hated the old Terrence; the Terrence who would succumb to drowning a seven-year-old boy just to keep his mouth shut and save his own skin. He hated the old Terrence who ridiculed teachers and talked back, even using profanity without fear or remorse. He hated the old Terrence who took things that didn't belong to him. He hated the old Terrence who couldn't control his temper. He hated the old Terrence who had returned in the cafeteria and slammed a tray of food into another person's face.

Terrence glared at the leather-bound Bible lying on the center of the chaplain's desk. That book was supposed to change who he was. It said he would become a new person, that the old him was gone. So why did the old him come back in the cafeteria, Terrence pondered.

"Terrence," the chaplain called from behind. He extended his hand toward Terrence for a shake. Terrence ignored him.

"Why do you want to see me?" Terrence asked abruptly.

"How are you?" the chaplain asked. He was a tall and very slender man, with long, afro-puffy brown hair. He didn't look as if he should have been a chaplain or anyone else with a religious title. He wore an earring in his left ear and sported tattoos on both arms. Terrence thought he looked more like he should have been riding a Harley down the highway rather than ministering to juvenile delinquents like himself.

"I'm a'ight," Terrence replied, avoiding eye contact.

"Good, good, I'm a'ight, too," answered the chaplain. "Things going okay for you?"

Terrence slowly turned his eyes toward the chaplain and glared at him. "I'm locked up in a prison," he answered sarcastically. "How do you think things are going?"

"I don't know," the chaplain replied. "That's why I'm asking you."

The new Terrence would have enjoyed a friendly chat with the chaplain, who was one of the most genuine people Terrence had ever met. He, too, had been raised in a foster home and was headed down the wrong path until a concerned teacher intervened. He seemed to really understand the guys in the facility and saw them as people rather than depraved animals.

But the old Terrence wouldn't have had anything to do with this geek, and the old Terrence was back. So he just crossed his arms, leaned back in his chair, and tried to tune him out.

"Heard you got into a fight," the chaplain said.

No response.

"You know that Grill fellow could really use some prayer. He seemed to be a bit disturbed when I talked to him."

"Aren't we all?" Terrence couldn't resist asking.

The chaplain shook his head. "No, some of the guys are, and some are not. Some of you just landed on a bad path, but this guy has an evil lurking about him."

"Thought you said nobody was evil, just misunderstood," Terrence retorted.

"I didn't say he was evil. I said he has an evil lurking about him."

"What's the difference?" Terrence asked with a shrug.

"There's a big difference. You see, Terrence, we're all just hosts, and there are three spirits. One is your own, one is God's, and one is from the devil. The spirit you are born with is your own, and it desires the things of the flesh, the things of this world. That's where things like pride and greed and envy come from. But when you accept Jesus as your Lord, you receive God's Spirit. That's the spirit that helps you have love and joy, peace and self-control."

"Then what happened to my self-control in the lunch room?" Terrence interrupted.

"I said that God's Spirit helps you have these things," answered the chaplain. "Do you know what free will is, Terrence?"

Terrence shrugged, not sure of the answer, and not wanting to give a wrong one.

"That means that God sends his Spirit to tell us what to do, but we have the free will to obey or ignore what we're told."

"So you're saying it was my own fault?"

"What was going through your mind while Grill was

taunting you?"

Terrence moaned and said with a sigh, "I can do all things through Christ who strengthens me."

"That was God's Spirit speaking."

"You're saying I ignored God's Spirit and chose to slam a tray in Grill's ugly face?"

"You said it, Terrence. I didn't."

Terrence groaned and turned his face away from the chaplain. "You saying I'm a failure?"

The chaplain shook his head. "There's a third spirit, re-member?"

Terrence nodded. "The evil one lurking around Grill, right?"

"We all get visits from demons, Terrence," the chaplain said, rubbing his tattooed arm. "Unfortunately, they take up residence in some people and have to be evicted."

"I guess you better call an exorcist then, cause we got a whole lot 'em up in here."

The chaplain laughed and shook his head. "No, Terrence, we don't need an exorcist, at least you don't. You just need to deny yourself."

"Deny myself? Deny what? I'm in prison."

"That demonic spirit tells you to think about yourself and no one else," replied the chaplain. "Resist the devil, and he will flee from you, remember?"

"Resist what?" asked Terrence. "I don't have anything! What do I have to deny?"

"Your pride."

Terrence fell silent for a moment. He stared at the wall, then blurted out, " Pride! What do I have to be proud of? I'm locked up in a prison."

"There is a difference in being proud of something and being prideful," the chaplain answered. He crossed his arms and leaned back in his chair. "A parent is proud when a child makes all A's. It just means they feel good about their child's achievements. But pride is when the parent is puffed up about that child's achievements, when the parents brags about it all the time, or when the parent thinks their kid is better than everybody else's."

"I'm not bragging about anything," Terrence interrupted.

"Pride can also be when you won't listen to what other people have to say, when their opinion isn't worth two cents to you. Why? Because you believe your opinion is the only opinion."

"I'm not like that either," said Terrence. "I listen to you, don't I?"

"Of course you do, Terrence. But what if Allen gave you some advice?"

Terrence sneered. "Sorry, man, my bad," he said. Then he laughed again. "Allen? Take advice from Allen?"

"Why not?"

"No offense, but Allen ain't the brightest crayon in the box," Terrence answered with a laugh.

"And whose opinion is that?"

"Everybody's!"

"Did you know that Proverbs says that a fool doesn't value other people's opinions?"

"I value other people's opinions. I just don't value Allen's," Terrence answered and sneered again. "Can we go to something else?"

"Okay, just remember that you need to at least listen to what other people have to say before you write them off as ignorant, understand?"

Terrence nodded. "But you could've at least used somebody else as an example," he added.

"What about Grill?" asked the chaplain.

"You just said he had an evil spirit," Terrence answered quickly.

"But your pride wouldn't let him get away with embarrassing you."

"That was self-defense! He called me a punk and stuck my fry up his nose!"

The chaplain just smiled.

"I'm supposed to let him get away with that?" Terrence shook his head. "Nobody is that weak."

"You mean nobody is that strong, don't you?" asked the chaplain.

"What! Strong? Only a fool would sit there and take that? That's weak, man!"

"It's not weakness, Terrence. It's meekness."

"Weakness. Meekness. Same thing."

"Meekness is knowing you have the power to do something but having the self-control not to do it."

"That's stupid, letting somebody embarrass you and get away with it."

"You calling Jesus stupid?"

"I didn't say that. I said it's stupid to let somebody embarrass you."

"You don't think it was embarrassing to be hanging from a cross, naked, in front of the whole city?"

"Ain't the same thing," Terrence answered, shaking his head. "I'm saying that'll be stupid of me," he said, pointing at his chest.

"The Bible says to be imitators of Christ."

Terrence laughed and shook his head. "Nah, Preacher, I ain't Jesus. I'm Terrence. And I ain't about to let some toothless fool mess with me like that."

The chaplain picked up the Bible from his desk. "Believe it or not, Terrence, this little book has transformed people who were a lot worse off than you think you are. Thieves, murderers, drug dealers, prostitutes, even slave traders."

Terrence laughed. "Yeah, I know," he said, then took a deep breath and paused. He and the chaplain sat quietly for what seemed like an eternity for Terrence. Terrence stared at the floor, while the chaplain stared at Terrence.

Then Terrence felt his once cold eyes suddenly bulging with tears. A tear began to slowly roll down his cheek. The chaplain handed him a box of tissues from his desk then looked away without saying a word. Terrence didn't make a sound either. He simply allowed the tears to roll quietly down his face.

"I'm sorry," Terrence finally said after he regained composure.

The chaplain nodded. "It's okay. We all-"

"Fall short," said Terrence.

The chaplain smiled.

"You got any exorcist experience?" Terrence asked.

"I've been known to scare off a demon or two," the chaplain answered.

"I think I have some I might need to evict," said Terrence. "Let's pray, man."

DON'T TEMPT GOD

Joshua took a deep breath and smiled. "Aaah, barbecued chicken wings," he said as he stepped through the front door of the apartment. "Finally a little peace and quiet," he whispered to himself as he headed toward the kitchen, where Sadie Belle hovered over the stove.

"Grandma, you losing weight?" Joshua inquired as he gave his grandmother a hug.

Sadie Belle smiled and shook her head as she turned back to the stove and poured boxed macaroni into a pot of boiling water. "Where y'all been all this time?" she asked.

"You mean where've I been?" Joshua asked. "Caleb in there sleeping."

"Sleeping?"

"Yep," Joshua answered as he took a cup from the cabinet. "Said he was tired, so he came home."

"I didn't hear him come in," said Sadie Belle. "You sure?"

"Yes, ma'am," Joshua said with a nod. "We went to the woods, but just past the fence like you told us," he added quickly. "And we were playing some games, and he said he was tired. So I told him to go on home, and I'll be there later."

"I didn't hear Caleb come in the house," Sadie Belle said as she quickly put the macaroni box to the side.

"I guess he came in and went straight to bed."

"Let me go check," Sadie Belle said as she brushed past Joshua. "You know that boy broke out today."

Joshua followed Sadie Belle into the hallway. "What you mean, 'broke out'?" he asked. "Caleb don't have no rash."

"I ain't talking about a rash," replied Sadie Belle. She stopped and turned to face Joshua. Her face was wrinkled with worry. "I'm talking about that boy that tried to drown you."

Joshua's expression went blank. "What you talking about, Grandma?"

"Didn't you just hear me? I said that boy broke out of prison."

"What boy? Terrence?"

Sadie Belle shook her head. "No. Not him."

"Ron?"

"That's the one."

Joshua suddenly lost his appetite for dinner. His body stiffened. He could still feel Ron's grip on his puny legs, even after three years. "He won't come this way, will he, Grandma?"

"He probably won't, baby," Sadie Belle answered. "But I want you and Caleb to stay in the house just the same."

Joshua's heart fell to his stomach. Caleb. Caleb was still outside the house, without protection.

Sadie Belle opened the door to Joshua's room. "Well, I'll be," she said. "That little booger slipped in here without making a sound and went straight to sleep."

Joshua peeped around Sadie Belle, with hopeful expectation, but all he saw was blankets stuffed under sheets.

"I'll let him sleep for a little while," Sadie Belle said, closing the door. "You probably ran him raggedy out there in this heat," she told Joshua.

Joshua forced a smile, then swallowed a hard lump in his throat. "Grandma, did they say that on the news?" Joshua asked as he followed Sadie Belle back to the kitchen.

"Say what on the news?" Sadie Belle asked without looking back.

"About Ron."

"Yes, sugar."

"What did they say?"

Sadie Belle took a deep breath as she stirred the macaroni. "I already told you he broke out," she answered.

"Did they say he was armed and dangerous?"

Sadie Belle shook her head.

"How come you ain't watching the news?" asked Joshua.

Sadie Belle placed her stirring spoon on the stove and retrieved milk and magarine from the refrigerator. "I sent Lisa to get you and Caleb. I turned off the TV and quit worrying about it. The Lord will watch over us."

Joshua silently watched Sadie Belle for a moment, then asked, "Is that true, Grandma?"

"Is what true, hon'?"

"That God will watch over us."

"Course it's true."

"What if we had stayed out there all night?"

"Now what kind of foolish question is that?"

"Ah, Grandma, just answer the question," Joshua said,

throwing his hands up in exasperation.

"God can watch over you wherever you are. He watched over you that night, didn't he?"

"Yes, ma'am," Joshua answered with a little uncertainty.

"But the Bible says, 'Don't tempt God', so I sent Lisa to get you. No sense taking chances. Now get yourself ready to eat. Food's almost ready. I'll let your brother sleep for a little while."

Joshua headed to the bathroom to wash his face and hands. He knew he'd have to change his dirty clothes, too, before Sadie Belle would allow him to eat. But, hunger was the last thing on his mind, regardless of how much the barbecue sauce glistened on the chicken wings. He just prayed that Caleb would be okay until morning. There was no way he was going back out to the woods before then, knowing that a killer was on the loose.

BREAK TIME

Ruth had always felt that she had been born into the wrong family. She had imagined that one day her real parents would come and claim her, announcing that there had been an accidental switch at the hospital on the day she was born. Of course, that never happened, and Ruth was stuck feeling like a stranger in her own home.

Nothing she ever did was good enough. Nothing she ever said made sense. She never wore the right clothes. She never had the right friends. And not one family member ever hesitated to call her weird. Remembering all this, there was no way she could ever go back and face the ridicule awaiting her.

"Excuse me," she called out to Basil.

Ron turned around, while Basil kept his eyes on the road. "What's up?" Ron asked.

"I was talking to Basil," Ruth answered.

"You didn't call a name," Ron said as he turned back in his seat.

Basil adjusted the rearview mirror and gave Ruth a quick

glance. "You talkin' to me?" he asked.

"Yes."

"What do you want?" Basil answered, his tone harsh.

"When we get to Saint Louis, can I just be on my way?" Ruth asked.

Basil laughed. "You won't be going to Saint Louis," he answered.

"What do you mean?" Ruth asked.

"Just what I said. You won't be going. We ain't taking you."

"Where's she going?" asked Ron.

Basil laughed again. "I don't know. You'll figure out somewhere to dump her body, won't you?"

Ron gave Basil a worried look. "What you mean by dump her body?"

"You're pretty good at dumping bodies, aren't you? Basil asked.

"Hol' up, now. Stop talking crazy," Ron said, shaking his head.

"I don't mean kill her," said Basil, laughing. "We'll just dump her somewhere then be on our way. No point in killing her. Everybody knows we've escaped. Our faces are all over the news by now."

"We just told her we're headed to Saint Louis," said Ron.

"Saint Louis is just a pit stop. I don't plan on staying. She doesn't know where I'm going." Basil spoke as if Ruth were not even in the backseat.

Ruth thought about the gun she had packed in the gym bag. She also remembered that she unloaded it. Foolishly, she had not thought that she would need it to defend herself.

"I need to go to the bathroom really bad," she announced.

"That's too bad," answered Basil. "We ain't stopping."

"Come on, Baze," Ron said pleadingly. "Give her a break."

"She doesn't have to go," Basil answered.

"I'm not lying. I really do," said Ruth. "I haven't gone all day."

"I could stand to go myself," Ron added.

"What do you think this is, a joy ride?" Basil barked. "We can't just stop on a whim."

"We can pull to the side real quick," said Ron.

"You expect me to pull over and let Bright Eyes run off to the woods?"

"No," Ron answered, shaking his head. "You see that patch of woods about a mile off?"

Basil looked in the distance. The entire scenery was nothing but woods. "Okay, I see woods. So?" he asked.

"That's where my treasure is," answered Ron.

"You hid the money in the woods?"

"Buried it," answered Ron.

Basil squinted his eyes. The setting sun was blinding his right side, and the sun visor was useless. If Ruth had been smart, he thought, she would have had the sense to bring them sunglasses. "How do we get to the money?" he asked.

"We can pull over to the side and walk, don't know where we'll hide the car though. Or, we can go through my old 'hood."

"I don't need choices," Basil said sharply. "I need the best way."

"Okay, then, the neighborhood," Ron answered.

COPS AND ROBBERS

Caleb had been in Mississippi long enough to recognize the chirping of crickets and the hoot of owls. He also knew that meant night fall was fast approaching.

"Joshua!" he screamed for the hundredth time. Then he struggled again with the strings that were bound tightly around his wrists, which were sore from all the struggling. By now he knew that Joshua had tricked him. He had been smart enough not to fall for the lie about the buried treasure, but he had been too excited about playing cops and robbers to think that Joshua would be tricking him again.

"You can be the cop," Joshua had told him. This got Caleb excited. He had always thought of police as bad people, since his mother was always running from them.

"I'll have to tie you up," Joshua said.

"Why?" asked Caleb.

"Cause," answered Joshua.

"Cause what?"

"Cause robbers always tie up the cops," Joshua answered.

"That doesn't make sense."

"That's cause you're a little kid," Joshua replied. "You see, cops are stronger than robbers. So when I tie you up, you have to show how strong you are by breaking loose."

Caleb frowned. "I don't get it."

Joshua groaned. "Just trust me, okay? I know what I'm talking about. Me and Marvin play this game all the time, and I'm always the cop cause I'm stronger than him." Joshua pulled some long strings from his pocket.

"Where did you get those?" Caleb asked.

"Grandma. She said I could have them."

"So you were the cop, and Marvin was the robber?" Caleb asked.

"Yup," Joshua answered with pride as he played with the string.

"I still don't get why the cop gets tied up," said Caleb.

"You ain't never saw no Clint Eastwood movies?" Joshua asked.

Caleb shook his head.

"You wanna play or not?" asked Joshua.

Caleb shrugged. "I guess so."

"Then I need to tie you up," said Joshua.

"Then what?" asked Caleb.

"Then I go pretend I'm robbing a bank, and you break loose and come arrest me. Okay?"

Caleb nodded. Joshua tied his hands behind his back, then had him sit on the ground and lean his back against a tree while he bound his ankles. Joshua then ran off mumbling, "See you, sucker," while Caleb struggled to free himself in order to go arrest him.

FALSE SECURITY

The last people Joshua wanted to see were the police. He was tempted to pretend Sadie Belle wasn't home when the police officer at the door asked to speak with her.

"Grandma!" Joshua called from the doorway. He kept his hand on the doorknob and his body between the police officer and the entry into the apartment. Sadie Belle, emerging from the kitchen, was as surprised as Joshua to see a police officer at her door.

"Good evening, ma'am," the officer greeted. Sadie Belle didn't invite her in. Instead, she shooed Joshua away from the door and stood in his place.

"Good evening, Officer," Sadie replied.

Joshua's heart was thumping so hard that he was sure Sadie Belle could hear it. It never occurred to him that someone might find Caleb tied up and call the police. Or, even worse, what if something bad had happened to Caleb, he worried.

"Sadie Belle Brown?" the officer inquired.

"Yes," Sadie Belle replied.

"I'm Officer Bridgette Lopez," the officer said. "I don't mean to alarm you. This is simply a formality. But it is our duty to inform you that there has been an escape from the juvenile correctional facility-"

"I heard," Sadie Belle interrupted. "It was on the news this evening."

"This is just a formality," the officer said again. "We don't think the escapee would bother coming this way. But, it is our duty to make sure you are aware of the situation."

Joshua breathed a sigh of relief. Caleb was still okay, and Ron wasn't headed his way. Two prayers answered in one breath.

"Any idea where he might be headed," Sadie Belle asked.

"We have a couple of leads," answered Officer Lopez. "One from a neighbor of the girl believed to have helped them escape, and another from a convenience store clerk. Not to alarm you, but they appear to be going north."

"North?" asked Sadie Belle. "But not headed this way," she said matter-of-factly.

"There is no reason to believe they would come here," answered Officer Lopez. "North is just probably the direction they chose, doesn't necessarily mean they're coming here."

"And it doesn't necessarily mean they're not," said Sadie Belle. "But I can't sit around worrying about that, now can I? I just need to keep my boys in the house. No sense being foolish."

"That's a good idea, Ms. Brown," Officer Lopez replied.

Joshua's heart melted, sensing that Sadie Belle's security was really false. He could tell she was worried, why else would she insist they stay in the apartment. But, Caleb was still out there, and it was all his fault. Joshua knew he would get the punishment of his life if Sadie Belle found out. He had to find a way to get Caleb home, and to keep him quiet. If he got him home before dark and found a way to bribe him, maybe he could convince him to keep it a secret, he reasoned. Now all he had to do was get to him before Sadie Belle found out.

Homeward Bound

"This is it," Ron said, with mixed emotions. "This is my exit. I'm back home, man."

Basil didn't respond. He was too nervous, but the money was worth the risk. It would increase their chances of not being caught. Ron had given him directions, and he had played them again and again in his head. Exit to the right. Take the very first right back toward the interstate. Go a half mile, then take a left onto a little country road called Westwind, which was a back road into town.

Basil followed the directions without saying a word. Ron was on edge. He was sure they would pass someone who would recognize him. He sank deep into his seat, with his head barely visible.

"Maybe I should get down," he told Basil.

"You can't," said Basil. "You've got to make sure I'm going the right way. Just duck if we see somebody."

Basil thought for a moment, then said, "Maybe we should put her in the trunk." He nodded toward Ruth.

"Nooo!" Ruth cried. "Please don't. I might suffocate."

"No, you won't," said Basil.

"Please," Ruth said. "I'll lie down. I'll make sure nobody sees me."

Basil looked around. There were no other cars in sight. He slowed down to pull over.

"Please," Ruth begged.

Basil stopped the car.

"Leave her alone for now," said Ron, surprised by his sympathy for Ruth.

"Get down and stay down!" Basil turned and snarled at Ruth.

Ruth obeyed. Basil sped off.

After a few twists on a winding, tree-lined road, Basil saw a neighborhood of well-kept homes with a seventies kind of appeal. "These used to be the burbs," Ron informed him, from low in his seat. "They built nicer houses on the other side of town. That's where all the big-money people live now." Basil nodded in disinterested agreement.

"Keep going and take a left at the corner," Ron said, trying to scoot even lower in his seat.

"Think anybody will recognize you?" Basil asked. "You put on a little weight since you got locked up."

Ron didn't feel much like joking, however. He had begun to sweat and his stomach was in knots. He knew that just one glimpse of him, and it would all be over. He just wanted to get his money and leave.

Basil took a left at a corner where there was a convenience store housed in a rickety old building. Beside it stood a boarded up auto shop.

"My daddy's shop!" Ron cried in a mix of panic and sadness.

"That's your daddy's shop?" Basil asked rhetorically. "You didn't know it was closed?"

Ron shook his head, his eyes still fixed on the abandoned building. "Mama didn't tell me," he said absently.

"Maybe he opened another," Basil added.

Ron shrugged and sank lower into the seat. "We'll have to get out and walk the rest of the way," he said, his voice still sounding blank and distant. "We can't drive through the apartments. Be too obvious." He studied the scene around him, glad no one was on the street. "That's the high school. Pull in here and drive 'round to the back," he told Basil. "We'll leave the car here. We can cut along the edge of the apartments to the woods."

"Where is everybody?" Basil asked. "I don't see anything but cats," he said, looking around carefully as he parked the car close enough to the side of the building that he could reach out and touch it.

"It's getting dark," said Ron. "Folks don't want to hang outside with mosquitoes."

"Hope you're right," said Basil. His heart was beating faster than it did the day the judge sentenced him to life in prison.

THE BOY WHO CRIED HELP

The sun was low in the western sky, making the trees cast frightening shadows upon one another, and every shadow looked like the shape of a wild animal to Caleb. His mouth and throat were dry, and his arms and legs were covered in mosquito bites. The tears on his face had now dried into flat white lines. Although hunger pains shot through his stomach, all Caleb could think about was whether Joshua would ever come back.

He had heard voices earlier, voices of teenagers into some type of mischief. Caleb had cried out, but they never came his way. Now the only sounds he heard were crickets, owls, and mosquitoes buzzing around his head.

He was completely exhausted from struggling to free himself and had given up. He wanted to sleep but was too afraid. He remembered what Joshua had said about snakes, so he kept his eyes open even though there was nothing he could do if one approached him.

Suddenly, Caleb again thought he heard voices. As the

voices got closer, Caleb was about to cry out for help, then he thought about the teens he had probably scared off earlier. He sat still and pondered what to do. If he remained quiet, they might bypass him anyway. If he called out, he at least had a better chance of being found.

"Help!" he cried. "Somebody, help!"

A CRY IN THE NIGHT

Ruth had a hard time convincing Basil that she needed to carry her gym bag with her, but after much arguing she was able to persuade him into believing that the bag held much needed personal hygiene items. She had no idea how she would get the gun out of the bag or how she would use it, she just felt safer having it with her.

"You remember where you buried it?" Basil asked Ron.

"Remember like it was yesterday." He grinned broadly. "Didn't think I'd be getting my hands on it so soon, though."

"Okay, Bright Eyes," Basil said to Ruth, "you said you have personal matters to take care of." He had been walking shoulder to shoulder with her in case she thought about trying to run. "You know you're not going alone, don't you?"

"What!" cried Ruth.

"Somebody's gotta keep an eye on you," Basil replied.

"You've got to be kidding!" Ruth stopped and planted her hands on her hips. "I've put up with enough junk from you already. The least you could do is let me have some privacy."

"Forget it, sistah," said Basil, standing face to face with Ruth. "We'll stand on either side of you with our backs turned. You can forget about privacy."

Ruth stared back, not answering, only thinking. There was no way she was going to do anything, even pretend, with Ron and Basil standing right beside her. Even if they turned their backs, she couldn't get a gun out without drawing attention.

"Never mind," she moaned as she turned from Basil. "I can wait."

"I thought you could," Basil replied. "It's almost dark," he said to Ron. "How far we got?"

"Just a little ways on this path," said Ron. "I can find it in the dark if I have to."

The trio continued along the path, fighting mosquitoes and hanging branches. Ruth fought back tears as she thought of the sorry mess she had made for herself. Her family would disown her for sure. There was no way she was ever going home again, if she ever got away.

"Right up this way," Ron said anxiously as he picked up speed along a wider path.

Then Basil suddenly stopped. "Did you hear that?" he asked.

"Hear what?" Ron asked, slowing down, but not stopping.

"Hold up," Basil said, raising his hand. Ruth stopped and crossed her arms impatiently. Ron stopped also, his face twisted in irritation.

"I thought you said nobody would be out here," said Basil.

"I didn't hear anything," Ron answered.

"Shh!" Basil said quickly. Then they all heard it.

"Somebody, help!" the voice came again, as clear as day.

NIGHT FLIGHT

Breathlessly, Joshua darted through the apartment complex to the fence leading to the woods. He quickly glanced around to make one final check that no one had seen him, then he dashed into the woods.

It was almost dark because he had spent too much time trying to sneak out. Sadie Belle had struck up an additional conversation with Officer Lopez, recounting every detail of the incident in the woods three years before. When Officer Lopez finally got away, Sadie Belle started the conversation all over again with Joshua. Joshua finally ended the conversation by saying he was tired and needed a nap like Caleb. And as soon as Sadie Belle had gone to finish cleaning the kitchen, Joshua ran to his room, locked the door, and slipped out the window, hoping to be back with Caleb before Sadie Belle decided to wake him.

~~~~~~

JaLisa was performing her usual evening routine of giving her baby a bottle before dressing him for bed when she spotted the hard-headed Joshua Tanner climbing out of his bedroom window. After she had finished feeding her baby, she asked her mother to watch him for her until she came back from helping Ms. Sadie with a little problem she was having. She left her apartment and headed to the woods, hot on the trail of Joshua Tanner.

SEEING GHOSTS

"I don't know who's out here," said Basil, "but we're not helping him. Let's go," he told Ron, as they both started walking up the path again.

Ruth, however, hesitated. "That's a child's voice," she said, after hearing the cry again.

"So?" replied Basil, stopping and glaring at her.

"So we need to see what's wrong," Ruth answered sharply.

"I don't think so," answered Basil. "Ron, let's find the money so we can get out of here."

Ron began walking faster, with Basil right on his heels. When Basil noticed Ruth still standing, he went back and grabbed her by the wrist, pulling her along.

"You're hurting me!" Ruth yelled.

"Keep up and I won't have to hurt you," Basil said, tightening his grip.

Then the cry for help was heard again, but this time it was louder and clearer. They all stared ahead, perplexed, because the cry came from the direction in which they were heading.

"You sure it's this way?" Basil asked.

"Positive," answered Ron.

"Then let's go," Basil ordered.

But, as soon as they had gone about ten steps, Ron froze in his tracks. He had found the spot where his money was buried, but they had also found the voice of the one crying for help. Ron stood with his mouth agape as he stared at the tree where he had buried his treasure. Right over his treasure sat a little boy, who could have been the ghost of Joshua Tanner.

GOOSEBUMPS

Joshua hadn't realized he had taken Caleb so deep into the woods. It would surely be dark before they made it back home, and he hadn't thought to bring a flashlight. He had also forgotten how afraid he was of the dark until he thought he heard footsteps behind him. "It's just my imagination," he whispered, but he hurried along through the woods, just in case.

GUARDED TREASURE

When she saw Caleb, Ruth broke free from Basil's grip and rushed to him. She could see that Caleb had been crying and was looking dehydrated. She quickly began untying the strings around his wrists.

"What do you think you're doing!" Basil yelled. He rushed over and shoved Ruth to the ground. "Leave him, girl! We don't have time for this!"

But Ron still had not moved. He just stood staring at Caleb as if he were seeing a ghost.

"Stop gawking!" Basil yelled at Ron. "Let's find the money and get out of here!"

"It's right there," Ron said blankly, pointing toward Caleb. Then he shook his head, trying to clear his thoughts. He walked over to Caleb and knelt down. "Joshua?" he whispered.

Caleb tried to hold his head up and look at Ron. He shook his head weakly and said, "Joshua left me."

Confusion spread over Ron's face. He shook his head again.

"Joshua sent you to get me?" Caleb asked, his voice rasping and weak.

Ron got closer to Caleb's face and touched it. He just had to be sure.

"Where's Joshua?" Caleb asked. "Did something happen to him? I've been out here all day," he said, stopping to catch his breath. "We played cops and robbers, and I couldn't break loose," he said, then sighed loudly.

"What's going on, Ron?" Basil asked. "Who's this kid?"

Ron slumped on the ground beside Caleb and dropped his head between his knees. "I don't know," he answered, looking up briefly. Then he laughed. "I thought he was a ghost," he said, rubbing the back of his neck. "Ah, man, he looks just like the kid we almost drowned." Then he laughed again, a kind of crazy laugh. "I thought he like died or some-thing, man, and came back as a ghost to guard my money, man."

"So the money's buried here?" Basil asked impatiently.

Ron, still laughing, answered with a nod.

Basil hastily pushed Caleb to the side and began digging with a screw driver he had found in the trunk of the stolen car. He tossed a second screw driver to Ron. "Get up and help me," he ordered.

With Basil and Ron distracted, Ruth saw an opportunity to run, but she couldn't bear to leave the kid behind. That's when she remembered the gun. With both of them concen-trating on digging, she could possibly get the gun out of the gym bag.

Ruth quietly swung the bag behind her left shoulder. With her right hand, she unzipped it behind her back. She reached in and pulled out the gun. Standing a safe distance away from Ron and Basil, she pointed the gun toward them and yelled, "Untie the boy!" She was fully aware that the bullets remained in her pocket.

IN THE HANDS OF A KILLER

Joshua wasn't certain he had heard voices until he had walked right upon them. He shrank back behind a tree when he saw the figures in the shadows of the trees. His heart was racing uncontrollably.

He saw a girl who looked about JaLisa's age pointing a gun at two men who were kneeling beside Caleb. One of them was untying Caleb's wrists. Joshua was so scared that he thought he would vomit. He leaned against the tree and lifted his eyes toward the sky for a prayer, but he didn't know what to say. Then he peeped around the tree to check on Caleb. Then it hit him. He did recognize the man untying Caleb. It was Ron!

Joshua wrapped his arms tightly around his stomach and doubled over, sure that his dinner was about to be expelled. He tried not to cry, but he couldn't stop himself. Because of him, Caleb was in the hands of a killer.

MONSTER

"What do you think you're doing?" Basil asked harshly, trying to intimidate Ruth.

"You just shut up and stay on the ground!" Ruth screamed. "I'm the one with the gun!" She tried, without much success, to control her trembling voice. Yet, she could tell that Basil sensed her fear.

"Give me the gun, Ruth," Basil said, as he slowly stood up.

"Stay down!" Ruth yelled, her voice cracking. She steadied the gun as best she could in her trembling hands.

Basil shook his head. "You won't shoot me," he said. "You're not a killer like me. You're a good girl. You could never hurt another human being."

"You're not a human being," Ruth answered with contempt. "You're a monster. You killed two innocent children."

Basil nodded his head slowly. "That's right," he said. "I am a monster." He stood up and faced Ruth, then began slowly walking towards her. "Yep, I'm a monster. The product of too much church and not enough Christ," he said mockingly. He kept walking toward Ruth, laughing.

Ruth backed up as Basil moved closer. "Stay back!" she yelled, feeling helpless, knowing the gun was not loaded, and not sure what she'd do if it were. But, before she had time to think twice, Basil was right upon her.

"I am a monster, and you should be smart enough not to pull a gun on me!" Basil yelled as he rushed on Ruth, snatching the gun out of her hand and knocking her to the ground.

~~~~~

As Joshua watched the scene unfold, he knew he had to run. He had to get help. He took one last peek around the tree. He heard the man yell at the girl that she would be sorry she ever met him. Then he ordered Ron to dig. Caleb just sat there, wiping tears from his face, his ankles still bound.

Joshua leaned against the tree, lifted his eyes toward the almost dark sky, and finally found some words to say. "God, help Caleb," he whispered. Then he ran as fast as he could back down the path.

~~~~~

"You know, if I were really a murderer, I'd shoot you right now," Basil hissed at Ruth. "But just to set the record straight, I don't know who killed those two little kids, but I do know that it wasn't me. Yeah, I was there all right. I was higher than cloud nine, couldn't tell my right hand from my left, but I know in my heart that I didn't kill anybody."

Ruth, still on the ground, rolled her eyes away from

Basil. She had believed that lie once before, and it had only gotten her into a cesspool of trouble.

SHH!

Joshua had not run very far when he ran head-on into JaLisa. JaLisa stepped back and angrily grabbed Joshua by the shoulders. "Joshua Tanner!" she yelled. "You are the sneakiest little boy I ever met! I oughta whip your butt right now for causing Ms. Sadie so much trouble." She shook him hard, then she noticed he was crying.

"Be quiet," Joshua whispered through tears. "They're gonna hear you."

"What? Who's gonna hear me?" JaLisa asked. "What you talking about?" she asked in a lowered voice, as she still held Joshua by the shoulders.

"They got Caleb," Joshua said, through sniffles and sobs. "We gotta get help him."

"Who got Caleb, Joshua? You ain't making sense."

"Ron and another man!" cried Joshua.

"Ron!" JaLisa felt as if a knife had gone through her stomach. Either Joshua was lying again, or he had lost his mind. There was no way Ron was in the woods, and how could he possibly have Caleb. Caleb was at home. "Stop playing games, Joshua!" JaLisa demanded.

Joshua shook his head firmly. "I ain't playing games. They got Caleb. We got to hurry up and get the police. They got a gun!"

JaLisa found Joshua's words hard to believe, but there was no mistaking his tears. She took her cell phone from her pocket and dialed 9-1-1. She got a "no-signal" tone. They were too deep into the woods.

"Dog!" she yelled with a whispered voice. "Where are they?" she asked.

Joshua pointed the way.

"You run back and get help. Run to the first apartment and tell them to call the police. I'll stay out here and keep an eye on Caleb."

Joshua stood there nodding. "Go!" JaLisa commanded.

EMPTY THREATS

Basil was getting anxious. "Dig faster!" he ordered Ron.

Ron stopped stabbing the ground with the screwdriver and held it up at Basil. "Does this look like a shovel to you?"

"Get the other one and help him," Basil ordered Ruth.

"What!" cried Ruth.

"You heard me. Help him."

Ruth shook her head, "I don't think so."

Basil grabbed her by the arm and yanked her to her feet. Then he pushed her toward Ron. "I said dig," he ordered.

Ruth crossed her arms and glared at him, knowing there were no bullets in the gun. "You want the money. You help him," she said.

Basil put the gun at Ruth's head. "I might not have killed those two kids, but I'll be more than happy to kill you."

"Go right ahead," Ruth replied, knowing that Basil's threat was as empty as the gun.

Basil, miffed that his bluff had been challenged, frowned, then pushed Ruth back to the ground. "I'll take care of you later," he threatened. "Hurry up!" he barked at Ron.

Caleb stopped wiping his eyes for a second when he thought he heard a sound coming from a nearby tree. He looked up just in time to see JaLisa in the distance peeping from behind the tree. She held up a finger to her lips, warning him to keep quiet.

I Am My Brother's Keeper

Joshua didn't bother knocking, knowing that no one locked their doors until after 8:30. He ran right into the first apartment he came to. "Call the police!" he yelled frantically. "Ron got my little brother in the woods!"

Talking Dogs

JaLisa knew that if Caleb had spotted her then she wasn't hiding carefully enough. One of the others might see her, too. But as she was moving to another spot, she tripped, making a loud 'umf' sound as she hit the ground.

~~~~~

"What was that?" Basil asked quickly as they all looked in the direction of the 'umf'.

"It was a dog," said Caleb. "I just saw it."

"Dogs don't talk. They bark," said Basil.

"I saw a dog," Caleb said again, his voice trembling.

Basil sighed and looked around, unsure what to do, figuring Ruth might run if he left her unattended. "Ron, go check," he said.

"It could be a dog, you know," said Ron. "They do sound like people when they sneeze."

"Go look," said Basil. "If this kid is out here, then somebody is sure to come looking for him."

Ron dropped the screwdriver and stood up.

"Take the screwdriver with you," said Basil.

~~~~~

JaLisa rubbed her aching knee. She had twisted it badly when she fell. She tried getting up, but the pain was too great.

"Let me help you," came a male's voice. JaLisa looked up and saw Ron standing right over her, holding a long screwdriver in his hand.

THE ROOT OF ALL EVIL

"Well, well, well," said Basil. "What a nice little party we have going on here," he said looking around at the crowd that had formed in the woods. "And all I'd hoped for was a quick little visit to Hickville to pick up some money."

JaLisa tried to resist Ron's grip as he shoved her onto the ground next to Caleb. The pain in her leg was excruciating, and all she could do was try to rub away the hurt and hope that Joshua had gotten someone to call the police.

The seconds slipped quickly away and felt like an hour to Basil, who had begun to sweat even though the heat of the day had faded away. Ron had gone back to viciously digging into the ground with the screwdriver, wishing he had not buried the money so deeply.

"Come on, Ron," Basil pleaded, "I know you can dig faster. If these two are out here," he said, waving the gun toward Caleb and JaLisa, "other people might come out here, too."

"Look, dawg, I'm using a screwdriver, okay," Ron replied. Sweat was popping from his face too. "I hadn't planned

on having to dig with this thing. Now just shut up and be patient."

"We don't have time for patience," said Basil, his eyes
darting back and forth from Caleb and JaLisa to Ruth. "Get
over there with them!" he ordered Ruth.

"Hol' up! Hol' up!" Ron said anxiously. "I got it! I feel
it!" he cried as he jabbed at the dirt like a hyper preschooler
in a sandbox. "Yes!" he cried. "Here it is! Come to Papa,
baby," Ron said, laughing. He tossed the screwdriver to the
side and began digging with his hands. Basil's eyes grew
wide when he saw Ron pulling on the strap of a backpack.

"You gotta help me," Ron said, his voice strained. "It's
stuck!"

Then they heard the siren.

"Hurry up, man!" Basil yelled. "I knew this was gonna
happen!" He looked around nervously, contemplating what to
do, as he watched Ron yank frantically at the unyielding
backpack. Then, out of desperation, he threw the gun into a
cluster of trees and rushed over to help Ron pull out the stub-
born backpack.

In an instant, Ruth picked up Caleb and began to run.
"Run!" she yelled at JaLisa.

"I can't!" JaLisa cried, her eyes filled with tears. "Just
go!" she told Ruth.

Basil, who was too concerned about the money to care
about Ruth, looked up for only a second. The backpack was
halfway out, and he wasn't about to leave it to chase after
Ruth.

"They're over there!" Basil heard Ruth yell.

"Forget the money!" he cried to Ron, but Ron kept tug-
ging. Basil got up and ran in the direction where he had

thrown the gun, wishing he had never tossed it.

Ron yanked one more time, and the backpack gave up the fight. "Basil, wait up! I got it!" he yelled. But he was too late.

"Police! Freeze!" the chilling warning came from behind him.

"The other one went that way!" cried JaLisa.

Two officers rushed quickly toward the cluster of trees. "Police! Freeze!" the warning came again.

"He's got a gun!" Ron heard an officer shout. "Drop your weapon!" the officer ordered. The officer again ordered Basil to drop the weapon, then, a few seconds later, a shot was fired.

QUITE CONTENT

It had been nearly a week since the adventure in the woods, and Joshua's rear end was still sore from the whipping Sadie Belle had given him. But Joshua hadn't complained. He knew that the discipline was well-deserved after what he had done to Caleb. On the other hand, Sadie Belle, who always said that everything works together for the good of those who love God, also praised Joshua for being a hero again, putting Ron behind bars for a second time.

"If it hadn't been for you trying to get revenge on your brother, those two boys would've escaped to who knows where and with money to boot," Sadie Belle had said. "God only knows how far they could have gone with that. And a gun, too?" she added. "Lord, have mercy."

"The police said they didn't even have bullets, remember, Grandma?" Joshua added.

"That little foolish girl had 'em in her pocket, though," said Sadie Belle. "They might've eventually figured it out. But all that's beside the point now. They're back where they belong."

Joshua had built a fort in the living room, using pillows and blankets. He and Caleb relaxed in it, watching cartoons, while Sadie Belle enjoyed a cup of tea. After seeing him in the hands of a killer, Joshua had promised himself that he would try not to ever be mean to Caleb again. He remembered all too well what it was like to think you were going to be killed.

"Grandma, you think Ron will ever get out again?" asked Joshua.

"Chil', I hope not," replied Sadie Belle. "They did it right this time and put him in a grown folks prison. If he ever gets out, he'll be too old to ever threaten anybody again."

"What about the one with the gun?" asked Caleb.

"They'll lock him up for good, too, whenever he gets out of the hospital, won't they, Grandma?" Joshua asked.

"Yes, they will," answered Sadie Belle. "But that bullet shattered his leg so bad that he might not be able to walk on it."

"How come that lady had to go to jail?" Caleb asked. "She was nice," he said with a shrug. "She tried to help me."

"'Cause she's the one who helped them escape in the first place," Joshua said, with a hint of anger. "That's against the law, Caleb."

"I know," Caleb said, shrugging again. "But she was still nice."

"She might be nice," Sadie Belle interrupted, "but look at all the trouble she caused. Even JaLisa's got to have knee surgery."

Joshua felt guilty knowing that some of this was his fault, too. But he did have a new appreciation for JaLisa, and so did Sadie Belle and everyone else in the neighborhood.

"Grandma, do you think our mama will ever come back?" Joshua asked, unexpectedly.

Sadie Belle, startled by the question, just sighed loudly. "I don't know, Joshua," was all she knew to answer.

"Well, it's okay if she don't," said Joshua. "I'm happy with you as my grandma *and* my mama."

Joshua stretched out under his fort, placed his hands behind his head, and planted a contented smile on his face. Caleb looked over at him and did the same. "Me too, Grandma," he said. "I'm happy with you as my mama, too."

About the Author

Linda Williams Jackson, a native of Rosedale, Mississippi, traded in her career in Information Technology to take on the challenge of full-time family management and writing. Her first novel **THE LIE THAT BINDS** gives readers a glimpse into the lives of seven-year-old Joshua Tanner and four teenage boys and takes the readers down a path lined with unimaginable plots and unsurpassed suspense. Her second novel **WHEN LAMBS CRY** gives readers a look at the lives of her memorable characters four years later, continuing down a path lined with unimaginable plots and unsurpassed suspense.

Mrs. Jackson lives in Southaven, Mississippi, with her husband Jeffery and their children Olivia, Chloe, and Benjamin.